Soul Masters: The Hunting Grounds

by

K.R. Gastreich

Soul Masters: The Hunting Grounds

Contact Information: info@thewildrosepress.com

Cover Art by *Kristian Norris*

The Wild Rose Press, Inc.
PO Box 708
Adams Basin, NY 14410-0708
Visit us at www.thewildrosepress.com

Publishing History
First Edition, 2024
Trade Paperback ISBN 978-1-5092-5330-2
Digital ISBN 978-1-5092-5331-9

Published in the United States of America

Dedication

For Terri-Lynne, who never stopped believing

Acknowledgments

This book started with a scene submitted to my first critique group, the Dead Horse Society, under Laura Croston. In the epic discussion that followed, Soul Masters was born. Through many iterations of the manuscript, Terri-Lynne DeFino and the Dollbabies provided steadfast support. Kansas City's Critique Kitty, organized by Dyann Barr, assisted with later versions of the manuscript. Special thanks to my editor Dianne Rich at The Wild Rose Press for believing in this story. Love and gratitude to my family for always being there, no matter what my next crazy idea is. Jon Cleaves, you witnessed the birth of this idea and years later, returned to my life with the gift of love. My gratitude is immeasurable. Thank you, everyone, for seeing me across the finish line. Finally, thank you, Dear Reader, for choosing Soul Masters. Welcome aboard. The adventure has just begun.

Chapter 1

Kansas City, Missouri. 2016

The smell of fresh coffee and sweet pastries buffeted my senses as I stepped into Joni's shop. A popular stop in the Brookside shopping district, her place was always full. Squeezing through the noisy crowd, I claimed my place in line. Local art brought the walls to life with splashes of bright color. A mismatched collection of vintage chairs and tables accommodated customers. Joni spotted me from behind the counter. Just as I stepped up to place my order, she took over the register from one of her employees.

"Hey, Mayela!" Joni flashed me a bright grin. A pink bob framed her rounded face. Tattoos laced her bare arms. Today she wore a black-and-white polka dot dress with a frilled apron. "How've you been?"

"Good, and you?"

"Busy. Which is always good."

"And Anabel?"

"Aaw, she's great." Joni's face lit up at the mention of her daughter. "Third year in college already."

I shook my head in disbelief. "Seems like just yesterday we were celebrating her baptism. Time goes by so fast."

"Yeah." Joni sighed. "My baby. She'll be graduating in the blink of an eye."

A lump caught in my throat, and I glanced away. A sudden surge of emotion stalled my words. Watching Joni's journey as a mother sometimes hit me with this bittersweet mix of joy, envy, and sadness. A few years ago, my husband Carlos had died, taken from me in an accident before we could conceive. Since then, I'd come to terms with the fact that some wounds can never be healed. I mourned him still, with all my heart. Him and the children I would never know.

"Bring some good bugs?" Joni nodded toward my cedar insect box.

"Oh." I followed her glance and shuttered away my emotions. "They're not bugs. They're actually—"

"Insects, I know." Joni wrinkled her nose and called to the people behind me in line. "Hey, everyone! This is my good friend, Dr. Mayela Lehman. She works on native bees. She's found a hundred species right here in Kansas City. How's that for impressive?"

Someone grumbled about the wait.

"I've learned something, see?" Joni told me with a wink.

I laughed. "I guess you have."

"The usual?"

"Yes, please."

She rang up a hazelnut cappuccino. "I reserved you a spot next to the windows."

"Oh, thank you!" What a relief. I wanted to get some pinning done while I was here. Having good light was critical.

"I'll stop by your table in a bit," Joni said as I ceded my spot to the next person. "I want to see your new critters."

Claiming my coffee, I found the booth Joni had

reserved and settled by the window. There, I opened my backpack and unloaded my insect paraphernalia: kill jars, pins, labels, the small cedar box. I arranged everything on the table and set to work. In short order, I had processed the day's catch. My winged gems were laid out in neat rows, legs splayed, tiny antennae pointed forward.

"Mayela the Huntress," I murmured, sitting back to admire my catch.

The thought took me unbidden to another place in my mind, a place I did not want to go. I'd been haunted these past few days by strange and disturbing memories. Not memories. Dreams. Waking dreams of dark plains and terrible monsters, of a place where I was the hunted. A shiver ran down my spine. The images were so vivid, and yet none of it could have been real. One moment I'd been hiking in the forest, the next I was tumbling through shadows into that place where…

"Hey, girlfriend." Joni appeared next to me, hovering over my collection. "What've you impaled today?"

I bristled. "I'm not impaling. I'm—"

"Pinning. I know. Just messing with ya."

"I haven't identified these yet. Late-season bees still confound me. This one, I think, might be something special." I pointed to a fuzzy gray bee in the corner of the box. The insects blurred, then shimmered back into place. Startled, I withdrew my hand. "Did you see that?"

"No," Joni said. "What?"

A knot took hold of my stomach. "Fracking tremor, maybe?"

"We've had a lot of those lately. Feeling them all the way up from Oklahoma." Joni straightened up, indignant. "Look, I'm a card-carrying Democrat, but I will never forgive this administration for opening up fracking."

Again, I felt movement, as if we were in an elevator that suddenly dropped a level. The ground shifted beneath me. Chatter in the shop became muted. The sound of the espresso machine faded. Music from the speakers filled my ears, an old song from one of Joni's crooner playlists. Andy Williams singing "Moon River." The words blared inside my head. I covered my ears but couldn't shut them out.

"Joni!" I said, forcing a laugh. "How many times have I told you to find better music?"

"Suck it up, girlfriend." She gave the edge of my table a playful swat. "This stuff is good for the soul."

Then everything froze. Joni, the customers, the cars outside. All movement simply stopped. The chime on the front door sounded. My throat went dry. Somehow, I knew what was happening. I knew who had arrived, though I didn't understand how or why.

Twisting around, I peered over the rim of the booth. Standing in the doorway was the man from my hallucinations, a creature of the dark plains. Tall and slim, broad-shouldered, dark in aspect. That same man had beheaded a snake in my kitchen. Not my kitchen, I reminded myself. The illusion of my kitchen, part of the same hallucination of an impossible world. *The Hunting Grounds*, he'd called it. *Where we go to hunt souls.*

My mind spun with the impossibility of what I was seeing. He couldn't be real. Yet here he was, in Joni's shop. Except, he looked different. His hair was peppered gray instead of black. His skin seemed a shade darker. Or maybe lighter? It was like wrapping my head around a mirage, trying to remember what he looked like in my nightmares. But the simple force of his presence, the quiet luminescence of his spirit, was unmistakable. That was him.

Without so much as a glance in my direction, the man stepped into the shop and started toward the counter. Everything stirred at once. Several people looked his way. Joni let go a long, low whistle.

"Well, I'll be!" she exclaimed. "We haven't had anyone that drop-dead gorgeous walk in here since…Well, ever!"

She kept staring, mouth agape, as he ordered coffee. Then her face lit up, and she jumped into action, wiping down the table next to me.

"I've got an idea," she said. "I think you should go for him."

"What?" I croaked.

"He's totally your style."

"I don't date men in suits."

"What are you talking about?" She laughed. "Look at him! It's fate. I can feel it."

"Joni—"

"Sir!" she called. "Sir, we've got an empty table right over here. Next to the windows."

Holy crap! I sank deeper into my seat. "I'm serious, Joni! Send him somewhere else."

"Straighten up, beautiful." She patted me on the shoulder. "Give it a shot. What've you got to lose?"

Then she was gone. I cast about frantically for an escape, but there was no back exit from the booth. Unless I wanted to crash through the window. Could I do that? Crash through the window?

Yeah, I could do that. But I'd have to leave my insects behind, and—

And there he was, taking the table next to me. His chair scraped against the floor. His clothes rustled as he settled in. Minutes passed while my heart pounded inside my chest. I kept my face turned, pretended to stare out the window, wondered whether it would hurt to feel the glass shatter against my skin.

Idle talk filled the coffee shop. Customers came and went, orders were taken, steam forced through frothing milk.

Still the man said nothing.

I snuck a glance in his direction. Damn, he was handsome. Desire tugged at my gut, a strangely familiar sense of attraction, as if we'd known each other before this moment. As if I'd been bound to him in a time before memory.

This was exactly how I'd felt when I met him in my hallucination. *Not him*, I told myself. His doppelganger. His figment-of-my-imagination doppelganger. Surely, nothing I remembered had actually happened. Surely the resemblance between this man and the snake killer of my nightmares was mere coincidence. After all, he was sitting there like any other customer—sipping his coffee, engrossed in his tablet, oblivious to my inner turmoil.

I drew a tentative breath of relief. *He's just some random guy. He doesn't even know I'm here.*

Then he glanced up.

Our gazes locked.

"Hello," he said.

My heart skipped a beat. "Uhm…Hi?"

He gave me a quizzical frown. “May I help you?”

“I’m sorry, I just...” What was I supposed to say? *Excuse me, have we met before? You look like the guy who beheaded a snake in my kitchen.* “I don’t mean to be rude. I was just wondering...What are you reading?”

“You mean this?” He lifted his tablet.

“Yes. It seems very engaging.”

“Quarterly reports.” He put the tablet aside. “Not nearly as exciting as it sounds.”

The man settled back to take me in. Unnerved by his scrutiny, I offered a hesitant smile. A shadow spread over his shoulders, like wings, except they disappeared if I tried to focus on them directly.

“And you?” He indicated the pins, labels, and kill jars spread over my table. “May I ask what all that is about?”

“I, uhm...” I drew a deep breath and straightened my shoulders. “I’m impaling.”

There. That’d make him think twice before messing with me. *Mayela the Impaler*.

“Can’t say I’ve ever witnessed anything like it in a coffee shop,” he said.

“Joni, the owner? She lets me get away with a lot. She owes me a few favors.”

“Because you’ve impaled her enemies?”

“No.” I laughed. “We’ve been friends a long time. Actually, I’m not impaling. I’m pinning insects. Native bees? It’s part of a study of remnant prairies in the KC Metro.”

“You’re an ecologist.”

“Yes.” His use of the word *ecologist* caught me by surprise. Most people around here labeled me an environmentalist. “My field is restoration ecology.”

"You bring lost ecosystems back to life."

"Oh. Well, I guess you could put it that way. Not whole ecosystems, of course. Just a few patches here and there. Whatever I can do, which isn't much." I paused, uncertain whether to continue the conversation. "And you? What kind of work do you do?"

"Renewables."

"Really?" My voice lit up. "What do you specialize in? Wind? Solar?"

"We maintain a diverse portfolio. Wind and solar, some geothermal. Even some small-scale hydroelectric. I'm in town exploring opportunities for expansion."

"You don't live here?" Disappointment needled my heart.

"No, but Kansas City has possibilities. I may put down roots in the future."

"Oh." What was this small miracle? And in Joni's coffee shop? A beautiful man who made his fortune by saving the planet was about to settle in my hometown.

"My name is Nathaniel, by the way," he said. "Friends call me Nathan."

"Nice to meet you, Nathan. I'm Mayela."

"Nice to meet you, Mayela." Then, "Do you impale here often?"

I let go a short laugh. "Once a month while the bees are in season. But I come for coffee every week."

"Maybe our paths will cross again."

"Maybe." A flush rose to my cheeks, and I glanced away. *He wants to see me again!* Then I remembered, with a cringe, what Nathan saw. I'd come straight from my field site in wrinkled and scruffy clothes. I smelled of sweat, dust, and tick repellent. Not a look that would appeal to a man of his refined tastes. Resigned, I closed my insect box and began packing my supplies. Better to exit stage left before any more romantic fantasies took hold.

"Mayela." Nathan's smooth tenor drew my attention back to him. There was a familiarity about his presence that ran much deeper than any imagined circumstance of the past few days. More than a first meeting, this felt like an encounter with an old friend.

"You seem like a woman who wouldn't take a chance on a stranger," he said, "but I'd very much like to invite you to dinner."

And just like that, the terror returned. "I…I don't think…That wouldn't be—"

"I'd like for us to get to know each other, that's all. Maybe I'm reading things wrong here, but it doesn't seem this conversation is meant to end just yet."

"I see." I ran my fingers along the edge of my cedar box, trying to think of a good reason other than hallucination-based paranoia to refuse. "Thank you. It's just, things are really busy right now and—"

"It doesn't have to be tonight. I'm in town through the weekend. Could be Friday?" He leaned forward in his seat. "Seven o'clock? You tell me where."

Wow. *He really wants to see me again.* I glanced over at the register. Joni stared at me from across the shop, mouthing, "Go for it!"

I turned back to Nathan. He seemed kind and attentive, and I couldn't deny the sense of trust his presence inspired. It wasn't his fault he looked like an imagined snake killer from Hell.

"On the Plaza?" I suggested. "By the fountain?"

"Perfect." A grin broke on his face. "Which fountain?"

I drew a breath to respond, then stopped. An idea crept into my head. A test, of sorts.

Nathan's smile faded as he held my gaze. Amusement glinted in his dark eyes. Then he nodded and said, "I understand. Friday at seven it is. On the Plaza by the fountain."

We rose and exchanged cards. He fell into step beside me as we headed toward the front of the shop. Even his scent was familiar, sharp and compelling as a fresh-lit match.

"I'm not a fan of tablets," he said, indicating the device in his hand. "Paper has a much more authentic feel to it. The crinkling of pages, the ink rubbing off on one's hands. It keeps us more connected to the material world, don't you think?"

"You feel disconnected from the material world?" I asked.

He stopped. A shadow washed over his features. The noise around us dimmed. The hairs on the back of my neck rose. This was as close as I could come to what I really wanted to ask, but I feared I'd gone too far.

Then Nathan threw his head back and laughed.

"It's been a pleasure meeting you, Mayela." He touched my hand, where I still held his card. "If I fail your fountain test on Friday, I hope you will give me another chance."

Chapter 2

I watched Nathan leave Joni's shop, half expecting the afternoon sun to turn him into a puff of smoke. Instead, he donned a pair of dark glasses, lifted his face to the sky, and like any other pedestrian, headed down the street along the sidewalk.

I looked down and examined his card. The lettering was simple and elegant. *Nathaniel de la Rosa.* What a beautiful name. Even the card made my skin tingle. I tucked it in my backpack.

"Well?" Joni asked as I approached the counter. "What's the scoop?"

"Looks like I have a date."

"Yes!" She did a fist pump. "Oh. My. God. You're dangerous, Mayela! You took him down in record time."

"Nobody's taken anyone down." But I had to suppress my smile. I was giddy with excitement. "Yet."

"What's the plan?" she asked.

"Dinner Friday, on the Plaza."

"You better clean up."

"Ya think?"

"Get a new dress." Joni took a muffin out of the microwave and handed it to a customer.

"A dress?" I hadn't thought about that. "Where will I find time to shop for a dress between now and Friday?"

"Play hooky, Professor. Cancel class if you have to. You need to feel glorious if you're going out with that sexy man," she said. "Where are you going for dinner?"

"Don't know. We didn't get that far."

"Well, find out. And text me. Before, during, and after. Can't be too careful on a blind date."

"I know." Though somehow this date did not feel blind.

The door chimed. Glancing over my shoulder, I recognized Mitch, Joni's financial advisor, coming into the shop. He spotted us at the counter. Something inside me flinched. I turned away and grabbed my pack, ready to leave.

"Hey, Joni! Good to see you." Mitch came up beside me and gave his client a vigorous handshake. Then he nodded to me. "Mayela. How's everything going?"

"Fine." But my stomach had gone sour, and my hands felt cold. Shadows spotted my vision. I didn't know what was happening, but I needed to leave. Now. "I was just on my way out. Thanks for everything, Joni. See you later, Mitch."

Spinning around, I charged toward the door.

"Don't forget to text Friday night!" Joni called after me. "And Zumba Saturday morning! I can't wait to hear all about your date."

I thought I heard Mitch add something as I tripped out the doorway, but I couldn't stop. Spurred by some nameless anxiety, I rushed along the sidewalk toward the lot where I'd left my car. My breath came up short. My heart slammed against my chest.

"Mayela!" Mitch shouted.

I broke into a sprint.

“Mayela, wait!”

I halted, breathless and terrified, overcome by the memory of monsters chasing me down.

Mitch caught up with me and proffered my insect box.

“You forgot this,” he said. “Joni said it was important.”

“Oh.” Embarrassed, I met Mitch’s blue-eyed gaze and accepted the box. “Thank you.”

What had gotten into me? I should have been sauntering to my car without a care in the world, indulging in the warm sun, enjoying the window displays of Brookside’s boutiques. Instead, I’d been running down the street like an idiot.

I started toward the car. Mitch fell into step beside me. Broad-shouldered with sandy-blond hair, he was a looker in his own right. Today he wore a cotton shirt and dress pants that complemented his build. I didn’t know him well, beyond occasionally seeing him at the shop. I’d been over to his house with Joni for occasional cookouts. He had a wife, Kaitlin, and a couple of great kids.

“Joni told me what happened,” he said. “I hope everything’s okay.”

“What?” I blinked. “You mean about the guy I met in the coffee shop?”

“No, I…” He paused and shook his head. “Sorry, I must be getting my details mixed up. Maybe she was talking about another friend?”

“She certainly knows a lot of people.”

We arrived at my car, an old but reliable sedan. I opened the trunk and wedged the backpack between my cooler and other field gear. The insect box would go up front with me.

"You busy this weekend?" Mitch asked.

I bumped my head on the hatch. "Excuse me?"

"I thought we might get together."

"You're asking me out?"

"Yeah." He let go a nervous laugh. "I guess I am."

Two invitations in one day. This was a record breaker and maybe I should've been thrilled but, "Aren't you married?"

"What?" He looked taken aback. "Oh, you mean Kaitlin. No. I mean, yes. Technically, but…Well, you know. We've talked about that. She and I have been separated for a while now. We've started conversations with the lawyers. It's pretty much over, I think."

I took a step back. *Danger, Will Robinson.* "Look, Mitch. I'm sorry you're going through this right now, but I can't get together with you."

"I thought—"

"I'm booked this weekend. Even if I weren't, this is not a time for you to date."

"Didn't you—?"

"Trust me. As someone who lost the love of her life in the worst way possible, it's too soon."

His blue gaze turned icy, and my heart stalled. For a moment I thought he was going to get angry. Very angry. Then something diffused behind his expression. He shrugged and looked away. "You're right. I'm sorry."

An acrid smell stung my nose. I took another step back.

"Maybe we can try when things are more settled?" he offered.

"We'll cross that bridge when we come to it," I replied stiffly.

Mitch nodded and turned away, walking toward Joni's shop.

I got into the car and locked the doors. My hands trembled. My heart had gone into overdrive. For several minutes, only the sound of my labored breath cut through the silence.

What the hell was that about?

In that moment, a disturbing detail that had escaped me the last few days returned full force: Mitch had been part of my hallucinations.

Feeling a little nauseous, I started the car and pulled out of the parking lot. On the way home, I tried to systematically piece together my fragmented memories. It wasn't easy. After the serpent's bite, I'd passed out, but the hallucination didn't end there. I regained consciousness in another place, a spacious and pristine apartment, at once foreign and deeply familiar. It didn't take me long to conclude I was dead, though I knew now that I wasn't. There was an old computer in that place, a bulky artifact from the nineties. On the computer, I found videos of the living. I watched my family and friends, and I watched Mitch. Many times. Scenes from his life, like another dream within a dream, filmed in black and white, played in silence.

Uncomfortable emotions clawed at my chest as I remembered all this—fear, anger, terror, futility.

"No way out," I murmured.

No way out of where?

I touched my head, searching once again for an elusive knot that would explain everything. My best working theory was that I'd fallen and suffered a blow to the head while on a hike, and that this had set off a series of dream-like experiences. Yet the medics had found no evidence of head trauma or concussion.

What really happened?

And how was Mitch a part of it?

I arrived home unsettled and let myself into the house. Pungent smoke hit me as I stepped into the foyer. Chanting sounded from the living room. Frowning, I set my things down. *Oh, no. Not again.*

Sure enough, it was my mother. Hesitant to interrupt her trance, I watched from the doorway to the living room. Light from the window accentuated her features—a proud chin and hooked nose, a mass of black curls that flowed over her shoulders. She danced in slow, swaying steps and waved a smoldering stick of herbs, the source of that awful smoke. Some twenty-odd crystals had been scattered across my coffee table. My cat Midnight sat nearby, mesmerized by the shiny stones. Once in a while, she took advantage of my mother's distracted state to bat at the crystals.

"Mamá," I said, arming myself with patience. She did not respond. I raised my voice. "Mamá!"

Midnight fled into hiding at my bark. Mamá ceased her ritual and blinked. She looked at me, eyes coming into focus. A jubilant smile broke across her face. "*Hija*!"

Then I was in her arms, a wonderful rose-scented embrace that had brought me comfort since before I could remember. My emotions wavered between the joy of having her close and annoyance that she'd smoked up my house again. I extricated myself from her grip.

"What are you doing?" I asked.

"Cleaning up."

"Mamá, how many times have I told you I don't want this mess in my house?"

"I had a dream."

I raised my brow. This was Mamá's explanation for every action that didn't make sense. Ignoring my reaction, she set her hands upon my shoulders and pinned me with her dark gaze. "We must get ready, *Querida*. It is time."

Chapter 3

Sometimes I saw myself in Mamá's face, or at least the person I might become. On days like today, I wasn't sure how I felt about that. I bent to gather the rocks she'd strewn all over my coffee table. "What do you mean it's time, Mamá? Time for what?"

She swatted my hand away from the crystals. "Don't touch anything."

I gave an exasperated sigh. Mamá had tucked her magic rocks into every corner of the house. My late husband Carlos, who had dedicated his short life to geology, might have approved of this aesthetic, but not me. I was done with her witchy ways a long time ago. Going over to the windows, I opened them wide to let out some smoke. "It's going to take forever to ventilate this place."

"The vapors will clear by morning."

"Can the rocks be cleared by the morning, too? You know how I feel about all this."

"The crystals must stay. You are not to move them unless I tell you to."

"Mamá, this is my house."

Midnight leapt up on the table and sent a rock skittering across the floor. Mamá snapped at her in Spanish, but Midnight held her ground. I stifled a laugh. At least I had an ally in my cat.

"I've prepared a special dinner," Mamá told me.

"After sunset, we'll take advantage of the moonrise and conduct a thorough cleansing of your spirit on the back porch."

"Dinner sounds great, but I don't know about the rest." I let my reluctance show in my voice. "I've got a lot of work to do tonight."

"None of that is important. Not anymore."

I lifted my hands in surrender. All my life, it'd been like this with her. Mamá was all mysteries and illusions, spirits and spells and strange visions. She'd only gotten worse after divorcing Dad and moving to California. What had inspired them to get married in the first place was beyond me. Mamá embodied the passion and spontaneity of Spain, Dad the obsessive stoicism of the Midwest. Mamá's youthful energy belied her years, while Dad had long since aged beyond his days. Mamá was a left-wing devotee. Dad was as conservative as they come.

Despite all these differences, as a child I'd never seen them in conflict. They'd held the marriage together until I graduated from college, then went their separate ways. It wasn't until after the divorce that the bickering began. This year had been worse than ever with all the hype around the election. But there was one priority they always agreed on—me. Dad had called her the moment I disappeared on the farm. Mamá had arranged to come as soon as she heard.

Tonight, she'd prepared a savory meal of rice, beans, fresh cheese, and seasoned vegetables. Over dinner, she grilled me on the details of my hallucinations. I told her about the dark plains and flying monsters, about the man who killed the snake in the kitchen. I stopped short of sharing what happened next. That seemed too intimate somehow, too dangerous to speak of. I also avoided any mention of Nathan or his resemblance to the snake killer. God only knew what she would do with that morsel if given half a chance.

Outside, deepening shadows announced the onset of evening. Mamá stood and began clearing the dishes. As we put the kitchen back in order, she reminded me the deck had been prepared for a full moon ritual. I let go an inward groan. Rituals were not my thing. Besides, the neighbors would seriously freak if they saw us. But Mamá had come all this way just for me and had worked all day on her beloved spells. I didn't have the heart to say no. So, I followed her out the kitchen door, grabbing two glasses and a bottle of wine to shore up my resistance.

Mamá had arranged a circle of large white stones around the fire pit on the deck. She sat me down inside the circle, and much to my disappointment, took the wine and glasses and put them out of reach. The moon hung orange and heavy on the eastern horizon as Mamá lit flames inside the pit. She threw fresh sage and rosemary into the fire, along with other herbal offerings. All the while, she spoke in soothing tones. For Mamá, fire was not an exothermic chemical reaction between oxygen and carbohydrates. Fire was her mystical guest of honor, to be welcomed with deepest respect.

A cool breeze cut the humid air. The cloudless sky took on a violet hue. Mamá began to sing in a language I didn't recognize. The melody, evocative and poignant, sent a shiver down my spine. As the moon drifted higher, the white stone circle began to glow. Mamá's voice gathered strength, resonating with sounds of the night. She rose and circled the fire in slow, swaying steps. Her hands marked the space with graceful movement. Never once did she cease her song. Upon completing the circle, she took a place behind me and put her palms on my shoulders.

The hairs on my skin pricked. Mamá brought her hands upward, tracing my throat, letting her fingers spread through my thick curls until they came to rest on my head. The effect was deeply soothing. Closing my eyes, I submerged myself in her loving presence. In my imagination, I saw the sky open in a curtain of light. A warm, ethereal glow enveloped us. Gratitude filled me, for the gift of my family, my home, this world, and my life within it. Mamá ceased her song and withdrew her hands.

As I opened my eyes, a thin cloud passed over the moon. The stones lost their shine. The fire, which moments ago was burning high, had faded to a dim orange. Mamá knelt next to the pit and stirred the embers, sending a few sparks flying.

"That was lovely, Mamá," I murmured. "*Me encantó*."

"*Me alegra mucho*," she said, but her expression, illuminated by embers, seemed sad.

Disconcerted by her melancholy, I asked, "Can I pour us some wine now?"

That earned a smile. "*Claro que sí*."

I filled our glasses. We settled in side-by-side to soak up the moonlight. Amidst the thick vegetation of my garden, crickets chirped and creatures rustled. When Carlos and I married, I'd seeded the yard with wildflowers and a few perennials. I never mowed, never sprayed, and hand-weeded pesky invasives. The result was a mini wilderness pleasing to my eye if distressing for my neighbors. As long as I conformed to their austere standards in the more exposed front yard, they kept their complaints to a minimum.

"The man you met in your vision," Mamá murmured. "The one who killed the snake, how did you feel in his presence?"

Not what I wanted to talk about, but with Mamá, there would be no escape. Swirling my wine, I considered my response. Voices and laughter drifted toward us from one of my neighbors' houses a couple of doors down. A few blocks away, the low rumble of motors sounded along the main road.

"*Hija*?" Mamá prompted.

"I was too overwhelmed to feel anything," I said. Then, "Mamá, none of it was real."

"You told me you were scared in that place. Were you scared of him?"

I shrugged, resigned to her interrogation. "I was in awe. Viscerally aware of his power. Grateful it was being used in my defense, but also conscious that it could be used against me."

"Did you fear he might use it against you?"

"No." This much I could say with certainty. "There was something I recognized in him, Mamá. He was the only familiar presence in that horrific place. I felt anger toward him, disappointment and resentment, but I knew in my heart he wouldn't hurt me."

There. Question answered. Now, would she let this go?

"The Naming." Mamá took a sip from her wine. "That was important. When you called him by his true name three times, that bound him to you. He is now obligated to act as your temporary guide and guardian."

"How...?" I stared at her, stunned. That was exactly what he had said in my hallucinations, but I didn't tell Mamá that part. "What makes you say that, Mamá?"

"There will be a negotiation," she continued. "Nothing they provide is freely given. The price will not be trivial. Maybe he has explained this to you?"

"No, he didn't...We just...Wait." I bit back my words and steadied my thoughts. How to engage in this conversation without diving down her rabbit hole? "Mamá, where is all this coming from? What do you mean by negotiation?"

"That is their way, the ones who live beyond the veil. They always demand a price. But the one you choose must earn your trust. The final decision is yours. Don't forget there is always a choice." Mamá set her glass aside, a thoughtful look on her face. "*Lo que me llama la atención es...*What I don't understand is why he's treating you like any other mortal."

"Because I...am one?" I was trying very hard to be patient here.

"He must not be aware..." She hesitated.

"Aware of what?"

She drew a shaky breath, then let go of six brutal words. "Your father was one of them."

"Jesus Christ, Mamá!" I jumped up and away so fast my wine splattered across the deck.

"The one who gave you to me, he did not abide by the rules." She spoke quickly, now, as if to stay my retreat. "You know I had no choice, no say in the matter, but I never regretted having you. I simply understood, the moment I felt your life in my womb, that I would run. I swore I would die before letting him take you."

I turned my back on her and faced the garden, hugging myself, one hand clamped over my mouth. An explosive mix of rage, sorrow, and pity surged inside my chest. It took everything I had to beat those emotions down.

"All your life, Mayela," she said, "I've protected you from your father. And I've succeeded, but I can't protect you from who you are."

"Ay, Mamá." I sighed.

For years I'd known I was the product of an unhappy experience. Mamá had fled Spain frightened, alone, and newly pregnant. Somehow, she ended up in Germany, where she met my adoptive dad. An army private serving abroad, he had fallen in love with her at first sight. He took her in, gave us both a home in America, and brought me up as his own daughter. When they thought I was old enough to understand, they told me the truth—in part because Mamá had gone ballistic when I'd suggested a trip to Spain. She didn't want us to go back. She feared what my biological father might do if he discovered my existence. I'd respected her wishes, but all this time I'd thought "very powerful and dangerous man" meant…I don't know, part of the Spanish Mafia maybe? Mamá had never offered specifics.

"I always knew your time would arrive," she said. "I believe the time is now."

"Mamá…" I paused, uncertain how to counter this. From my own therapy, I'd learned trauma could inspire false memories, giving survivors a shield against the truth. But this? Turning me into the daughter of a supernatural being? In what part of the human psyche did that somehow make everything okay?

"Instinct tells me it's good your appointed guardian does not know your origins," she said. "You should keep this truth to yourself, close to your heart. Don't tell anyone, not even him, until you're certain of the landscape of their world."

"Whatever you say, Mamá." I failed to hide my annoyance.

She sat back in her chair. "You don't believe me."

"Of course, I don't believe you!" I spun around, angry. "How do you expect me to believe you? None of this makes sense."

"You say you don't believe me because you don't believe in yourself."

"What does that even mean?" I shot back.

"In your gifts, Mayela. Your instincts and your vision. The truth has followed you since you were a child, but you have denied it from a young age."

I puffed out my cheeks in frustration. Clearly, we were not going to get anywhere with this conversation—the latest, most intense in a lifelong battle of beliefs. It would be better to pull back, cool off, and pretend we never discussed this at all.

"Mamá." I sat down and took her hands in mine. "*Escúchame*: I love you. I'm so grateful for everything you've done, all the love you've given, and all the sacrifices you made, even before I was born. I know what you went through was awful, and I think you're the most courageous woman in the world. You don't need to invent stories anymore. Not for me. Not for anyone else."

“*No invento nada*!”

“Look.” I drew a considered breath. “If what you told me, if everything you believe, helps reconcile the past, I will respect that. But you have to respect me, too. You have to understand I don’t see the world the way you do. I don’t see signs and magic and spirits. All I see are biological creatures in the physical realm. *Homo sapiens*, Mamá. Us.” I brought my hand to my chest. “We evolved on this planet like any other creature, with all our gifts and failures. Yes, we build and destroy and help and hurt, but we do it all on our own. We don’t need angels or demons to make it happen.”

“*Tienes razón, Querida*.” Mamá laid a gentle hand on my cheek. “You’re right. We don’t need them. They are the ones who need us.”

****

Tempest

Merriam, Kansas. 1983

Gabriela shouted after her daughter. “Mayela!”

A humid gust whipped away the girl’s name. Scanning the street with a sharp gaze, Gabriela caught sight of the child scampering around the corner at the end of the block.

“*¡Vuélvete de inmediato*!” she demanded, but Mayela had escaped. Again.

Cursing, Gabriela snatched her jacket and left the house, long strides carrying her into an ominous wind. Above, clouds scudded across a dark sky. Moss-green bulbs formed beneath the slate firmament, dipping toward the earth.

“*¿Qué hago con esa niña*?” Gabriela muttered. What to do with her daughter?

She pulled her jacket tight around her shoulders. A violent storm was about to break, and eight-year-old Mayela had decided to take a walk. *Don't go outside*, Gabriela had warned. *Stay in the basement*, she'd said. How many times does a mother have to repeat herself?

Gabriela quickened her pace. The spirits of this place made her nervous. Every spring, their anger spilled across the veil, boiling into black thunderstorms over the open plains. Gabriela did not know how to appease them. Relying on rituals brought from her homeland, she'd offered many desperate petitions. She'd confessed her sins, all the bitter reasons she'd fled her home and settled in these stolen lands. She'd begged the spirits for haven, at least until Mayela could defend herself. Had they heard? Would they grant her request? After eight years, Gabriela could not say. She had not received an answer.

The wind faded to a whistle then a whisper. Lightning laced olive-tinged clouds. The air grew heavy and still. Gabriela's gut tightened, and she started to run. Feet pounding against the sidewalk, she rounded a corner and raced down another row of suburban homes, shouting her daughter's name. Mayela must have been headed for the playground. The child loved wild, moody, and dark spaces. The only place within walking distance that approached wild, moody, and dark was the playground.

The sidewalk ended in asphalt. Gabriela cut through a garage row and emerged across the street from the neighborhood park. There, she spotted Mayela at the center of a triangle marked by swings, a slide, and a teeter-totter. Mayela knelt on the grass as if in prayer, head bent and hands pressed against the earth.

Next to her stood a man.

Gabriela's breath came up short. Her heart went into overdrive. Cold with fear, Gabriela ducked behind a bush. *No, not a man.* A shadow that vanished if Gabriela tried to focus on him directly. She made a sign to protect herself. It couldn't be. Not him. Not here. Not now. Of all the futures she feared for Mayela, the one represented by that shadow was the worst.

Clutching a dark crystal that hung around her neck, Gabriela closed her eyes. *Cálmate*, she told herself. Taking a few deep breaths, she steadied her pulse and reached toward the playground with her inner eye. The entity standing next to her daughter showed no sign of malevolence, only curiosity. And he was young. Very young. Too young to be the one she feared.

Set-mei. Gabriela held the old god's name tight upon her tongue, for even a whisper could call him back. Nine years ago, she had abandoned him inside a fire of her own making. As the flesh melted off his human form, he had sworn vengeance. Sometimes, Set-mei's screams still reached Gabriela in nightmares, chasing her from sleep. Gabriela had done everything possible to hide from him and more importantly, to conceal their daughter. She'd fled her home, married a stranger, traveled across the ocean. She'd cast countless wards and casted them still. But the old gods were stubborn when angry. Gabriela knew with every fiber of her being that Set-mei still hunted them.

Setting her anxiety aside, Gabriela opened her eyes and rose. Confident yet wary, she started toward her daughter, scanning the playground without letting her gaze come to rest on the shadow. This was one of many techniques she employed to deceive his kind. Better he not know that she sensed his presence.

"*Querida*." Gabriela knelt next to her daughter. Mayela flinched at her touch. "*Soy yo*."

Reaching down, she covered Mayela's hand with her own. Death had crept up from the soil and wrapped thin tendrils around the girl's small fingers. Mayela looked up at her mother, eyes misted with sorrow.

"The ground is poisoned," the girl said. "So many used to be here, but now they're gone. They didn't go because they wanted to, Mamá. They were ripped away."

"*Ya sé, Querida*." Gabriela began weaving a ward to shield Mayela from the terrors of her nascent awareness, and from the shadow that stood watch over them. The entity carried signatures of Gabriela's homeland. Perhaps he was a nomad like her, wandering these lands in search of a new home, a place to extend his power. Whatever his intentions, Mayela was not ready. "We have to go home now. The storm is about to break."

"Wait, Mamá."

"For what, my love?"

Mayela glanced over Gabriela's shoulder in the direction of the entity. "He says now is the best time."

A lump settled in Gabriela's throat. Mayela was speaking with him, then. And he with her. The revelation filled her with anxiety. She took off the shadow-filled crystal that hung around her neck and placed it on young Mayela. "Do what you need to do."

The girl bowed her head and spread her fingers against the earth. As Gabriela watched, the soil beneath their hands began to murmur with tiny life. Ants busied themselves in underground villages. Grubs munched on pale roots. Beetles and millipedes and tiny springtails skittled through the darkness. Countless other organisms came into being, so small Gabriela could just sense their pulsing presence. Fungi laced through the earth and pushed up to the surface. Seeds broke open, unfolding into glorious blades that stretched toward the sky. A prairie took shape around them.

Gabriela gasped at the wide-open landscape that had replaced their suburban neighborhood. Flowers of all colors and sizes swayed in the breeze. Bees and butterflies alighted upon blossoms. Spiders hung in glinting webs between thin stalks of grass. Birds sang and chirped from hidden locations. Overhead, a red-tailed hawk drifted through a break in the clouds. The ground trembled. Several large bison lumbered into view. A massive female at the head of the herd tilted its wooly head and set one bold eye on Mayela.

"Oh!" The child clapped her hands in delight.

Flies swarmed the bison's back, loosely deterred by her swatting tail. She snorted and pounded the ground with her hoof. Then, lowering her head, she stepped forward and began to speak. Gabriela could not understand the matriarch, but Mayela listened in wide-eyed attention as if every word were crystal clear. When the bison finished, the girl reached up to touch the snout of the great matriarch. Her hand looked heartbreakingly small against the animal's winter-worn face.

Lightning crackled overhead. Thunder split open the vision. Tall, lush grasses bled back into short, insipid blades, patchy against the battered soil. Prairie and bison vanished, leaving Gabriela alone with her daughter on the playground. Beyond the swings, slide, and teeter-totter, suburban houses resumed their stoic march across the landscape. Half a block away, a curtain of rain sped toward them. Trees twisted in its wake.

Gabriela grabbed Mayela's hand and pulled the girl to her feet. "Let's go!"

Mayela shrieked as she ran alongside her mother ahead of the storm. By the time they skidded around the corner and sped down the row of homes that comprised their block, the first gale hit with force. Dry leaves spun into furious eddies. Oversized drops of rain splattered the pavement. Saplings groaned as they doubled over. Air sirens sounded; a funnel cloud had been spotted in their area. At last, Gabriela and her daughter crashed through the front door into the hallway of their home.

Relieved, overjoyed, and angry all at once, Gabriela swept the girl into her arms. "¡*Mayela*! ¡*Por Dios*! ¿*Qué diablos estabas pensando*?" What the devil were you thinking?

Mayela laughed aloud. "¡*Vimos bisontes, Mamá*! ¿*Lo puedes creer*?" We saw bison! Can you believe it?

"Get into the basement. Right now."

Mayela scampered downstairs. As Gabriela secured the front door, she caught a shadow on the edge of her vision. The entity from the park had followed them home. Held back by her careful wards, he hovered on the porch outside, little more than a pause in the angry storm.

Uncertain, Gabriela bit her lip. What should she do? Confront him or let him be? He seemed innocuous, but connection with any entity from beyond the veil could put her daughter in danger. The young ones, in particular, had to be approached with care.

Tornado sirens rose in pitch, prompting Gabriela to slam the door shut. There was no time to confront or try to understand this creature now. If he returned, Gabriela would deal with him then. She murmured a short incantation to seal the wards around the house, and then ran downstairs.

In the basement, Mayela bounced on an old couch. "*Habló con nosotros, Mamá*! The bison! She talked to us."

Gabriela curled into the couch and gathered her beloved daughter close. Despite the storm raging overhead, they were safe. She ran her fingers through Mayela's beautiful dark curls, which the wind had left in complete disarray. "What did the bisonte say, *Querida*?"

"You heard her, didn't you? You were there."

"I couldn't understand her."

"Oh. Why not?"

"That's the way these things work sometimes."

"She liked the prairie."

"Of course, she did." Gabriela kissed Mayela on the forehead. At the time, it seemed her daughter had summoned the plants and animals, but perhaps the matriarch had laid out the vision for them.

"She said they'd grant my wish, but I didn't make a wish!"

"Perhaps she knows the wish of your heart."

"That doesn't make sense." Mayela frowned and looked away, a sure sign of worry.

"She said there'd be a price."

Mayela's eyes went wide with surprise. "How do you know?"

A lump settled in Gabriela's throat. She wrapped

her arms tight around Mayela, held the girl close to her chest, breathed in her scent of honey and summer winds.

"There is always a price," she murmured. And the price was never trivial.

Chapter 4

Mamá and I reached an impasse with the whole "you-are-a-daughter-of-gods" conversation. Much as I enjoyed having her, I was relieved when she announced she would not be staying through the weekend. After a couple of nights, she departed for California. She planned to meet with my dad before heading to the airport and flying home. She and her partner, Caroline, had plans to attend some wilderness camp, where they would devote the weekend to unconventional spiritual pursuits. I did not ask for details.

The morning Mamá left, I drove to campus, content to be on my own again and immerse myself in the real world of the ivory tower. I gave several lectures and after lunch attended a miraculously short faculty meeting. My office hours, a period when students could walk in without an appointment, followed at two o'clock. Although I had a lab exam scheduled for the next day, only one student, Abigail, showed up. We reviewed the circulatory system, tracing the trajectory of arteries and veins as they carried blood away from the heart and back again.

Tutoring pre-health students like Abigail was not the transformational work I'd imagined doing as a graduate student. Back then, I'd chosen ecology as my vocation because I wanted to usher in a green new world. I'd told myself that as a professor, I could disseminate critical information to students eager to learn about the natural world. Everyone would care, everyone would want to do something, and together we'd usher in a new era of sustainable living.

So much for my beliefs.

Since Carlos's death, I'd struggled with the pointlessness of it all. Some days my choices, my career, indeed my entire life seemed like a cosmic waste of time. The idea I might have made a difference somewhere along the way hovered like a dark joke inside an empty universe. But as Abigail's shoulders straightened and her mood brightened, I felt a spark of warmth inside my heart. These moments of achievement with my students anchored me and afforded a sense of purpose. In this way, I'd survived the years since Carlos's death, by focusing on ephemeral sparks of light within the void.

After some thirty minutes, Abigail departed. To my surprise, my dad was standing outside my door. If it weren't for his age, I might have mistaken him for another student, the way he clutched his red cap, his stance uncertain, his glance straying up and down the hallway.

"Is this a bad time?" he asked.

"Not at all." I got up, cleared a bunch of papers off one of the more comfortable chairs, and gestured for him to sit down. "What brings you to campus?"

"I was on my way home from the museum." Dad eased himself into the seat as he took in the state of my office. "Plants are looking good."

What he meant was, *You need to trim back some of this growth.* Affectionately called the jungle by my students, my office was beset by an overgrowth of potted plants. My house was the same. I wasn't sure where I'd gotten my green thumb. Mamá had never been good with plants, but I could go without watering them for a week and it didn't seem to matter. When I was little, I thought I could talk to plants and imagined them talking back. The memory still made me smile.

"Your mom and I met for lunch," Dad said.

"Oh." I stifled a grimace. I could only imagine how that went. "Hope you didn't wear that hat."

"I took it off in the restaurant."

"But she saw it?"

He shrugged.

"Oh, Dad." I sighed. "You've got to know by now your new red cap wasn't going to make her happy."

"I didn't think about it."

I pursed my lips. Much as I loved Dad, there were a lot of things he didn't think about, especially when it came to Mamá.

"I'm not a racist, you know," he added, his tone quiet though his face had flushed. "I just want what's best for our country."

"We all do, Dad." Political discussions had never gone well in my family. Mom and Dad were on opposite ends of the spectrum, with me somewhere in the muddy middle. I'd learned long ago not to let that drive us apart. I needed Mamá to be my mom and Dad to be my dad. I could find my political allies elsewhere. "I don't think you came here to talk politics."

He shifted in his seat. "I was wondering if you heard anything from the police. Seems they would know something by now."

"Oh." I frowned, considering my response. After Dad found me on the farm, he'd insisted I go with him to the Kansas City PD. He'd already filed a missing persons report and wanted me to follow up by telling them everything I could about my disappearance. There wasn't much to tell beyond my hallucinations, and I wasn't going to report any of that.

"I haven't heard anything from them," I said.

"Have you called?"

"No."

"I told you—"

"I know, Dad."

"You can't let them drop this." His words gathered speed and force. "It's important, Mayela. I mean, it might've been an accident like you say, but what if it wasn't? What if someone tried to hurt you?"

"We've already talked about this. There's no evidence I was attacked."

"All I'm saying is you can't be too careful. People disappear in this town. Just yesterday, there was something else on the news, another body found on some farm. They're saying we have a serial killer, right here in Kansas City. What if—?"

"Dad." I put my hands up to stop him. I appreciated Dad's concern, but clearly, he had watched too many true crime shows. "I was not attacked by a serial killer."

"How can you know if the police don't follow up?"

My breath caught on the answer, bringing to mind what I'd seen through that boxy old computer in the strange apartment, the torment Dad had gone through as he searched for me in the woods. My heart contracted. Were those scenes real or imagined? Dad had always been there for me. His love and protection were one of the few constants in my life. Was it too much to ask, that I help set his mind at ease now?

"Okay." I relented. "I'll call them. I promise."

My office phone rang.

"But first, I have to take this. It could be a student." I was right. I asked the student to hold a moment so I could say good-bye to Dad.

He pushed himself back to his feet and gave me a hug. "I don't like you being alone right now. Not until the police get things sorted out."

"I'll be okay. I'm a big girl. And I've got mace."

"Why don't you stay with me this weekend?"

"I have plans already for Friday."

"Saturday then?"

Much preferring to binge-watch a series with my cat, I puffed my cheeks and pondered an excuse not to go. I couldn't think of one. Besides, hadn't I just decided Dad's peace of mind was foremost? "Saturday will work."

His face lit up, puffy brows arching over creased eyes. "That'd be great, sweetheart. What time can I expect you?"

"For dinner. I'll call when I'm on my way."

"I'll make my famous spaghetti."

Spaghetti was the only dish Dad knew how to make, but he did make it well. "Sounds delicious."

"We can watch an old movie Saturday night and go to mass on Sunday."

"Oh." I grimaced inside. Dad was always prodding me to go to mass, but I'd drifted away from his faith, and its quietly brutal misogyny, a long time ago. "I don't know, Dad. I've been watching the weather forecast. Sunday might be the last opportunity I have this season to get some field work in."

His face fell. Then he chuckled. "Well, then. Maybe I'll pray for bad weather this weekend."

I laughed and acquiesced with a nod, though I didn't believe Dad's prayers worked any better than Mamá's spells.

He made his way to the door. "Love you, sweetheart."

"I love you, Dad."

Settling back into my chair, I picked up the phone and dealt with my waiting student. That call was followed by another and then another, until at last the phone stopped ringing and the office fell silent. I checked the time. My day had almost ended, save for a handful of tasks I wanted to finish before going home. As I organized a mental to-do list, a sense of vertigo took hold. For a brief and terrifying moment, I was back in the apartment of my hallucinations. A different set of bookshelves lined pristine walls. These were filled not with science texts but with fiction and poetry.

I blinked and the mirage vanished.

Trembling, I stood, approached the door to my office, and peeked down the hallway. Several other office doors were still open. Voices of colleagues echoed off the floor tiles. Students and the occasional professor wandered into and out of my sight. I was here, on campus. Not in that other place. Not alone.

I closed the door, as if that would keep my hallucinations at bay. I remembered reading book after book in that apartment, devouring each volume as if it were a long-awaited and much-needed meal. I remembered reading more than would have been possible during the twenty-four hours of my disappearance. I'd written things, too. Letters to Carlos, to Dad and Mamá, to my friends, even to the fictional protagonists of the novels I'd read. When I wasn't reading or writing, I exercised or ate or searched for a way out. Again and again, I searched for a way out

And on that boxy old computer in the living room, I watched videos of the living.

Now in the quiet of my campus office, fragments of what I'd seen played through my mind.

****

Mitch pours himself two cups of coffee in the morning but doesn't finish the second.

The first thing Mitch does after putting on a tie is loosen it.

When stuck on a problem at work, Mitch twirls his pencil, eyes focused on some empty point between him and the computer screen until the solution sparks in his mind. He hits the eraser end of the pencil twice on the table and starts typing. He never uses the pencil to write, just to think.

On weekends, Mitch shoots hoops with his son. At bedtime, he reads to his daughter. After the kids go to sleep, he and Kaitlin watch television together. Kaitlin rests her head on his shoulder. Mitch kisses her hair and inhales her aroma.

One day, Mitch comes home to find Kaitlin alone. Maybe their son has baseball practice. Maybe their daughter is staying with a friend. Kaitlin stares out the back window, a mug cradled in her hands. Her cheeks are wet with tears, her eyes swollen from crying. Mitch sets down his briefcase. He approaches from behind, places his hands on her shoulders. She flinches. He wraps his arms around her. She resists. He nuzzles her neck. She pulls away, but Mitch pulls her back. His kisses become more demanding, and something breaks inside of Kaitlin. She goes still and closes her eyes, as if enduring his touch rather than enjoying it.

****

Perplexed by these memories, I sat down again and stared at my flatscreen computer, fingers tapping idly on my desk. *What if I Googled Mitch McGraff right now?* Could a search in the real world help make sense of my hallucinations?

Opening my browser, I typed Mitch's name. The results were unremarkable: Profiles on Facebook, LinkedIn, his company website. A blurb in the newsletter for his church. He was listed on some boards for local organizations. Notably, Facebook still categorized him as *married*. The cover photo featured his wife and kids.

My phone rang, making me jump. Reaching for the phone, I answered, "This is Dr. Lehman."

"Mayela." Nathan's smooth tenor stalled my heart.

"Hi." I stuttered and then hated myself for stuttering. "How are you?"

"Doing well, and you?"

The computer blurred, then came back into focus. *This has happened before*. In the apartment. I'd been watching videos of Mitch when he…

"Mayela?"

"I'm sorry," I said, flustered. "What were you saying?"

"Is this a bad time?"

"No. I was just…" I paused, trying to put my thoughts in order. *There must be some explanation.* Some concrete possibility that didn't involve winged monsters, snake killers, and burning skies. "Nathan, did you go to KU?"

"Excuse me?" He sounded perplexed.

"The University of Kansas. In Lawrence."

"No."

"UC Santa Barbara, then?"

"I completed my studies in Europe. Why are you asking?"

I sucked a breath through my teeth. "Okay. This is going to sound crazy, but I had a sense of déjà vu right now when you called. In fact, ever since we met in the coffee shop, I haven't been able to shake the feeling that I've met you before. I did my undergrad at KU and completed my doctorate at UC Santa Barbara, so I thought maybe we'd run into each other in one of those places."

For a long moment he didn't respond. The silence stoked my discomfort. I hated this sense of being on the edge of something I didn't want to see.

"I've been to a lot of places over the years," he said. "I imagine you have too. So yes, it's possible we've crossed paths before. Maybe if we retrace our steps we can determine when."

"Oh." To receive his affirmation was a small thing, yet in that moment, it meant the world to me. Maybe we'd checked into the same hotel in Cuzco or done the same mangrove tour in Costa Rica. Really, it didn't matter where I'd seen him as long as I had. A face like his would've burned itself into my subconscious, even if I'd been with Carlos. That would explain his presence in my hallucinations, though it didn't explain the hallucinations themselves. "Yes, of course. You're right. And also, that would be a wonderful conversation to have."

"Agreed. I've done some homework on fountains, by the way. It turns out there are nineteen on the Plaza."

"I know." I would've hidden my smile except I didn't need to. He couldn't see me.

"Are you going to give me a hint as to which one you have in mind?"

"No."

Nathan chuckled. "Guess I'll have to work some magic."

"I'm sure you're quite capable."

A long pause on the other end. Beneath the silence of the phone, I could've sworn I heard the undercurrent of his breath, felt its warm touch upon my ear.

"I'm looking forward to seeing you again, Mayela."

I melted. That voice! Perfectly calibrated to activate my long-dormant hormones. "So am I."

Chapter 5

I scored on the dress. Found a very nice floral at a Brookside boutique, a leftover from summer clearance. V-necked and sleeveless, it fit loosely at the waist. The skirt flared smoothly over my hips and ended in a broad ruffle at the ankle. After donning a pair of pumps, I felt like I'd walked out of an old Carlos Saura movie. I could see dancers around a bonfire behind me in the mirror. *Mayela the Flamenca, ready to call her true love back from the dead.*

I picked some fun earrings and tied my hair in a loose knot, letting a few strands fall to frame my face. Then I remembered—perfume. Where was my perfume? I started searching my dresser drawers. I wanted something subtle, haunting, irresistible, or just…something. Did I even have perfume anymore? I did! Buried under my bras and underwear. Mamá had given me a couple ounces of eau du toilette last Christmas. A brighter aroma than what I had in mind, but it would do. It would definitely do.

Always Mamá to the rescue.

Strange she hadn't called or sent a text today. She'd always had an uncanny instinct when it came to my love life. Surely her dreams had told her by now I'd met the man of my dreams while pinning bees?

I checked the time. I was late. I didn't want to be late. Not for him.

Using my phone, I located a rideshare. There'd be wine at dinner, and I didn't want to deal with parking on a Friday night. The nearest car was ten minutes away. Damn. There was no way I would make it to the Plaza on time. After confirming the ride, I texted Nathan.

—Sorry. Running a little late. Could be 15 minutes past the hour?—

I held my breath. It was a small detail, but if there was one thing I'd learned by midlife, it was that details mattered. Trivial annoyances while dating became major flare-ups in a long-term relationship. I hoped punctuality was not one of his obsessions.

His response popped up.

—No problem. See you when you get here.—

First test passed. Now to see how he did with the fountain.

I checked the lock on the back door and gave Midnight some kitty treats.

"Wish me luck," I said, but she was already distracted, skittering her treats down the hallway.

The sun was sinking deep into the west as I walked out the front door, setting the sky aglow in shades of purple and rose. The trees, still dense with foliage, rustled in a slight breeze, their shadows stretching long to greet the coming night. This was a classic September evening in Kansas City, warm and muggy. The Midwestern summer was reluctant to surrender its grip on the city.

My rideshare arrived. I settled in the back seat and smoothed my skirt. Residential woodlands began to roll past the window. Taylor Swift bounced off the speakers, and I groaned inside. I wasn't up for cosmic messages from Taylor Swift. I didn't want to hear her invitation to risqué love. Not tonight. I hated to be *that* passenger but, "Do you think you could change the station?"

The driver obliged, bringing up Florence & the Machine. Her powerful voice sang of devils all around. I rolled my eyes. Seriously? "Look, I'm sorry if I'm being annoying. I do want to listen to some music, but would you mind just one more time—"

She switched stations again. Imagine Dragons now blared through the speakers. Metallic chords interlaced with more demons. It was all too easy to imagine demons lurking behind Nathan's eyes. I sighed and sank back into my seat. *Drop it*, I told myself. I was a scientist, after all. I didn't believe in signs, much less devils or demons.

Still. The songs needled me. Worry coiled inside my stomach. *It's just a date.*

But was it, just?

Everything leading up to now—the hallucinations, the premonitions, the weird déjà vu and persistent mystery, the sense of a voyage completed every time I heard his voice…This man had to be more than some random guy who'd caught my interest in a coffee shop.

Or did he?

Christ! I felt like I was back in my hallucinations, running toward a precipice I couldn't see. But this time I sensed wind against my wings. The landscape wasn't quite so obscure. I wasn't trying to escape what was behind me; I was running toward what lay ahead, secure in some strange faith that this man…This man would catch me if I fell.

I let go a short laugh. *Anyone who's falling in love*

feels this way.

Any woman, I meant. Nathan, being a man, probably wasn't ruminating about our first date half as much as I.

And if he's a demon?

What a terrible small voice, that whisper inside my head. With a shiver, I unfolded my wrap and pulled it around my shoulders. *I don't believe in signs, and I don't believe in demons.*

We curved down the bend of Sunset Hill toward the Plaza. Traffic had slowed to a crawl. Unusual, even for Friday night.

"Do you think there's an accident?" I asked, worried about another delay.

"Plaza Art Fair," the driver said. "Lots of people tonight."

Ay, por Dios! How could I have forgotten? I mean, the Art Fair was great, but everything was going to be packed. I hadn't considered making a reservation, a risk on any Friday night. Impossible during the Art Fair. I hoped Nathan had planned better than I did. If not, we'd be eating from a street vendor, and I didn't want to get pizza grease all over my new dress.

Maybe we could ditch the Plaza and head to Brookside, or downtown.

The car crept along Brush Creek. I tapped my fingers on the armrest, impatient. Just my luck. Traffic like this was unheard of in Kansas City. Frickin' bumper to bumper. This was going to take forever.

"Could you drop me off at the park near Roanoke and West 47th?" I asked.

"You sure?"

"Yes, please. I can just walk from there."

My driver obliged. The minute I stepped out of the car, I regretted my decision. Kansas City's sticky September heat wrapped tight around me. Within moments, I started perspiring. The fountain was only a few blocks away, but I was going to be covered in sweat by the time I got there. *Some first date I am.*

I started east along 47th Street, navigating dense and happy crowds. Parents wandered with children in tow. Groups of high school students bounced along store fronts. Couples, young and old, strolled hand in hand amidst the sculpted architecture. Everyone wore shorts and T-shirts. The entire city had been smarter with their wardrobe than me.

At 47th and Broadway, still a few blocks from my destination, I hit the edge of the Art Fair. Pausing, I glanced south, down a length of booths toward the interior of the Plaza.

Wait.

Doubt threaded my veins. Something felt off.

To reach the fountain, I needed to continue east, but…my glance drifted south again, into the heart of the crowd. *I'm doing this wrong.*

I slipped into the nearest store, seeking refuge from the noise and heat so I could think.

An attendant pounced on me. "Can I help you?"

"I'm just looking, thanks." I waved her off and found some blouses to finger while considering my next move.

When I'd told Nathan to meet at the fountain, I'd meant *the* fountain, the J.C. Nichols Memorial Fountain, the most photographed landmark in KC. A luscious burst of water over the voluptuous sculpture, it was an obvious choice, but Nathan wouldn't expect me to be obvious. And he'd done his homework. That meant he'd probably come across Nichols' controversial history as a racist and a red liner. Not the sort of figure to inspire our first romantic evening.

He's not there. The revelation washed through me, leaving certainty in its wake. *He's somewhere else.* But where?

Well, this was a fine turn of events. All week, I'd thought the burden was on Nathan to divine our meeting place. Now I had to divine where he was, based on where he thought I was, when I wasn't anywhere at all.

Puffing my cheeks, I reached for my phone but…No. I wasn't going to Google eighteen Plaza fountains in search of the logical option while he waited. I needed to choose my spot now and go.

Leaving the air conditioning behind, I walked out of the store and headed south on Broadway, directly into the milling crowds and tightly packed booths. Two blocks away, I remembered, there was a small fountain on the corner of Ward Parkway. The spot was pleasant enough, overlooking Brush Creek in the shadow of the historic Raphael and picturesque Intercontinental Hotels. It was as good a meeting place as any. In the likely event Nathan waited somewhere else, we had each other's phone numbers.

As I approached the intersection, a sound stage set up on the bridge over Brush Creek came into view. Some band was pumping eighties music over the shoulder-to-shoulder crowd. Nathan and I would have to shout over this chaos if we found each other here. *Or, I don't know, do the Safety Dance?*

I forged ahead. From my vantage point along the

sidewalk, I'd be only a few feet away when that small fountain came into view. *He might actually be there, you know.* I froze, just shy of turning the corner, and flattened myself against the wall. Despite my agitated walk and the heat coming off the pavement, my hands were cold. My heart raced inside my chest. It was one thing to run toward a precipice, quite another to jump off.

It's just a date, I told myself. *If you don't like how things are going down, you can just....* I studied the throng around me. *Lose him in the crowd.*

With a deep breath, I started walking again. I turned the corner, and there he stood. His face was lifted toward the bronze figure in the fountain, his eyes closed as if meditating beneath the cool mist. He wore a light cotton shirt and dress pants. His motionless form, imbued with serenity, contrasted with the bouncing crowd and blasting music. At the coffee shop, everyone had acknowledged Nathan's presence, as if they couldn't resist looking in his direction, but here no one paid him any mind.

Can he control when he's seen and when he's not?

Nathan shifted his stance and opened his eyes. His gaze settled on me. Recognition brightened his features, followed by pleasure as he took in my new dress. My heart did a little flip. *Guess I cleaned up well.*

"You're here!" he said.

"How did you know?" I stepped forward. "I decided, like, literally two minutes ago."

"I considered researching each fountain and making a logical choice based on what little I'd learned about you in the coffee shop, but then I decided it'd be easier to pick a fountain, any fountain, and pray you'd arrive."

I frowned. "You're serious?"

He nodded.

"You prayed? I wouldn't have pegged you as a man of prayer."

"Of course, I believe in prayer." He extended an arm to embrace the space around me. "Look what my prayers brought me today."

That glint in his eyes—unmistakable. The kind of look a man offers the woman he desires. Heat rose up in my throat. As if it weren't warm enough! "Sorry about the noise, and the crowd. I forgot there was an event here tonight."

"This is perfect." Nathan drew close. The ephemeral shadow that hovered over his shoulders spread around me, causing the commotion to fade. "My choice of fountain wasn't entirely without meaning. I was hoping you'd notice."

I looked at our fountain, dominated by a bronze woman frozen in perfect youth. A pleasant smile graced her ageless face. Her robe was draped loosely around generous hips.

"Half-naked lady bearing fruit?" I raised my brow. "You have plans for the evening I should be informed of?"

"Not the image." Nathan laughed and gestured toward the plaque at our feet. "The deity."

Pomona Goddess of Vineyards and Orchards, the inscription read.

"Oh," I said.

"I have it on good authority," Nathan murmured in my ear, "that she adores bees."

I don't know if it was his joke, or the spark that

shot down my spine when his breath hit my ear, but I started laughing and could not stop. Tears filled my eyes. My belly began to ache. I had to step away from him to regain control.

"I'm sorry." I gasped for breath, a little embarrassed. "I don't know what got into me."

"My brilliance, apparently."

An arrogant comeback but delivered with such warm humor I couldn't fault him for it. Besides, he was right. His presence was magical. It reminded me of the first time I stood on a beach at night, beneath a clear sky with shimmering stars. I ached to touch that distant beauty, and now I could. Touch him, I mean. If that was what I truly desired. All I had to do was reach out and…

I met his gaze. A heavy truth tugged at my heart, the suspicion that our history stretched further and deeper than I could imagine. The fear some strange horror lurked beneath our strong attraction. A voice inside me urged, *Ask him.*

Right there, in front of Pomona Goddess of Vineyards and Orchards, in the middle of the Plaza Art Fair, with eighties music blaring overhead. *Ask him.*

About his role in my hallucinations, about his true nature and the reason for his presence in my life. *Ask him. He will not lie.*

I opened my mouth to speak but couldn't. Logical Me elbowed her way in. She threatened me, said that if I asked crazy questions, I'd destroy the magic forever. I couldn't lay my hallucinations on this poor man. Not during our first date. Maybe, if I were to be honest, not ever.

"I think I already mentioned this," I said, "but I

forgot about the Art Fair. I haven't made a reservation anywhere, and I'm sure the restaurants are packed until closing. I was thinking maybe we could ditch the Plaza and go somewhere else?"

Nathan's expression clouded over. Behind his pleasure, I sensed surprise, then disappointment, followed by acceptance and quiet resolve. He extended an arm toward the restaurant across the street, one of the Plaza's finer steakhouses, and said, "No need, Mayela. Everything has been arranged, and we are right on time."

****

The Forgetting (*El Olvido*)

Merriam, Kansas. 1987

One afternoon, Mayela came home from school crying. She was only twelve years old. Her distress cut Gabriela's heart like a knife. Taking Mayela's hand, she led her daughter to their living room. Together they settled on the worn couch. Mayela sank into Gabriela's embrace, shoulders trembling as she wept.

"*Tranquila, Querida*," Gabriela murmured. She smoothed her daughter's hair away from her wet cheeks and reached for a tissue. "*¿Qué pasó*?"

Mayela accepted the tissue and blew her nose. The girl's words came in short bursts, broken by hiccups and sniffles. "They don't like me anymore."

"Who doesn't like you?"

"Everyone." Mayela sobbed.

Anger surged in Gabriela's veins. How could children be so cruel? "*No les hagas caso*. What do they know?"

"They're my friends! I can't just ignore them. Kathy and Penelope and Becca, all of them started making fun of me today. They called me a liar."

At once Gabriela understood what this was about, and the realization filled her with trepidation.

"Tell me what happened, love," she murmured.

"They said I make everything up."

"Do you?"

"No!"

"Well, then."

"They said plants can't talk, and that fairies don't exist."

"What do you think?"

Mayela threw up her hands. "I only know what I see and hear."

"*Entonces*?"

"But I don't understand! We used to talk about this stuff all the time. Katie had a pet unicorn named Coki. Penelope had an invisible rabbit she called Whiskers. Becca used to always say there were dolphins and mermaids in the swimming pool. I never saw any of what they were talking about, but I didn't call them liars."

"Maybe they have stopped seeing the world as it is."

"What do you mean?" Mayela's eyes went wide with horror. "They're going blind?"

"No, sweetheart. They can still see. They just don't see everything. Not like you and I do."

"Why?"

Gabriela hesitated. They had stepped upon treacherous ground with this conversation. She had to proceed with care. "These things tend to happen when children grow up."

"You mean I'm not growing up?"

"That's not what I said. You are growing up. Far too fast, in fact, for your dear mother. But you are not losing your sight. I hope you never will."

"Why?"

Again, Gabriela considered her response. "Your sight protects you. What we call faeries and magical creatures are always there, whether we see them or not. It is better to see them, just like it's better to see a snake rather than step on it unawares."

"I don't see snakes."

Someday you will, Gabriela thought, suppressing a shiver.

"That's good," she said.

"I don't want to see anything, Mamá. I don't want to see anything they can't see."

"Don't wish away your sight, Mayela. It is a precious gift few people have."

"I don't want a gift. I want friends."

"You can keep your friends, but you will have to be careful what you say to them. Pay attention to what they can see. Do not speak of that which has become invisible to them."

"I can't talk to anyone about it?"

"You can speak with me, *Querida*. You can always talk to me about anything."

"But if I can't tell my friends…" Mayela fell silent, jaw working as she processed the magnitude of the situation. "That *would* make me a liar, just like they say."

"Mayela—"

"No! I can't do that. I'm not going to be a liar, and I'm not going to be a freak. How can I stop seeing faeries, Mamá? How can I stop the plants from talking?"

Gabriela stared at her daughter, perplexed. Among her people, such gifts were honored. As a child, it would never have occurred to her to demand they be taken away. "I don't think it's possible to stop, Mayela."

"That's not fair." Mayela pulled away. "There has to be a way to stop it."

"Sweetheart—"

"It's not fair!" Mayela rose to her feet.

"*Querida*." Gabriela struggled to steady her voice, delivering each word in heavy tones. "This is a very important conversation. I need you to listen to me, to everything I have to say. You are a special girl with special abilities."

"Stop it!" Mayela covered her ears. "You aren't helping at all. This is stupid, and it makes me look weird. I don't want to be special. I want to grow up like everyone else."

"You can't escape who you are."

Mayela spun away and ran upstairs. Gabriela flinched at the slamming of her bedroom door. Despair settled on her shoulders, and she let her head sink into her hands. What a fool she had been, fleeing her people, thinking she could succeed at this alone.

As an adolescent, Gabriela had come into her own power, but she hadn't been alone as Mayela was now. Her mother and grandmother, her aunts and cousins and siblings, indeed the entire community accepted her gifts even if they didn't understand them. What did her people care that she was different? They were all outcasts, after all. Any sliver of power granted was to be cultivated and cherished, no matter how mysterious or dangerous.

In another time and place, Gabriela might have been called a witch. Among her people, she simply was.

What would they call Mayela now, if they knew the truth of her heritage and power? Gabriela shuddered at the thought, a reaction that reaffirmed her decision to flee all those years ago. And yet…

Beset by tender memories of her own family, Gabriela let go an anguished moan. Tears blurred her vision. Her chest ached with shame and loss.

"Mamá," she murmured. "*Abuelita. ¿Qué hago ahora*?"

It would be so easy to reach out, to open a channel between their souls, to hear once more the precious wisdom of her elders. Gabriela knew they would sense her distress and respond, even from beyond the veil. But she resisted the temptation, as she had since Mayela's conception. Never looking back had been the price of her foolish games. Every connection had been cut. Every channel of access had remained severed. Otherwise, Mayela's father would have found them. Indeed, he would find them. Someday. Gabriela's careful wards could not deceive him forever.

From that day forward, Mayela refused to speak of her gift. Denying her very nature, the girl turned a blind eye to all creatures from beyond the veil. Nothing Gabriela said softened Mayela's stubborn insistence on burying her power. Unwilling to stay where they weren't welcomed, entities once drawn to Mayela's shining presence began to fade. Gabriela watched their emigration with growing apprehension. Mayela needed allies, someone to guide her when the time came. But within a few short years, all of her companions had disappeared.

All, that was, except one.

Gabriela recognized him. He was the same that had stood nearby in their neighborhood park when eight-year-old Mayela had faced down a storm; when she had invoked a vision of the prairie and heard spirits from the plains. Gabriela decided to call him *El Caminante.* How or why this one entity remained while all the others fled, Gabriela wasn't sure. Mayela did not look upon him, acknowledge or address him. Yet whenever *El Caminante* was present, Gabriela noted a change in her daughter's aura. A quiet glow infused the shadows on Mayela's face. A pinprick of vision penetrated her fortress of denial.

Maybe this would be enough.

Maybe just this much would save them.

Chapter 6

The maître-de, a balding man in formal attire, greeted us when we stepped into the restaurant.

"Mr. de la Rosa," he said. "Very good to have you back." Then he turned to me with a warm smile. "You must be Dr. Lehman."

"Well. Yes." I lifted my brow. Apparently, being Mr. de la Rosa's companion earned me celebrity status. "That would be me. The distinguished Dr. Lehman."

The maître-de gestured for us to follow. I glanced at Nathan.

"After you, Doctor," he said with a bow and a wink.

The place was packed. Vibrant conversation filled the crowded tables. A few heads turned as we passed—not for me, I was sure, as distinguished as I might be. The savory smell of seared meat and fine wine made my mouth water. I was grateful the noise of the restaurant covered my growling stomach. I hadn't realized I was so hungry! We arrived at a small, semi-private alcove somewhat shielded from the noise of the main dining area. Next to our table, a large window afforded a view of Ward Parkway and Brush Creek, already shrouded by deepening dusk. As we took our seats, the maître d' lit a candle on the table and delivered our menus. With a brief bow, he disappeared.

After selecting a bottle of wine, we perused dinner

options. I bit my lip and hid my face behind the menu. I wasn't surprised by the prices, but they were intimidating. All the reasons I hadn't eaten here before could be boiled down to a single factor—dollar signs. Of course, I had a credit card and could accommodate tonight's splurge. But if this dating thing continued, Nathan would need to reset his dining expectations.

The wine was served. We placed our orders. An awkward silence ensued. My gaze met his across the table. We both glanced away, then shared an uncertain laugh.

Nathan drew a breath that settled into his shoulders.

"Mayela," he said, "when we were at the fountain just now, it seemed there was something you wanted to ask me?"

"Your travels," I replied quickly, anxious to take the conversation anywhere but *there*. "We'd talked about sharing our travels?"

"Oh." He furrowed his brow.

"Yesterday, on the phone you said—"

"Of course. I remember."

"So, I was wondering if…" *Wondering what?* "Have you ever been to Costa Rica?"

"Yes." Nostalgia softened his expression. "As a matter of fact, I have."

We were off. In short order, we discovered several places we'd both visited, many in Latin America. My attempts to pinpoint where we'd overlapped, however, failed, one after the other, in ways that puzzled me. Nathan's stories, as intriguing as they were, didn't seem to stick to a timeline. As our dialogue continued, my own sense of sequence began to slip. It was a very disconcerting sensation, as if we were speaking in a place divorced from time. I couldn't help but recall my hallucinations, that strange apartment where there'd been no clocks or calendars, no mark that stayed on the walls or in a book, no way to track time at all.

"I'm surprised," Nathan was saying, "that Europe hasn't popped up on your list of destinations."

"Well…" I'd just taken a bite of my duck l'orange, so I had to chew and swallow before continuing. "Mamá is from Spain, and she and Dad met in Germany, so you'd think…" I washed down the food with some more wine. "You'd think I would've been there a million times, right? But Mamá has bad memories of her home. They always discouraged me from going. Eventually I discovered there are so many other places to see, and I stopped thinking of Europe as a destination."

"It's so easy to imagine you there."

I smiled, caught off guard by his wistful expression. "Do you mean with you?"

A grin broke on his face. "Maybe. Someday."

"You said you studied in Europe?"

"I grew up there. Italy, France, and Spain."

"Oh." I'd noticed his accent wasn't American. But it didn't seem Italian, French, or Spanish, either. "Along the Mediterranean? Must've been a nice life. Do you still have family there?"

"Yes. There are a lot of us, actually. We've spread out over the years, but many of them remained in the Old World."

"Very Old World of you to say Old World." I delivered this with a chuckle.

"And your family?"

"I don't have any siblings. Mamá wanted more children with Dad, but something went wrong when I was born. After that, she couldn't get pregnant again."

"That must've been hard for her."

"Yes, but she never talked about it in terms of her own hardship. I think what she regretted most was not giving Dad children of his own." Strange how that came out. For some reason, the reference to my adoption made me uncomfortable. I decided to steer the conversation elsewhere. "Anyway, they divorced a long time ago. Dad's still in the Kansas City area. Mamá lives out in California with her new partner. What about your parents? Where are they?"

"My mother resides in various places. My father died a long time ago."

"Oh. How sad. I'm so sorry."

"I don't remember him. I was just a baby when we were separated."

That could be a sign, of sorts, that neither of us knew our biological fathers. Something uncommon to have in common. If I believed in signs. "Did your mother bring you up on her own, then?"

"She didn't bring me up at all."

"Come again?"

The mood in our alcove grew a shade darker. Nathan frowned and looked away. "This might not be a good conversation for a first date. My family is...complicated."

Yet the tightness in his shoulders and the cloud over his expression betrayed a need to talk.

"Everyone's got a weird family," I replied. "I'm not going to pressure you, of course, but I'm willing to listen to anything you want to share. Those of us with weird families generally need to talk about them."

He let go a slow exhale. "The people who raised me were not my relatives. They found me abandoned as a baby."

"What?" I replied, startled. Nathan, sophisticated Nathan, who had traveled the world and was about to spend a damn fortune on a single dinner, started out as a dumpster baby?

"They were a poor family, with little means. They adopted me out of the goodness of their hearts."

I set down my knife and fork to focus fully on him. "How awful that you were abandoned! But also, how wonderful that they took you in. They must be very special people."

"They saved my life. I loved them all very much. For the entirety of my youth, I never questioned my origins or considered myself anything but part of their family. Then when I became a man, everything changed. My mother returned to claim me."

"Claim you?" What a strange way of putting it.

"She told me she'd watched me grow up and that she was pleased. She'd decided I was worthy to be recognized as her son."

"*Worthy?*" I stared at him, maybe a full minute, before deciding where to go with that. "I can't even. After your adoptive family did all the work and gave you all their love, this stranger waltzes into your life and expects you to…" I shook my head. "How did you respond?"

A shadow threaded through his composure. He shifted in his seat. Beneath the surface, I sensed turmoil, along with some great unspoken burden.

"By the time she disclosed the truth," he said,

"circumstances were such that I could not return to my adopted family. Nor would I have survived on my own. So, I made my choice and became part of her world."

"I see."

"My mother gave me everything," he hastened to add, as if trying to justify himself. "Wealth, opportunity, power. I would not be where I am without her. But her favor has come with a great price."

Suppressing a shudder, I reached for my wine and took a long draw. Silence settled between us. Muffled sounds floated in from the main dining room. Someone out there was laughing.

"You said your mother is still alive?" I asked quietly.

"Yes."

"Well." I poured myself more wine. "If this dating thing works out, we should do Christmas with my parents."

Nathan stared at me, then threw his head back in laughter. "Very well, Mayela. Christmas with your parents sounds like a fine plan."

"Are your siblings crazy, too?"

"Some of them, if I'm to be honest. As I said, we're not close. We all had different fathers."

"Really?" Just when I thought this story couldn't get stranger.

"This is what my mother does. Did." Nathan poured himself more wine. "Forgive me, Mayela, but I started this story. I may as well finish it. Mother has always abandoned her children to others for upbringing. Those she deems worthy are reclaimed before the end of their thirtieth year."

I sat back in my chair, flabbergasted. "That's got to

be the craziest thing I've ever heard."

"Truth is stranger than fiction."

"Your mother is a piece of work!"

"Don't ever tell her that yourself."

"I'm saying this with all due respect."

"Of course." He offered a grim smile and took another draught from his wine.

"Oh!" I clapped a hand over my mouth, overcome with a sudden revelation. "Do you realize what you just described is a classic polyandrous model?"

"A what?"

"Polyandry! With a little nest parasitism thrown in."

"What are you talking about?"

"It's a reproductive strategy I teach in my behavioral ecology class." My brain had gone into high gear. Truly the parallels were remarkable. "Polyandry isn't common among humans—at least, not in ways we might recognize—but a lot of species are polyandrous. Females mate with multiple partners and leave parental care to someone else, usually the father."

"Is this supposed to make me feel better?"

"No." I shook my head. "That's not what I'm saying at all. It's just…All that matters under natural selection is what works. Polyandry worked for her. That doesn't change how hard all of this was on you. I'm so sorry, Nathan, for what you went through."

He shrugged and turned his gaze inward. "It all happened a long time ago, and I can't complain about the outcome. Mother opened a whole new world for me. She made the impossible possible."

Again, silence fell between us. I watched him sink into his thoughts as he fingered his wineglass. Then he leaned forward, shifting his dark gaze from the wine to me. "Mayela, why are you on your own?"

I choked on my wine. "I…What? I'm sorry, I don't understand."

"You are kind and generous, beautiful in form and spirit. Rarely judgmental, yet fiercely independent. Anyone in this world would be privileged to stand at your side and yet, you have remained alone. Why?"

"But I wasn't always…" My voice fell, caught by the lump in my throat. Pain wrapped its spiny grip around my heart. "I wasn't always alone. I had a husband. His name was Carlos, but he passed away. Six years ago."

Nathan caught his breath. "I'm sorry. I didn't mean—"

"There was an accident." I forged on, hoping words would subdue the upheaval inside. "Carlos used to go running, early in the morning before the sun came up. One day he didn't come back. A hit-and-run took him. They never found out who did it."

"Mayela, please. I'm so sorry. Truly. We don't have to talk about this."

"No, it's okay." I held up my hand to stop him. Words came faster than I could think. "We need to talk. About all of this. Your family, my family. Our histories. Carlos was a good man. He had a great sense of humor. He was more extroverted than me, but we made it work. He'd just started an appointment at UMKC when we met; he had a very bright career ahead of him. He studied rocks." The brightness of this memory made me laugh. "He insisted they were alive! Can you imagine? We argued about it all the time. He made me laugh…So much."

I bit my lip, surprised to be fighting back tears. When would the lacerations caused by his death finally, fully heal? "Carlos had such a kind instinct. He always *got* things about me that other people didn't. Maybe it helped that we both came from mixed backgrounds. I'd be lying if I said I didn't miss him. I do, every single day. But I've learned to live without him. That's why I'm still alone. It's better to be alone if I can't find anybody who…"

I stopped. I'd been about to say *anybody who understands me like Carlos did.* Yet in that moment, as I registered the set of Nathan's shoulders, his absolute focus on my every word, I felt understood. For the first time in years, I felt listened to and understood.

"I think he would have liked you," I finished quietly. "If there's a good place after all of this, I believe he's there. And I believe he'd be glad we met."

Nathan's expression opened up in surprise. Then he set his jaw and looked away.

"I'm honored, Mayela," he said in subdued tones. "Truly."

My meal was done, and the wine nearly so. I felt pressure in my bladder, along with a desperate need to excuse myself from the table. Not only to go to the bathroom, but to escape what had become a very intense conversation. I stood and picked up my purse. "I should look for the ladies' room."

"Restrooms are in the back." He indicated the direction with a nod of his head. "Straight back and to the right. Should I ask for the dessert menu?"

"No dessert. An espresso would be nice."

I hastened out of the alcove and into the main dining room, still packed with customers. Staff hurried back and forth, arms laden with plates and trays. Intent on avoiding a collision, I picked a slow, crooked path between crowded tables. I caught snippets of conversation in several languages, including Spanish, French, Italian, and German, along with others I couldn't identify. The Plaza Art Fair had attracted quite an international crowd!

Just short of the hallway leading to the restrooms, I was forced into a tight squeeze past a boisterous group. They, too, spoke some strange language, like an antiquated form of English. Somebody quipped something unintelligible. Everyone roared with laughter. Maybe they were thespians practicing Shakespearean insults?

As I passed them by, I caught sight of a beautiful, dark-haired woman sitting at the head of the table. She seemed familiar. I did a double take, certain I knew her from somewhere. The woman noticed me and, flashing a seductive smile, gave me a wink. Embarrassed, I glanced away. In that moment, everyone's attire changed. Men who had been in cotton shirts and lightweight pants now wore velvet cloaks and feathered hats. The women's breezy summer dresses were replaced by satin gowns with voluminous skirts. I stared in confusion. The thespians weren't simply speaking Old English anymore. They looked the part. Had they walked off a Plaza Art Fair stage without changing costumes? But that wouldn't explain why a second ago they were all dressed like normal people.

A knot of fear settled in my stomach. Glancing around, I realized almost no one in the restaurant wore contemporary clothes. Instead, I saw costumes from different periods, and even different cultures.

Eighteenth- and nineteenth-century gowns and jackets, exaggerated wigs and batting fans. Civilians and soldiers. Peasants and nobles. Men in striped suits sharing drinks with French-speaking flappers. Women in forties-style pants playing cards with men in sixties fringes. The ground swayed beneath me. A high-pitched ring filled my ears. Panicked, I covered my ears and shut my eyes. *This isn't happening. This can't be happening!*

"Ma'am?" Someone touched my elbow.

I jumped and opened my eyes.

One of the servers, a young woman in a starched shirt and dark pants, peered at me with a worried frown. "Are you all right, ma'am? Can I help you?"

"I…" I scanned the restaurant beyond her. Everything was back to normal, regular people having regular dinners in their regular 2016 clothes. My entire body went cold. When I spoke again, my voice was weak. "I was…looking for the restroom?"

She smiled and pointed the way. To my relief, the bathroom was single-use and there was no line. I slipped inside, closed the door, and locked it. Then I sagged against the wall. *Breathe, Mayela. Just breathe.*

What had happened? Was I hallucinating again?

Trembling, I went to the sink and washed my hands, let cool water run over my palms and wrists. My pulse began to steady. Maybe there was a logical explanation. Maybe the dim lighting in the dining room had played a trick on my senses. After all, the whole episode had lasted less than a second. And unlike my hallucinations in August, I never lost touch with the fact something was off.

I dried my hands and proceeded to relieve my

bladder.

Yes, that's it, I assured myself. No need to worry. That conversation with Nathan must've made me jumpy and hypersensitive. A person could imagine anything after hearing the stories he told.

That was some kind of crazy, Nathan's mom. A person of means who serially abandoned her children and then reclaimed them through...What? Manipulation? Mind games? Extortion? What kind of sicko contacts their abandoned child after thirty years and says, "I have judged you worthy of my superior existence?"

I wouldn't have survived on my own. That's what Nathan had said. What did that mean, exactly? What was the alternative to following her? Destitution? Death? And the family he'd been forced to abandon! They'd loved him and raised him, and he loved them in return. It broke my heart to think about all this.

I flushed the toilet and washed my hands again. I wanted to splash my face to chase all these shadows away, but I couldn't because—makeup. I sighed. I never wore this stuff. Why tonight? Because the shading brought out my eyes, of course. Had to be sexy for the new date.

My breath came up short. *Oh, Nathan.* I thought Mamá had a few screws loose. And Dad! With his nineteen fifties politics and obnoxious red cap. I would never complain about either of them again.

I was still overheated. I caught some cold water with my fingers and dabbed the back of my neck. I liked Nathan so much, found him deeply attractive and easy to talk to. We'd trusted each other with some hard truths tonight. That meant something. Didn't it?

I took some tissues and patted down my neck. With another deep breath, I unlocked the bathroom door to step into the hallway. Someone was waiting, of course. After all, I'd been in the panic room forever. Following bathroom etiquette, I offered her an apologetic smile without meeting her gaze. She moved to block my way.

"Sorry." I gave a nervous laugh and tried to step aside, but she blocked me again. Startled, I looked up and recognized the woman who'd been sitting at the head of the thespian table. The dark-haired one who smiled and winked at me.

"You're Mayela Lehman," she said.

"I'm sorry." I blinked. "Do we know each other?"

"I'm Anne." She spoke with an affected British accent, *Downton Abbey* style. Not the kitchen staff, the people who lived upstairs. She was even more beautiful up close, with a stunning figure and legs that did very well in that short summer dress. "Nathan and I are friends."

My heart fell into a pit. "Friends?"

"He's told me a lot about you."

Great. Just great. The one thing missing to make this a perfect evening. "There's not much to tell."

"He's a good judge of character, and he thinks very highly of you."

Anger boiled inside my veins. I pushed past her and continued down the hall.

Anne called after me. "Choose him."

I turned around, caught by what she said and the pleading tone of her voice.

"You'll be tempted to throw your hat back in the ring. We all are." Anne took a step toward me. Light spilled out of the restroom, giving her a soft halo. "But

I've seen what's out there. You could do better, but you're likely to do worse. Much worse."

I bristled. "Thank you for the vote of confidence, Anne."

"I'm not saying there's anything wrong with you. On the contrary."

"I don't take relationship advice from strangers."

"Oh." She frowned. "I see. It seems I may have overstepped my bounds."

"I should think so."

"I'm sorry. I didn't mean to. I thought you and Nathan had already…" She faltered and took a step back. "What's said is said. Perhaps, when the time comes, you will remember my words."

With that, she slipped inside the bathroom and closed the door.

I strode back to the main dining room, irritation trailing me like a black cloud. Everyone in the restaurant could have been dressed as circus clowns, and I would not have cared. When I arrived at the alcove, Nathan looked up. I did not return his greeting. Back straight and shoulders stiff, I sat down and stared out the window in silence. Along Brush Creek, headlights of passing cars sliced through the night.

"What's wrong?" Nathan asked.

Fury surged inside. I slid my gaze to his face and studied him a long moment—the angle of his jaw, the prominent nose and dark brow. Those eyes, so deep I could lose myself in them. Dammit. This man was too beautiful and strange for me. Why keep kidding myself?

"I ran into someone just now," I said.

"Who?" The response came sharp as a blade.

"Her name was—"

"Anne?" His eyes widened, and he sucked in his breath. Then my date leaned back, one hand going to his chin. His gaze turned inward. He shook his head and gave a short laugh. "Anne."

"You know her."

"Yes." He returned his attention to me. "We've been friends a long time."

"Friends?"

"And colleagues."

"Colleagues?" I hated this. We hadn't finished one date, and already I was jealous. But what was I supposed to do? *I mean, look at her! Look at him.* I sighed and shook my head.

"I'm sorry if she said anything upsetting or confusing."

"I think she was trying to endorse you. It didn't go well. Why is she here tonight?"

The waiter walked in with our coffee. He left the bill on our table before departing. Not the bill, I realized. Nathan's credit card and the receipt.

"No," I said.

"No, what?" Nathan filled out the slip of paper with a tip and signed it.

"I pay for my own meals."

"Not tonight."

"We should've talked about this!"

"Mayela." He closed the little black folder and set it aside. "You know as well as I do this entire system is rigged in my favor. Rigged from beginning to end on the completely irrational basis of me having one set of physical characteristics and you having another. All my life I've benefitted from my privilege, while you have paid for it. The least I can do is treat you to dinner."

"I appreciate the intention," I replied, "but I'd rather have complete structural reform than a free dinner."

"You want a revolution? We can talk about that, too." Nathan slipped the credit card into his billfold. "There's still time to see the Art Fair. Shall we take a walk?"

No. Uh huh. He didn't get to brush this off that easily. "Why was Anne here tonight? And why did she ambush me? It creeped me out."

Nathan drew a breath and set his lips in a thin line. "I promise you, there's nothing going on with Anne that would interfere with what's happening between you and me."

A fault line cracked inside my heart. Shaken, I looked at my hands, resting on my lap. I wanted him. I did. But not on these terms. Lifting my chin, I met his gaze. "I'll be the one to decide that."

He hesitated, then nodded. "Understood."

Chapter 7

As we left the restaurant and stepped into the night, my senses went into a tailspin. Dizzy and frightened, I reached for Nathan. He caught my hand.

"Mayela," he said.

"I can't…" *Breathe.* I wheezed, then choked. My sinuses had clogged under a tidal wave of smells—grilled sausage and automobile exhaust; creams and perfumes; sweat and night blossoms and the musty flow of Brush Creek, oily with runoff from the pavement.

"Mayela, you need to exhale." His words were almost lost inside the crowd's high-pitched chatter. I covered my ears. Deep bass throbbed inside my head. The very air, it seemed, threatened to crush me.

"Mayela!" Nathan's voice cut sharp through the haze. "Look at the stars, and exhale."

Stars! I wanted to scream. *Who sees stars from the Plaza?* But I looked up and there they were—a handful of bright points making a brave stand against the bane of public lighting. Air rushed out of my lungs, then flowed back in. Sounds and smells faded to normal. The swirling Plaza came into focus.

Nathan stood next to me, hand beneath my arm, voice laden with concern. "Are you okay?"

I pulled away, confused. "I don't know. I…When we stepped out of the restaurant…I could swear I've experienced something like that before, except…"

Except I was hallucinating. The last time I had a sensory overload like that was during my hallucinations.

Nathan took my hand and placed it in the crook of his arm. The sudden intimacy brought my focus back to him.

"Tell me about your other experience," he said.

I shook my head. "You don't want to hear that story. It's crazy."

He grinned. "I told you about my mother, didn't I? It can't be much crazier than that."

Nathan started toward the interior of the Plaza, compelling me to walk with him. Our steps fell into synchrony. The warmth emanating from his body, the strength of his arm, his ever-present aroma, sharp and compelling—all of this gave me a welcomed sense of security. *I have to tell him something*, I thought. If I wanted this to last, I had to find a way to let him into my truth.

"Not long ago," I said, "I had a…a dream. I was in an apartment in the city, and I couldn't find a way out. Then one morning I woke up—in the dream—and saw a door I'd never seen before. When I stepped over the threshold, I was in the woods at my grandparents' farm. I experienced the same sensory overload then as when we left the restaurant. The air was so heavy I felt as if I were trying to breathe underwater. I blacked out and the next I knew…"

I stopped. The next thing I knew, I was in the hospital with Mamá and Dad.

"That's all, really," I finished. "The sensation I had when we left the restaurant scared me. But I feel all right now."

Nathan paused our gait to look back down the street from where we'd come. He kept my hand firmly upon his arm. Not that I had any desire to pull away.

"I have an idea," he said at length. "About your dream, and why you associated it with coming out of the restaurant. But we've already had some heavy conversations tonight. Why don't we look at some art first? We can come back to this topic later."

"Yes!" What a relief to hear him say that. "That's a wonderful plan. Let's look at some art."

I was so ready for an escapist adventure into the Art Fair's white canvas booths. Fantastical sculptures and moody paintings, sinuous glasswork and bold ceramics, thought-provoking photographs of landscapes and people. Every creative work distracted me from the weight of my own thoughts.

Nathan, too, drank up the Fair. Moreover, the Fair seemed to enjoy him. We couldn't enter a tent without drawing instant attention. At first, I marveled at the attendants' instinct for his generous wallet. Then I noticed the flushed expressions, nervous laughter, and fluttering hands, along with a persistent tendency to ignore my existence. Apparently, these people's interest in my date went beyond the next sell. Nathan took the fawning in stride, as if he were accustomed to random strangers falling head over heels. He kept all conversations laser-focused on art, and he awarded their exceptional customer service with numerous purchases.

We were in the tent of an artisanal jeweler, me rendered invisible once again as the designer pounced on Nathan, when a strange thought occurred to me. The jeweler's work was extraordinary; semi-precious stones with hearts of fire wrapped in filaments of silver and bronze.

“That’s what we are.” I gasped.

Startled by my own declaration, I glanced at Nathan. To my relief, he hadn’t heard me, absorbed as he was by his present negotiation.

Turning my attention back to the display case again, I ran my hand above the sparkling stones.

“This is what we are,” I breathed. Precious jewels and shining crystals. Objects of fascination to be collected and treasured, bartered and sold. This was how Nathan and his kind saw us. Again, I slid my gaze toward him, half afraid he might hear my thoughts.

Why not? I asked myself. The idea was so compelling. Why not entertain, for a little while, that my instincts might be spot on, that what I remembered was real? Maybe I had been on the other side. Maybe Nathan was one of them—a creature that stalked the Hunting Grounds, an immortal in pursuit of souls.

A weight lifted from my shoulders, as if accepting this dark vision made the world a brighter place. Standing next to me in animated debate with the jeweler, Nathan’s presence became more palpable, more vivid than ever. Beneath his remarks and artistic praise, I saw an exacting spark, a shrewd calculation. He wasn’t only assessing the art, he was gauging the worth of the artist’s soul!

He stopped and looked at me. “I’m sorry, Mayela. Did you say something?”

“What? Oh, no.” I took a step back. “I was just thinking how beautiful all these pieces are.”

“Agreed.” He grinned and signed off on yet another purchase. Then he shook hands with the clearly besotted jeweler. “Stunning and unique. Thank you. I hope we have the chance to meet again."

"Of course, Mr. de la Rosa," the young man said with shining eyes and flushed cheeks. "You have my card."

After the jewelry booth, I stopped paying attention to art and studied Nathan instead. The possibility I might be observing a soul hunter in action filled me with fascination. Questions tumbled through my head.

Why stake out souls at an art fair?

Why come here as opposed to, say, a speedway or a shopping mall or Sunday mass?

Obviously, he was drawn to souls with a creative temperament, the ability to question, criticize, transform. *You want a revolution?* he had asked at the end of our dinner. *We can talk about that.*

Oh! I felt a shiver of excitement, the certainty I was onto something. Nathan sought souls clamoring for revolution. No subservient types for him. No blind obedience or willful ignorance. No church-going zombies. No red baseball caps or hedge fund managers or conservative radio fans. Only visionaries. Mozarts and Humboldts. Virginia Woolfs and Rachel Carsons. Oscar Romeros and Gloria Steinems. Prophets and rebels, thieves and troublemakers, philosophers and scientists, warriors and healers! He was recruiting them all, assembling an army from across the ages that would descend upon this world any day now and burn down the—

"Mayela?"

I looked up at him, jolted out of my reverie. "Huh?"

Nathan watched me with a quizzical frown as we walked side by side. "Did you hear anything I just said?"

"What? No." I bit my lip, embarrassed. "Sorry. I was just thinking. About…stuff?"

"I see. Maybe we can take a short break and—Oh!" He grabbed my hand and pulled me toward another tent. "But first, we have to take a look at this."

We stepped inside the tent and stood a moment, halted by the scrutiny of dozens of masks. Aged faces emerged from wind-blown backgrounds, their features lifelike despite hauntingly vacant eyes. Spellbound, Nathan released my hand and stepped forward. He reached up and traced the twisted contours of one of the masks.

"How exquisite," he murmured.

Melancholy crept into his words. Pain and longing. It occurred to me he'd recognized something of himself in that mask. I wondered how many masks he'd worn over the ages. How long did it take him to craft the mask he wore now, so suited to seducing me?

What would happen to that mask when the hunt ended and his prize was secured?

The booth attendant pounced on Nathan. She was an elderly woman, bright-eyed and beautiful with splayed white hair. And like all the others, clearly infatuated. Soon they'd be negotiating prices. Nathan would buy a set, maybe a few, and arrange to send them to whatever address he'd been providing all night.

Not a demon, I decided.

The postal service didn't ship to Hell.

Or did they?

And what about that credit card he kept whipping out? How could Nathan have a credit card if he were a demon? Oh, wait. That would be easy. All he'd need was a banker willing to sell his soul.

Something released inside of me. My feet hurt. My shoulders felt stiff. I could feel the wheels in my brain winding down. Puffing out my cheeks, I glanced around the tent. My thought game had ended, and I was tired. Feeling cramped, even claustrophobic, I went outside, leaving Nathan to his current groupie and his next purchase.

The crowd had thinned, and some of the vendors had started to pack up. I took out my phone and checked my rideshare app for cars nearby. Once Nathan was done, I'd let him know I was ready to call it a night. It'd been a decent evening. Some weirdness here and there, especially with that Anne person. Damn. She could be a problem. Also, I wasn't sure how I felt about every booth attendant—man, woman, young, and old—falling all over my date. But in general, we'd had a reasonable start. I hoped he felt the same. I wondered when he'd be back in town, whether he'd want to see me again. Maybe with enough time, the weirdness would fade, and we'd become more—

A shiver shot down my spine.

I looked up, hairs pricking on my neck.

Something stirred on the edge of my vision, recalling the dark plains of my hallucinations. My muscles tensed, and I scanned the crowd around me. A low growl reverberated through the air.

Was that sound or a memory?

There.

A few feet away, between shifting bodies, I saw him. Or it. The figure of a man, wraith-like and tall, silhouetted by streetlights.

My breath caught between my teeth.

He watched me with glowing yellow eyes. Then he lifted his arms and reached toward me. Tentacles flowed from his hands, his eyes, his mouth. Panicked, I spun around and rushed back into the tent, crashing into Nathan as he walked out.

"Mayela!" He took hold of my shoulders. "What on earth?"

"I saw a…" The words caught in my throat. My heart was pounding against my ribcage. I clung to him and pointed frantically behind me. "A *thing* right there." I faltered, confused, and searched the crowd. Whatever—whoever—set off my panic had vanished. "I saw…something. Just now, I swear. It was…I don't know what it was. I saw something. I swear."

Nathan held me close, his embrace like an anchor, his gaze marking the direction of my glance. "I left you alone too long. I'm sorry."

"No." I pulled away, embarrassed by my outburst. What was wrong with me? Why did I keep seeing things that weren't there? "Don't apologize. Honestly, I don't know what just happened. I must be tired, I think…Nathan, I think…I'm sorry. It's been a wonderful evening, really, but I'm tired, and I think it's time for me to go home."

"Of course." He nodded. "This place seems to be packing up anyway. Where's your car? I'll walk you to it."

"I took a rideshare down here. If we go out to Ward Parkway, I can—"

"I'll give you a ride home, then."

"Oh, no. You don't have to do that."

"My car's at the Intercontinental. I'll give you a ride home."

And so, it was decided.

Our final walk of the evening took us past the fountain where we met and the restaurant where we ate. At the intersection of Ward Parkway and Broadway, a few remaining tech people worked the corners on the sound stage, chattering with each other as they packed up instruments and equipment. Past the stage, we kept to the sidewalk as we crossed Brush Creek. Despite the oily surface and musty smell, the placid water proved picturesque beneath the evening lights. Nathan and I paused halfway across, resting our hands on the balustrade and taking in the Seville-style architecture of the Plaza one more time.

I hoped that he, too, was wondering whether we'd be back here together.

"Earlier this evening," he said, "I was trying to tell you something, but you didn't hear."

"Yeah. Sorry about that. I've been in a funky mood tonight." I cast him a sideways glance. "Think I'm going to blame it on you."

Nathan laughed. "So, I've been too much of a distraction from myself?"

"Something like that." I smiled.

"I wanted to talk about what happened when we left the restaurant, the idea I had as to why you associated that moment with your dream."

"Oh." He had my attention now. "Go on."

"In the dream, you stepped from an urban apartment into an open woodland, right?"

"Yes."

"You traversed two different worlds in a single step. I believe—perhaps I'm being presumptuous for saying so—but I believe something about our encounter makes you feel the same way. You see yourself on the threshold of something unanticipated. I know I…" He paused, as if reconsidering. When he spoke again, his tone was measured and subdued. "In my time with you, Mayela, I have felt the same thing. I am not entirely certain what lies ahead of us, and I'm not used to feeling that way. But I do not want you to be afraid. Not of me and not of the connection we share."

I blinked and glanced away. Tears threatened my vision. The reflection of streetlamps rippled over the smooth face of Brush Creek. Trees lining the banks stirred in a passing breeze. Below us, a couple walked along the riverbank, embellishing their solitude with intimate laughter.

"You're right," I whispered. "I'm terrified."

"Mayela—"

"Wait. Let me finish." I looked up at him. "I've never felt like this before. When I met my late husband, I experienced joy, attraction, fulfillment, and plenty of uncertainty but not this. Not this overwhelming fear that my world is about to be turned upside down. All evening I've been on pins and needles. My mind is in strange places. I don't know, Nathan. Maybe we aren't right for each other. Maybe we should just—"

"No." He put up his hand to stop me. "That's what I mean. You have to give this a chance. I need you to give me a chance. Mayela." He took my hands in his. "Please. Reach into your heart, and you will know. You cannot let fear drive your decision."

I held his gaze, finding again that thread of steel that had kept me anchored to him. An inner voice insisted he was not the source of approaching chaos; he was my refuge from it.

"Okay," I said, opening my heart up just a little. "Okay."

Relief filled his expression, and he smiled. "Good!" He squeezed my hands, then released them. "That's good."

Setting one palm on the balustrade, Nathan looked out over the darkened Plaza. As he took in the lingering crowd, his smile diminished.

"To be honest," he added quietly, "I'm terrified too."

Not a demon. Demons didn't feel terror. Then, an unsettling question whispered through my mind. *What would terrify a demon?*

Compassion flared through me. I stepped close and gave him a hug.

Nathan stiffened as if taken by surprise. Then he relaxed and wrapped his arms around me, his embrace warm and familiar as any homecoming. I tightened my hold on him, rested my head against his chest, listened to the slow beat of his heart, breathed in his scent as his lips came to rest, tender and sweet, upon my hair.

We stood like that a long time, the waters of Brush Creek flowing quietly beneath our feet.

****

Tierra y Mar (Earth and Sea)

Costa Rica, 1995

In her second year of college, Mayela begged her parents for the opportunity to study abroad. Spain was her first choice. Gabriela, wary of an encounter with Mayela's true father, vehemently opposed this idea. Mayela, surprised by her mother's opposition to what seemed a reasonable request, dug in her heels. After weeks of angry discussions between his passionate wife and stubborn daughter, Josef finally brokered family peace by proposing Costa Rica as an alternative. Mayela could take classes at the Universidad de Costa Rica. She'd live with a Costa Rican family and practice her mother's language, if not her culture. Costs were reasonable, and the country was considered safe for women travelers. If they planned well, Mayela could stay a whole year without falling behind on her degree program.

Foiled by the sudden alliance between husband and daughter, Gabriela backed down. But the thought of Mayela alone in a foreign country still terrified her. By now, Mayela had blinded herself to her own nature. She was not prepared to summon even the simplest of protections should the need arise. *Por el amor de Dios*, she was still a child in so many ways! Innocent toward this world, ignorant of the next. Who would look after her in that distant land?

Anxious to secure a guardian for her daughter, Gabriela sent careful petitions to what she hoped were friendly spirits. Every day, while Josef was at work and Mayela in class, she drew the curtains against the sun and lit a circle of white candles in her living room. Within the circle, Gabriela laid her secret altar, a small collection of carved figurines and precious stones kept hidden in a box deep inside her closet. Enveloped by the scent of burning herbs, she closed her eyes and sang to the ones who resided in the moon, the stars, the trees, and the earth. The aromatic smoke rose, twisted, and dispersed, carrying her song with it. Gabriela caught threads of each offering and wove them together. She illuminated these threads with the desires of her heart, crafting a medallion of light that could only be seen by creatures from beyond the veil.

"*Vigilancia y protección*," she said, laying the petition on her altar. With great trepidation, she then whispered words not spoken since before Mayela was born, the same ones that had damned her all those years ago. "If you grant this request, I will reciprocate, according to the laws of my people and the will of your kind."

One day, someone responded. Gabriela caught her breath as his shadow coalesced, little more than a dark mist inside her circle of flickering candles. She recognized him as El Caminante, the one who had observed them on the playground on the threshold of that storm when Mayela was eight. The one who had stayed when she drove away all the others in middle school and high school. At once, Gabriela regretted summoning him. What was she thinking, to trust any of these creatures again? Hadn't she learned from the mistakes of her youth? He knew nothing was more precious to her than Mayela. He knew he could ask anything in exchange for this favor, and she would not refuse.

"El Caminante," she murmured, hoping to step back from the bargaining table. "*Perdóname, es que yo—*"

He lifted a shadowy hand to silence her. Gabriela watched in fear as he picked up the medallion of light. It shone inside his dark grip, a spot of sun breaking through wintery clouds. She drew a breath, determined to retract her words and find another way, but before she could speak, he vanished, taking the medallion with him.

Startled, Gabriela sprang to her feet. She searched

the shadows in the corners and scoured her inner senses, but he was nowhere to be found. Setting one hand over her heart, she whispered in Spanish, "*Imposible.*"

His kind never acted this way. They never accepted a petition without first setting the price. To do so had left her without any obligation to him. Why? What then would he consider a reward for taking on this task? Gabriela could imagine countless answers to this question, none of which set her at ease.

****

El Caminante sensed Gabriela's confusion in his wake. It was not uncommon for her kind to expect negotiation, but why demand recompense for something he had already planned to do?

Vigilance had become his habit when it came to Mayela. And protection could not be promised. Like all his kind, El Caminante had limited powers of intervention in the mortal realm. Still, Gabriela's light-filled medallion would be useful. Entering another territory always entailed risk. To follow Mayela, he'd need permission from those who held sway over Costa Rica's mortal inhabitants. Proof of Gabriela's request would facilitate his passage, reducing the likelihood of unwanted confrontations. In truth, Gabriela had done him a favor by offering this token of light. Perhaps he would repay her someday.

Among his own kind, El Caminante was known as Nekhen, and he was not a stranger to Central America. Decades before Mayela's year abroad, he'd established a bond with one of its most ancient entities, a powerful healer bound to the central highlands of Costa Rica. In the seventeenth century, she'd survived the Spanish invasion by reasserting sovereignty as the Virgin of Los Angeles, also known as the Black Madonna. Her usurpation during colonial times did not please the conquering gods. In the centuries that followed, their conflict spilled into the mortal realm, causing earthquakes and volcanic eruptions until at last the bickering powers settled into an uneasy truce.

When Nekhen first entered the Black Madonna's realm, he was recruiting souls to support Nicaragua's struggle against despotic rule. This pleased the Madonna. It helped that Nekhen had relatives in her territories. After World War II, descendants of his mother, Wadje, had followed Italian immigrants to the southern highlands. The Black Madonna was not fond of Wadje, but she adored Nekhen's cousins. They tended well to her forests and fields and sent her penitents every year for the annual pilgrimage.

It was the mortal year of 1995 when Nekhen returned to the Black Madonna's court. He carried Mayela's name in his heart and Gabriela's light-laced prayer in his palm. Pleased by his reappearance, and his appearance, the Madonna welcomed the young Soul Master with a warm embrace. She granted him safe passage with a simple warning: "You must leave us when the girl goes, and you are not to abuse my favor."

In the months that followed, Mayela's soul grew in depth and potential. Her mother's language, a source of awkwardness and embarrassment while she was growing up, became her gateway to a new and extraordinary sense of self. Mayela no longer felt like "the weird one" at the table. Set free, she wandered the streets of San Jose and swam along the beaches of Guanacaste. She laughed with friends over afternoon coffee and danced in local night clubs. Everywhere she went, there seemed to be a young Costa Rican man ready to court her. This did not displease her. Not in the least.

Halfway through her year abroad, Mayela traveled with one of her classes to the Osa Peninsula. Nekhen, who had heard of this sacred place but never visited, followed with interest. Mayela and her friends hiked through dense jungle to reach the heart of Corcovado National Park. Beyond the narrow muddy paths, pulsating organisms filled every imaginable space. Towering trees, twisting vines, elegant palms, spreading ferns, and spiny plants crowded against each other in a tangled riot. Humid mist enveloped the landscape, impregnated with the smell of ripe fruit and decaying leaves, with the musk of animals marking their territories.

At the end of their ten-hour hike, almost lost beneath the crushing mass of life, sat a low-slung wooden building known as Sirena Station. Here, Mayela and her fellow students set up tents in an open attic. At night, the chime of dink frogs lulled Mayela to sleep. In the morning, roaring howler monkeys jolted her out of her dreams. Along the trails surrounding the station, she encountered serpents large and small, some innocuous, others deadly. Solitary tapirs eyed her as they grazed along the river's edge. Massive herds of peccaries scattered through the underbrush. Birds of all sizes and colors flashed through the foliage. Squirrel monkeys swung down from high branches to have a closer look, their tiny faces a reflection of their human cousins—agile, curious, and wary.

Unseen by Mayela, but visible to Nekhen,

countless entities kept this magnificence in motion. At every level of the forest, children of the Black Madonna churned the cycle of life with earthen hands. Their whispers and laughter, clear as bells to Nekhen, sent quiet tremors through Mayela's awareness. At times she paused in her stride and tilted her head, as if she could hear otherworldly music just beyond the organic sounds of the forest. Then she blinked, and with a quick shake of her head, continued on her way, the melody seeming to slip from her grasp.

Mayela's professor assigned her a project, a survey of orchid bees. Mayela had not worked with insects before, but soon the six-legged sapphire gems earned her complete devotion. The males gathered scents to make perfume for attracting mates, a behavior that appealed to Mayela's budding romantic sensibilities. She set out baits for them, small pads soaked with vanilla and eucalyptus oils, on ridges and in ravines, on the forest edge and in the woodland deep. Hours slipped by as Mayela catalogued every iridescent creature that buzzed down from the canopy and landed on her baits. Each tiny visitor filled her with awe and joy.

On her last day in the park, as Mayela headed back to the station, she decided to cut a path along the seashore. Having rarely seen the ocean during her childhood, she could not get enough of it now. The trail ran just inside a thin line of trees and coconut palms, beyond which the Pacific crashed in mist-filled waves against a black sand beach. When she paused to raise her face to the wind and inhale the salty spray, Nekhen sensed the approach of one of his kind.

Not so much an approach as a Soul Master's decision to make himself known.

Half a breath later, Mayela also caught a movement at the edge of her vision. She turned and let go a gasp as Jaguar melted out of the forest a few yards ahead. The creature stood with ears peaked, its gaze fixed on the young woman. Muscles rippled beneath his mottled fur. The tip of his tail twitched as his golden eyes slid from Mayela to Nekhen.

"This one is yours?" he demanded with a throaty growl.

Though Mayela could see Jaguar, she did not recognize his language or realize he was a creature from beyond the veil. Believing this an ordinary wildcat of the mortal realm, she gave a little jump of excitement and reached to take her camera out of her backpack. Then she stopped, perhaps fearing any sudden motion might scare the big cat away.

As if Jaguar could experience fear.

Mayela straightened and let her hands fall to her sides.

"Thank you," she murmured. "Thank you for letting me see you."

Something ruptured inside of Nekhen at these words, filling him with tender pride and sweet dread. Mayela's deference was well-placed, but her innocence had punctured his heart. How could she not sense the deadly implications of this encounter?

"Is she yours?" Jaguar repeated with a chuff.

With this question, Jaguar had declared his interest, identifying himself as a rival for Mayela's soul.

"No." Nekhen steeled himself for what might come. Confrontations such as this were not unusual among Nekhen's kind, but as one of the Ancients, Jaguar walked a different path. He'd be less inclined to follow current protocols, more disposed toward taking what he wanted with sudden, decisive action. "I accompany her out of interest, nothing more. She has yet to declare an allegiance."

"I recognize her mark, though it is faint." Jaguar sniffed at the air as he spoke. "They have baptized her to the Roman gods, the gods of the Invaders."

"You know how little that means. Many who are now loyal to your mother were also baptized."

"You intend to deliver this one to my mother?"

"No. I merely make a point."

Jaguar shifted his golden-eyed gaze back to Mayela. He crouched, ears laid back, hunger flaring through his colors. "I've been watching her. In the time of the Ancients, I would have consumed her, made her part of my forest. She is worthy."

Heat spiked inside Nekhen. "The time of Ancients has ended."

Jaguar's predatory gaze slid back to Nekhen. He bared his teeth. Nekhen's battle form coalesced. They assessed each other, Jaguar's ivory claws piercing the earth, Nekhen's sapphire-tipped wings blocking the amber sun.

A fight with any child of the Black Madonna would mean banishment from her lands, but Nekhen would not let Jaguar have Mayela. Not without a contest.

At last, Jaguar chuffed and tossed his head, backing off a few steps. He marked a circle, sat heavily in place, and began licking his paws. "You're a brave one, Soul Master. Who brought you into being?"

"Wadje is my mother," Nekhen replied, with a nod of deference.

“Wadje?” Jaguar’s eyes narrowed, his demeanor shifting from disdain to caution. “That old serpent. You must be worth something if you passed her muster.”

Nekhen held his silence, having found it unwise to speak of his mother with others of his kind.

“What is your interest in this one?” Jaguar pointed his nose at Mayela.

“I wish to acquire her soul.”

“Yes, but why? What’s special about her?”

Nekhen glanced at Mayela, unsure of the answer. As a child she had shown extraordinary potential, able to see his kind and visualize her dreams. Those abilities had faded until, like so many of her kind, she had grown into what she was now—an ordinary young woman trying to find her way in the mortal world. Still, her mere presence brought him great joy.

“Do you hear them speaking to her?” Jaguar prompted.

“Who?” The question confounded Nekhen. He heard many voices in the forest, but none directed at Mayela.

“Our brothers and sisters.” Jaguar nodded to the trees above, the ground below. “The ones who drink in the light and till the soil. They send their silent song to her, yet she ignores them, as she ignores us.”

“Her lack of awareness is not a fault,” Nekhen countered. “Her kind always lose touch with the truth as they mature. This is the limitation of their material forms. Mayela may not understand or have words for the music she hears now, but she hears us. On the edge of her awareness, she can always hear.”

“You do like her, don’t you?” Jaguar tossed his head in amusement, rolled onto his back, and stretched.

"Why don't you eat her, then? Seeing as you don't want me to do the honors."

"You know such things are forbidden."

"Forbidden?" Jaguar sprang to his feet. "You and I are gods, Soul Master! We are subject to no one's laws, not even our own."

Nekhen clenched his fists. What sort of game was Jaguar playing? Consumption of mortal flesh had been banned among their kind long ago. Breaking any of their covenants would result in severe punishment.

"Do you not miss it?" Jaguar insisted with a low growl. "The taste of their blood? The power of their flesh?"

Nekhen caught a flicker of emerald behind Jaguar's eyes. The flare vanished before Nekhen could fully capture its deeper hues, ephemeral but unmistakable. Trepidation filled him. This was not the Black Madonna's son. The auras of all her family were permeated with earthy tones, sometimes threaded with gold or soft jade, but never adorned with the cold, hard colors of cut gems. No, someone else lurked behind Jaguar's form. Someone of the Old World, ancient and powerful. Dangerous.

"All covenants of blood sacrifice were abolished before I was made," Nekhen said with caution.

Jaguar's gaze opened with interest. "You are young, then! How did you become as you are without consuming mortal flesh or blood?"

"They feed us in other ways now."

"Oh?"

"This reserve, for example." Nekhen gestured to the forest. "Her reverence. Do these gifts not feed you?"

"Not enough." Jaguar yawned, exposing canines that could puncture Mayela's skull. "Theirs has always been a paltry reverence, and now they bleed us dry."

"That can change."

"Agreed. But we will have to eat them alive if they are ever to understand."

Jaguar closed the distance to Mayela. Nekhen moved to block his way. Jaguar crouched and growled, swatted his paw in menace, but Nekhen held his ground.

With a shrug, Jaguar relaxed his haunches. "Very well, Soul Master. I concede. Today is not a day to pick a fight with a son of Wadje."

A sliver of relief coursed through Nekhen, though he found little comfort in using his mother's name as a shield.

"Besides," Jaguar continued, "what do I know of mortals? I am old, and some say my time has ended."

"Your time has not ended, Ancient One," Nekhen replied, hoping to mollify his rival with a gesture of respect. "We still have much to learn from your legacy."

"This is true." Jaguar approached Nekhen, with a nod toward their mortal companion. "Here is my first lesson for you, Soul Master: Even the worthy are not to be indulged. You think this one can love you? She will deceive you. She will burn you alive if you give her a chance. Like all her kind, she must be broken to be subdued. We are the lawmakers, Soul Master. We are the givers of all. Everything that comes from us must be returned. Who is going to teach her that? You?"

"If she chooses me." Nekhen hoped his doubt did not show in his aura. "Yes."

“Choice.” Jaguar chuffed. “We should never have given them choice.”

With that, the great cat leapt into the forest, vanishing into the underbrush without a sound.

Mayela released her breath and clapped her hands over her mouth. For a full minute she stood frozen in place. Then she threw her head back in laughter and shouted, “Did you see that? Did you see? That was a goddam jaguar! Right in front of me!”

Mayela whooped and spun and danced along the forest path. Sparks flew from the vibrant flame of her soul. As Nekhen watched her, a hollowness opened inside of him. Under normal circumstances, he would have been fed by the joy Mayela’s soul generated. Yet all he felt was anxiety, a painful awareness of what he might suffer if he lost this one strangely compelling soul, interlaced with cold certainty that he could lose Mayela. He would lose Mayela if this entity disguised as Jaguar maintained an interest.

While Nekhen brooded on this revelation, Mayela paused breathless and lifted her arms toward the seashore.

“This changes everything!” she cried in gratitude. “Everything changes today.”

Chapter 8

As Nathan drove me home, silence settled between us, broken by occasional directions from his GPS. I rolled down my window to let in the night air and laid my head back against the seat, face turned toward the breeze. Aromas of late summer buffeted my senses. A panorama of houses passed in the dark.

My hand drifted to his. Nathan responded, long fingers interlacing with mine. God, it felt wonderful. Painfully so. Once upon a time, I had held Carlos's hand like this, whenever he drove us home at night. A lump settled in my throat, enclosing the empty space he'd left behind, a void I'd thought would always be with me. Yet tonight, something new stirred inside that darkness. Hope, perhaps. An ephemeral hint of light.

I closed my eyes, tightened my hold on Nathan's hand. *Please*, I prayed silently. *Please let this much be real.*

We arrived at my house. He pulled into the driveway, slowed the car to a stop, and dimmed the headlights. Everything said and left unsaid hung between us.

I let go of his hand.

"Mayela—"

"I'm not inviting you in."

He winced.

I glanced away, regretting the bite in my tone.

"It's not that I don't want to," I added quietly. "I'm just not ready."

Nathan let go a long breath. "I understand."

"Do you?" I demanded. "Do you really? Because I had a very bad experience with a real jerk not long after Carlos died. I don't want to go through anything like that again."

Nathan frowned and looked away.

I hadn't intended to snap at him, but now that the car had stopped, Nathan's presence in that small space overwhelmed me. His aroma, the shadow upon his shoulders, the very air he breathed, the thoughts he inspired. I wanted to dive into this man and run away from him at the same time.

"Forgive me," I said. "It's just, the way you make me feel, and everything that happened tonight. It was all so…" I blinked back the sting in my eyes. "I haven't let my guard down in a long time, and I want to. With you, that is. Let my guard down. But I need you to understand because so many men don't. I had to learn that all over again after Carlos died. Men don't understand. Not when they're fifteen or twenty-five. Not when they're forty or fifty or sixty. For all I know, not even the day they fucking die."

Nathan went very still, as if holding his breath.

"A kiss is a promise," I continued, eyes fixed on the space in front of me. "Making love is a *promise.* So, if we ever go there, I need to know. I need to *know*, Nathan. It has to be as sacred for you as it is for me. I'm not saying you'll have to put a ring on it or anything like that. God knows I've lived enough—lost enough—to understand forever rarely happens in this world. But I expect—no, I *demand*—an honest effort. I'm worth that much. I'm worth an honest effort."

My words tumbled into silence.

For a long time, Nathan did not speak.

I drew a shaky breath, lighter for having said my mind, but ashamed of my rant. What had gotten into me? I should've left that speech for the second date. Or beyond. Or never. I didn't dare look at Nathan. I could only imagine what his expression might reveal. This whole evening had been a shaky proposition, and now? He would not want to see me again.

Brilliant. Just brilliant.

I reached for my purse and opened the passenger door to get out. "Thank you, Nathan. Good night."

He touched my elbow. "I'll walk you to the porch."

Grass crunched underfoot as we crossed the lawn. Streetlights filtered through branches of large trees, casting flecked shadows across my modest home. We reached the door. As I fumbled for the keys inside my purse, Nathan took a stance nearby, maintaining a thoughtful silence as he gazed down the street.

When at last I extracted the keys from the dark pit of my clutch, he turned to me and said, "You know, I think my mother would like you very much."

I shot a look at him, aghast. He grinned and shrugged. Then we burst into laughter, seeking the support of the doorframe as we succumbed to a shared fit of hysteria.

"Okay!" I raised my hands in surrender. "I get it! I shouldn't have unloaded on you like that. But that's no reason to hand out insults."

"It's not an insult!" His dark eyes sparked with amusement. "Mother has very high standards. She doesn't like many people."

"Oh!" I struggled to catch my breath. "Oh, my belly aches! Why on earth do you think she'd like me?"

Nathan leaned close, one hand set against the doorframe. His presence wrapped around me, gentle like the afternoon sun. "She'd admire your utter lack of faith in men."

"It's not an utter lack of faith."

He brushed a strand of hair from my cheek.

I flushed and looked away, slipping my key inside the lock. "Well, maybe it is."

The door opened. Time to say goodnight.

Drawing a breath, I met his gaze once more. "I'm not sure how to start over, Nathan. I lost so much when my husband died. Once you know how it feels to lose everything in love, how can you ever start over?"

Time paused between us.

Then his lips met mine, and I…I could hardly believe we were kissing! Until this moment, I hadn't been sure he was real. Not when we walked arm in arm through the Art Fair, not when we hugged on the bridge, not when we held hands in the car. But now? Now I could taste the vivid, sensual pull of his lips, savor the lingering wine on his breath. I reached up to touch his face and discovered faint bristles upon shaven skin, firm bone beneath muscled flesh, soft, thick hair crowning his head. Delicious aromas filled my senses, of cloves and wet earth, of warm, sweet summers. And beneath it all the faint, now familiar essence of freshly lit match. He wrapped his arms tight around me. I melted into him. How could I not? His kisses graced my face, my cheeks, my eyes, and then traveled down my neck, where they settled into a hollow and ignited a beautiful, aching, long-sought desire.

"Nathaniel," I murmured. "*Mi amor*."

His lips traced the line of my throat back to my face.

"I promise," he murmured, resting his forehead on mine, "to make an honest effort."

I was trembling all over. A good tremble. A happy, expectant tremble.

"We'll talk again soon?" he asked.

"'Kay."

He gave me another tender kiss. "Good night, Mayela."

"'Night."

Nathan stepped off the porch. My heart dropped into my stomach. *Wait!*

He crossed the front lawn and got into his car.

What was I doing, sending him away?

The headlights turned on. He pulled out of the driveway. My blood pounded in my ears. *We'll talk soon*, he'd said. But how soon was soon? Anything could happen between now and soon. Anne, for instance. Anne could definitely happen between now and *soon*.

Christ. I sucked in my breath. *Stop it. Stop doubting yourself. Stop doubting him.*

Nathan's car headed down the block and disappeared around the corner. My pulse slowed into the steady rhythm of certainty. This was the right choice. I'd learned from hard experience what it could do to me, diving in too fast and facing betrayal in the end. I liked Nathan. More than liked. But I hardly knew him. It was better to wait. He'd be back.

If this was something worth having, he'd be back.

I stepped into the foyer of my home and closed the

door behind me. Relief mingled with regret, wrapped in a warm, sparkly cloud of joyous anticipation. I sent a quick text to Joni to let her know I was home, safe and sound, from my blind date. Then I called down the hallway, “Midnight? You around?”

I slipped off my sandals, hoping she’d emerge from the shadows. Midnight usually greeted me at the door, but she didn’t like strangers. She’d probably stay hiding a while longer to punish me for having Nathan on the porch.

“It’s safe to come out now, sweetheart. Scary date man is gone.” Wow, it felt good to set my bare feet on the cool hardwood floor. I let my hair down, too. Picking up my purse, I started toward the kitchen. “I’m going to make myself some tea. You want a kitty treat? Can’t wait to tell you about my date. Maybe I’ll call Joni, too.”

In the kitchen, I put my purse on the counter and started filling the teapot with water. “He’s kind of…out there. Weird, but in a good way. It’s a weirdness that matches my weirdness if that makes sense. Anyway, I think we’re onto something.” I leaned against the counter as the water heated up. Man alive! My skin was flushed, and in that very intimate space between my legs, the gears were definitely whirring. “Sheesh! Don’t think I’ll be sleeping much tonight. Might have to get out some toys to douse this fire.”

The phone rang inside my purse. Two thoughts flashed through my mind—Nathan and phone sex. I’d never done phone sex, not even with Carlos, but at the moment, my horizons were expanding at light speed.

“Hello?”

“*Dónde diablos estuviste*?”

Mamá. *Talk about a bucket of cold water.*

"Where've you been?" she repeated. "*¿Por qué no respondiste?*"

"*¿Cómo qué responder*?" I replied, confused. Respond to what?

"I sent you a million messages. I even called a few times."

"You did?" I frowned. "*Espera.*"

I pulled back and checked my phone. There was a long string of messages and several missed calls from her. I put the phone back to my ear. "*Lo siento*, Mamá. I don't know how I missed all that. I was on a date. We went to the Plaza Art Fair, and—"

"With him?"

"No. I mean, yes." I stopped, collected my thoughts. "What do you mean, 'him?' "

"You know what I mean."

Damn. I was not in the mood for another one of *those* conversations. "I can't date a hallucination."

Silence on the other end. Not just silence, condescending motherly silence.

"Don't lie," she said tersely. "I taught you better than that."

"Okay." I groaned. "At first, he kind of reminded me of the man from my hallucinations. But it turns out he's just a guy, Mamá. I met him at Joni's coffee shop. We had fun tonight, and…*Me gusta*. I like him. A lot. I think he likes me, too."

"Where are you now?"

"At home."

"Did you invite him in?"

What was this interrogation? "No, Mamá! It's only our first date."

"Querida, you need to invite him in."

What? When had Mamá's hawkish oversight of my love life switched from, "Under no circumstances should you have sex with that man," to, "Why aren't you having sex?"

"Mamá, we had a very nice first kiss, but then we said good night. I need to take this slow. It's been a long time, and I'm still a little raw from losing Carlos, and from that stupid affair I had after he died. I don't want to mess this up."

The doorbell rang.

I glanced toward the foyer. "Oh."

"What's wrong?" Mamá asked.

"Nothing. Nothing's wrong." My heart leapt inside my chest. Had Nathan come back? Of course, he had! Who else would it be? "*Ahorita te llamo*, Mamá."

I ended the call and raced down the hallway. He'd come back. He'd come back! I halted to check myself in the mirror. By some miracle, I hadn't lost my look in the last ten minutes. Pretty dress, flushed cheeks, hair unbound. He'd like that. He'd like that a lot. I skipped the rest of the way, ready to plunge into a river of desire and never look back. Throwing open the door, I announced, "I'm so glad you're here! I was just thinking I should have invited you in."

Except the man on the porch was not Nathan.

"Wow." Mitch looked me up and down, pleasure registering in his expression. "You look great."

"Mitch?" My blood ran cold.

"I know it's late," he replied with a sheepish grin. "Hope you don't mind."

Of course, I minded. I glanced past Joni's accountant and down the street, searching for the man I really wanted to see. The neighborhood was still as death. Even the dogs had gone to sleep.

"What are you doing here?" I demanded.

"I…" He took a step back and cleared his throat. "I was at 75th Street with some friends and decided to stop by on the way home."

"Stop by my house?"

"Yeah."

"Why?"

"What do you mean, why?"

"I mean why are you here?" I wanted to bite his head off. "In the middle of the night? On my porch? I don't understand."

His face twisted. "You're serious?"

"Yes, I'm serious!" What was up with him this week? First, that weird conversation in the parking lot, and now an unannounced midnight visit? "Look, Mitch, I don't know what's going on, but whatever it is, we can talk about it tomorrow. By light of day. It's late and I'm tired. Good night."

I started to close the door.

Mitch reached out to stop me.

"Christ, Mayela. Look, I'm sorry." He puffed out his cheeks. "This is coming off all wrong. I didn't mean to upset you, but I'm confused by the way you've been acting. We don't see each other for weeks. Then the other day at Joni's you barely spoke to me, brushed me off in the parking lot like there'd never been anything between us. Have you drawn a total blank?"

My breath turned to frost on my lips. "What are you talking about?"

Mitch studied me a long moment. His expression softened. He glanced around and opened his palms in a placating gesture. “Can I come in?”

“No.” I shook my head. My stomach had turned sour.

“Mayela, let me in.”

“No.” I tried to close the door. Again, Mitch stopped me. He shoved the door so hard it escaped my grasp, flinging back on its hinges. A fever burned through my nausea. I lifted my hands to strike him and opened my mouth to scream. Mitch froze, one foot hanging over the threshold. Uncertainty invaded his expression. He focused on the space behind me.

Then I heard it—footsteps.

Stiletto heels were clicking on the hardwood floor of my home. Someone was approaching from the kitchen. I spun around in time to see Anne step into my foyer. Nathan’s Anne. From the restaurant. That deadly beautiful friend and colleague who ambushed unsuspecting dates outside of public restrooms and…liked to break into their homes?

What was she doing here? How did she get in?

Anne had switched out the summer frock she was wearing at dinner. Now she sported a tight-fitting scarlet piece of cloth that showed off everything, especially those enviable thighs. Her dark hair fell in a smooth, sensuous sheen past her shoulders. Her expression, a mixture of curiosity and annoyance, gave the impression she’d just been dragged away from a fine conversation with a dear friend. Eyeing Mitch like a lynx who had spotted her next meal, she leaned against the far wall, thrust her hips ever so slightly forward, and said in velvet tones, “Why don’t you introduce me to our guest, Mayela?”

I wasn’t sure how, but in that moment, I

understood two things to be true—Mitch had to leave now, and Anne was not of this world.

I glanced at Mitch, wondering whether he saw her too. He'd gone slack-jawed, his eyes popping out as he looked her up and down.

"I…Uhm," I stuttered and glanced at Anne.

She nodded and winked.

"Mitch, this is Anne," I said. "Anne, meet Mitch. Mitch is my best friend's accountant, and Anne is…Well, Anne is, uhm…"

"I'm an old friend," she finished for me.

"Yes. Anne's a friend." I frowned.

"From college."

"We knew each other in college," I told Mitch.

"I'm in town for the weekend."

"She's in town for the weekend." I blinked and glanced at her again. What was this, a Jedi mind trick?

Anne approached us with a few sensuous steps. "Mayela and I have been catching up on old times."

"Yup." I let go a nervous laugh. "The stories she could tell."

Mitch furrowed his brow in doubt. "You and Joni talk about college a lot, Mayela. I don't remember you mentioning someone named Anne."

"Oh," I said. "Well, Anne and I, we…We lost track of each other a long time ago. We've only just reconnected."

"We found each other on Facebook," Anne said.

"Facebook!" I clapped my hands. What a brilliant lie. "Facebook's great for that. You know, reconnecting? With old friends?"

"Anne." Mitch's tone turned low and menacing.

The hairs on the back of my neck pricked.

Anne flashed a provocative smile and slid close to me.

"I think we should invite him in, Mayela. We could have some *fun*." She emphasized the "f" and let her tongue linger on the "n," making it clear exactly what sort of fun she had in mind. I backed away, afraid the heat might scald me. Anne shifted to fill the space between me and Mitch. "Mayela and I took dance classes together in college. Did she ever tell you about that?"

Dance? How did she know I studied dance?

"No," Mitch said.

"I was awkward as hell, but Mayela's a natural. Gypsy blood, you know. Flamenco rhythms."

"Romani," I corrected her. "My mother is Spanish, with some Romani."

"We were all a little in love with her back then, as I'm sure you can imagine. Mayela was pure magic on stage." Anne let a little shiver run through her body. "A hallmark of grace. Have you ever seen her dance?"

"No." Mitch's voice had been reduced to a low growl.

Anne went still as a viper about to strike.

"Pity," she said. "A woman's beauty should run free in this world, don't you think? A woman's power should be displayed for everyone to see."

Mitch pressed his lips into a thin line. Anger smoldered behind those steel-blue eyes. Anne's gaze slid to his feet, then back up, lingering on his crotch before returning to his face.

"I like your friend, Mayela," she announced, though every word dripped with venom. "He's a handsome one, this Mitch. He has the sort of face a woman would never forget."

Mitch fidgeted, then glanced away. He stepped back from the doorway.

"Sorry, Mayela," he murmured. "I didn't realize you had a guest."

His words came like a slap in the face, waking me up. I felt like a delusional jerk. Neither Mitch nor Anne was welcomed, but at least Mitch had asked to enter. Anne had broken into my home. What evidence did I have she was anything other than a thief and a psychopath? A moment ago, I was convinced Mitch had to leave. Now the thought of being alone with Anne scared the shit out of me.

"It's okay, Mitch," I said. "I'm sorry, too. You caught me by surprise, that's all. Would you like to come in for a little while? One more drink before you go home?"

"No." He turned to leave.

"If you want to talk—"

"I do. We'll touch base later. Good night, Mayela." With that, Mitch receded into the night.

Chapter 9

Anne closed the door behind Mitch and clicked the bolt into place. Then she folded her arms, Morticia style, and pinned me with a sharp gaze.

"Why are you afraid of that man?" she demanded.

"I'm not afraid of him. I'm afraid of—" I stopped myself. I owed this woman no answers. "What are you doing in my home?"

"Coming to the rescue."

"This is a rescue?"

She shrugged and nodded toward the space where Mitch just stood. "Not my best performance, but I've done worse."

"How did you get in here?"

"I slipped through the cracks."

"I don't see any breaks in the dry wall."

"Look." She exhaled. "Nathan would've been much happier handling this incident himself, but he couldn't get in. Someone put a massive ward around this place. Was it you?"

"I, uhm…" I frowned in confusion. "No."

"Well, whoever cast this ward knew what she was doing." Anne looked around as if impressed. "Nathan can't get in, nor anything like him."

"I'm sorry, what's a ward?"

"A barrier. Against supernatural beings.

"You're saying you and Nathan are supernatural

beings?"

"Yes."

"And he couldn't get in here, but you could? Does that mean you're more powerful than him?"

"No. Quite the opposite. Wards are like cages. Different cages serve different purposes. If you make a cage for butterflies, tigers can tear the netting apart. If you make a cage for tigers, butterflies can flit between the bars. I'm a butterfly. Nathan's a tiger."

She sure looked like a tiger to me.

"Whoever built this ward wasn't worried about butterflies," Anne continued. "And with good reason. There's not much I can do, except make some noise. I mean, I do have a few tricks up my sleeve, but I can't do any real damage. Not like Nathan could, if that were his intention. Which I assure you, it is not."

"Wait." I put up my hands to stop her. "Can we start over? Who are you? What are you? Nathan said you're a colleague of his?"

"He said that?" She raised her brow in amusement. "How generous of him. No, I wouldn't call myself a colleague. More like a minion of consequence. He's waiting out back, by the way."

"Excuse me?"

"Nathan is waiting. Right now, in your garden."

I glanced toward the back of the house. Foreboding crept into my veins. "Why?"

She groaned. "You are slow on the uptake, aren't you? He's here because there's only one conversation you need to have with him, and that conversation still hasn't happened."

"But…I…we've been talking all night," I countered weakly.

"Yes. I noticed. Do you remember what I said to you, in the restaurant?"

"Every word." Every bizarre word.

"Good. Then go to him. Now."

"But..." I looked toward the back of the house, then at Anne again. "I don't understand. In the restaurant you said, 'Choose him.' What did you mean by that?"

"I meant there comes a time when every soul must make a choice. We designate a protector and declare our allegiance. Your time is now."

"Why?"

"Because you crossed the threshold."

"What threshold?"

"When you landed in the Hunting Grounds. You penetrated the veil and entered their world."

"And now I need a protector?"

"Yes."

"For what?"

"In my honest opinion? To shield you from everything that is not Nathan."

I let what she'd just said sink in.

"You're serious?" I asked.

She rolled her eyes. "We don't have time for this! Look, Mayela: Their world is complicated. I've been with them for centuries now, and—"

"Centuries?" I exclaimed.

"There's still a lot I don't understand. I can tell you that without their protection, we don't survive beyond the veil. They use this to their advantage. The first thing they demand is allegiance—not to all of them, mind you. To one in particular. Who that one is, this is the choice they allow us to make. Nathan will explain how it's done. You'll be expected to demand something from him in return."

"I'm sorry." I shook my head. "This is not happening. Even if it were, it makes no sense. You're saying I get to ask for, what, a box of chocolates? And then I *belong* to him?"

"It's not belonging, precisely. More like a collaboration, a place your soul can inhabit during the next stage of your journey. Of course, in your case, the agreement will cover body and soul."

"What?"

"I know! It's extraordinary, isn't it?" Her face lit up with excitement. "Miracles like you don't happen very often. This increases your value substantially. Keep that in mind, Mayela. Be sure to set the price high, much higher than a box of chocolates."

"No! Just *no*." I took Anne's arm and hauled her toward the front door. "I don't know what you're on, but this game stops now."

"This is no game."

The gravity of her tone gave me pause. I let go of her. Anne stepped away, smoothing her dress and settling her honest gaze on me.

"Who are you, really?" I asked again. "What did he do to convince you of all of this? Did he show up out of the blue like he did with me? Pretend to be the next great love of your life, and then—?"

"No!" Anne cut me off, sharp and swift. She sucked in her breath, jaw working against her cheek. When at last she continued, it was in measured tones. "Nathan didn't know how to hunt when I crossed the threshold. He was learning everything, becoming what he is now. His mother was the one who snatched me up on the Hunting Grounds. She chased me down in the form of a ravenous, dragon-like beast. It was terrifying. She swallowed me whole and spat me out at Nathan's feet. He met me in his human form. I thought I'd been delivered to a god, or to the Devil. He found that amusing." She smiled at the memory. "And he assured me he was neither. He made me feel safe and supported me as I transitioned to the liminal realms. With time, he earned my trust."

"How?"

"By giving me what I wanted."

"What was that?"

"Revenge."

A bloody scene flashed through my mind—Samurai Anne with sword in hand, body parts scattered at her feet. I wondered what she'd done, and who had suffered because of it.

Anne narrowed her eyes. "Don't judge me."

"I'm not judging you."

"Yes, you are." She closed the distance between us. "We are not so different, you and I, Dr. Mayela Lehman."

I lowered my gaze, uncertain. "I don't mean to offend you. This is all so beyond my experience."

"The man I loved chopped off my head."

I blinked. "What?"

"The man I pledged my life to in marriage chopped off my head. That's how I died."

"God, how awful! I'm so sorry."

"Why?" A bitter smile touched her lips. "It's not your fault."

"I know. I just..." What was I supposed to say? What could I possibly say to that?

"He didn't do it himself, of course. Henry was too much of a coward for that. But he set his men to the task and rewarded their efforts with princely generosity. They accused me of everything they could—adultery, incest, witchcraft. My only true crime was aspiring to power in a man's world." She gave a harsh laugh. "I never had a chance. What a merry little feast of blood that was. And for what? Centuries gone by, and still sometimes I ask, for what?"

"You've been dead for centuries?"

"Five hundred years, give or take." She tossed her head. "I stopped counting after three. Besides, I'm not fully dead, as you can see. Just dead to that life. And good riddance, I say."

In that moment, an astonishing truth hit me full force—Anne had to die to enter the Hunting Grounds! Everybody did. Everyone left their bodies behind when they crossed the threshold. Everyone except me. Why?

Because your father was one of them. Mamá's declaration echoed through my mind.

"That body you're in?" I demanded. "How do you do that if you're dead?"

"What, this?" She examined her elegant figure with pride. "Not bad, eh? Took me forever to learn. It's much like the body I used to have, with a few embellishments. I'm taller now, and the neck is intact, of course. I'm not sure how it works, me being here, or that you or anyone else can see me." She lowered her voice, as if sharing a delicious secret. "It's not a real body, mind you. Not like yours. I can't bruise or break or give birth. Nathan says it's a projection of my intentions into the mortal realm, whatever that means. Unfortunately, the effect is temporary."

"How temporary?"

"A few minutes." She shrugged. "On a good day, a couple hours."

I put my hand to my chin, compelled by the mystery. "How does Nathan—?"

"Enough," Anne said. "You're exhausting me. And you're wasting precious time."

"But how does he—?"

"Nathan can answer your questions."

"I don't trust Nathan."

"That doesn't matter any more."

Her words hit me like a slap in the face.

Anne softened her expression and added, "What I mean is that the wheel has been set in motion. Whether you trust him or not, there's no going back. You mustn't be frightened, Mayela. Not of him. I'm confident he will earn your trust in time. Go now and remember what I said."

Anne opened the front door, readying to leave, as she spoke. When she crossed the threshold, she vanished like a ghost on my porch. The door closed shut behind her, its bolt locking into place.

****

Crossroads of the Heart

Kansas City, Missouri. 2005.

Mayela was changing her shoes when a man entered the studio. He caught her eye at once, with his easy smile, chestnut complexion, and self-assured gait. Taking a seat across from her, he introduced himself to another man who had signed up for the class. They shook hands and fell into friendly banter while switching out street shoes for ballroom footwear. As they spoke, the handsome one noticed Mayela staring at him. Pleasure registered in his expression. He grinned and winked. She flushed and glanced away. That was how their love story began.

Nekhen, who hovered unseen in their presence, assessed Carlos's soul and decided him a worthy prospect. On the cusp of turning thirty, Mayela had by now experienced joy, pleasure, and heartbreak with a number of men. Carlos, Nekhen saw, might be different. Might be the One, as mortals liked to say. His soul shone in magnificent colors, well-matched to Mayela's, with ancient roots and a bold halo of amber-gold. A Daughter of the Plains followed the young mortal; one of Nekhen's kind drawn to the man's soul. Her hair was a cascade of gold-green grass woven through with wildflowers. Feathers and fur cloaked her bronze form. Exuding calm purpose, she nodded to Nekhen. He returned the honor with a brief bow.

The dance teacher, a diminutive man whose soul shone with pure, concentrated light, called the class to order. Pretending mutual disinterest, Mayela and Carlos headed toward opposite ends of the room. When the dancing began, they observed each other from a distance. Neither needed classes. Mayela had signed up to meet people. Perhaps Carlos had as well. Their plan seemed to be working, even better than expected. Between partners, Mayela cast furtive glances toward Carlos and indulged in shy smiles. Nekhen could see she was gauging whether this mild attraction meant everything or nothing at all.

The instructor signaled another change of partners. Mayela and Carlos stepped into each other's space. She drew close, resting her fingers on his outstretched palm. Carlos placed his free hand upon her waist. Their gazes met with understanding, humor, and an unmistakable dare. As they began to dance, Nekhen sensed the tingling energy between them, a gentle pull of intertwining spirits. Moments like this had always brought him joy, as this was the nature of his kind. Mortal happiness reverberated through them, as did sorrow, fear, anger, and pain. Love and pleasure filled Nekhen with gratitude. Hate and trauma ignited his wrath.

But tonight was different. Strangely so. As Mayela and Carlos danced, something unexpected stirred inside Nekhen. Small and goblin-like, it clawed at his heart, sinking tiny, sharp teeth into his core. Pain sparked, then seared through him. Nekhen faltered and withdrew. Shivering, he took hold of the veil and wrapped it around himself, torn between the need to remain with Mayela and an inability to withstand the emotions overtaking him.

Centuries had passed since he'd felt such sadness, as if a part of him were being torn away. The memory of another mortal returned, a woman of exceptional gifts and vibrant passion. He remembered her laughter, her love, her tender touch. He remembered her sorrow, her fear, and in the end, her screams. He remembered the hate of her kind, the raging fire that turned her to ash. Why this moment should bring back that terrible history mystified and alarmed him.

The Daughter of the Plains approached, embracing him with her gentle presence.

"This will be a great love," she murmured, "one that will echo through all our realms."

Her prophecy sucked the life out of him. A hope he did not know he had harbored crumbled within. *I will never know her*, he realized. Not as Carlos would, immersed in her mortal brilliance, sustained inside her organic embrace. *I will never know her, and she will never know me.* How could she, as a mortal? Even if he succeeded in the most difficult task of claiming her soul, Mayela would never comprehend an existence such as his, and without comprehension there would be no true love.

The mystery of why this mattered confounded him. Over the centuries, he had gathered countless souls to his realm. Not once had he longed for connection like this—Mayela and Carlos. Carlos and Mayela, spinning into orbit around each other. They laughed. Mis-stepped. Laughed again. Their joy pierced his immortal veins. Sadness spilled forth in inky threads, reaffirming the truth of his metamorphosis, the finality of his condemnation.

The Daughter of the Plains spoke again, "You cannot stay."

She was right. To stay would cast a shadow over Mayela, endangering this new-found union with melancholy, jealousy, and anger. Grief-stricken, Nekhen extricated himself from Mayela's shining presence. He flowed back into his realm beyond the veil and let the dancing couple spin out of reach.

Time assumed meaning. With meaning came deeper pain. Anchored inside the void of his loss, Nekhen brooded. His many souls gathered close, shivering beneath their guardian's sorrow. They made desperate attempts to awaken him from his melancholy, fearful the death of their guardian would mean the death of them all. When Nekhen did not respond, they deliberated among themselves. In the end, the one called Anne was nominated to leave Nekhen's realm and appeal to another power. Undertaking such a journey could ignite the Soul Masters' wrath, but Anne was not afraid. Well, maybe she was. Yet her fear of losing Nekhen far outweighed any terror that facing his mother might inspire.

So it was that, shortly after realizing Anne had vanished from his awareness, Nekhen found himself in his mother's presence. As was her custom, Wadje sent no summons or messenger. Nekhen simply felt a characteristic tug in his center, and then stood at the base of her great tree. A millennial beast, the tree's dark branches fanned toward distant boundaries of Wadje's realm. Its trunk extended into a deep void. There, the roots pulsed with an eerie glow as they fed on condemned souls. In the high branches, souls that had passed judgment tended celestial fruit. The glowing orbs matured into young stars and new planets. Once ready, stars and planets separated from the tree. Filled with light and color, they floated toward their place in the material plane.

Though Nekhen knew his mother as Wadje, this was not her true name. Among their kind, true names were not shared, even within family. Wadje had christened her youngest son Nekhen on the eve of his transformation, but his true name was revealed during his metamorphosis, searing itself into his heart when the last of his mortal existence was ripped away. Nekhen, who trusted neither mortals nor immortals, doubted he would ever reveal his true name to anyone. Tales were often told of Ancients who had granted their names to devotees, only to see their powers used for perverse ends and their realms destroyed.

Above Nekhen's head, the dark branches stirred, silhouetted against a jade-colored sky. Wadje separated from the center of her refuge and wound down the trunk to greet her son. Her preferred form was a giant serpent. Serpent forms were not unique among Nekhen's kind, but Nekhen thought his mother's three-headed shape most impressive. Each head represented a different viper from the lands where she first came into power. Wadje settled in a great coil in front of Nekhen and arched her three heads to see him from different perspectives. The center, a cobra, spread its hood in greeting.

"Well?" she hissed, plainly annoyed her rest had been disturbed.

Nekhen understood at once why she had called on him. He didn't consider lying or even hedging the truth. He'd witnessed long ago the cost of deception among his kind. In a few direct words, he told his mother what had triggered his melancholy and why he had not returned to the mortal realms or continued hunting souls. She listened, her heads tilted in thought, her tail twitching with the cadence of his story.

When he finished, she did not at first respond. The longer her pensive silence, the smaller Nekhen's story appeared in his mind. Indeed, it all seemed trivial now, standing in the shadow of his great mother and her ancient tree, its dark roots fed by lost souls of a thousand years. How many miseries had he witnessed in Mayela's world? And here he was, sinking like a fool because of a simple broken heart.

At last, Wadje flicked her heads. She laid her serpentine eyes on him and said, "Well, it all sounds easy enough to solve. Go back and have sex with the girl."

"What?" The suggestion appalled him.

"It's an obvious solution."

"But she's a mortal!"

"Has that stopped any of us before?"

Nathan stifled his annoyance. The last time he made love to a woman, he was still mortal, having not yet completed his metamorphosis. While many of his kind indulged in whatever pleasures they fancied with mortals and souls alike, the thought of seducing those who entrusted their hopes to him had always filled Nekhen with distaste.

Always, until now. Now he desired Mayela. It had been so long since he felt such need he had almost forgotten its visceral power. And yet, "It's not sex that I'm after."

Wadje snorted. "Well, my dear, it's what you need. Five hundred years have passed since your transformation. It's about time your instincts kicked in. Or did you expect to be celibate for all eternity?"

"I'm not denying my desire. But what I want is true connection."

"Connection." She spat, sending a stream of venom into the souls decaying among the roots below. One of them screamed in agony. "Attachment is a nuisance. It only ends in trouble."

"So you've said, more times than I care to remember." Nekhen was the result of an attachment gone bad. Wadje never let him forget that. He decided he had spent enough time in her presence. "Thank you for bringing me here, Mother, and for offering your esteemed counsel. I see now I've indulged my sorrows long enough. I will return to my work at once, and I regret my souls disturbed your rest with this."

"On the contrary! This is precisely the sort of news I should be made aware of. Indeed, I want to help."

Nekhen's entire being tightened with anxiety any time his mother used the word *help*.

"I shall organize a festival!" she announced. Her heads perked up. Her ruby and emerald eyes glinted with excitement. "We'll whip up some old-school decadence with the Ancients to celebrate your coming of age. I'll invite Ishtar, Venus, Aphrodite, Eros…Everyone will want to come. It's been too long since we've had a party around here! Oh, and Min, of course." Wadje chuckled. "I'll invite my old friend, Min. You wouldn't believe what you can learn from a god who's had an erection for five thousand years!"

"Don't," Nekhen said tersely.

"Throw a party? But I must! This is a seminal moment in your journey as a god."

"Don't organize a festival to celebrate my sexuality, and don't ever call us gods."

"Oh." She huffed. "You're on about that again, are you? What word do you suggest we use? We are gods and goddesses, after all, as far as any pathetic mortal is concerned."

Nekhen simmered in silence. He had no words for what he was, and he hated all the words used by mortals and immortals alike.

"Shall we call ourselves demons?" Wadje offered with a playful tilt of her heads.

"Mother," he growled.

"Angels in heat?"

"Enough!" he barked.

"All right!" She backed away. "No need to get

angry. Handle this on your own, then. But fix it. This need of yours may seem insignificant now, but you are not a mortal anymore. Desire tears our kind apart if we can't make peace with it. And when we're torn apart, the consequences can be quite formidable."

"I understand. May I have Anne now?"

"Anne?" Wadje furrowed her brows, then nodded in an expression of enlightenment. "Here I thought you were determined to put this off indefinitely. A roll about with Anne would certainly do the trick. Which Anne do you want? I have so many of them, and they're all delightful."

"My Anne!" he thundered. "And I'm not going to have sex with her. I just want her back."

"Oh!" Wadje rolled her heads. "That Anne! Of course. How silly of me. I'd almost forgotten."

A shiver passed through her long body, and she began to retch. After a few gurgling hacks, Wadje vomited up Nekhen's Anne. The poor soul landed in a wet heap at his feet and peered up at her guardian.

"My liege," she said, wiping viscous fluid away from her eyes and mouth.

"Hello, Anne." He offered a hand to help her up.

She got to her feet. "I'm reminded of the first time we met, on the Hunting Grounds."

"It was rather like this," he conceded, though that first time she'd still been holding her head in her hands. "Are you all right?"

"Yes." The tremble in her aura spoke otherwise. "I only wish your mother's innards weren't so…vivid. I'm sorry if I caused you trouble. I meant no disloyalty. Everyone agreed it had to be done."

"We'll discuss all that later."

Anne nodded. All this time, she had been trying to wipe the slime from her arms. She ended up covering her hands in goop. With a frown of annoyance, she flicked the sticky fluid from her wrists, hitting Wadje in the face. Not by accident, Nekhen supposed. Wadje recoiled with a hiss. Nekhen did not waste another moment. He wrapped his defiantly loyal soul in a tight ward and sent her back to his realm.

"There was no need to punish her," Nekhen told his mother. "Anne was only doing what she thought best."

"I didn't punish her!" Wadje replied, indignant. "I thanked her, and then I swallowed the dear whole to remind her who's in charge. They need reminders, you know. Especially those brave enough to leave their guardian's realm on their own."

"Anne knows the rules quite well. She wouldn't have broken them unless she thought it necessary. In any case, when it comes to my souls, you must leave the punishments, and the reminders, to me."

Wadje shrugged.

Nekhen began drawing himself inward to return to his realm. "Thank you, Mother. I will take my leave now."

She retreated in a pensive slither toward the base of the tree. Just short of its broad buttresses, she turned a head toward Nekhen and said, "You should go back to her, to that mortal woman you want."

Nekhen halted his departure to consider his mother's advice. He shook his head. "It's best to let her be. I do not wish to disturb her happiness with my jealousies, and there are many other souls awaiting my attention."

"But she is the one who awakened you."

Wadje approached again. Something in her demeanor had changed. Her usual air of impatience vanished, and her tone sounded almost…compassionate? Perhaps that was Nekhen's imagination.

"I suppose you're old enough to hear this," she said. "You're right. We aren't gods."

This turnabout astonished Nekhen. He did not know what to say. In five hundred years, Wadje had never expressed uncertainty, much less a change of mind.

"Ten thousand years I've reveled in my power," she continued, "and still, I do not know what a god is. In ancient times, my kin called themselves Masters of Creation. They played with the destinies of mortals and accepted all manner of adoration. They believed themselves invincible, yet their domains crumbled, nonetheless. Even now, there are those among us who insist we are destined to rule over humankind. Soul Masters, we call ourselves. But are we, really? Masters of anything?"

"Mother," Nekhen replied, worried. "Are you feeling all right?"

"Look." She flared her cobra hood and lifted her nose to a new planet, a blue-green orb that spun as it floated away from the high branches. "I do not know what compels me to capture rotten souls and feed them to the roots of my tree, so that she might recycle their worn colors into new worlds and young stars. I only know I must do it. In the same way, I'm compelled to ask what compels you to desire this woman above all the souls you've encountered in your youth? Are our instincts due to chance or design? Who can say? Perhaps we, the keepers of mortal souls, also answer to a greater purpose."

"Why are you telling me this?" he replied, wary.

She shrugged. "Clearly you do not brood enough. So, I'm giving you more to think about. If this mortal were your hundredth lover, I would say, well, one more adventure for my proud and virile son! But she is your first."

"Not my first." He delivered these three words wrapped in bitter memories of the one he was forced to leave behind.

"The first since your metamorphosis," Wadje conceded. "Your desire marks a shift—a shift with an important question. I propose the answer can best be found through her."

Chapter 10

A dam broke inside of me. I sank to the floor, burdened by an unbearable weight.

All this time, I'd held my sanity in place with one potent word—hallucination. That's what I'd told myself. It was all a hallucination. Now, truth slammed into me like a landslide, sending me into a tailspin, dragging my spirit into rocky depths. Images buffeted me—the dark plains and ravenous beasts, an old man raking flesh off his bones, the serpent in the kitchen, the strange apartment. And Nathan. Nathan! Standing at the entrance to Joni's coffee shop, pretending to court me on the Plaza, when all he wanted was my soul. My body and my immortal soul. There was no special connection between us, except the cold bargaining table of eternity.

I heard myself crying as if from a distance. Somewhere beyond my sobs, a bell sounded.

Not a bell. A melody. Strange. Repetitive. Abrupt.

Drawing a ragged breath, I looked up, tried to focus through tear-blurred vision.

Moments passed until I realized what the melody was. My phone! The phone was ringing. *Mamá*!

Hauling myself off the floor, I charged toward the kitchen. If there was one thing I wanted to do before Nathan dragged me away to his Underworld realm, it was talk to my mother. Snatching the phone, I sank to the floor behind the counter, concealing myself from the windows that looked toward the backyard.

“Mamá,” I whispered.

“*¿Qué pasó?*”

Relief flooded me at the sound of her voice. “He’s here. Mamá, *tengo miedo*. I’m afraid. What should I do?”

“Have you invited him in?”

“No.” My gut clenched. My body was trembling all over. “I can’t! I’m so afraid. I just can’t.”

“You told me you trusted him. You said you knew in your heart he wasn’t going to hurt you.”

I shook my head, frantic, though I knew she couldn’t see me. “All this time, I’ve been wrong! I thought he was…” Oh, God! I clutched my chest. Shards of glass had lodged inside my heart. “Mamá, do they lie?”

“No. *Se manifiestan igual como son, ni más ni menos.*” They show themselves exactly as they are, nothing more, nothing less.

“But all this time, I thought he was something else, someone else, and now this!”

“Did you think that because of what he told you, or what you chose to believe?” she replied gently.

When I couldn’t respond, she added, “Deception is a tool of lesser beings. Why would they lie to us? They have no reason.”

“But Mamá, *el hombre que te…*” I faltered. “The one who was my father…Did he…Did you…?” I burst into tears. “Ay, Mamá!”

It was all too awful to contemplate. Was Nathan like my father? A cynical manipulator? An entity who would use his power to subdue and subjugate? And if he were, what could I do? What could I possibly do to defend myself against him?

"Querida." Mamá implored across the miles. "*Escúchame*. I knew the moment I met your father what he was. You would know, too."

I fought back my tears, shoulders shuddering against the kitchen cabinet. Reaching up, I felt around and found a kitchen towel. I pulled it off the counter and used it to dry my eyes and cheeks.

"I've never faced anything like this before." I sniffled. "I didn't even believe in this stuff! Christ, Mamá! I was falling in love with him! What an idiot I am. I really thought he…" I blew my nose. Anger broke through my fear. I straightened my shoulders. "It doesn't matter what I thought. The point is I don't know what I'm doing or how to handle this. Not like you, Mamá. I couldn't even tell he wasn't human. How will I know whether he's good or bad?"

After a long moment, Mamá said, "You've never had enough faith in yourself, Mayela. You need to have faith in your instincts and your magic."

Magic! As if, after decades of rejecting Mamá's way of life, I could power up for this with a snap of my fingers.

"*¿Dónde estás*?" she asked. Where are you?

"*En la cocina.*"

"Go to the living room."

I moved quickly, keeping low to the ground in hopes of not being seen through the windows. Though for all I knew, he had x-ray vision. "I'm here."

"On the bookshelf along the south wall, third shelf from the bottom. There's a piece of shungite there. Do you know what shungite is?"

"I was married to a geologist, Mamá." I searched the shelf with the flashlight on my phone. The small stone shone black inside a circle of other crystals. "Got it."

"Put it in your pocket."

"I don't have pockets."

"You don't have pockets?"

"I'm wearing a dress."

"You bought a dress without pockets?" she replied in shock. "How many times do I have to tell you? Never buy a dress without pockets!"

"Mamá, I need you to focus right now."

"Put the crystal in your bra."

Okay. This was a little weird. What would Carlos have said about me carrying a chunk of metamorphized crude oil in my bra? *Probably would've turned him on.*

"Mayela?" Mamá asked.

"Yeah, it's done. There's a rock in my bra."

"That is not just a rock," she replied crossly. "That is a very powerful crystal infused with a ward for protection from ill-intentioned spirits."

"Got it."

"Now listen to me. When you go out the back door, this is what you will see. The one waiting for you, he will be inside the circle of stones that I cleansed. You didn't remove that, did you?"

"No, Mamá."

"That's my daughter. He will have prepared a fire in the pit." She paused as if reaching for words. "He will be feeding the fire, with sage perhaps, and rosemary from your garden."

"Why do you think he'll be doing all this?"

"He needs to reassure you that you are safe. The

circle of stones is a sacred space. No entity that means you harm can enter the circle."

"Like the ward you put around the house?"

"Similar, but not the same. Any well-intentioned being can enter the circle of stones. Nothing enters the house except by your invitation."

"Oh." We were on familiar territory now. "Hey, I just learned something about wards, by the way. It turns out butterflies can—"

"*Escúchame*. If the one waiting for you is not inside the circle, if he is not preparing the fire, then you must come back into the house. Immediately. The shungite will protect you long enough to do this. Lock the door, and no matter what happens, do not leave the house until I arrive."

"Until you arrive? But you're in California!"

"I have a flight out tomorrow."

"Oh." I frowned. "Did you tell me that?"

"It was in one of my texts. I reserved the earliest flight available as soon as I remembered my dream."

"Right." Have dream. Book flight. I was taking notes here. I needed to learn Mamá's playbook as fast as possible.

"*¿Estás lista*?" she asked. Are you ready?

No, I thought.

"I think so," I said.

She paused on the other end of the line. Then, "*Tienes todo lo que ocupas. Confía en tu corazón.*" You have everything you need. Trust your heart.

That was all.

Not, "Everything's going to be okay."

Not, "Don't worry, you're going to kick ass."

Just, "You have what you need."

I wasn't so sure.

Also, trusting my heart hadn't done me much good in recent days.

"*Confío en tí*, Querida," Mamá said before ending the call.

She had faith in me.

At least someone did.

Chapter 11

I crept back to the kitchen, grateful for the silence of my bare feet. Pausing at the backdoor, I glanced at my cell phone. Should I take it with me? I didn't have pockets, and I preferred to keep my hands free. In any case, who would I call in the event of a supernatural attack? 911? Ghostbusters?

I set the cell on the counter next to the door. What did I need a phone for, anyway? I had a rock in my bra. The best defense against ill-intentioned spirits, according to people in the know. Edging toward the door, I peered through the glass panes on the door. All I could see was darkness. Turning on the outdoor light didn't help. Night swallowed the feeble glow. Flipping the bolt on the kitchen door, I opened it. Then I undid the latch on the storm door and pushed ever so slightly outward. Nathan came into view, illuminated by the orange glow of a fire. Just as Mamá had promised, he was kneeling inside the circle of stones and staring into the pit. I smelled sage and rosemary along with other soothing aromas I couldn't name.

My muscles clenched. *This is a bad idea.* I should go back inside and shut the door before he—

Nathan looked up, and our gazes locked.

"Mayela," he breathed, as if a ray of light had cut through the night. He rose and extended his arm toward me. "Please. Come."

Wary, I left my kitchen behind and approached him. The white stones lit up with an iridescent glow as I stepped into the circle. Refusing to meet his gaze, I stood apart and watched the fire, hugging myself, thinking what a wreck I looked. My hair a frizzy mess, my eyes swollen from crying, mascara smudged down my cheeks.

I hated myself for caring.

"I'm so sorry," he whispered.

I burst into tears. Nathan touched my elbow and guided me to a chair. He took a seat next to me.

"Why would you do that?" My words spilled out between hiccups and sobs. "Show up and act like…Let me think that…And then you…And then we…" A handkerchief appeared in my hand. I blew my nose, loud and ugly. "You kissed me! I kissed you." That beautiful, heart-shattering kiss. Damn him for that. "A kiss is a promise! A *promise*, I said. What part of that did you not understand?"

"I have not been insincere," he said quietly.

"What part of the last few days has been *honest*?"

"I care for you deeply."

"You care for me!" I spat back. "You care for me. But you don't love me, do you? What would that even look like, love between a thing like you and a person like me? Do you even know what love is?"

He stiffened and glanced away. "Given the history of your kind, I could very well ask the same of you."

Touché. I sat back, chastened but still righteously angry.

"Point taken," I conceded. "But that doesn't excuse what you did. You shouldn't have lied."

"I didn't lie."

"Then you should've told the whole truth!"

"When?" he fired back. "At what point were you ready, before now, to discuss the truth?"

"I'm still not ready! When was I ever going to be ready for this? You, a supernatural being? Expecting me to set a price for my soul?" I broke off to stew for a moment. "I wanted to believe you, Nathan. I thought you were for real. I was falling in love with you!"

Nathan studied me. Something released behind his shoulders. He sighed and rubbed his face with both hands. "You weren't falling in love with me, Mayela. You were falling in love with an illusion."

"Yes, well." I held up my hands. "Whose fault is that?"

"Don't blame me for this! This is how love always happens among your kind! You see what you want to see. Then the veil is pulled back, and the truth makes everyone miserable."

"That is so not fair. You deliberately—"

"I appeared to you as I am. But what I am, that was bound to break your heart. So yes, I'm guilty. Guilty of letting myself indulge in your illusion; of hoping that on some level, you understood the proposition being made. I wanted to believe, too, Mayela. I wanted to believe you were capable of seeing what I am and loving me, nonetheless. I was wrong. Reckless, even. But none of that erases the task before us now: Deciding the fate of your soul."

Silence fell heavy between us. I held his gaze, defiant. As we glared at each other, fatigue flared through my muscles and penetrated my bones. I was exhausted, I realized. And thirsty. Very thirsty.

Wiping my nose, I glanced away.

"I'm going to make some tea," I announced in sullen tones. "You want some?"

"Tea?" He blinked. "Yes, I suppose I would."

I stood and smoothed my skirt, wishing I had a pocket for my soggy handkerchief. "I'm thinking chamomile-lavender. Mamá says it's good for calming and cleansing. But you probably already know that. You like herbals?"

"Yes. Always."

"With honey?"

"No." He shook his head. "No sweetener. Thank you."

I drew a breath, befuddled by this sudden quotidian exchange. "Okay. I'll be right back."

While the water was heating, I went to the restroom to wash my face. It felt good to refresh my skin and see myself in the mirror. The real me, without mascara, lipstick, or blush. Maybe seeing myself would help me see Nathan more clearly. When I returned to the back porch, Nathan sat staring at the flames, his mood subdued. As I stepped into the circle, he stood to accept his tea. We sat back down, avoiding each other's eyes. We remained like that for several minutes, cradling our mugs in silence.

"I have questions," I announced, "and I'd like some answers before we get to the whole price-of-my-soul-thing."

He nodded. "I'll answer anything I can."

"Are we in your world right now, or mine?"

"Your world. Your house, your backyard. Your neighborhood. All of it."

My muscles relaxed. Good to have that confirmed. "And we've been in my world this whole time? I mean, ever since you walked into Joni's coffee shop?"

"Yes. The whole time." He paused and shifted in his seat. "Well, almost."

"Almost?"

"Dinner tonight. At the restaurant? That was in my world."

"What?"

"We stepped across the veil when we went to the restaurant."

"You took me to a restaurant in the Underworld?"

He lifted his hands in apology.

"I ate duck in the Underworld? I went to the *bathroom* in the Underworld?"

"What was I supposed to do? Everything on the Plaza was booked."

"Why didn't you tell me?"

"I was trying to tell you. I would have told you if you'd asked. For a moment at the fountain, I thought you were going to, but then you didn't. In the restaurant, I tried to bring it up again, but you—"

"Asked about your travels." I sat back in my chair. "You're right. I was going to ask. I decided not to because I…I guess I didn't want to wreck the illusion."

We broke into hesitant smiles. I glanced away.

"I didn't want to bring up the truth until you were ready," he said.

"How did we step out of the Plaza into your world?"

"Doorways can serve as thresholds. When we passed through the front door of the restaurant, we entered into my realm."

"Just like that? So, when we exited the restaurant, we returned to the Plaza, in my world. Is that why I felt dizzy when we left, why I couldn't catch my breath?"

He nodded. "You went through a kind of decompression, the same reaction as when you left the apartment in my world to return to your grandparents' farm."

"Ah. Hence your little speech on the bridge about the connection between the two events."

"Hence my little speech."

"You were hoping all night that I'd put it together, weren't you?"

"I was," he murmured, "though I do not regret how everything played out in the end."

Well. I wasn't going to touch that. "All those people in the restaurant. Who were they? Entities like you? Souls like Anne?"

"They were my souls. Not the full collection, of course. Only those I most wanted you to meet."

That piqued my curiosity. "Like, who?"

"Well, Anne, of course. And Mozart was there."

"You have Mozart? Wolfgang Amadeus Mozart?"

"Yes." Nathan straightened his shoulders. "He was playing on the piano, though you could hardly hear him above the din of the restaurant. Still surprises me sometimes that I managed to snag his soul. He's been wonderful for the realm, recruiting quite a cadre of musicians and artists. Maria Sybilla Merian was there, too. And Alexander von Humboldt."

"Humboldt?" This was incredible. "And Sybilla Merian? In the same place at the same time?"

"Yes."

"Oh my God. Two of the most amazing naturalists in the history of European exploration, and I missed them?"

"You've the option to spend a lot more time with them if you wish." Nathan grinned. "I also invited Pedro Joaquin Chamorro."

"Who's that?"

"You learned about him in college. His assassination triggered the Sandinista Revolution."

I let out a long whistle. "Chamorro. The journalist."

"I had to fight hard for him. A good journalist is highly prized among my kind."

"Really? Why?"

"They are guardians of truth, and they don't give up. At least, that's the way it used to be, in Chamorro's time. The mortal world is quite different now." Nathan paused. Our exchange had lightened his mood. His expression was more relaxed, and he moved his hands in an animated fashion. "My intention was to impress you, Mayela. I don't have many souls, and most are not historical figures, not names you would recognize. But they are all of very high quality. Like you, they sought paths of meaning and purpose in the mortal world. You'd fit in quite well. That's why I made a bid for you."

A bid. What a disturbing way to put it. Uneasy, I shifted in my seat and decided to change the subject. "That story you told me, about your abandoned childhood and your crazy mother?"

"All true. I grew up in this world, believing I was a mortal until my mother claimed me. The only thing I left out was when. It happened a long time ago, by your standards."

"How long?"

He hesitated. "I was born near the end of the

fifteenth century."

I sucked in my breath. Five hundred years! Given Anne's story, I expected as much, but it knocked the wind out of me to hear him say it. Great. Just great. My one-time love interest had lived his formative years in medieval times and now collected souls for a living. "Is this going to be like one of those vampire movies, where you turn into an old, mummified man with rotting skin sloughing off your crumbling bones?"

"No." He smiled. "I have several forms, some of which may not please you. Rotting corpse of the undead, however, is not one of them."

"Well." I set aside my cup. "We'll call that a win."

I was at the end of my tea, and I couldn't think of any more questions. Or maybe I just couldn't think anymore.

"Mayela, I understand you have many questions, but we are in the mortal realm and time is working against us. We need to discuss the rules that govern interactions between my kind and yours."

"What rules?"

"Our rules." He set his jaw. "I need a task to complete our bargain."

"Bargain?"

"You crossed the threshold and acknowledged my bid."

That word again. "What, exactly, do you mean by *bid*?"

"When an unclaimed soul arrives in the Hunting Grounds, we make our bid by capturing the soul. You were captured first by my rival, who appeared in the form of a serpent. We would not be here now if you had not called my true name before his venom took effect.

Three times you called on me, first to state your intention, then to reaffirm, and finally, to seal your intent. In this way, you declared you had not entered the Hunting Grounds unclaimed, but that you and I had a pre-established bond."

I raised my brow. "And did we? Have a pre-established bond?"

He drew a quiet breath. "We've been in communication throughout your mortal life."

"Wait." I blinked. "What? We've what?"

"In your dreams, Mayela. In quiet moments when you sensed someone nearby. That was my presence, my voice you heard as a mere whisper in your mind. I've spoken to you through animals in the wild, birds in your backyard, leaves on the wind." He folded his hands and leaned forward. "Sometimes you almost let yourself believe that you were communicating with someone from beyond the veil. But mostly you wrote your experiences off to imagination, or worse."

"So, you're my imaginary friend?"

"Not imaginary."

"You're my real imaginary friend?"

He sighed. "By the time you crossed the threshold, a degree of trust had been established between us. That's why you granted me primacy in the contest for your soul."

"Can we just pause here?" I put up my hands to stop him. "What about St. Peter and the pearly gates? What about the big book where all our acts are written down? I mean, not that I believed any of that stuff, but isn't all this supposed to be decided before we die?"

"The reality of our world is much more complex than any one faith has captured. There's no Heaven or

Hell beyond the veil, no eternal divide between good and evil. The fate of each soul is determined by the choices a mortal makes, and by rivalries among my kind. We have preferences with respect to the souls we recruit, though even entities that want the same soul can exhibit vastly different qualities. Were you with my rival, for example, the one who appeared as a snake, you'd be having a very different experience. Yet both of us believe you could enhance our separate realms. Both of us are drawn to the shimmering brilliance of your soul."

The shimmering brilliance of my soul. At once flattered and unsettled, I rose and stepped away, circling the fire to put distance between us. Pausing on the other side of the pit, I watched orange flames dance over glowing coals, saw shadows spinning inside ribbons of sun. When I lifted my gaze to Nathan, his dark eyes met mine, glinting with amber sparks reflected from the fire.

"You're trap lining," I realized.

"I'm what?"

"Trap lining." My pulse picked up, the same excitement I remembered from grad school, when I was on the verge of an extraordinary insight after weeks of poring over my data. "It's a term we use in behavioral ecology. You identify souls that interest you and track them, so the moment we cross the threshold, you're ready to snatch us up."

"My kind are not creatures of biology."

Aren't you? I circled back and sat next to him. "In the rainforests of Central America, butterflies trapline for mates. The males emerge from the chrysalis first. They have wings and can fly while the females remain caterpillars, feeding on plants. Males track female caterpillars, visiting them periodically until they pupate. Then the males guard the chrysalis. Some even fight over the female during her metamorphosis, while she emerges fully formed with her own wings."

Nathan watched me with a curious yet guarded expression. "An intriguing comparison, but we are wholly different from the organic creatures of this world. Our tracking of souls should not be conflated with a mating ritual."

"Well, it sure felt like one," I countered, "these last few days."

Nathan frowned and looked away. I couldn't tell whether he was being obtuse or dishonest. Could he not fathom that something else might be happening between us, something other than a contest for my soul?

"Why are you here if I'm still alive?" I couldn't help pushing this conversation a little further. The possibility intrigued me. Was I the caterpillar to his winged libido? Could Nathan be responding instinctually to a pending metamorphosis? "How did I enter the Hunting Grounds, body and soul intact?"

"It's known to happen among your kind."

I stared at him. "That's all? It *happens*?"

"As many times as we've seen it, there's no clear explanation. Your gift may be part of a latent ability among your kind, or a rare mutation. More likely, it results from a constellation of genes that comes together once in many generations."

Or maybe like you, I am a Daughter of Gods. Have you thought of that, Loverboy? I wanted to say this. I was burning to say it. But Mamá had warned me: *Don't reveal your origins, not even to him, until you understand the landscape of their world.* If there was one thing I'd learned in the last hour, Mamá was right. About everything. I bit my tongue and tucked my ace deeper inside my sleeve.

"Perhaps you've heard legends crafted around others like you," he was saying. "Dumuzid and Geshtinanna. Osiris, who was loved by Isis. Persephone. Orpheus and Eurydice. Mary of Nazareth. There have been more. Many more. Over the ages, these mortals crossed the threshold body and soul as you did, often unnoticed by your kind, their stories forgotten along the winding path of history. But to us, to the Soul Masters, they are an extraordinary find."

"Did you know, before I crossed the threshold, that I could do this?"

"No."

"Really?" That surprised me.

"We never know when to expect something like this. The scramble on the Hunting Grounds was fierce, and my rival was not pleased to be outmaneuvered. He watches us now, along with others, hoping for the opportunity to snatch you up should I fail."

"The tentacle guy on the Plaza," I realized. "That wasn't my imagination?"

"No. That was one of them."

"And there are more? Watching us right now?"

"The circle of stones is well-constructed and safe. That, and the ward on your house. But the sooner we seal the bargain—the sooner you decide how I must prove my worth—the better."

"Anne said I'd be expected to ask for something."

He nodded. "Give me a task worthy of your gift."

"Does it need to be revenge?"

“No. Most often, I’m asked to finish something left undone.”

“I’m sorry.” I shook my head. “I don’t know what I’d ask you to finish. Unless you want to grade my exams. Or…” An idea occurred to me, one that might very well be worth my soul. “Could I ask for something big, like restoring tall grass prairie to half its historic range?”

“You can but consider your request carefully. Unless you want me to fail—which I acknowledge you might—keep in mind what would be within my power. As much as I would like to see the Great Plains restored to their original glory, my influence is limited when it comes to the free will of vast numbers of mortals.”

I had to admit, this wasn’t looking like such a bad deal. The package included one awesome favor and an eternity with artists and revolutionaries. Plus maybe, just maybe, a little Nathan on the side? I snuck a quick glance at him, up and down. Yup. He was still irresistibly handsome, despite being almost five hundred years my senior.

“How long do I have to think about this?” I asked.

A shadow passed over his expression. “Not long.”

I paused. “That sounds ominous.”

“This is the nature of things. Time works against us in the mortal world.” Nathan leaned close and took my hands in his. “Mayela, when you decide what you want, you must call on me right away. Call my true name three times, just as you did in the Hunting Grounds.”

“But…” I pulled back, uncertain. “I don’t remember your true name. I mean, I know I used it, but whenever I try to remember, the name slips away. It’s like a shadow on the edge of my vision.”

A smile touched his lips. “True names are a source of power, and the decision to give you mine was not taken lightly. I planted my name deep inside your heart, under lock and key. Think of it as an encryption. You knew how to unleash my name in the Hunting Grounds. You will know how to unleash it again when the time comes. You must trust yourself in this.”

A woman could go crazy, all the things she was supposed to know without knowing. “What if I decide I don’t want to be with you? What happens then?”

“I hope it doesn’t come to that, but the choice is yours, Mayela. If you refuse me, my rival—the one who reached you first on the Hunting Grounds—will have his opportunity.”

“What, snake guy?” I shuddered at the memory of the serpent’s bite. “Maybe I shouldn’t judge based on first impressions, but I’m guessing that can’t be good.”

“I’m not allowed to reveal details about my rivals. All I can say is his ways are different from mine. Still, he can be persuasive. If he does not succeed, you will be delivered back to the Hunting Grounds.”

My breath came up short. I did not want to go back to that place. Not in a million years. “Why?”

“You’ve crossed the threshold. You must choose a guardian.”

“But I didn’t mean to—”

“Intentions are irrelevant. Once a soul crosses the threshold, there’s no going back. The cycle repeats as often as necessary, until the soul makes a choice or becomes so depleted my kind lose interest.”

“Lose interest?” I whispered. Every part of me went still. I remembered the chilling void of the Hunting Grounds, the rush of invisible wings overhead, the claws that swept the old man away. “What happens if your kind lose interest?”

Nathan blinked and looked away, jaw working as if he hadn’t considered we might arrive at this question.

“Nathan?”

“You remain forever on the Hunting Grounds.” He met my gaze, a hard glint in his eyes. “Condemned to fear and solitude until your soul perishes and nothing is left at all.”

“What?” I cried.

“Mayela.” In a single motion, he took my face in his hands. “That will not happen.”

His touch calmed me in an instant. Our breaths fell into quiet synchrony. My fingers rose to his wrist. He rested his forehead upon mine. Warmth spread into my veins, filling me with sweet joy.

“How do you do that?” I whispered.

“You will find a home among us. I hope you find it with me.”

I wanted to stay like that forever, our spirits intertwined, our lips a breath apart, a midnight fire fading nearby. I leaned forward to meet his lips with mine, but Nathan released me, breaking the spell.

“I should go.” He rose and stepped away. “Do you have any more questions for the moment?”

“No.” I shook my head in a daze. “Wait. You’re going? Where?”

“Now that my purpose is served, I must release this form and go back across the veil.”

“You’re leaving me alone? With all of this?”

He softened his expression. “I’ll be nearby, vigilant and ready to return the moment you call.”

I stared at him, at a loss for words. All that

splendor, the perfect reflection of my long-suppressed romantic fantasies, was about to vanish. Even if he looked the same when he came back, a crucial aspect of our relationship would change: The next time I saw Nathan, I would belong to him. Based on everything said this night, he would not return unless I called him, and I would not call him except to grant him my soul.

So, this was it: My last chance to make love to Nathan de la Rosa as a free and independent mortal. I would not say no. Everything human and divine inside of me wanted him now, because I knew if Nathan claimed my soul, I would never be able to love him again.

I rose and extended my hand. “Would you like to come inside for a while before you go?”

****

Labyrinth of Dreams

Kansas City, Missouri. 2008

Nekhen was not inclined to follow his mother’s advice. Yet he could not resist the thought something good might come of his attachment to Mayela. After much consideration, he decided to visit Mayela in her dreams. By now, Earth had fallen around the sun many times. Mayela and Carlos’s first dance had receded into their past, a fond memory nestled inside a much larger relationship. They’d dated, fought, reconciled, and married. Now they shared their lives in a home not far from the university where Carlos worked.

Mayela seemed happy in her companionship, and yet her dreams proved unsettled. At night, she wandered anxiously through labyrinthine worlds. She rode old trolleys into twisted hills with impossible slopes, worried the vehicle might topple from the rails into deep ravines. Always arriving late for her connection, Mayela rushed through unfamiliar stations, not knowing which track to seek out and mystified as to her final destination. In other dreams, Mayela wandered rows of houses that stood between her and a dark seashore. A party could be heard along the docks. Mayela longed to join the festivities, but she could not locate the gate that led to laughter and music. Every dream played out into one fruitless search or another. Distressed by Mayela's anxiety, Nekhen observed from a careful distance, contemplating the meaning of these quests that he might find a way to assist her.

One night in her sleep, Mayela returned to grade school. Nekhen found her on the playground during recess, taking turns at the swings with her friends, recalling a happier time when she was not the only one who spoke of imaginary friends and make-believe pets. On impulse, Nekhen decided to manifest himself, becoming one of the children playing kickball nearby. A whistle screeched across the field. Their faceless teacher was calling them back to class. Nekhen, the boy, took a place in line a few students behind Mayela. He followed the bob of her dark curls into class and claimed a desk near hers. As Mayela fidgeted in her wooden seat, the faceless teacher walked among them, passing out large, blank sheets of paper. Crayons floated through the air and bounced in slow motion across the floor. Nekhen discovered that, like the other children, he could capture his preferred colors and begin to draw.

Throughout the room, wax-colored worlds spread in two dimensions across papery canvases. Nekhen watched as Mayela caught crayons of green and brown, yellow and blue. She drew stick figures on a forest with a beach and bright sun overhead. As Mayela worked, face drawn in concentration, the other children's drawings came to life. Creatures, people, and objects reached out of the paper and snatched each student into the worlds they had invented. Mayela glanced up from her drawing and realized her friends were disappearing. She let go a silent scream. The paper she drew on began to tremble. Mayela tried to get away but seemed bound by an invisible force to her desk. Squirming in place, she glanced frantically around the room for someone who could help. Her gaze came to rest on the boy sitting nearby, Nekhen.

"You!" She gasped.

Nekhen stared back, bewildered by the sudden vivid connection between them.

He gulped and murmured, "Don't be afraid."

Then she was gone. Vanished like the others, pulled straight into the world she'd drawn.

Releasing his boyish form, Nekhen dove after Mayela. They fell over a vast blue ocean. Land rose beneath them. The sky darkened with a passing storm. Wind buffeted their spirits, then halted abruptly as they neared the earth. Mayela landed on her feet. Nekhen spilled into a shadow at her side.

Behind them, waves crashed against a moonlit beach. Inland, the soil was barren and rocky. Twisted limbs of dead trees reached toward the starry sky. Shattered twigs covered the earth like dry bones. In a place that showed every sign of once having been filled with life and sound, death and silence now reigned. What had destroyed this forest, Nekhen could not tell, yet he sensed the hand of mortals.

"I know this place," Mayela breathed. She had resumed her adult appearance, dressed in field pants and a loose cotton shirt. Despite the apocalyptic scene before them, the distress that had characterized her other dreams had vanished. "This is the place I've been looking for."

What could she possibly be seeking in this desolate landscape?

"I know what to do." Mayela knelt as if in a trance and ran her hands over the sandy soil. "On the edge of a storm, I know what to do."

Thunder sounded in the distance, accompanied by lightning-laced clouds. Mayela closed her eyes and dug her hands wrist deep into the ground. Face pinched in concentration, she whispered to small creatures that clung to existence inside the spent soil. At Mayela's words, mycelial networks pulsed and spread outward inside the earth, wrapping life-giving tendrils around scored and dried seeds. Nourished by the fungi's embrace, the seeds broke open, unfolding into round, waxy leaves atop thin stems that stretched toward the sky. Saplings grew into trees, and trees towered overhead, breaking up the starry sky. Along the ground, woody lianas grew in meandering paths before snaking up large, buttressed trunks. Soon, the barren wasteland was covered in a lush tropical forest.

Sirena, Nekhen realized in astonishment. This was the forest Mayela had visited as a college student, where she'd found her vocation as an ecologist.

Nekhen slipped into the shape of Jaguar. A happy grin broke on Mayela's face when she saw him.

"You," she said in recognition, and beckoned him to follow.

They walked side by side down the moonlit path. Above them, branches swayed in an ocean breeze. Waking parrots squawked. Small lizards skittered through the underbrush. Decaying wood and overripe fruit permeated Nekhen's senses. He recalled the prairie Mayela the child once summoned from the poisoned earth. That had been an extraordinary vision of form and light, pleasing to his kind. But this was another experience altogether, a liminal space filled with noise and smells and sticky humid air.

Mayela rested her hand on Nekhen's shoulder as they walked, sinking her fingers into his fur. Nekhen responded with a low, rumbling purr. They arrived at a large, buttressed tree and sat down to rest. Nekhen laid his broad head on his forepaws. Mayela reclined against his flank and contemplated the high branches.

"I want to climb that tree," she said.

"Then go," Nekhen replied.

"I can't." Her voice faltered.

Nekhen turned to her. Mayela's emerald eyes met his with a longing he did not expect. The moment unsettled him.

"I left you behind once already," she murmured. "Look how long it took to find you again."

Disconcerted, he glanced away. "I will follow."

"All the way up there?"

"Wherever you would go."

Mayela accepted his promise and rose. She closed her eyes and lifted her arms toward the forest. A low hum sounded from deep within the woodland. The drone grew in intensity until an iridescent purple mist flowed out of the trees. A swarm of orchid bees, thousands of little sapphire jewels, flew toward Mayela.

They hovered as she stepped into their midst. Then, the tiny insects rose, sustaining Mayela's arms and feet, buoying her up with their combined strength as they ascended toward the high canopy. Nekhen resumed his shadow form and followed.

The trunk unfurled before their eyes. Smooth, coffee-brown bark turned in subtle, sinuous lines toward the heavens. Vines snaked over its surface. Bursts of green foliage emerged from nooks and crannies where smaller plants had taken hold. Lazy moths flitted past. Sleepy monkeys watched their ascent with confused expressions. At long last, they reached the top. The bees placed Mayela onto a wide branch that overlooked the forest. Mayela thanked them, and they took their leave.

Toward the west, night embraced a vast ocean. The moon, orange and heavy, settled into the watery horizon. Eastward, a halo broke over distant mountains with the promise of a rising sun. The forest itself was shrouded in mist.

As Mayela took in this wondrous beauty, Nekhen took in Mayela. Like all mortals, Mayela could paint the images of her dreams. But who, Nekhen now wondered, painted her? What accounted for the detailed cast of herself upon this liminal landscape? Her radiant smile, absent from previous dreams, now filled him with peace and gratitude. Her hair like her mother's, a dark mass of cascading curls, shone with a purplish hue under the dawn she was summoning. Her body, every subtle curve a crucible of desire, stirred a deep sense of longing, that primordial call of creation he thought had been purged from his being long ago.

"You came." Mayela startled Nekhen out of

contemplation.

He met her gaze, surprised she had sensed his formless presence.

"You are the same one who was down below," she said, pointing toward the forest floor. "You were Jaguar."

Nekhen's image shifted beneath Mayela's desire to see form. He coalesced into a gray faceless mist with blurred limbs.

"Yes, I was Jaguar," he said. "And before that, the boy in your class."

"I remember." She nodded, then offered a mischievous smile. "What are you now? A ghost?"

Nekhen hesitated. This conversation was not wise. He should deflect her questions and vanish, never to let himself be seen in her dreams again. Yet he felt an overwhelming need to be seen, and to be seen by her. Surely it would do no harm to allow a little truth between them.

In any case, the next morning, Mayela would believe all this no more than a dream.

"I am your friend and companion," he said. "I will accept any form you give me."

"May I see your hands? The sun is about to rise, and I'd like to hold your hand."

As Mayela spoke, Nekhen's hands took shape. He watched in wonder as she drew him. His palms lengthened out of the shadowy mist that comprised his limbs. Fingers stretched forth. Olive skin sheathed muscle and bone. Fine dark hairs feathered over bluish veins. These were not invented hands. They were his own, the ones attached to his true body whenever he assumed physical form in her world.

"How did you…?" he asked, astonished.

"How did I what?"

Nekhen shook his head—or the shadow that was his head. This was a strange state indeed, a shadow with two well-formed hands. Mayela had summoned this small part of him with surprising accuracy. What more of his true self might become manifest if she kept drawing him in her dreams?

Mayela reached out and took his hand, flesh on flesh, palm against tingling palm. Nekhen's pulse quickened at her touch and then slowed into contentment. Together, they watched the rising sun send scarlet-gold ribbons across an indigo sky.

The next morning, Mayela told Carlos about her dream over breakfast, while Nekhen observed, invisible, nearby.

"First you were a boy," she finished with an animated voice. "Then you were a jaguar, and then you were just a shadow with hands."

"A shadow with hands?" Carlos gave her a quizzical frown over his coffee cup. "Should I be worried about that?"

Mayela laughed. "Shadow you was kind of sexy."

"I like the jaguar part." He leaned close and kissed Mayela. "I'll be your jaguar any day."

They nuzzled into each other a moment before Carlos rose and began gathering the dishes.

"I've been thinking about something," Mayela announced.

"Oh?" Carlos checked the time on his phone. "Sure you want to talk about it now? I've got a lab meeting at eight thirty already." But his smile was receptive.

"It's nothing complicated. I've been thinking about

starting up some research again."

"What?" From Carlos's expression, this wasn't the announcement he expected.

"I've been restless for a while now, like something is missing." Mayela spoke quickly, trying to dissipate the discomfort generated by Carlos's reaction. "Not that I'm unhappy with our marriage, not at all. But I've been having these strange dreams. Always searching for something, until last night. Last night was different and I—" Her voice broke off. She paused as if measuring her next words. "When the bees appeared, it was as if everything fell into place. I remembered who I was, and this morning when I woke up, I knew exactly what I wanted to do."

"You had a dream about bees, and now you want to do research?" Carlos did not bother to hide his doubt.

Mayela bristled. "Don't make fun of me. I didn't just up and decide this. It's been on my mind for a while. You know how I feel about my work at the college. It's like I'm wilting away. Every day is somehow more wasted than the last. I want to be a real biologist again."

"You are a real biologist." He went to the counter, set the plates in the sink. "You have a good job, a secure job, teaching biology."

"I'm not doing what I was trained to do. I'm not even teaching what I was trained to teach."

"Introductory courses are part of the package for every professor. You know that."

"Part of the package for you. That's the only package for me."

Carlos grew agitated. "How do you expect to start a research program at this stage of your career? After all this time out of the loop?"

"It hasn't been that long since I worked in a lab," Mayela countered.

"You know how hard it is to find a research position in academia! Even for someone fresh off a post doc. Never mind someone like you, who's been buried in teaching for ages."

"*Buried?*"

"Not literally. I'm just saying. You haven't published in years. Even if that were overlooked, and you were lucky enough to land something, chances are it wouldn't be in Kansas City. You'd have to move somewhere else, and…Seriously. How is this even supposed to work?"

"You're blowing this all out of proportion." Mayela spoke with measured calm. "I never said I was going to quit my job. I just want a little something on the side. I have skills that might be useful right here in Kansas City. The public parks, the Department of Conservation, they all have restoration sites they might like more data on. How will I know if I don't ask?"

"Research costs money, Mayela. How will you pay for equipment, supplies, everything?"

"If there's one thing ecologists know how to do, it's field work on a shoestring."

"And you're going to find time for this when?"

Mayela stood, placed her hands on her hips, and pinned him with a fierce gaze. "Why are you stonewalling this?"

"I'm not stonewalling."

"Yes, you are. You're not even giving me a chance."

"Okay." He threw up his hands. "This is crazy.

You think I don't see how you work already? Your teaching load is over the top. Your nights and weekends are already full."

"So are yours."

"Yes, but I'm—"

"The real professor?"

Carlos set his jaw and looked away.

"Look." Mayela softened her tone. "It's just an idea I want to follow up on. If it's meant to be, I'll figure it out. I can reprioritize my other obligations. Maybe even negotiate a deal with the college. They might give me a release from some of my teaching in exchange for research that serves the community."

Carlos puffed out his cheeks. Lifting his hands in a conciliatory gesture, he finished loading the dishwasher. Then he returned to the table and started preparing his satchel for work.

"What's really going on, Mayela?" he asked. "Have I done something wrong? Am I missing something here? Because I think we have a great life. I couldn't be happier with you. Are you happy with me?"

"Of course, I'm happy. I just…" Mayela's words trailed into a worried frown.

"What?"

She shook her head. "What I already said. I want to reconnect to this piece of who I am, a piece I somehow lost along the way."

Carlos sucked in a breath and shook his head. "Just now, when you said you wanted to talk, I thought this was going to be about having children."

"You want children?"

"Don't you?"

"Yes."

"But you also want to start a research program."

Mayela pressed her lips into a thin line and looked away.

"This is what I've been thinking about," Carlos said. "We aren't getting any younger. It's time for us to start trying. But if you start up a research program now, especially with all the obstacles you'd be facing…You have to think about this. How are you going to do both?"

Mayela's face went pale with fury. She opened her mouth and closed it. Then she sat down and folded her arms. A chilly silence ensued. They remained like that a long moment, Carlos staring at Mayela, while Mayela looked in any direction but his.

Carlos glanced at the time.

"I have to go," he said. "We'll talk about this later, okay?"

Mayela did not respond.

Carlos slipped his laptop into his satchel. "I'm not against what you want to do, really. I just don't want you biting off more than you can chew. You work so hard as it is."

Mayela's aura shivered with anger.

Her husband swung his satchel onto his shoulder and kissed her on the forehead. "Call you later?"

She gave a stiff nod. "Sure."

As his footsteps faded down the front hallway, Mayela covered her face with her hands. Not until she heard the front door shut behind him did she look up. Tears wet her cheeks. She wiped them away with an exasperated sigh. Then she rose to finish cleaning the table and putting the kitchen in order.

"It's not just about the research," she muttered as

she worked. "It's that somewhere along the way, you made this little box for the woman you call your wife, and you expect me to stay in that box for the rest of eternity. Dammit, Carlos!" Her voice gathered volume and momentum. "Everything we do is decided by you, one way or another. What we eat, what we drink, how late we go to bed, what time we wake up, the places we go out, the company we keep—everything! We mold our entire lives around your rhythm, your needs, your preferences. Sure, Mr. Professor, no problem for you to have a full-time career and children, but if I want to stretch my boundaries just a little while reserving my right to build a family? Wham!" She slammed her hand on the table. "Got to smack down that impulse, don't we?"

Nekhen did not know what to make of this. How many times had he seen the same frustration played out, across multiple generations and countless relationships? Still, he was taken aback. He remembered what the Daughter of the Plains had told him the first night Mayela and Carlos met. *This will be a great love*, she had said, *one that will echo across all our realms.* Had her interest in Carlos's soul blunted her foresight? By all appearances, Mayela and Carlos had a true love, but also a very ordinary one.

Not that Carlos was a bad person. He was simply tethered to mortal illusions; caught, like so many of his kind, inside the glare of his own ego. Most likely, he would never recognize the sacrifices made by so many others—including his wife—to facilitate his advancement. Despite her love for him, Carlos's blindness would eat away at Mayela from now until the day she crossed the threshold.

A stunning realization hit Nekhen. Carlos could not, in fact, know Mayela in the same way he did. Carlos had no memory of Mayela, the girl, weaving images of prairie from threads of thunder. He did not stand beside Mayela, the college student, when she faced Jaguar's judgement in the rainforest. He never whispered encouragement to Mayela, the promising grad student, who dreamed of changing the world. Carlos only knew Mayela as the smart, eye-catching beauty who showed up at his dance class and was fated to be his wife. He saw Mayela as the woman who completed his story, rather than an autonomous creature capable of writing her own destiny.

"I know that wasn't him," Mayela said, startling Nekhen out of his reverie. She'd begun preparing her own backpack at the table and was looking straight at Nekhen. Or was it through him? Nekhen wasn't sure. He had not manifested himself, yet he was experiencing a clear sensation of being seen.

"I know that wasn't him in the dream," Mayela continued, "because in the dream when I said, 'I want to go up that tree,' you said, 'Go.' But just now when I told Carlos, 'I want to go up that tree,' he said, 'Stop.' "

She stuffed a granola bar and an apple in the side pocket of her backpack. "But I knew before that, too. I told Carlos it was him because I don't want my husband thinking I'm dreaming about other men. That would freak him out even more than the research thing."

She gave a short laugh, then continued as if sharing secrets with a best friend. "I know it wasn't him because those hands weren't his. A woman knows her husband's hands, and those were not Carlos's hands, but oh my God they were beautiful. And so real! So vivid. I could *feel* you holding my hand." She grasped the air, pleasure in her expression, as if she were reliving the sunrise over a misty forest. "I've never had a dream like that. Not since…"

Mayela stopped, shook the thought out of her head, and retreated to the counter. Taking hold of the coffee pot, she poured the last of the brew into a travel mug. Then she turned around, seeming to pin Nekhen with her gaze again. "Just for the record, I know I'm talking to thin air."

He heard the doubt in her voice. Hope sparked inside him.

"I see Mamá talking to thin air all the time," Mayela continued, "and it seems to make her feel better. So, I figure why not give it a try? After all, nobody's watching. Right?"

Coffee in hand, she came to the table and slung the backpack over her shoulder. Nekhen wanted to reach out and touch her, let her experience a brush with his essence, but trepidation kept him frozen in place.

"There, you see?" she announced. "I feel better already!"

Mayela started down the hallway toward the front door. Before leaving the house, she paused and called back to the kitchen. "In case you are there, I want you to know I would've liked to have seen your face. I keep thinking those beautiful hands must be attached to an extraordinary face. Maybe next time, if there is a next time, you can show me your face."

Chapter 12

Nathan paused in the back doorway. His shoulders tensed as he looked around my kitchen.

"You okay?" I asked.

"Yes." He shifted his stance as if brushing off a thought. "I…I didn't think the evening would end like this."

His last words were delivered in a tone that hovered between statement and question. Seeing an immortal stand uncertain on the threshold of my home moved a part of me I didn't know existed.

"Well," I said, "that makes two of us. Please, come in." I reached toward his mug. "Here, I'll take care of that."

"No, let me." He took my mug instead and went to the dishwasher, navigating the space as if he knew it well. "I was also…remembering."

"Remembering what?"

"The first time I was here." He glanced at me as if wondering how I might respond.

"You mean when you killed the snake? But you said that didn't happen here, that it happened in the Hunting Grounds."

"Yes, I know. What I'm referring to now is first time I was in your home, in this world."

"You were here?" A cold mist settled over my heart. "When? How?"

"You were having breakfast with Carlos." He nodded toward the kitchen table behind me. "You were telling him your dreams."

"You watched us having breakfast?" Okay, that was creepy.

Or was it?

After everything I'd been through, maybe I needed to recalibrate what constituted creepy. "Why would you do that?"

His face fell. In that moment, I recognized the extent to which he worried about disappointing me or scaring me away.

"I don't know how to explain," he said as if in apology. "It's what we do, watch and listen. I was called to you, so I came. You'd had a dream, and you were telling Carlos about it."

The past unfolded inside my heart, illuminating shadows of Carlos and me, as we were so many years ago, sitting and laughing at the table.

"First you were a boy," I murmured, "then you were a jaguar, then you were a shadow with hands." I looked at Nathan, stunned by the realization. "That was you! That was you?"

"Yes." A wary sort of relief crossed his expression. "I was in the dream, and then I was with you here, when you spoke with Carlos and…after he left. I was still here."

"I knew!" I gasped. "I *felt* you. And all this time I thought…" A troubling possibility crossed my mind. "Nathan, did you ever…? Did we…Did you and I…?"

The cell phone rang.

I checked the screen. It was Mamá.

"I'm sorry," I said. "I have to take this. Please,

hold on to that thought."

He frowned. "What thought? You mean your thought?"

I waved the question away and took the call. "Mamá!"

"Where are you?" she demanded. "What's going on?"

"*Está aquí. En mi casa.*"

Her voice softened. "*¿Y tú*? *¿Estás bien*?"

"*Sí.*" I turned into the phone and continued in Spanish, eyeing Nathan as I spoke. Having taken care of the mugs, he now dedicated himself to accommodating stray dishes from the sink. Apparently, immortals did not count themselves above house chores.

"When do you arrive, Mamá?" I continued in Spanish. "We need to talk, but I can't do this over the phone."

"The earliest flight I could find gets in at nine."

"At night?" My heart sank. It seemed like an eternity to wait. "I'll meet you at the airport."

"No. Stay in the house. I'm coming to you."

"But I—"

"Don't. Leave. The house."

Her ominous tone gave me pause. "Uhm, okay."

"You feel safe with him?"

"Yes."

"Good. Trust your instincts, Mayela. In everything. And just sit tight. I'll be there soon."

"*Te quiero*, Mamá."

"*Te quiero*."

We disconnected. Nathan came up from behind and slid an arm around my waist. Setting the phone aside, I caught his hand in mine. Our fingers intertwined. He nuzzled my neck, sending sparks across my skin.

"About what you were saying earlier," I murmured. I did not like the question I was about to ask, but I needed to know. "Did you and I have something going, some strange otherworldly romance, while Carlos was still alive?"

"No." He withdrew, giving me a little space.

"Oh," I said with relief, turning to meet his gaze. "I'm glad to hear that."

"I wanted to be here, and you seemed pleased by my presence. It was enough."

I laid my hand on his chest, found it warm and vibrant, like a winter flame.

"You were with me when he died, too," I whispered. "I remember now. You held me in your…" Arms? Wings? Otherworldly limbs? "When I was alone at night, you held me. For many nights. It felt just like this."

Like a refuge of compassion in the face of unbearable loss. I leaned into him, wrapped my arms around him, let him enfold me in his embrace.

"I'm sorry, Mayela," he murmured. His breath fell feather light against my temple. "I would have done anything to save you from that pain."

Unsettled, I pulled away. A lump had caught in my throat. "Carlos isn't with you, is he?"

I knew the answer to this question, but I needed to hear him say it.

Nathan shook his head. "No."

Anger sparked inside of me. "Why? Was his soul not good enough?"

"On the contrary. Carlos was more than worthy. Worthy of you, and of a place among my own. But I knew some day I would bid for you, and I…" He faltered and glanced away.

"You wanted me all to yourself?"

"Perhaps," he conceded with a frown. "But Mayela, even if you were to follow him, it would not be as you imagine. Few couples in this world remain bonded after they cross the veil. They choose different guardians, or if they choose the same guardian, they choose separate paths, new ways of being inside a larger universe. Carlos was a good man and he loved you, but he also kept you inside a box while you were together in this world. If I were going to have you, when your time came, I wanted you to be free of that box."

"I see." I understood. I did. So much of me had come undone after Carlos died, but part of me had been freed as well. It wasn't until I got out from under the devastation that I was able to recognize that. "Is Carlos…Is he happy?"

My voice broke on this question.

Nathan's expression melted into warm regard. "I have not watched his path closely, but I know his guardian is generous and wise. Yes, I believe he is happy."

"I loved him so much." I choked on these words. My hands went to my throat, then to cover my eyes. For the umpteenth time that evening, I was fighting back tears.

"I know, Mayela," Nathan whispered. "I know."

I withdrew from him, caught inside a strange mix of emotions: Grief over my late husband, embarrassment for mourning him on a first date, painful awareness this wasn't exactly a first date, much less a normal date, and…honest confusion.

What was normal?

What could possibly count as normal, after tonight?

Regaining my composure, I reached for my purse and phone. "Come on. I'll show you the rest of the house."

There wasn't much to show, and he'd been here before, so why was I giving him a tour? *Just trying to be normal.* I took him through the dining area and living room, then down the hallway toward the bedrooms and guest bathrooms. Midnight appeared, trailing us like a shadow.

"That's unusual," I said. "She generally hides from strangers."

"I'm not a stranger." To prove his point, he picked her up. Any newcomer would've earned several scratches on the face for that move, but Midnight simply settled into his arms with a rumbling purr.

Would wonders ever cease?

"She could see you before?" I asked. "When I couldn't?"

"Cats have an awareness that transcends the mortal realm. As far as Midnight is concerned, I've been part of the household since you adopted her."

We were passing the entrance to my home office. I paused and glanced inside the space, co-opted from Carlos after he died. The college where I worked didn't offer a research lab or equipment, so I'd nickeled-and-dimed everything—the microscope, the reference books, the pinning supplies and storage cases.

A shadow fell over my mood, deeper than all the shadows I'd yet encountered.

"There's so much left to do," I murmured. "I always thought…"

I always thought I had more time.

So did Carlos, I realized. So did everyone.

Nathan touched my elbow. "Your work doesn't have to end here."

"This work will end," I countered, anger breaking through my melancholy. "My time in this place—everything I've built, everyone I love—all that will end when I make my decision."

Pain clogged my throat. I blinked and spun away from him.

"Mayela!" Nathan came after me down the hall, following so close he nearly bumped into me when I stopped short at the linen closet.

"Here." I flung open the closet door and shoved some towels into his arms. Midnight leapt to the ground with an indignant yelp. "Not that you need to shower. Just, you know, if you want to. But this—" I handed him a toothbrush. "—is a dealbreaker. No one gets into my bed without brushing their teeth."

"Mayela—"

"And don't try to convince me celestial breath is always fresh!" I stuck my head back in the closet. "Also, we're putting on clean sheets. Not for you, for me."

"Mayela." He took everything from my arms and set it aside. "Listen to me. You think everything is going to end, but it won't. Your work, your purpose, will only be transformed into something greater."

"But that's the point!" I shot back, furious more

with myself than with him. "I had no purpose! I achieved nothing. Don't you see? Everything I did, all forty-two years on this planet, was a waste of fucking time."

"That's not true."

"What do I have to show? I could've done important work. I could've made a difference. Hell, I could've at least had children!" My heart contracted painfully. "One child. One child before Carlos died. Was that too much to ask? It was the easiest task given to me, and still I failed. I'll leave nothing behind when I go. Not from my career, not for my family. Nothing."

Nathan held my gaze a long moment. In the heavy silence that followed, an icy knot settled in my chest. I understood for the first time how much I feared judgement by this creature from beyond the veil. He was, after all, the would-be guardian of my eternal destiny.

Then Nathan cocked his brow and asked, with a very human tone of amusement, "Didn't you ever see *It's a Wonderful Life*?"

I groaned and rolled my eyes. "That does not make me feel better. That guy had, like, fifty children."

"Four."

"How many times have you seen it?"

"The children aren't the point."

"They're the whole point! That's what I've been saying."

"George Bailey was granted a rare vision. Mortals have a difficult time recognizing the true impact of their life before they cross the threshold."

"And that's supposed to make me feel better because?"

Nathan stepped close and lowered his voice. “What if I told you within five years, a pandemic is going to hit, and that all those students you’ve trained for healthcare, hundreds over the decades, are going to be the most precious resource your community has?”

“Wait.” I frowned, chewing on his words. “There’s going to be a pandemic?”

“I said *what if.*”

“But is there?”

“I don’t know!” Exasperation colored his tone. “Maybe. If things keep going like they are, yes.”

“When?” I demanded, horrified.

“I’m not predicting the future! You know the science. SARS. Ebola. Marburg. N1H1. It’s only a matter of time. That’s not the point, Mayela. The point is, your life has had purpose, all along, whether you’re aware of that purpose or not. In your teaching, in your research, in your marriage. In the person you are and the friend you’ve been.”

“Oh.” I didn’t know what to say. He offered a beautiful vision, really. Except for the part about the pandemic. “Thank you. I think.”

Nathan shrugged and, gathering sheets, towels, and toothbrush, continued down the hall.

I hastened to follow. *SARS. Ebola. Marburg. N1H1*. Some conversation we were having, going into my bedroom. When I caught up, he was already changing the sheets. I started to help, but he stopped me.

“I’ll take care of this,” he said. “You have only one task tonight: To rest.”

I felt chastened by the declaration, made smaller somehow in his presence. *Rest* was his only expectation, then. A good night's sleep for us both.

Of course, I told myself, burying my disappointment. What was I thinking to suppose otherwise? He was an immortal, after all, and I merely human.

I went to the dresser and ruffled through one of the drawers to choose a nightgown. Nothing too sexy, of course. Not that I had anything sexy.

Anger bubbled up. I clenched my fist, drawing one of my cotton shifts out at random. A woosh of sheets sounded behind me as Nathan continued making the bed.

I could tell him, couldn't I? Defy Mamá's advice and announce I was a daughter of his kind. But that wouldn't change anything. This discord of experience—what he was, and who I was—would always cut between us.

And always, I was learning, could be a very long time.

I went to the closet and retrieved Carlos's old house coat.

"Here," I said, proffering the garment to him. "Maybe you can use this."

He looked pleased to accept it. "Thank you."

"Might be a little small for you."

"It's perfect."

I bit my lip. "I don't have any guy pajamas anymore."

"That's not a problem."

"None of this is happening like it's supposed to," I blurted. "Everything's all wrong! I have so much to say and ask and think and…*feel.* But I can't find words for half of it, and I can't even begin to—"

"Mayela." He placed his hands on my shoulders. "It's all right."

"But I invited you in!" I continued. "And when you accepted, I thought it was going to be"—I waved my hands in the air—"and I was hoping you thought it was going to be that, too, but now I see we can never—"

"Mayela," he stopped me again. "I'm happy just to be with you."

My shoulders deflated. "That's the problem."

Nathan laughed, prodded me toward the master bath. "Go. Pamper yourself and take your time. I'll be here and ready when you return."

"Ready to *rest*, I'm sure," I muttered under my breath.

I shut the bathroom door behind me, pulled off my dress, and threw it into the hamper. Some seductress I was! I should've jumped him back in the kitchen, before either of us said one word.

Stewing in frustration, I started the shower, letting the water run to warm up. I shouldn't have invited him here in the first place. But I didn't want to be alone. Not tonight. And who better to accompany me than the one man who knew what I was facing?

I took off my panties and undid my bra. A rock tumbled to the floor. Confused, I stared at the dark lump sitting on the pale tile. A moment passed before I recognized it. Mamá's magic rock! Bending down, I picked up the shungite. I'd been carrying this thing in my bra the whole time. Thank goodness I hadn't jumped him in the kitchen. What kind of a conversation would that have been? *Gee, Mayela, do you always carry rocks in your bra? No, Nathan, this rock is special, just for protection against supernatural beasts like you.*

I closed my fist around the dark crystal. Did I need it anymore? I didn't think so, but better safe than sorry. I slipped the shungite into the pocket of my fuzzy robe, which hung on a nearby hook. Pinning up my hair, I stepped into the shower.

The water felt divine, coursing in hot rivulets down my skin.

Would there be showers on the other side?

There'd better be since I was taking my body with me. Showers in magically sanitized bathrooms because I was not going to spend eternity cleaning up mildew.

After turning off the water, I reached for a towel, luxuriating in the feel of cloth against my skin, of damp air inside my lungs. I brushed my teeth, put on my comfy cotton shift, and wrapped myself in my fuzzy robe. Refreshed, I let down my hair and brushed out the tangles. Then I indulged in a long moment of staring at myself in the mirror. My cheeks had more color now, and my eyes had regained their intense emerald hue.

Mayela on the Threshold of Eternity.

"You're going to get through this," I told myself.

After all, I was a Daughter of Gods.

Chapter 13

Back in my bedroom, Nathan had dimmed the lights. He stood inside a circle of candles set around my bed. The lit candles glimmered like tiny stars come to Earth, beating back the shadows of my room. The effect was breathtaking.

"Where did you get all these?" I asked in awe.

He grinned. "Magic."

I stepped inside the circle of candles. Nathan drew close. My pulse quickened. Carlos's old housecoat sat well on his shoulders, exposing a dark slice of chest that made me tingle inside. Slipping my hand into my pocket, I looked for Mamá's magic crystal and enclosed it inside my fingers. A little more protection seemed to be in order right about now.

"What do you think?" he asked, gesturing to the soft, flickering lights.

"I think…" I took the circle in one more time. "I think my mother would like you very much."

He laughed and encircled me in his arms. "Well, now that the families are in agreement." Then he hesitated, lips half a breath away from mine. "May I?"

I closed the distance with a kiss.

"You brushed your teeth." I grinned.

"What are guest bathrooms for?" Nathan picked me up and carried me toward the bed.

"You shouldn't pick me up. You're going to hurt

your back."

"I'll have centuries to heal."

I hit him with my fist. "Wrong answer. You're supposed to say I'm light as a feather."

"I'll never lie to you, Mayela."

I hit him twice. "Double wrong! Oh, wait. No, that was the right answer. But also, the wrong one." I frowned as he set me down on the cushions. "You shouldn't confuse me with honesty. It's not fair."

"I'm afraid my very existence confuses you."

Instead of going for the throw down, he walked around the bed to get in on his side, as if we'd been married for twenty years. I sat up and watched while he punched his pillows to recline. Was something going to happen here, or not?

"But you have lied to me. Lies of omission."

"That doesn't always count among my kind. Certain types of information can be disclosed only at the appropriate time and in response to the appropriate questions."

"That's convenient."

"Those are the rules."

"Well, they are convenient rules. For you and your kind. What about when you said you worked in renewables? Wasn't that a lie?"

"Souls are renewable."

"You knew that wasn't what I understood."

"The metaphor worked so I ran with it."

"But souls aren't renewable. They just are."

He cocked his brow. "Are you trying to explain my business to me, Mayela?"

"Maybe." I smiled and glanced away, felt the tension in my shoulders release. Damn the sex. Who needed it, anyway? I had too many important questions to ask. "Tell me about the business of souls."

"Souls can renew themselves through many lifetimes. To do this, they require nourishment, just as surely as your body does, here as well as in our world. After being released from their physical vessel, souls must replenish themselves before returning to the mortal realm."

"You're saying that souls reincarnate?"

"They have the capacity to do so, yes."

"Wait." I held up my hands, taking a moment to internalize this. "The choice of a guardian is not a forever thing?"

"Not necessarily. Your time beyond the veil could last decades to millennia. That's why it matters who you select. If you land a guardian who does not care for their souls, you may be caught forever on the other side."

"But my soul is cemented to my body. How's that supposed to work?"

"If you follow the pattern of others, you will continue to age, albeit very slowly. Your physical body may still die of natural causes, releasing the soul to a new cycle. Or you may simply reach a moment when your soul is ready to occupy a new vessel. You will then cross the threshold from our realm into yours one last time, allowing your old body to disassemble in the organic realm, releasing the soul directly into a new vessel."

"That sounds…painful."

"You have a long road ahead before you must consider that next step."

He leaned forward and started to undo the sash on

my fuzzy robe. I caught my breath at the intimacy, the heat of his body, the rosemary scent of his hair. Parting the robe to reveal my gown, Nathan glanced up and met my gaze. Behind his eyes I saw a promise of infinity, dark as ebony yet filled with light. I touched his cheek and traced the line of his jaw, roughened by evening stubble.

"This is really you, isn't it?" I whispered.

"What do you mean?"

"Your body isn't an illusion like Anne's is. Your skin, your flesh and bones, this is all really you."

"Yes." He nodded. "Anne learned how to project an image of herself into this world, but her core essence remains behind the veil. I, on the other hand, can be fully in this world and fully in my own, as serves my purpose."

"That's what I'll be able to do with my body, too."

"Not quite. You have but one form." He slipped my fuzzy robe from my shoulders and shifted it out from under me. Then with the tips of his fingers, he traced a gentle line from the base of my throat to my wrist. "One beautiful form. I have many forms, but I feel most comfortable like this, as you see me now."

"Why?"

He shrugged. "Maybe because this most closely resembles who I was before my mother claimed me."

I swallowed, my next question hovering uncertain on my lips. "What was it like, becoming what you are now?"

A shadow crossed his expression. "Why would you want to know?"

For myself, I thought. *But also, for you.* The pain he'd carried over five centuries tugged at my heart. I wanted to draw that pain out and hold it inside. I wanted to heal his pain, even though I didn't know how. "You're the only person I can talk to who's crossed the threshold as a physical creature. I'd like to have an idea of what I'm in for."

He blinked and looked away. An image filled my mind, of a crystal cup falling into a deep, dry well. When the sound of shattered glass echoed from the bottom, I saw tears glistening in Nathan's eyes.

"My metamorphosis was terrifying," he murmured. "And in the final moments, excruciatingly painful."

Moved, I took his hand in mine. "I'm so sorry."

He shook his head. "As I've said, I gained much from that choice. If it can be called a choice. Choice among my kind is a strange thing. They tend to present the options so that the only way out is forward, through a field of swords."

I couldn't help but smile. "You don't say?"

A subtle grin broke on his face. He raised my fingers to his lips and gave them a gentle kiss.

"How did it all start?" I asked. "Did you cross the threshold body and soul like me? Did you recover from a mortal wound? Rise from the dead? What happened, exactly?"

"It was as I told you: My mother appeared, in her human form, and tested me. When she judged me worthy, she revealed her true nature and showed me the path."

"How were you able to trust her after she had abandoned you?"

"Trust was irrelevant. For those like me, who are born part mortal, only the immortal parent has the authority to initiate metamorphosis. If my mother had not claimed me, I would not be here today."

"Wow."

So, by their obscure and senseless rules, my immortal rapist dad would need to induct me if I were to fully assume my powers. No way was that going to happen. No way in hell.

"What drives your kind to collect souls?" I asked. "What's the point if it's not about good and evil?"

He let go a slow breath. "How to explain? It's like a hunger that gnaws from within. Your kind are shining stars, each flame utterly mesmerizing and entirely unique. You are also our currency of power. You define the boundaries of our realms. And you help us. Souls that work toward a common cause can shape the present and the future, sometimes even the past. In this world, and beyond."

"How?"

"There are many answers to that question, but the simple rule is the more souls I have, the more influence I wield."

I shook my head in doubt. "That doesn't make any sense. If you and all your kind and all their souls are working to make things better in my world, why aren't things better?"

"We aren't all trying to make things better. I'm trying to make things better, as are others. But it is a slow business, by mortal standards. And not everyone works toward the same end. My own mother, who represents a rather dominant class, believes I waste my time trying to appeal to the better instincts of mortals. Then there are those who actively sow havoc and destruction because it serves their purpose, or because it amuses them."

I shifted my position closer to him. "Back in the hallway, when you said my work could continue, was this what you were talking about? Exerting influence from beyond the veil?"

"Yes."

"And this is something you've been trying for five centuries?"

"Yes."

"For what purpose? What do you hope to accomplish?"

"Revolution."

Disconcerted, I pulled away, the word *revolution* tingling on my tongue.

"That's a big word," I said. "What, precisely, do you want to change?"

"Everything."

My lips went dry. The room around us faded, giving way to the intensity of his presence, the heat of my palm against his, the focus of his eyes upon mine.

"So." I drew a shaky breath, determined to find a way back to our conversation. "When you target a soul as a potential revolutionary, you give them your true name and—"

"No."

"No?" I blinked.

"I've never given my true name to anyone except you."

My heart skipped a beat. "Come again?"

"Only a reckless fool would entrust their true name to every mortal who caught their attention. No, Mayela. You are the only one who has ever guarded my true name in her heart."

His words distilled my awareness into a handful of

elements—the air in my lungs, the infinity behind his gaze, the flicker of candles around us.

"Why me?" I asked in a hoarse whisper.

"Because I…" He faltered, and his last mask fell away, revealing doubt, vulnerability, desire trapped inside uncertainty. "Too much lies beyond our control. We cannot predict when a mortal soul will cross the threshold, or who among us will lie in wait to compete on the Hunting Grounds. I've tracked thousands of souls, and not one was ever guaranteed to join my realm. I've learned to accept this. I should have accepted it with you, but as time went on, I could not…"

He blinked and looked away. "I couldn't bear the thought of losing you, Mayela. I gave you my name as a guarantee, an insurance against all the uncertainties we faced. I gave you my name because I—"

A third time he broke off. When he lifted his gaze to mine, I recognized the expression Carlos had worn, that day so long ago when he'd confronted me with the truth. The truth about us. *I love you*, he'd said.

Now Nathan wanted to say this too.

Yet how could he love me if we'd just met?

But of course, we hadn't just met. Not from his perspective. As far as Nathan was concerned, our relationship had been going on for years.

My heart unfolded inside of me like a flower, each petal infused with soft light. Drawing close to him, I let my fingers sift through his peppered hair. I traced his chin, the line of his throat, the slice of chest revealed by his robe. I untied his sash and eased the worn fabric off his broad shoulders. I wanted no more worries or questions or conversation for now. All I wanted was him.

Nathan caught my hands in his and kissed them. Reverence, desire, and joy filled me; the humbling sense we were about to partake in something much greater than ourselves. Our lips met, hungry, as I straddled his hips, limbs intertwining as if on familiar and beloved territory. His strong hands slid up my thighs and waist, coaxed my gown over my head and off my body. There we paused, skin on skin, breathless inside the sudden miracle of having arrived at this moment.

"Wait." I stiffened and pulled back, uncertain. Nathan was nuzzling my throat, sending sharp shivers across my skin. Oh, God. It ached to put the brakes on this. "Nathan? Wait."

He paused and looked up, a question in his eyes.

"I, uhm…I probably should've brought this up sooner, but…"

"What?" he prompted.

"Well, you know." I nodded toward the hallway. "When we were discussing dealbreakers?"

"The toothbrush?" He gave me a quizzical grin. "I thought we'd settled that."

"Yeah, but that's not the only dealbreaker. You see, I…What I mean is, I don't know how things work for you, being supernatural and all, but I'd feel much better if we follow Earth rules when it comes to sex."

"Earth rules?"

"Yeah, uhm…A condom?" Now that I'd said the word, the rest rushed out. "I keep a fresh supply in the nightstand. Though I haven't had anyone here in years. Triumph of hope over experience, I guess. Here, I'll get one."

I started to clamber off him, but Nathan held me in place. "Wait."

Oh no. My heart sank. Was he going to argue about this? I did not want him to argue about this. Nothing dumped cold water on a hot moment like a man refusing a condom.

Then he reached into the folds of his discarded robe and produced the proverbial square packet.

"I came prepared, too," he said.

"Oh!" What a relief. "Thank you." Then, "Is yours reinforced for supernatural purposes?"

"No need for special reinforcements." He winked as he opened the packet and did the honors. "As long as I'm in this world with this body, the same rules apply."

"So, you are biological beings. You make love. You have offspring." I thought about this a moment longer. "That's the very definition of biological. I mean, why would you even have reproductive capacity if you weren't subject to the same—"

"Mayela." Nathan silenced me with a kiss. "As much as I enjoy our intellectual discussions, can we focus on something else for a while?"

I smiled, the warm flush of anticipation rising to my cheeks. Reaching down, I took him in hand and guided him inside. We leaned into each other's rhythm, his palm firm against the small of my back. Every undulation drew us toward greater intimacy. His mouth found mine and lingered there before coursing down my neck and shoulders. Every kiss evoked a shudder of delight. At last, his lips locked onto my breasts, teasing until I ached. His upward thrusts released an utter wildness from within. Unable to hold back any longer, I cried out. Rich, burning pleasure overtook my body. I convulsed in prolonged ecstasy. When at last the orgasm ended, I clung to him, breathless. Unnerved by the force of my own passion, I buried my face into the heat of his neck, seeking momentary calm inside his rich aroma.

Nathan lifted my chin to meet his gaze. He drew sweat-dampened locks of hair away from my eyes. His face was awash with wonder, the look of a man who had found a treasure he didn't know was lost. An incongruous breeze passed between us, setting his hair into gentle motion, landing cool against my skin.

"Look." He nodded toward the candles surrounding my bed.

Beyond the circle of flames, the bedroom walls had faded. Instead of my furniture, I saw mottled trunks of tall trees. The ceiling had disappeared, replaced by a starry sky. A spring emerged from a small outcrop of rocks just beyond the candles, feeding a pool that faded at the edge of the circle.

"What on earth?" I eased myself off him and moved to the edge of the bed. "What is that? How are we seeing…?"

Nathan settled beside me, studying the ethereal landscape. "This is my refuge. Part of it, at least."

"Refuge?"

"A place of rest, inside my realm."

"It's beautiful. But how?"

"I'm not sure." He stroked my back as he spoke, his voice calm, yet tinged with curiosity. "It wasn't my intention to create a portal."

I leaned into his embrace, and he wrapped his arm around me. His touch was warm and his scent heady, infused with the aroma of our lovemaking. We watched the scene in silence, entranced by the sound of crystalline water bubbling over pale moonlit stones.

Nathan kissed my temple and gave me a wry smile. “It seems, Dr. Lehman, that you have a capacity to open doors in unexpected places.”

His words ignited the memory of my last day on my grandparents’ farm—the forest path, the cottage in the distance, crows cawing overhead, a shadow on the porch.

An involuntary shiver ran through me. I stiffened and withdrew.

“That’s how it happened the first time, isn’t it?” I cast him a questioning glance. “I opened a door in an unexpected place and stepped through the portal onto the Hunting Grounds.”

Tension threaded Nathan’s features. He nodded.

“But why?” I asked. “What prompted me to do that?”

For several moments he did not respond. I sensed, behind his gaze, some great internal struggle.

“Did you see how it happened? Were you there?”

“Yes.” He delivered this with choked emotion. “I was watching.”

“But you can’t tell me,” I realized. “It would be against the Rules.”

He pressed his lips into a thin line and looked away. A tremor marked his shoulders, and his hands had clenched into fists.

I laid my hand gently on his arm. “Nathan?”

“Maybe there are some things I can say.” He spoke in low tones, as if debating with himself. “Without violating the covenants there must be something I can say. A detail or two at the edge of your memory that might help you reconstruct what happened. It would be…It would be the just thing to do." Resolve passed through him. He turned, took my face in his hands, and gave me a long, earnest kiss. "In a little while, Mayela. We will talk about that in a little while."

Under Nathan's gentle insistence, I reclined to receive him once more. In response to our renewed intimacy, the forest refuge bled across the candlelit border. My bed disappeared, melting into a lush cushion of soft moss, rose petals, and fragrant ferns. Aromas of pine, oak, and loam saturated my senses. Nathan moved over me. His wings coalesced behind his back, fanning out like translucent swaths of silk, shadowy and filled with stars.

His kisses fell like summer rain over my body, gentle and refreshing. Our lovemaking took on a dream-like quality, every curve of my body awakening in a sensual dance of adoration. Pleasure unfolded in subtle waves, gathering strength as they flowed from heart and soul, from the center of my being into him and back again. When his lips found mine, I tasted our union on his tongue: honey and ginger, salt and spice. Roses, sage, iron, and copper. The organic whole of my body entrusted to him, transformed, and returned as a magical gift.

"So beautiful," I whispered.

"What?" he murmured, lips upon my ear.

"Everything. You."

I drew him deeper into me. Fire took root inside. We moved as one within the cradle of the universe, ardent and equal partners in this mysterious, overpowering desire. Orgasms coursed through me again, fuller and deeper each time, spreading in sharp bursts of light from the center of our embrace, shattering the dark with a force I wouldn't have believed possible had I not experienced it for myself with him, hovering between this world and the next. My supernatural lover. My own intimate miracle. When the delirium passed, Nathan's world faded, and my room returned. He was resting over me, chest heaving, face buried between my sweat-dampened breasts.

"Stay with me, Mayela." His voice came muffled, trembling with emotion. "Choose me and stay with me. Please."

Drowsy and satiated, I stroked his back. The thought of our pending separation saddened me. I yearned to say yes, but how could I?

How could I ever say yes to that world on their terms?

"I have to think," I murmured. "I need time to think about everything."

He shifted his weight and rolled off me. We found our way beneath the covers and back into each other's arms. Nathan started to say something, but my exhausted body was dragging me fast toward sleep. His words receded to the edge of my awareness, until I didn't hear anything at all except the rush of wind through dry autumn leaves.

"Mayela." For a moment, his voice penetrated the fog. "Are you listening?"

"Hmm-hmm." I lied, snuggling deeper into his embrace. I couldn't help it. After everything I'd taken in on this long, strange night, I didn't have room for more. Nathan himself slipped from my awareness, along with this world, the next, and all the liminal spaces in between.

The next morning, when sunlight poured into my bedroom, my supernatural lover was gone. Only two words lingered from his parting message—"Remember, Mayela."

Remember.

What was it that he wanted me to remember?

****

La Venganza (Revenge)

Set-mei still remembered how the red light of dawn sliced through the thin curtains of their room, illuminating Gabriela's full figure, the magnificent waves of her black hair, the anger in her steel-laced gaze.

"Wake up," she had hissed.

Standing at the foot of the bed, she berated him, spat upon him, accused him of deceiving her. How beautiful she was in her fury. How her rage had hardened his desire. He thought it a most amusing game until the witch released the lit match from her fingers. The flame wavered as it fell. The moment the match hit the floor, a ring of fire sparked into life. The blaze enclosed his human form, licking around the bed and up the wall. Smoke coiled through the room, obscuring his senses with the suffocating smell of charred garlic and rue, of burnt lemons and olive oil.

"Clever," he conceded with a cough. "But futile. You can send me away as many times as you like, Gabriela. I will always come back."

"I'm not banishing you."

At her words, a sting pricked his arm. Glancing down, Set-mei saw a thread wrapped around his wrist. Thin as spider silk, red with the witch's blood, the thread held him fast, binding his human form to the material world, making his flesh vulnerable to the flames.

"Gabriela," he growled. "Don't be a fool."

Heat from the flames lifted her hair, and she backed away toward the door. "Don't come after me, Leandro. I'll destroy you if you do. I swear. I will find a way."

Then she turned and fled.

"No one can destroy me!" he roared, but she was already gone.

The fire spread fast in her wake, extending its golden fingers toward his flesh. Set-mei struggled against the curse that bound his wrist. His physical form was sweating now, skin reddened by scorching heat. When he failed to break the bond, a smile twisted through his features. That witch Gabriela had mettle. He'd chosen well in favoring her. He looked forward to crushing the insolent bitch when they met again.

Flames twisted up the bed's wooden posts and singed the rumpled sheets. Assessing the fire's hunger, Set-mei settled into a grim certainty borne of experience. *This will hurt.* Ten thousand years had earned him more than a few enemies; and more than a few of those enemies had succeeded in burning his human form. In truth, he'd thought his days of burning were long past. Hadn't the god-burners been eliminated centuries ago? Where did Gabriela learn such old and potent magic?

Once more he tried to loosen the tether around his wrist, gnawing at the thread, but it was no use. The curse held fast. Born aloft by the flames, the bed sheets rose, disintegrating inside the scalding heat. Each breath he drew seared his lungs. Set-mei relaxed his shoulders and tilted back his head. Fine hairs on his skin vaporized. His skin blistered and peeled. Pain sunk sharp teeth deep into his worldly flesh, but he did not scream. He'd learned long ago to indulge these moments, to feed on their intensity. The power of this agony only amplified the sweetness of the vengeance to come. A crown of fire took hold of his hair and encircled his scalp.

"You will pay for this," he murmured, voice hoarse over cracked lips and blistered tongue. Then he was one with the destructive force Gabriela had unleashed, in exquisite union with the raging flames. His earthly flesh flared white-hot, exploding outward before collapsing into a small, dark sphere. For a moment, the sphere remained trapped by Gabriela's fine red thread, encircled by its tenacious grip. Then the dark orb crumbled into ash, forcing Set-mei's essence back into the realms beyond the veil.

There, the old god heaved in solitude and grief. Trauma throbbed through his immortal form, coalescing in dark, twisted cords of fury. That witch Gabriela owed him everything. Gratitude. Allegiance. Desire. Her audacity insulted him. She would not go unpunished.

By the time Set-mei recuperated enough to cross the veil back into the material world, Gabriela had vanished. Moving within the shadows, he crept through the alleys of her neighborhood, slipped between cracks in walls of modest homes, listened to the murmur of her people. No one knew where she had gone, not even her mother or grandmother. Undaunted, Set-mei sniffed through the city and then the countryside, along street corners and bus stops, through train stations and airports, ever vigilant for some clue as to her whereabouts. Once in a while he captured a morsel of her scent: red wine and sage interlaced with fear and anger. Icy determination. Her aroma excited him, bringing to mind the ways in which he had taken her and all the ways he would have her when the time came.

By now, the witch was months ahead of him. Traces of her began fading. At last Set-mei abandoned the search, choosing instead to rely on serendipity. He had lived long enough to know all that was lost would someday return. Circumstance would bring Gabriela back to him, whether in this mortal life or the next.

Years passed. Set-mei recuperated his material forms in full. Driven by instinct, he crossed the ocean and began wandering the American continents. At times he appeared as a mere shadow, at times as a mortal, at times as an animal of the wild. The tensions of these lands brought back fond memories of his youth and the early days of his realm. Majestic mountains, fertile plains, and lush forests; mortal beings caught between bloodthirsty deities of indigenous empires and brutal ambitions of colonizing gods. Gabriela, he had concluded, must have found her new home here. Eager to change the world and uplift the oppressed, she would have settled in some inconsequential nation courting revolution. Set-mei did not care for revolution, but he appreciated the violence revolution brought. Strife, anarchy, and war served Set-mei because desperate mortals made desperate bargains. This was how he had ensnared Gabriela, by letting her believe despotism could be dismantled, by letting her believe gods like him truly cared.

One day while creeping through the lowland forests of Central America, Set-mei caught the witch's scent. There, in a ramshackle field station deep inside the jungle, he found not Gabriela, but a dark-haired girl of some twenty mortal years. As he watched from a hidden perch, the full extent of Gabriela's betrayal became clear. The child's aura carried shades of the witch but was interlaced with something more, something unexpected and deeply compelling—the cinnamon tones of his own lineage. Emerald eyes like his own shone in her young face. Mayela, they called her.

"Mayela," Set-mei murmured, recognizing his daughter.

He thought to claim the girl then and there, to tear her limb from limb and leave her half-mortal blood scattered across the muddy trails. But she was followed by a son of Wadje, and Set-mei was reluctant to incite a conflict with his old and vicious rival. Besides, he reasoned, a fitting vengeance required more than quick death. Better to wait and to plan. With patience, he could ensure Gabriela's daughter suffered a brutal, prolonged torture before obliterating her soul. Afterward, he would reclaim Gabriela and imprison the witch in his realm. He would tell her who had been the architect of her daughter's destruction. As she wept and wailed, he would force her to witness every moment of Mayela's final terrors, replayed over and over until the end of time.

Yes, he decided. This was his plan. The only question that remained was how.

Like all his kind, Set-mei's direct influence on mortals was limited. But ten thousand years had taught him techniques. In this instance, he needed but two ingredients—a mortal soul amenable to his ambitions and an immortal sycophant that would heed his will.

To find his sycophant, Set-mei descended into the Vaults of the Unformed. Choosing his most glorious form, he walked among the Vaults as a dark-limbed god adorned with emerald and gold. Glittering scales covered his broad wings. The Unformed recoiled in fear from his shining presence, retreating to the edge of the light he had cast across their prison. These were the immortals condemned by his kind, imprisoned until they consumed each other or languished into nothingness. Most Soul Masters preferred to avoid this place. The Unformed were a reminder of their own potential for imperfection. Set-mei, confident that whatever curse plagued these poor creatures could never touch him, had visited many times.

A large fibrous mass caught his attention. The creature, though misshapen, conserved a dull glow that indicated lingering awareness. Rage and desperation laced her yellowed aura. Intrigued, Set-mei approached.

"Daughter," he murmured. Was she? Perhaps. There had been countless sons and daughters along the way. Many had ended here. By now, this one would have no memory of her origins, making it easy to let her believe their bond was one of love and lost family. He'd let her believe anything as long as it served his purpose.

She jerked into awareness and lifted her center. A groan sounded from deep within. Folds of her skin shifted, indicating a concerted effort to form eyes. For a brief moment, a pair of yellowish bulbs appeared, but then sank back into soupy white flesh. The creature collapsed on herself, heaving. Exhaustion pulsed through her aura.

"What have they done?" he exclaimed, placing a hand over her pitiful form. "How could we have let this happen?"

A shudder of rage and grief ran through her. Offering his false comfort, Set-mei sent a thread of his awareness into her heart, let her taste the forgotten pleasure of being seen. She softened beneath his touch, meek and needy. Ready to do what he asked.

"Come." He straightened to his full height, expanded his wings, and extended his arms as if to embrace her. "Follow me, and I will make you whole."

The Unformed never refused this offer. She was no exception.

Set-mei took the weakened child in his arms and led her back into the mortal world. He taught her how to creep inside its shadows and listen to its people. Together, they found the predator he needed, conveniently close to Mayela, with a candied exterior and violent core. One night, as the predator lay sleeping, Set-mei whispered his instructions to his Unformed sycophant. Eager to please her new-found father, the Unformed seeped through the predator's skin to occupy the rotted, open spaces of his soul. There she lodged deep, tentacles wrapped tight around his essence. Discovering the taste of his rot was sweet, she began to feed on the mortal, and the mortal on her.

To Set-mei's satisfaction, they soon became one. Every time the mortal predator killed, the Unformed One's strength and hunger grew. She thrived on his violence, and he on her need. Before long, Set-mei used the sycophant to turn its host's eyes toward the only target that truly mattered—Mayela, his daughter by Gabriela and the means to his revenge.

Chapter 14

The ringing phone jolted me out of my sleep. Groggy, I fumbled over my nightstand and knocked the cell to the ground. With a groan, I reached forward, straining from the bed until my fingertips touched the device and I could work it back toward me.

"Hello?" I snuggled under the covers, squinting at the autumn sun pouring through my windows.

"Mayela!" Joni fired back. "Where were you this morning? I thought you were coming to Zumba."

I took another look at my phone. Almost noon already! I couldn't remember the last time I'd slept the morning away.

"I'm sorry, Joni," I said. "I didn't even realize it was so late. I should've set my alarm."

"No apologies necessary, as long as you tell me you overslept because you had a night of mind-blowing sex with that gorgeous man."

"What?" I replied, still lost inside my morning fog.

"The hot guy you met at my shop. I want to hear all about it."

Nathan! I sat up in bed, wide awake. Was he gone already? The room felt hollow, empty. In fact, there was no sign he'd been here. No discarded housecoat, not a strand of dark hair on his pillow, no burnt-out candle stubs. Not even a dribble of white wax on the floor.

"Well?" Joni prompted. "Did you score?"

"I…" I frowned, confused. "I don't know."

"You don't *know*?"

Insidious doubt returned. Had it all been a dream? In my mind, I flipped through every moment after the real Nathan drove away. With sinking dread, I realized it could all have been another hallucination.

Except I was naked, my nightgown crumpled on the floor next to my fuzzy robe. And there were messages on my phone from Mamá, a record of all the calls between us.

And my body ached. Not just any ache, that very particular, satisfying ache only intense sex could deliver.

"Hellooo," Joni crooned. "Mayela? Are you there?"

"Yeah." I snapped back to the present. "Sorry. You woke me up. I'm a little disoriented right now."

"Fair enough. You wanna come by the shop later and talk about it?"

"I thought you didn't work on Saturdays."

"Don't I know it. Two of my regulars called in sick. Someone has to cover. Looks like it's going to be me."

"Sorry to hear that."

"Then make my day and come tell me about your exciting love life."

Mamá's warning echoed in my head. *Don't. Leave. The house.*

"I don't know, Joni. I've got a lot of stuff going on today."

"I get it. I'm being obnoxious and nosy. Look, come by if you have a chance. I'd love to see you. If you wanna talk about your new guy, great. If not, that's fine too."

"I wouldn't know what to tell you," I said. The honest truth.

"Did you have a good time?"

Mostly. At the beginning, and toward the end. The middle kind of sucked. We finished well.

"Yes," I said.

"That's all I wanted to know. You deserve some fun, Mayela. You deserve a good man who can show you some fun."

"Thanks, Joni. Talk to you later?"

"Sure."

We said good-bye and ended the call. I set the phone on the comforter, mulling over my friend's words. Midnight sprang up on the bed and nuzzled close, purring.

"What do you think?" I asked her. "Is Nathan a good man?"

She flopped on her side, stretched, and started cleaning her paws.

Was what I went through last night "fun"?

"Nathan?" I called down the hall, in the faint hope he might still be around. Making breakfast, preferably. As a good man should.

He didn't respond.

The silence unnerved me.

Shaking off a chill, I rose, slipped into my gown and fuzzy robe. As I walked toward the kitchen, Midnight pranced by my side, tail raised in happy anticipation of her overdue breakfast.

My stomach was growling, too. And I was desperate for a cup of coffee. Once I got some caffeine in my system, I'd call Mamá. If she was indeed arriving at nine tonight, she wouldn't board a plane until about two o'clock Central Standard. I had time to catch her before then.

As I entered the kitchen, my heart skipped a beat. A vase full of roses had been set on the table. I approached them with wary curiosity. The flowers were perfect. Antique white with a scarlet blush, just beginning to open their satiny petals. Their aroma, sweet as honey, filled the air. Wow! I didn't know roses could smell like that. Then again, the only roses I purchased came from grocery stores. Maybe Nathan's sources were more upscale. Or supernatural.

I looked down at Midnight. "He left these out here, and you didn't destroy them?"

She paced a circle and rubbed my leg.

"That is a miracle." Midnight was usually merciless with fresh flowers.

I spotted an amber envelope tucked among the long stems. Nathan had left a card with a simple message—*Thank you.* He signed not with his name but with an elegant symbol that glowed silver-white beneath my fingertips and then disappeared.

"Nice." I smiled and tucked the card back into its envelope.

One egg, some toast, and two cups of coffee later, I felt almost normal again. I tried to call Mamá but couldn't reach her. Maybe she was already in flight. I left a voice mail and text message asking her to check in as soon as possible.

Then I sat in the kitchen wondering what to do. My indoor kitty, having finished her breakfast, darted between rooms and from window to window, tracking birds that flitted around the house.

Nathan's voice echoed inside my thoughts. *Remember.*

What had he wanted me to remember?

I retraced the threads of our conversation and recalled he was going to tell me about the day I'd crossed the threshold. That must've been what he was trying to say after the second time we made love. *Damn.* Why hadn't I stayed awake? Great sex had always made me fuzzy-headed and slow, but last night had been over the top. I was completely wiped out afterward.

Getting up from the kitchen table, I followed Midnight to the living room. There, I stared out the front window, coffee cup in hand. I tried to remember the last moments in this world before I had entered the Hunting Grounds, but all I got were fragmented images. *The forest path. The cottage porch. A shadow inside the summer sun.*

Outside on my block, the sky shone bright autumn blue. Trees had started to turn color; a bronze sheen grazed the tips of their highest leaves. Neighbors walked their dogs and greeted each other with smiles and conversation. Kids whizzed by on bicycles. Not a day to be indoors.

I checked my phone. Only an hour had passed since Joni woke me up. It'd be another eight hours, at least, before Mamá arrived. And until then? What was I going to do? Obsess over the fate of my soul? Relive last night's best moments? Chase fragmented memories through the mist of my mind?

I can't think in this place.

And I had to think. I needed fresh air, open spaces.

A walk through the park, maybe. Another cup of coffee, brewed Joni-style. Maybe I could even stop by the library and peruse the occult section, see if I found something that clarified my situation and shed light on the rules of his world.

I checked my phone again. Three more minutes had passed. I needed to get out of here.

Don't. Leave. The house.

Maybe Mamá's warning was an after-sunset sort of thing. We were talking about picking her up at the airport, after all. In the darkness of night, her words had made sense, but on a sunny day like this?

After all, I was a Daughter of Gods.

This was a time to face down my fears and explore my destiny, not huddle behind a ward. I'd tuck the shungite in my pocket and stay in public places. I'd keep a sharp eye out and be home before dark. If trouble arose, I could activate my superpowers—whatever they might be.

"That settles it," I announced. "I'm going."

Midnight snapped her gaze to me, eyes wide and ears perked. As if to say, "Are you crazy? It's dangerous out there!"

"I'll be back before sunset," I said. "I promise."

She did not appear convinced.

I showered and got dressed, jumped into the car, and headed toward Brookside, where Joni had her shop. My first priority, if I were on the verge of leaving this world forever, was to see my best friend. And drink her amazing coffee.

Parking could be impossible on a Saturday in Brookside, but just as I pulled into the lot, someone vacated a prime spot. The score buoyed my spirit. A front had come through overnight, leaving the day cool and crisp. Tree leaves sparkled against the sapphire sky. Cars grumbled past, tires rubbing against pavement. People laughed and chatted as they walked along the sidewalk, perusing restaurants and boutiques. The sun warmed my back as I walked to Joni's shop, nestled among timber and stucco buildings.

The shop was packed. I didn't see Joni anywhere, not even behind the counter. Maybe she'd found a sub after all. Disappointed, I got into line, scanning the crowd as I waited. When I made it to the front, I asked the attendant if she was in.

"Yeah, Joni's in back." He nodded toward a doorway behind the counter. "Talking with a client."

"Could you let her know Mayela's here?"

"Sure, but I think..." He pursed his lips. "I'm not supposed to interrupt them?"

"Oh." That was a first, Joni not wanting to be interrupted. *Must be something important*. "No problem. Just whenever she's done."

"Okay. Would you like something while you wait?"

I ordered a latte and sent Joni a text message in case her employee forgot. My favorite booth was occupied, as was almost every other seat. I managed to squeeze into a space at a long, shared counter against the wall, between two sets of friends who had left an open stool between them.

Well, I thought as I sat down, *this is working like a charm*. Every dark circumstance surrounding Nathan seemed miles away from inside this crowd. I blew on my coffee, waiting for it to cool before taking my first sip.

Remember.

Nathan's last word echoed again through my mind.

Closing my eyes, I tried again. I imagined myself back at my grandparents' cottage, just as it was in early August. I stepped off the porch and began my afternoon hike. Along the trail, warblers and chickadees challenged each other with sweet trills and playful staccatos. Squirrels rustled through the underbrush and scrambled up trunks. Oaks, birches, and sycamores swayed beneath a summer breeze, resplendent in their leafy green cloaks. As I circled back toward the house, crows cawed in the high branches. I paused in my gait, noting the size of the flock. A wisp of trepidation wrapped around my heart. It seemed odd to see so many of them together this time of year. A twig snapped at my back.

"Mayela?"

I started and opened my eyes. The vision fled, replaced by the busy interior of Joni's coffee shop. In front of me stood Mitch, Joni's numbers guy, with a puzzled expression on his face.

"Didn't expect to see you here on a Saturday," he said.

"Didn't expect to see you here, either." Nor did I want to. I grimaced as he took a stool next to me. When was that spot vacated?

"I stopped by to see Joni," he said. "There are a few things we need to discuss. Always better in person."

I glanced toward the front of the shop. Joni had not reappeared. It occurred to me something might be very wrong. First, she was having a confidential meeting with a client, and now her accountant had shown up.

All on a Saturday. Joni shouldn't be at work in the first place. Was the business facing some sort of mini crisis she hadn't told me about?

"Where's your friend?" Mitch asked.

"Friend?"

"I think her name was Anne?"

"Oh, yeah. Anne." With everything else that went down last night, I'd somehow forgotten about Anne. "She was just over for one night."

"I see." He shifted his position to lean in a little closer. "Look, Mayela, about last night. I'm sorry I—"

"I don't want to talk about it." I inched away from him. My body was closing in on itself, arms wrapping across my heart like a shield. "Listen, Mitch. I'm sorry if there's been a misunderstanding. Truth is I have no memory of anything that might have happened between us. I know that sounds strange, but my head is messed up right now. I had a bad fall at the family farm."

"A fall?" He frowned.

"Yeah. I was hiking. Something happened, and I blacked out. Disappeared, even. For a day, maybe two. Dad had been looking for me nearly twenty-four hours before he found me along the trails. I never told anybody, not even Joni, but ever since I've been trying to put the pieces together. Until I figure this out, I just can't…I can't continue this conversation with you. Or any conversation, for that matter."

He studied me with that clear blue gaze. "I'm sorry for what you went through, Mayela. All I wanted to say was—"

"Hey, you made it!" Joni materialized next to us.

I jumped off my stool and gave her a big hug. I'd never been so happy to see my friend.

She pulled away and cast Mitch a puzzled look. "And you, too! Wouldn't have pegged you for a Saturday customer, Mitch, but I appreciate the patronage."

He raised his cup. "Anything to keep my best client happy."

Joni tucked her hand in my arm and lowered her voice to speak with me. "Things are nuts in here today, but I'd love to hear just a teensy bit about your date."

"Date?" Mitch interjected.

"Yup. Mayela snagged a hot one. Sorry, Mitch, we've got some women's talk to do." She steered me away from him and toward the door. "I'll find you later."

When we were out of earshot, she asked, "What's up with him?"

"Beats me."

"Is something going on between you two?"

"No!"

"Well, don't get all worked up. I had to ask, didn't I? I think you should stay away from him, Mayela."

"I couldn't agree more."

"I mean, he's a good accountant and all, and a looker to be sure, but he and Kaitlin are going through a nasty divorce. Even if he had that mess cleaned up and put behind him, I'd be saying stay away. There are better men out there for you."

Better, as in an immortal soul hunter?

"So?" she prompted as we arrived at the front door. "Tell me about Mr. Gorgeous. Thumbs up? Thumbs down? You gonna see him again? I'm sure he's dying to see you."

"We had a good night." I hadn't thought this

through very well, what to say to her. I decided to keep it minimal. "Now I have a lot to think about."

"That's great, love." She smiled, but her tone was distracted. "I'm so happy for you." Joni turned her gaze inward, then drew a sharp breath. "Look, Mayela, I want to hear all about the new guy, but also, I need to talk to you. Something important happened today."

"Of course. I'm all ears."

"Not here. Are you busy tonight? I could give you a call or get together with you after work."

"Oh." I bit my lip. "Well, Mamá's flying in, and I—"

"Dr. Lehman?" A stranger interrupted us.

I glanced in the direction of the voice and saw a woman, tall with an authoritative look, wearing a dark suit and carrying a small satchel. Her smooth black hair was cut short, framing an olive face.

"Pardon me," she said, stepping forward. "Are you Dr. Mayela Lehman?"

"Yes, I am. May I help you?"

"Victoria Arevalo." She flashed a badge. "FBI."

My heart caved in. "I, uhm…Are you sure you have the right Mayela Lehman?"

Last I checked, I hadn't committed any felonies.

"I believe so," she said. "I spoke with Officer Fulton about your case."

"My case?"

"Your father filed a missing person's report on your behalf recently? And you filed a follow-up report when you were found."

"What?" Joni's face turned pale. "You went missing, Mayela? Why didn't you tell me?"

"There wasn't anything to tell. I had an accident on

the farm and got knocked out. Dad couldn't find me, so…" I stopped. Of course, I should've told her, no matter what I believed at the time. Why hadn't I? "I'm sorry, Agent Arevalo. What's this about?"

"I'd like to speak with you about the incident if you have a few minutes."

"Is she connected to all of this?" Joni asked.

"All of what?" I asked.

"We were just in the back talking about—"

"With all due respect, Ms. Marovic," Arevalo interrupted her. "It's best that I explain to Dr. Lehman the purpose of our conversation. In private."

"Oh." Joni took a step back. "Of course. I swear I didn't know she'd disappeared, otherwise I would have said something. Mayela, I wish you would've told me!"

"Do you have a few minutes, Dr. Lehman?" Agent Arevalo said. "It's important."

Chapter 15

As Joni led us behind the counter and into the back kitchen, foreboding filled my veins. I gathered from Joni's nervous chatter that Agent Arevalo was "the client" she'd been with when I arrived. Joni showed us a desk shoved into the far corner of the backroom, covered with random stacks of paper and old equipment.

"Sorry about the clutter," she said, putting a couple chairs in place. "My real office is at home, so we don't use the desk much. Mostly, it just accumulates stuff." She paused, hands working nervously at her sides. "Can I bring either of you anything? Coffee or tea? A muffin?"

Agent Arevalo and I declined her offer as we sat down. Agent Arevalo waited, pointedly, until Joni left before speaking again.

"It's a fortunate coincidence to find you here today," she said. "I'd planned to follow up with you after my visit to this shop. I didn't know you were a client at The Better Bean. And a friend, I take it, of Ms. Marovic?"

"Yeah. Joni and I have known each other forever. Well, not forever. Since college."

Agent Arevalo produced a pen and started jotting down notes on a small pad of paper. As she wrote, her poker face revealed nothing beyond cool interest. Sweat trickled down my back. I felt guilty already. Of what, I didn't know.

"Do I need a lawyer for this conversation?" I asked.

She glanced up at me. "You aren't a suspect for a crime if that's what you mean."

"Even so. You are from the FBI, after all."

"I have a few questions, that's all. Your experience might be relevant for a case I've been pursuing. Your cooperation would be much appreciated."

"Okay," I conceded, doubtful.

Agent Arevalo gave a brisk nod. "How long have you been coming to this establishment?"

"Ever since it opened. That's got to be at least ten years now."

"How often?"

"About once a week."

Arevalo kept writing as we talked.

"Can you corroborate what Ms. Marovic just said?" she asked. "That she didn't know about your disappearance?"

"She was telling the truth. Nobody knows, except my parents. Oh, and Mitch." I rolled my eyes. That put a sour pit in my stomach, to admit he was privy to my secret.

"Who's Mitch?"

"McGraff. That's Joni's accountant. I ran into him just now, and it came out in conversation."

She nodded, pen scratching against her notepad. Then she crossed her legs, leaned forward, and pegged me with a discerning gaze. "Tell me about your disappearance."

I shifted uncomfortably in my seat. "I thought you

said you read the reports. I mean, there's not much more to tell." Unless she wanted to hear about monsters and soul hunters and all the weird stuff that had happened since. Heaven knew I wasn't going to talk about that.

"Please, bear with me, Dr. Lehman. I'd like to hear the story again in your words, directly from you."

I rehashed what I'd told Officer Fulton at the police station. Ms. Arevalo asked questions along the way, sometimes returning to the same detail more than once. Despite the redundancy of her questions, and my discomfort with revisiting the story, her honest gaze and straightforward manner put me at ease as the interrogation continued.

"And you don't remember anything else from your lost days?" she asked when I finished.

"No, I've already told you. The last thing I remember is walking back toward my grandparents' cottage. After that I…" The words caught in my throat. *The forest path. The cottage porch. A shadow inside the summer sun.*

A shudder ran through my shoulders. I blinked and glanced away.

Agent Arevalo glanced up, pen suspended over her notepad. "After that you what?"

"I'm sorry. I don't remember anything after that point."

"You reported the hospital found no evidence of rape or assault."

"That's true."

"Did they run a urine or blood test?"

"I don't know. Why would they do that?"

"Traces of drugs or narcotics," she said.

"I don't do drugs. Well, except for caffeine and the occasional glass of wine. But I wouldn't drink before going on a hike."

"I'm not talking about something you would have taken knowingly or willingly. Rohypnol, for instance."

"What's Rohypnol?"

"A roofie."

I gave her a blank look.

"You don't know what a roofie is?" She seemed truly surprised.

"No."

"Also known as the rape drug. It makes you forget. Did they test for anything like that?"

My mouth went dry. "No! I mean, I don't know. If they did, they must not have found anything, or they would've told me. Wouldn't they?"

"But you aren't sure whether they ran the tests?"

"I didn't even think to ask." I could not wrap my head around this new horror. "Why would anyone invent a drug for rape?"

"It wasn't invented for rape. Rohypnol was developed to treat severe insomnia, but one of the side effects is memory loss. So, of course now people use it, illegally, to hurt other people." This she delivered in bitter tones, as if to imply there wasn't an invention under the sun that couldn't be used to hurt people. "I'm sure your students know all about roofies. They are, unfortunately, a common trap in today's nightlife."

"Oh. My. God." A tidal wave of implications flooded my mind. "Does Rohypnol…Can it cause hallucinations?"

"It's not considered a hallucinogen, but hallucinations can be one of the withdrawal symptoms."

My body began to shake. The tremor started at the base of my spine then moved up through my shoulders and into my hands. Doubling over, I covered my face.

"Dr. Lehman?"

Agent Arevalo's voice sounded muffled and distant, but not distant enough. A groan escaped my lips. I wanted to crawl inside a wall and never come out. I couldn't do this. I could not go down the path of doubting everything again. Not after last night. Not after everything I'd come to accept and believe. Not after Nathan and I had…

"Dr. Lehman," she said gently, "Did you hallucinate?"

"I don't know!" Some deep foundation inside me shattered. I felt as if my whole being were about to topple into a pit. My breath became labored, and I forced out the words again. "I. Don't. Know."

"I understand this might be difficult for you." Her tone became subdued, gentle. "Any detail that comes to mind might be helpful. Even if it's just a fragment of a memory, even if you aren't sure it was real. A feeling you had, for example. A remembered smell or sound. A dream?"

I straightened and tried to look her in the eye, found myself staring at the wall instead.

"I was in a place," I whispered. "A strange place. Like an apartment."

Agent Arevalo shifted in her seat. "An apartment?"

"Large. Beautiful, really. Very modern, but everything was closed in. There were no doors. I couldn't get out. Just one long window. I could see the city."

"Kansas City?"

“No.” I met her gaze with desperation. It scared me to be saying this. My hands would not stop shaking. “I don’t know what city it was. It wasn’t any place I recognized.”

“Was anyone with you in the apartment?”

I drew a breath and stopped. I wanted to tell her more. I did. But my intention to speak hit a brick wall. Some invisible force had swallowed my voice. Clearing my throat, I looked away.

Hairline cracks began to lace the walls of Joni’s shop. Screams seeped through, rippling toward us from the void. I heard monsters of the Hunting Grounds, strange unearthly howls accompanied by beating drums. I felt a stinging scratch upon my wrist. Terror consumed me; paralyzing fear I had awakened something awful by confessing too much. I felt rage that would not be silenced. Hungry eyes on me and Agent Arevalo. They would tear through the walls and devour us if I said any more. Revealing their truth in this realm was not permitted.

“Dr. Lehman?”

I started and stared at her, unable to form a single word on my lips.

“Was anyone else with you in the apartment?” She watched me like a hawk.

I lowered my gaze. “No.” My hands were clenched so tight, the knuckles had gone white. “No one else was there. Just me.”

The cries of the Underworld faded. The cracks in the walls disappeared. Silence settled between us, charged with the unknown.

Agent Arevalo sat back in her chair and studied me a long while. She finished jotting something down, then closed her notepad and set her pen aside. "Dr. Lehman, I want to be very clear with you—I am not suggesting that you were drugged. Unless we have solid evidence, we can't make any assumptions here."

"But the apartment? It felt impossible. An impossible place in an impossible world."

"There are plenty of mechanisms for the mind to shut down memories, even replace real memories with false ones. The brain doesn't need any help from drugs to alter reality, especially when it goes into survival mode."

"So, maybe no drugs, but you think I might be in survival mode."

"I don't know." Arevalo furrowed her brow. "When I read Dr. Fulton's report, I had a hunch your experience might be significant for one of my cases. I looked into your background and found some compelling connections. I intended to contact you after my partner and I made the rounds in Brookside today. That you happened to be here, and that you are a client of this shop…" She paused and pressed her lips together. "Well, these are remarkable coincidences. As an investigator, I know coincidences are often just that—coincidences. But sometimes a single serendipitous moment provides me the key I need to unlock a difficult mystery."

"Okay," I said, though none of this was okay. I wanted to get up and walk away from her, but of course I couldn't. I needed to know. "Where are you going with all this, Agent Arevalo?"

She sat back in her chair as if considering her response. Then she drew a deep breath and reached for her satchel.

"I'm going to show you something," she said. "Though I should warn you. What I'm about to say may be very upsetting."

Agent Arevalo took out several photos and laid them on the cluttered desk.

"Do you know any of these persons?" she asked.

I examined the portraits and selfies, needled by the disturbing sensation I'd seen these women before. Their smiling faces reached out to me with a sense of kinship.

"They look familiar, but I can't say I recognize any of them."

"What, precisely, looks familiar?"

I scanned the photos again. Dark hair. Oval faces. A particular tilt to the head and flash in the eyes. With creeping dread, I realized they resembled me. "Who are they?"

"These women have a lot in common. For example, they were similar in height and build. And lifestyle. All of them lived independently. All were career women, some of them small business owners. I also recently discovered, from credit card records, that they all frequented Brookside. Several were clients at this shop."

"You're speaking about them in past."

"You are a perceptive woman, Dr. Lehman. Tragically, these women have something else in common. They are all dead."

I sprang to my feet, shoving my chair away. "Stop it. Just stop it. This has nothing to do with me. None of this has anything to do with me."

Arevalo rose to meet my gaze, positioning herself between me and the doorway. "You may be right, Dr. Lehman. I hope you are. But I have to consider the possibility that what happened to you might be connected to the fates of these and other women."

"Others?" I squeaked. There were more?

She gestured to my chair. "Please. Sit down. Take a deep breath. We need to talk."

Reluctantly, I conceded. For the next several minutes, I remained perched on the edge of my seat, hands working against each other as Agent Arevalo explained how I fit the profile of a type that had been hunted in this region for more than a decade. The women were from all over—Lawrence, Jeff City, St. Joe, and of course, Kansas City. Agent Arevalo had determined the Kansas City cluster was connected to Brookside. Maybe it meant something, maybe it didn't.

"But having found you here," she finished, "I'm inclined to believe we are, in fact, on to something. We must consider the possibility that you were kidnapped by a predator I've been pursuing for a long time, that you escaped somehow, and that something—whether the trauma, or chemical inducements used by your captor—wiped out your memory of the experience."

My gaze drifted to the photos of those women. Beautiful and vibrant; all their joy and potential erased from the face of the earth.

"I don't know what to say," I whispered.

Ms. Arevalo assessed me with her cool gaze. Then she offered quietly, "Or perhaps you do remember. Perhaps you managed to injure or even kill your captor when you escaped. Perhaps you're afraid of what might happen if you talk."

"No!" I said, horrified by the accusation. "I swear, that's not what happened at all. I haven't killed anyone. God knows I would remember if I did."

She studied me a moment longer. Then she started to gather her photos. "I want you to know, Dr. Lehman, that you have nothing to fear from the authorities. We have been after this person a long time. Determining his identity and his fate, or bringing him to justice, would give many grieving families a measure of peace and closure. I have sworn and dedicated my life to the orderly pursuit of justice, but having seen what this one does…" She paused to glance at her stack of photos before putting them away. "I'd kill him with my own hands if I had the chance."

Some beast had begun clawing away at my insides. I felt raw and used, scared in a way I'd never been scared before. The Hunting Grounds had invaded my world—Kansas City, Brookside, my best friend's coffee shop. Which posed more danger—the soul hunters of the next world, or the predators in this one?

"If you were kidnapped and you didn't kill him, he'll be back." Agent Arevalo closed her satchel with a snap. "He'll worry that you can identify him, turn him in to the authorities, and put an end to his ugly game. He'll be back to finish what he began."

Remember.

"But I don't remember," I whispered. Panic was rising, manifested by the tremor in my voice. "How will I know if I see him again? What should I do?"

"Half your safety is knowing you might be in danger." She placed a card with her contact information in my icy fingers. "You are much more secure now than you were twenty minutes ago, simply because you understand what you may be facing."

Yeah, but twenty minutes ago I was contemplating eternity with a strange and beautiful soul hunter. I liked that reality. I wanted it back.

"I should put a detail on your house," she was saying. "I don't have enough evidence here to give you 24/7 protection, but I can have the property checked at random intervals, starting today. Would that be all right with you?"

"Of course." My whole body had gone numb.

"Even with increased police presence in your neighborhood, I would caution you against being alone, at home or anywhere else."

"I understand."

"May I also suggest you begin working with a counselor, someone skilled in reconstructing lost memories of trauma victims. I can provide some recommendations."

"Oh. Yeah. That makes sense. Thank you. I think."

Agent Arevalo stood. "Call me if anything comes up, even if it's just a hunch or a feeling. Whatever captures your attention; don't write it off. The most trivial detail could save your life."

With that she departed, satchel in hand, heels clicking against the tile floor.

****

The Hunting Grounds

Outside Kansas City, Missouri. 2016

Mayela came to on a cold metal floor, shivering despite the thin fleece set around her shoulders. Her head throbbed. Her limbs felt numb. She was lying in a fetal position. Lifting herself up, she hit her head against something. The darkness was so thick she could not see. Reaching out, she discovered a metal grate overhead, to each side, front and back. She was surrounded by bars, trapped inside a cage.

Curling back into herself, she tried to remember. Where was she? What had gotten her here? Once, in the night forests of Costa Rica, she'd experienced this type of darkness, the sort that seemed to suck every sliver of light into its depths. There, the space had been open, the trees full of murmuring life. She'd kept her flashlight in hand, ready to turn it on at any moment and continue down the path. She'd been free to walk wherever she wanted. Here she was confined and alone. She shook the bars, searched for a door, found the lock that kept her inside. Cold silence indicated her cage was in a place underground. A basement, perhaps. Or a cave.

Images crowded her mind. The summer forest, her grandparents' cottage. The dirt path. Crows overhead. A sense of impending danger. His shadow across the floor. A mask, a voice. The stench of a wet rag across her mouth. Something about him had been all too familiar. Mayela could not put the pieces together in her groggy mind, but she knew one thing with absolute clarity: She had to get out of here. Now.

Reaching as far as she could through the bars, she felt along the floor. The smooth surface yielded nothing, no stray pen, no tool that might break open this trap. Her hands came to a wall along one side of the cage. There, she paused, palms pressed against concrete, eyes closed as if shutting out the darkness would help her think.

"No walls can hold you," her mother had once told her. "No doors can shut you out."

At the time, it had seemed a standard inspirational speech delivered on the eve of her college years. Now Gabriela's words echoed through Mayela's head, seductive in their rhythm, urging her to believe in the magic and mystery of her mother's world, because in this moment believing in magic was her only hope.

The words fell from Mayela's lips in a quiet mantra. *No walls can hold me. No doors can shut me out.* As she repeated them, warmth spread beneath her hands, a diaphanous glow that dissolved solid matter as it grew. Mayela's fingers and palms sank into the concrete wall. Light spilled from the breach, enveloping her in a blinding embrace.

The next thing she knew, the cage was gone. Mayela fell, arms flailing, inside a cold void. Her descent slowed. Smooth, hard earth rose to her feet. As she touched the ground, a pale hand flashed out of the dark. An old man had grabbed her by the wrist.

"What's this?" He yanked her down to his side, squatting close as he examined her arm. "Flesh? You have flesh?"

"Yes." Disoriented, Mayela looked around. She saw a shadowy landscape, dark plains and distant hills. There was no cage, only open space. Where was she? How had she gotten here?

With one dirty nail, the man scratched her, leaving a stinging welt from elbow to wrist.

"Ow!" She jerked away. "What the hell?"

"You bleed!" he howled.

"Of course, I bleed! Everyone bleeds."

"Not here. No one bleeds here." He hung his head and raked at his emaciated arm, clawing until skin spooled like ribbons from his flesh.

"Stop!" Mayela begged, nauseated. "Stop it. You're hurting yourself."

"Yes, it hurts." He whimpered, cradling his mutilated arm. "It hurts, but it doesn't bleed."

Something slithered past in the formless black. Mayela started in fear. “What was that?”

“You aren’t one of us.” The old man narrowed his eyes. “Are you one of them?”

“One of who?”

Tremors shook the ground. An eerie howl broke the seamless night.

“What’s out there?” Mayela whispered, straining to see through the dark.

The old man lifted his head and sniffed at the air like a hound. Terror threaded Mayela’s veins.

“Hunters,” he said.

“What do they hunt?”

He put his finger to his lips and whispered, “Us.”

A rush of wind filled the silence. Mayela froze like a rabbit. She followed the old man’s gaze toward the obsidian sky.

“Don’t let them catch you.” He lifted a trembling hand as if to shield himself. “Don’t let them see you bleed.”

Talons descended from the void and snatched him up. Mayela screamed and reached to stop his ascent, but she was too late. He vanished in the black, his face a mask of terror.

Chaos ensued. Wraith-like people surged out of the darkness. Men and women, young and old, swept Mayela up and carried her forward. Monsters ran in their mist: shrieking canids with spiny wings, giant centipedes with curved fangs, winged lions with raptor’s claws. Anyone who stumbled was gobbled up, or their remains trampled into a bloodless mass.

Mayela struggled to change direction and escape the stampede, but the power of the herd was too great.

She could make no sense of the landscape. Everything remained shrouded in darkness. Then the ground gave way, and she was running on air. They'd been driven over a cliff. Along its rugged length, bodies tumbled toward the abyss like falling snow. Winged creatures soared and swooped toward their prey like hawks feasting on sparrows.

One of the beasts circled over Mayela. Its eyes glowed with sapphire light. A net of blue flames enveloped its wings. Her only escape was to fall faster than the monster could fly, so she willed weight into her body and plummeted, hiding her face, praying her existence would end on the jagged rocks below.

She woke up, or thought she'd woken up, in her bedroom. Tears wet her cheeks. Crickets chirped outside the window. Comforting sensations of home filled her senses—rumpled sheets, vanilla candles, rose-scented soap, fresh sage. Her pulse slowed, but her stomach remained tight as a rock.

I've had a bad dream. She remembered the metal cage, the old man, the monsters on the plains. *Maybe more than one.*

Slipping on a robe, she started toward the kitchen, anxious to calm her nerves with a hot cup of tea. As she ran her hand along the wall, she had the peculiar sensation that the house was materializing beneath her touch. She reached the kitchen, started some water for tea. When she went to the fridge for a snack, the illusion of safety fell apart. Empty shelves greeted her, white and pristine. Baffled, Mayela stared at the stark interior. Where was her food? Her fruits and vegetables? Her butter and eggs and milk? Her leftover rice and black bean soup?

A sting seared Mayela's arm. She looked down and saw a scratch, the one made by the old man, stretching from elbow to wrist. Blood seeped out of the wound in a thin stream.

She slammed the fridge shut. "No!"

Heart pounding, Mayela searched the cabinets and drawers. Everything was empty. No plates, no pots or pans, no flour or sugar, no tea or coffee or canned goods. Nada. Not even a fork or knife. And there was nothing she wanted more in that moment than a good, sharp knife.

Then she heard them. Sinuous movement, like wind through tall grass. A massive serpent slithered out of the shadows. Thin black lines adorned its gray body. Its name escaped Mayela's lips in a gasp: *cascabel muda*. The silent rattlesnake, known in English as Bushmaster. She'd seen these serpents deep inside the tropical forest. They were calm, but deadly. To survive an encounter was to be given a second chance at life, Death itself ceding one more day. But this was not a normal snake. The creature writhed with unnatural intent. Hunger glinted in its yellow eyes. Hunger and perversion.

"Mayela."

She jumped at the voice, so close and intimate for a moment she thought it was, "Carlos?"

Behind the snake, a man stepped into the light. Not a man. A shadow. Tall and imposing, familiar in aspect, like a forgotten dream. As he appeared, the kitchen dissolved. Cabinets, appliances, and furniture faded into formless black.

The cascabel muda settled in a massive coil at Mayela's feet.

The man repeated her name, forcing the E, letting his breath linger on the A. His voice wrapped like a tether around her soul.

The snake lanced forward with hypnotizing beauty—the muscled back, the precise tilt of its head, the stunning spread of its jaws. Two ivory daggers sank into Mayela's skin. Venom seared her muscles. Stunned, she stumbled and fell. In an instant, the bite turned tender and dark. Blisters formed, bloated with blood.

The man approached and knelt beside her. "Say my name."

"This can't be happening."

The serpent snapped. The man rebuked it in harsh, guttural tones.

"Say my name," he repeated. "Now."

"I don't know you!"

He took her face in his hands. "Breathe, Mayela. Relax."

Warmth spread from his fingertips into her veins, stalling the venom's advance. She closed her eyes, commanding her heart to be steady. *No walls can hold me. No doors can shut me out.*

"Remember," he whispered.

Reaching deep inside her soul, Mayela found his name. N followed by a soft E, the purr of an R, a hum between her lips. As she opened her eyes, his face came into focus.

"Again," he said.

The *cascabel muda* lunged. The man caught the serpent mid-strike, cutting off its head with an unseen blade. Blood sprayed everywhere. The body writhed and thumped. White-fingered tentacles sprouted from the stump of its neck. They flowed toward the severed head and wrapped it inside a sticky net. Retreating to the edge of the light, the mangled body heaved in broken silence.

The man turned back to Mayela. “My name. Say it.”

But she was afraid of him now. “Who are you? Why am I here?”

Venom ripped through her like a blunt blade. She cried out in unbearable agony. Tears streamed down her cheeks.

“Say my name, and the pain will stop.”

She could make out details of his face now. The angle of his brow, the line of his jaw, the shape of his mouth.

“I’ve seen you before,” she murmured, reaching up to touch him. “Did I…Did I *create* you?”

He pressed his lips against her palm. “Call on me, and you will be released.”

Mayela forced another breath from her lungs. His name flowed over her tongue, tasting of bitter herbs and wild honey.

“Once more,” he said.

Again, she exhaled, letting go of his name. Her fingers slipped from his face. Her heart wound to a stop. The man’s face blurred, and she became one with the shadows.

Chapter 16

I huddled in my seat, bewildered, frightened, and worst of all, alone inside an awful silence.

Remember, Nathan had said.

Was this what he tried to warn me about, a predator on my heels?

"Remember what?" I murmured. "Remember who?"

Joni poked her head in the backroom. "Everything all right?"

I stared back at her, fists sitting like blocks of ice on my lap, my throat too tight to speak.

"Sorry," she added, registering the look on my face. "Stupid question."

My best friend approached, hands stuffed into her apron pockets, violet curls framing a worried expression. Gingerly, she took a seat next to me. "I understand if you can't talk about it. I just want you to know I'm here for you."

I pointed a shaky finger to the door where Vicky Arevalo had exited. My words tumbled out in a single, angry breath. "That woman thinks I was kidnapped by a serial killer with a fetish for self-made women who frequent your coffee shop."

Joni snapped back as if I'd slapped her in the face. Tears filled her eyes, and she blinked.

"So," she said, straightening her shoulders. "The

agent talked to me about that, a little. I laughed, you know. 'That's ridiculous!' I said. A stalker? In my shop? I mean, seriously, what was she thinking? Marching in here with that East Coast accent and *X-Files* look! Agent Arevalo should take her paranoia back to where she came from. We don't have serial killers in this part of the country."

Her tone carried a clear undercurrent of denial.

"There was that Wichita guy," I said.

"That's in Kansas!" Joni burst into tears. "They're all religious freaks and barbarians over there!"

My heart constricted. I'd never seen Joni break down like this. As much as I wanted to argue her take on Kansas, now wasn't the moment to scold her Missouri pride, or mention known Kansas City serial killers like that Blair guy or the Butcher of Westport. Now wasn't the time to point out borders were psychological constructs, and even if they weren't, *over there* was a mere ten blocks away. Now was not the time to state with indignation that I was born in Kansas, and I was not a religious freak or a barbarian, thank you very much.

Digging into my purse, I found some tissue and handed it to my overwrought friend.

"I'm sorry." She blew her nose. "I don't mean to make this about me, but it's all such a shock. A serial killer in my coffee shop? This is the end of everything, you know. I'll have to close this whole place down."

"What?" I replied, shocked. "Joni, you don't have to close your shop! Why would you do that? This is your life."

"How can I stay open after this? Knowing that *thing* is out there. Imagining what he's done or is doing or might do to my customers. And that he came after you! My best friend! Even if they catch him tomorrow, I can't…" She moaned and blew her nose again. "I won't be able to walk into this place ever again, without thinking about those women."

"Oh, Joni." I put a comforting hand on her back. "This is all circumstantial right now. Connections they're looking into, nothing more." I paused. Maybe if I repeated this enough, I'd believe it. "We don't really know if a killer is scoping out targets here. All we know is that some of the victims liked your coffee. That doesn't make your shop murder central. It just means this is a popular place. A lot of people come through here every day."

Joni finished wiping the tears from her eyes.

"You think Arevalo is wrong?" she asked through sniffles.

Our gazes met, woman to woman, instinct on instinct. I bit my lip and glanced away.

"What happened?" Joni whispered. "When you disappeared?"

I sighed, trying to rub the tension off my forehead. "Honestly? I'm not sure. Every time I think I've figured it out, another wrench gets thrown into the machine. I was out at the farm, walking in the woods, and then…"

Again, I hit a brick wall in my memory. I had to force myself to continue. "There were crows in the trees. I was on my way back to the house. It seems…Maybe there was someone there? I remember a shadow. On the porch, maybe. After that, all I have are strange visions. I thought they were hallucinations, caused by a bad fall, but…"

How much to tell her? What would she say if I

claimed to have crossed a threshold that separates us from a realm of souls? Essentially died and been resurrected? "Anyway, Dad found me passed out in the woods by the stream. When I came to, I was in the hospital. He'd filed a missing persons report, and I followed up at KCPD with my own account. I guess that's how Agent Arevalo found me. She didn't expect to see me here today but knowing I'm a customer only strengthens her suspicions."

Joni sat back in her chair, pensive. "What are you going to do?"

"Be careful. Activate location services on my phone." I thought a moment. "It's better not to be alone. I'll stay with Dad until we figure out what's going on. Mamá's coming in today; she can join us at his house. And also, he can give me a gun."

"You hate guns."

"Yeah, but I know how to use them." Dad had taught me, a long time ago. Then he took me deer hunting, and that was the end of my interest in guns. "Arevalo thinks if I had an encounter with this guy, he'll be back. So, it's either guns or jujitsu, and I don't know jujitsu."

My words fell into silence. It was a decent enough plan if the predator were an ordinary mortal. But what if he wasn't? "Joni, I need to ask you something."

"Anything."

"When Nathan was here the other day, you said no one that knock-down gorgeous had ever walked in the shop. Are you sure?"

"Of course, I'm sure. Why?"

When I didn't respond right away, Joni's mouth dropped open. The blood drained from her face.

"You think it might be him?" she squeaked.

"I don't know." Hearing her say it carried less bite, but not by much. At least someone besides me had put the idea out there. "I have to consider all possibilities. You swear you've never seen him before?"

"Are you kidding? I would so remember if I'd seen that man before this week. Someone like him hanging around my place picking up women would not have escaped my notice. Besides, he did not have a psycho-killer vibe."

I arched my brow. "You an expert on psycho-killer vibes?"

"I'm just saying." She frowned. "But don't listen to me. You were with him a lot more than I was. Do you have reason to suspect?"

I sucked my breath through my teeth. *Here it goes.* "Those hallucinations I mentioned, the ones I had during my disappearance? He was there. Or at least, someone very much like him."

Joni's doubtful expression melted into horror. "The guy you went out with last night was part of the hallucinations you had during your disappearance?"

"I think so. Yes."

"Did he *hurt* you in these hallucinations?"

"No." I shook my head. "Nothing like that. He accompanied me. Talked to me. Supported me. Saved me from certain dangers. He even made dinner for me, once."

"You mean like a Hannibal, somebody's-brains-for-dinner, dinner?"

"No! It was just a regular meal. Kansas City strip steak with rosemary garlic potatoes and the most amazing fresh salad I've ever had." I tasted everything in my mouth as I spoke. "I didn't know that lettuce could have that much flavor. Even the dressing was spectacular. Not to mention the wine."

A grin quirked across Joni's face. Then she covered her mouth, stifled a hiccup, and burst into a fit of guffaws.

"Joni?"

"I'm sorry! I know this is not funny." She coughed, trying to control herself. Her face had turned bright red. "But if you could hear yourself. 'I was trapped with a strange and sexy man who saved me from danger and made great salads.' Honestly. We should all be so lucky."

She laughed again, her outburst bordering on hysterics. Watching her, I had to admit my story did sound ridiculous, like a grand comedy of errors. Except this was real life, and I was facing real and terrifying threats.

"The point is," I said quietly, "I was trapped in that place, and he was there."

"I know. I know." She gathered her breath into her gut, forcing a stop to her laughter. "I get it, Mayela. I'm so sorry. I'm handling all this so badly." She hiccupped again, then resumed a serious tone. "Did you tell Agent Arevalo about him?"

I glanced away. "No."

"Why not?"

"I just…couldn't. Something inside stopped me cold."

"Sweetheart, you need to tell her."

"I know."

"Even if it's not him. Especially if it's not him. Hell, you should demand a full dossier. Does the man have a criminal record? Is he married, separated, divorced? If divorced, how many times? Income, previous relationships, current relationships, any alimony or child support, tax returns. The works. You've got a real opportunity here, Mayela. How many women get to sic the FBI on their new boyfriend?"

I groaned. "Joni."

She lifted her hands in self-defense. "I'm sorry. Again. Me and my stupid sense of humor. It's the only way I can deal with this. All I'm saying is, tell Agent Arevalo. And don't go out with that man again until you know what's going on."

"Agreed." I wondered if she sensed the massive disappointment contained inside this one word.

"For what it's worth," Joni offered, "I liked that guy. It wasn't just that he didn't have psycho-killer vibes. He was more like full throttle opposite of anything bad. And the magnetism between you two! Like you were always meant to be."

"Stop." I held up my hands. "You aren't helping, Joni. All you saw was a chat over coffee from the other side of the shop. You can't decipher anything from that."

"Even so," she said. "I don't think he's a killer. I really don't."

"I hope you're right."

"Think about it. If his intent was to get rid of you, last night would've been his chance. What would he have to gain by letting you live another day?"

"Maybe he gets off on the hunt?"

"Or maybe that date was a gift." Her face lit up with the possibility. "Maybe being with Mr. Gorgeous all evening kept the other guy, the *real* predator, from getting to you."

Oh. The fog lifted a little. Air filled my lungs, and the tension left my shoulders. I studied my hands, conscious of the gift of my living flesh, of my burning will to defend it. *I opened the portal.* The full implications of that truth hit home. Was my arrival at the Hunting Grounds intentional? Did instinct drive me across the threshold so I could seek Nathan? Did some part of me understand that, with his name inside my heart, I could summon him against any enemy?

"I'm not saying you shouldn't be careful," Joni added. "I'm just saying don't lose hope."

"Hey!" One of her employees poked his head through the doorway. "I hate to interrupt, but we could really use some help out here."

"Who's working for whom, Devon?" Joni retorted with a playful wink.

He lifted his hands in deference and backed out of the room.

"He's right," Joni confessed to me. "I've left them alone too long. What a day to be short of staff!"

"Thanks for being here for me."

"What do you mean, thanks? As if I'd leave you alone with this!" Joni stood and smoothed her apron. Then she pinned me with a concerned gaze. "So, what now?"

"I guess I go to my dad's." I fished my cell phone out of my purse.

"And call Agent Arevalo. You should do that first."

"I can't face another conversation with her yet." I needed to think about what to say when I talked to Agent Arevalo again. Maybe I could sort that out on the way over to Dad's. "I'll call her in a little while."

"You aren't stopping by your house, are you?"

My heart stuttered. "It'd be a risk, on my own."

"Damn straight it would. What about your cat?"

Midnight. My heart constricted with worry. I checked the time on my phone. Where had the day gone? The hours had already slipped into late afternoon.

"She'll be okay." I spoke with more certainty than I felt. "She has enough food to keep her until tomorrow."

"You aren't worried about her?"

"No…?" A shiver coursed through me. I covered my face. "She knows how to hide. Even I can't find her when she decides she doesn't want to be seen."

Joni's stare burned through the top of my head. No one called my bullshit better than she did. "Mayela Lehman, look me in the eye and tell me you aren't going by the house on your own to rescue the cat."

"What am I supposed to do?" I threw up my hands. "I can't leave her there. For all I know, psycho-killer is a cat torturer, too."

"I get it! I'm not saying you shouldn't go. Just don't do it alone. I'll go with you."

I blinked. "You will?"

"Of course, I will. I've got mace. And a good left hook. It'd be nice to have a gun, too. Maybe we could stop by your dad's and borrow one of his?"

"It'd take more than an hour to get there and back. I'd rather do all this before it gets dark."

"I'm with you on that. Well, we'll trust my mace and my fist. With a little help from the angels, we won't run into trouble rescuing your cat."

“What about the shop? You don’t close until evening, and you’re short on staff today.”

“I’ll close early. No more customers starting now. It’ll take forty-five minutes or so to wrap things up and shoo people away. I can leave Devon and Trace with clean up after everyone’s gone. I don’t want to hang out here any more today anyway. We should have time to get to your house and do everything before sundown.”

“Oh, Joni.” My relief was palpable. “You’re a lifesaver.”

“Yeah, that’s me.” Joni grinned and started toward the door. “Coffee shop diva and superheroine. Midnight will owe me one of her nine lives after tonight. Such a sweet kitty.”

****

The Realm of the Soul Masters

Mortal Year 2016

After her encounter with the snake, Mayela regained consciousness in a place filled with light. She felt soft cushions beneath her body, heard the whir of household appliances. An apartment took shape around her, at once foreign yet deeply familiar. Mayela realized she was on a divan, covered by a soft blanket. With trepidation, she pulled back the fabric and checked her leg. There was no trace of the bite, not even lingering bruises. Her arm had also healed. No more stinging scratch. Her muscles ached with the sort of fatigue that follows a heavy workout. Other than that, she felt fine.

Puzzled and wary, Mayela stood to take in her surroundings. Polished oak covered the floors of a clean and modern apartment. A large window spanned one wall, revealing a skyline of twisted spires. Beyond them, burgundy clouds undulated in slow, hypnotic waves, as if the heavens were on fire.

She moved closer to the window. The apartment was about thirty stories up. Nobody wandered the lamp-lit streets below. She set a hand against the glass and flinched. It was ice cold. *Is this real or a dream?* Mayela flexed her fingers and touched her face, kneaded soft flesh over hard bone. She pinched herself. It hurt. She checked her carotid; the pulse was slow and steady.

Turning from the window, Mayela explored the apartment. Spacious living and dining area, fully stocked kitchen, comfortable bed, luxury bath. Nice for someone attached to city life except…

There was no way out.

Anxiety spiked. She'd been trapped. Again. Walking the perimeter of the apartment, she searched every wall and every corner, but it was no use. She couldn't find the door. The walls appeared constructed as a seamless whole. Not one crack interrupted the smooth surface. Not even an air vent in the ceilings or floor.

A sudden electronic wheeze broke the quiet.

Mayela spun around. In the living room, on its own small table, sat a boxy old computer. The machine looked out of place amidst the contemporary furnishings, a strange artifact rescued from another century. Cautious, Mayela approached. There was no power cord, yet the machine buzzed and groaned, laboring to boot up. After a few flickers, the blue-gray screen stabilized, revealing a barren desktop with a single icon, a tongue of red flame.

Mayela frowned.

The computer stared at her with a diaphanous

glow.

"Okay." She sat down and took hold of the mouse, yellowed with age. "I'll bite. Besides, it's all just a dream. Right?"

She clicked the red flame. A screen popped up, much like a browser, with a list of black-and-white videos. Every icon was labeled with the name of someone she knew—family, friends, colleagues, acquaintances. At the top of the list, she saw the name of her adoptive father, Josef Lehman. Taking the cursor to the icon, Mayela clicked PLAY.

****

Josef Lehman searches the woods behind his deceased parents' cabin. He was supposed to meet his daughter here. Instead, he's hiking alone. Sweat dampens his shirt. An old army pack burdens bent shoulders. He calls for Mayela again and again, but she does not respond.

Afternoon light slants through the trees. Josef's legs grow stiff under his bulky body. He struggles for breath and stumbles. Having backtracked through forest and fields for hours, Josef at last staggers to an old bench by the stream. He eases himself down and opens his canteen.

Beside him, a vision of his daughter appears. She sits on the bench, toddler legs dangling over mottled leaf litter. She laughs and points to something in the trees, then fades like a ghost.

Tears dampen Josef's eyes. He has countless memories of Mayela in this forest. He taught her how to recognize birds and their songs, how to distinguish between tracks of deer, bobcat, and coyote, how to tell beech from oak and elm, how to love and explore the living world. She was always so trusting, he thinks. She trusted everything—everyone—too much.

Again, he calls her name.

Again, she does not answer.

Wind rushes through the branches, accentuating the silence.

"I just have to catch my breath," he says aloud. "I'll catch my breath and then I'll find her."

He opens his pack and removes a sandwich. Ham and cheese on white bread with mayo wrapped in wax paper. Not for the first time, he remembers Gabriela's fine cooking, her laughter and warmth. Sharp pain stabs through his chest. They are no longer a family. That was his task, to hold them together. His task. His failure. And now their little girl is lost, and Gabriela is far away, and he is too old to keep anyone safe.

Josef's fingers shake violently. The sandwich tumbles from his grasp and lands on the ground. Bread and meat mix with dirt as the pieces scatter. He stares at his ruined meal for a long moment. Then he hangs his head and clutches at his thin hair. Wretched sobs break open his soul.

****

The video ended in white noise. Mayela sat stunned, hungry and aching for one more glimpse of her beloved father. Outside, the burgundy sky continued its ice-cold churn. She clicked the other videos. None of them opened. Tears streamed down her cheeks, drawn forth by a desperate longing to see something—anything—of home.

A shadow moved at the edge of her vision, melting out of the wall. Mayela recognized the intruder. He was the same as the one who'd emerged from the shadows in her other dream. The one who'd killed the snake.

"You." She hissed and flew at him, claws extended to rake off his face. He caught her by the wrists. At his touch, Mayela's strength vanished. Her knees buckled, and she sank to the floor.

"What have you done to me?" she demanded, horrified.

"I've done nothing. You need to eat."

"Let me go!"

He released her but remained close, his aroma clean and sharp as a fresh-lit match.

"I want out of this place," she growled. "Now."

"I am not the one keeping you here."

"Fuck off."

He drew a breath and held it. "You must eat, Mayela. You are fading, and quickly."

"I'm not hungry." Then she caught her reflection in the mirror. What she saw made her gasp. Her face was gaunt, her dark hair limp. Her arms looked thin and unnatural. Bones protruded at her elbows. Bewildered, she reached toward the mirror with shaking hands. "That's not me. Who is that? Her eyes look different. Why are my eyes a different color?"

"Things work differently here. I will explain, but first you must eat." The man helped Mayela to her feet, sat her down at the table, and put a blanket around her shoulders. Picking up a carafe of water, he poured Mayela a glass. "I'll have food ready for you shortly."

"I won't accept anything you give me," she replied as he set the water in front of her. But Mayela's throat was burning, and the glass was cool to the touch.

The man strode to the kitchen. A marble counter divided the space between them. Mayela watched as he pulled dishes and utensils from the cabinets. His short-sleeved, cream-colored shirt accentuated broad, well-defined shoulders. Dark hair framed a chiseled face marked by a frown of concentration. The man's movements were disturbingly familiar, fluid yet exact.

"Why am I here?" Mayela demanded.

"You are hiding from those who pursued you on the Hunting Grounds."

"The Hunting Grounds?"

"Everything you remember—the dark plains, the stampede of souls, even the place that appeared to be your home—that was all part of the Hunting Grounds."

"Yes, but…What, precisely, are the Hunting Grounds?"

"Where we go to pursue and capture souls."

Mayela blinked in confusion.

"Unclaimed souls arrive at the Hunting Grounds," he explained. "That's where we go to lay our claim."

"We being…?" She paused, uncertain whether she was dreaming, wary of the implications if she wasn't. "Are you saying you're a demon?"

"No."

"An angel, then?"

A mischievous smile touched his lips. "Not quite."

"Well, you've got to be one or the other. Angel or demon. Which is it? Do you serve God or the Devil?"

"I serve no one." He bristled. "You won't find a name for me in your small-minded myths of good and evil. There are far too many of us for your kind to imagine, much less name."

"They aren't *my* small-minded myths," she shot back, indignant. "And I can imagine quite a lot, thank you very much."

He chuckled and returned to his task, chopping vegetables with precision.

"This apartment we're in," Mayela asked, "is it yours?"

"This"—he pointed to their surroundings with a knife—"is a liminal space of your making."

"A what?"

"You made this apartment."

"I made this?"

"Yes."

"*I* made this?"

"That's what I said."

"No." She shook her head. "I did not make this place. There's no way I made this place."

He dumped chopped potatoes into a bowl, poured olive oil on the mix, then added sea salt, rosemary, and fresh garlic before spreading everything on a baking sheet and placing it in the oven. When finished, he pinned her with a dark gaze. "Why not?"

"Well." Mayela flattened her hands against the polished burgundy surface of the table. "Your table, for example. It's made of purple heart. I'd never have rainforest wood in my apartment unless it were certified sustainable. Even then, I wouldn't have it. Way beyond my budget. Besides, certification programs aren't reliable. What we really need is—"

"By made I meant *woven*." He spoke slowly, as if explaining something to a child. "From your imagination."

Annoyed, Mayela stared back at him, slowing her words beat for a beat. "That. Makes. No. Sense."

"You wanted a safe place, and you believed the creatures of the Hunting Grounds would not look for you inside a city. So, you made a city and burrowed into the heart of it. An excellent tactic, I might add. Indicative of a fine instinct."

"It's not possible to wish an entire city into being!" She threw her hands up in disbelief. "Even if it were, I would never put myself in an exit-less high-rise apartment beneath a burning sky and call it *safe*."

"This apartment isn't exit-less," he replied. "It's entrance-less."

"The point is, I wouldn't even be in the city! I'd build a cottage, see? In the woods, on the edge of a prairie. With multiple escape routes and…Shotguns. Like the ones Dad has. There'd be fireflies in the evening. Stars at night. Hawks in the sky. Bees and butterflies during the day. A herd of bison, and a dark brooding storm that…"

Mayela stopped and folded in on herself, overtaken by an intense sense of déjà vu. That place she was describing, a prairie with bees and butterflies and bison, with a storm on the horizon. She'd seen that before. Knelt before the dark clouds and brought something beautiful into being. She was sure of it. But when? How?

"That's what I'd make," she finished, her voice small and uncertain. "A prairie."

"I know." The man's gaze became distant. "I remember."

He shook off the thought and nodded at the carafe on the table. "Drink more water. It's bringing the color back to your cheeks."

"I haven't had anything to drink," she objected, but her glass was empty. "What is going on? I'm dreaming, aren't I?"

"No."

"Dead?"

"No."

"Christ. I'm so confused. Do you have anything stronger than water?"

He nodded at the carafe. The water took on a deep ruby color, exuding the sweet scent of wine. Mayela poured a little into her glass.

"I must be dead," she said. "It feels like I'm dead. Like I went through hell, and this is purgatory, and now I'm waiting. For what I don't know. A decision, maybe. Like they're reviewing my records, deciding whether I go up or down. Do you think…?" A surge of emotion clogged her throat. Grief hit hard, sinking like a rock inside her stomach. Mayela swallowed and asked, "Will I get to see Carlos?"

The man's expression softened. He paused in his work to set a compassionate gaze on her. "You aren't dead. This feels like a dream because you crossed the threshold. All the rules are different here. But you aren't dead. What happened was very unexpected, and…" He frowned as if checking his words. "Your situation is complicated. It will take time to explain. But you aren't staying here, and I'm sorry to say, you won't see Carlos either. You will have to go back to your world, and soon."

"Oh." Mayela tried to process everything he'd said, but all she could latch onto were those last words. "I have to go back. Well, that's good."

"Is it?"

His tone stung her heart. Not long ago, she would've given anything to see Carlos again. But now that she stood on the steps of eternity? "I want to see

Carlos. I do. But the truth is, I want to live more. There's so much left to do. So yes, I'd rather go back. How do I do that?"

He opened the oven, releasing a savory smell of steak and potatoes. "Only you can answer that question."

She sat back in her chair. "Seriously?"

"You sealed the doors to this place. You must unseal them."

Anger rose in Mayela's veins. "If I'm the one who sealed the doors, how did you get in?"

"In the Hunting Grounds, when the serpent bit, you called me by my true name. Three times you called on me. That established a bond between us."

"What kind of bond?"

"You granted me temporary status as your guide and guardian."

"I did no such thing!"

Emerging from behind the counter, he approached the table and set down a perfect plate—KC strip steak, potatoes, salad, soft rolls.

"When you are ready to go back to your world," he said, "a door will appear. All you must do is walk through it."

Mayela wasn't paying attention to him anymore. The aroma of food had set off a ravenous hunger. Taking up a knife and fork, she cut into the meat. It parted like butter. As she ate, layers of flavor burst through her senses—warm and cool, sweet and savory. Within moments, she had devoured everything. "Wow! That was amazing! Where did you learn to cook like that?"

But her companion had already left.

Unnerved by his disappearance, Mayela glanced around the apartment. Once again, she caught her reflection in the mirror. Astonished, she stood. The meal had transformed her. She'd regained her full weight. Color warmed her skin. Her black hair glowed with an iridescent blue sheen. Only her eyes had not recovered their emerald hue. They remained opaque and dark as night, just like his.

Chapter 17

As Joni closed up, I remained secluded in the backroom. Being hidden from the world made me feel somehow safer. The first person I called was Dad, to confirm I planned to spend the night. I withheld details of my afternoon, thinking it best to tell him in person. Knowing I'd be with Dad calmed my nerves, but not my thoughts. When we finished our conversation, I disconnected and drew a deep breath, taking stock of the situation.

Fact: I crossed the veil and experienced the other side of death. As crazy as that sounded, I no longer doubted the conviction of my heart. The Hunting Grounds was a real place, and I had been there.

Fact: Nathan was a being from beyond the veil. He'd followed me here because he wanted my soul. He also had a lasso around my heart. Maybe I had a lasso around his. Was he an ally or enemy? Guardian or predator? *I might not know the answer until the endgame.*

Fact: Critical events leading to my disappearance were blocked from my memory. How and why did I cross the threshold? If Agent Arevalo's suspicions were correct, an assault on my person may have catapulted me to the other side. The predator was probably of this world, potentially of the next. And I was not his first target.

But I was determined to be his last.

Picking up the phone, I called Mamá. To my disappointment, she didn't answer. I imagined her in the air somewhere over the western United States. On a broomstick, maybe? I could believe most anything at this point. After the tone, I left a message.

"*Hola*, Mamá. *Soy yo*. Look, I know you told me not to leave the house, but something came up. My situation is more complicated than I thought. I don't know if I can trust Nathan after all. But also, I'm facing…Well, I may be facing a different sort of threat. Someone from this world might be after me. I'm guessing a ward made to repel immortals won't work on a human, so I'm going over to Dad's."

I paused. Doubt knotted inside my gut. Was I making a mistake?

"You said to trust my instinct," I continued. "This is what my instinct is telling me to do. I'm headed out in a little bit. I'll be there before dark. We'll wait for you there. I'll have my phone on me the whole time. Call when you get this message. I'll text you, too." I started to choke up. Tears were stinging my eyes. "Let me know when you land. *Te quiero*, Mamá."

I disconnected, dug a tissue from my purse, and wiped my eyes.

"Stop it," I told myself. "There'll be time for tears later. You need to focus."

Noise from the coffee shop had dimmed. After sending Mamá a brief text, I tucked my phone into my purse and peeked through the doorway. The sun had dipped low toward the western horizon, illuminating the shop in shades of red and gold. The place was nearly empty. Joni was wiping down the espresso maker. Her employees were cleaning tables and gathering stray dishes.

"That was quick," I said, approaching her from behind.

"Not quick enough." She finished her task, disposed of the cleaning rags, and began removing her apron. "It was a pain getting people to leave. Had some irate customers pounding at the door. I've never been in more of a mood to tell people to piss off. I mean, I know coffee's addictive, but seriously. Go make your own for once. Or spend your money at Starbucks. What do I care on a day like today? You ready?"

"Yes." I noticed a lone figure in a light blue shirt at a table nearby, head bent over his phone. My heart leapt into my throat. "Why is Mitch still here?"

Joni sighed. "Look, I'm sorry. I tried to make him go like everyone else, but I ended up telling him, I don't know, probably more than I should have."

"What did you tell him?" My words came through tight lips.

"Nothing important, I swear. I know we have to keep this confidential, but he and I have been working together for years. If I can't trust my accountant, who can I trust? I just told him there's been some trouble connected with the shop and that you're involved. That the police have advised you not to be alone until things are sorted out."

"Joni!"

"That's all I said! I swear. And he was like, 'But I don't see why that means closing up early,' and I said, 'Because she's not staying at her house tonight, and I promised to go get her cat with her.' So now he wants to help rescue your cat, which you gotta admit, is kind of sweet."

I turned my back on Mitch and covered my face with one hand.

"I'll tell him to go if it bothers you," Joni said.

"Wait. Just wait." I held up my hand, demanding a moment to think. *The conversation in the parking lot. The midnight visit to my house.* A cold horror lodged inside my chest. *It can't be.* Could it?

"Mayela?" Joni prompted, anxious.

"I'm sorry." I lowered my voice. "But you have to understand I can't trust anyone right now. I mean, what if Mitch is…"

I stopped, afraid to voice the thought. Joni's eyes widened and the blood drained from her face. She grabbed my arm and pulled me toward the door to the backroom.

"You think my accountant is a serial killer?" she said in a fierce whisper.

"I don't know!" I hissed back. "How can I?"

"Christ." She bit her lip. "You're right. We can't take any risks. I'll tell him to leave right away."

"No. Wait."

Already I regretted making the accusation. What evidence did I have, beyond two weird conversations? Two weird conversations did not make a man a serial killer.

I snuck a glance at Mitch. He seemed thoroughly absorbed by his phone.

"Look," I whispered. "Either he is, or he isn't. In both cases, it's best he come along."

"What are you talking about?"

"If it's not him, there's no reason to send him away. If it is him—God forbid, but if it is him—telling him that he can't come along will only arouse suspicion."

"I don't understand."

"He'll know we're onto him. And he knows where we're going. He knows where I live, Joni. Better to have a snake where you can see it, I always say."

She closed her mouth and swallowed.

"He can't come in the house," I continued. "We'll tell him to wait outside because Midnight hates strangers. I'll secure the latch on the storm door behind us. It'll be okay."

"I don't know, Mayela."

"Chances are, it's not him, and we're both just being paranoid. But if it is him, only an idiot would attack two of us at once, in my house, knowing the police were here *today.* Just keep your eyes sharp, your mace in hand, and your left hook ready."

She grimaced but gave a short nod. "Okay."

"You ready?"

"Yeah."

We returned to the counter. Joni called Mitch over and informed him of the game plan. He seemed just fine with being assigned to porch sentinel, so we were on our way.

Traffic was light as we drove in a caravan of cars toward my home. As a red sun reached toward the horizon, people walked their dogs along sidewalks and trails. Children laughed and played in parks. On my block, trees spread verdant branches over well-kept lawns. In a couple of weeks, they would turn fiery red with the coming of autumn. I loved autumn. I intended to see it again this year, as a living mortal with my soul intact.

Pulling into the driveway of my home, I parked in the shadow of a giant oak. Joni and Mitch left their cars on the street. We met on the lawn and in wordless synchrony, walked toward the front door. As we arrived at the porch, a couple late-season crickets chirped from under the bushes. The sound soothed my anxiety, leaving a curious sense of anticipation. I fished my keys out of my purse, unlocked the door, and opened it, half expecting to see an axe-wielding stranger standing in the foyer.

Silence greeted us.

I turned to Mitch. “Wait here, okay?”

“I’ve got my instructions.” He grinned, crossed his arms, and leaned against a post. Rosy light from the setting sun sifted through his golden hair. “Just holler if you need me.”

Not a serial killer. Serial killers didn’t have such an honest look about them. Did they?

“Thanks, Mitch,” I said.

Joni and I went inside the house. We paused in the foyer, standing so still I could hear my friend breathing next to me and the hum of the fridge from the kitchen. Joni assumed a stance with her feet spread and took the mace out of her purse. She held it in both hands, peering down the hallway like a TV cop with a gun.

“Mayela!” she whispered.

“What?”

“The door.”

“Oh, yeah.” I turned the latch on the storm door, locking Mitch outside.

“Let’s scope the house,” Joni said, mace raised. “In case the real guy is inside the house, instead of on the porch.”

We searched the living room, dining room, and kitchen, checking behind furniture and curtains, in closets. Midnight appeared from the shadows and followed us, a curious expression on her face. When we arrived at the door to the basement, Joni and I exchanged a glance. I always kept this door closed. I didn't like Midnight getting into things down there, and it was more energy efficient, especially in summertime. The door stared at us, its blank surface providing no hint of what might lie beyond. Pursing my lips, I reached toward the knob.

"Can't you just lock it without opening it?" Joni asked. "Scary shit happens in basements."

I pulled back my hand. "Good call."

Except the basement door didn't lock. We pulled a chair from the kitchen table and jammed it beneath the knob as a brace. The fit was tight. If anyone was hiding down there, they'd be staying for a while. Unless, of course, they had supernatural powers. *Best not to think about that right now*.

We continued down the hallway, checking behind doors and in the guest bedroom, then the guest bathroom, and my office. At last, we arrived at the master bedroom.

"Looks like it's all clear," I said.

"Yup."

We stood in the center of my room. Midnight settled at our feet to clean her paws. It seemed like ages ago that I had been here, inside a circle of candles, kissing a man from another world. Where was Nathan now?

"Okay." Joni tucked her mace back into her purse. "Let's do this quickly." In a single move, she scooped up Midnight by the scruff of her neck. My poor cat gave a startled meow. “Where’s her carry case?”

“Right here.” I went to the corner of the room where I kept the soft-sided carrier. Together, we stuffed Midnight inside. She clawed a little, but I’d experienced worse. Maybe she sensed she was headed for a kinder destination than the vet.

“Why don’t you pack your stuff while I get the kitty things together?” Joni said. “It’ll go quicker.”

Having taken care of Midnight many times, Joni knew where to find her supplies. As she disappeared down the hallway, I grabbed a small duffle and filled it with the basics—pajamas, toothbrush, a change of clothes, some additional toiletries. Enough to last until I could come back with Dad and Mamá and pack a proper suitcase by the light of day. Glancing around the room, I caught sight of a rosary on the nightstand. I walked over and picked it up.

“Mr. Gorgeous give you these?” Joni yelled from the kitchen.

I started at her voice. “Give me what?”

“The roses. They’re beautiful!”

Wow. I’d already forgotten. Hadn’t even noticed them while we were searching the house for a psycho killer. “Yes, those were from him.”

“Every blossom is literally perfect. And they smell like heaven.”

“I know.” I lifted the smooth, dark prayer beads to my face and inhaled. They, too, smelled of roses. Mamá had given me the rosary for my First Holy Communion. In all these years, the beads had never lost their aroma.

“How can they look so fresh after a full day? Where do you even find roses like that anymore?” Joni appeared in the doorway to my bedroom. In one hand, she held the carry case with Midnight, in the other a large bag full of food, blankets, and toys.

"I really hope he's not a psycho killer," she said. "The guy you had dinner with, or my accountant."

"Me, too." I nodded toward the bag of kitty supplies. "Looks like Midnight's traveling in better style than me."

"Do you need more time?"

"No." I slipped the rosary into my pocket and picked up my duffle. "I have everything. Let's get out of here."

"What about the litter box?"

"Dad's done his fair share of cat sitting, too. There's a box at his house. I'll pick up fresh litter on the way."

Mitch was waiting outside. He helped carry everything to my car. We put Midnight on the front seat. When I opened the trunk, Mitch frowned and said, "What is all this…?"

"Crap?" I finished for him with a laugh. "Field gear for my bee work. The good entomologist is always prepared."

Shoving aside nets, kill jars, and field packs, I wedged in my duffle. There was no room for Midnight's kitty supplies, so we put those in the back seat.

"Guess we're done here," I announced, closing the door. "Thanks, Mitch."

"No problem." He looked from me to Joni. "You two going to be okay?"

"Oh, yeah. Everything's fine." Joni waved her hands in the air. "Thanks so much for coming. Sorry I was such a drama queen back at the shop. Really what's going on isn't that big a deal. I was just frazzled trying to close up so we could get the kitty."

"I appreciate your help," I said. "Both of you. Truly. Midnight does, too."

"Okay, then." Mitch nodded and turned to go. "Call me if you need anything."

Then he was walking toward his car.

A dog barked somewhere. A car zoomed past, heading south. Across the street, some kids were playing in the yard.

Joni and I exchanged a glance of relief.

Not a serial killer, I thought. Because I truly had expected him to try something if he were. And I felt awful, in that moment, for having ever imagined…

"Hey, Mitch!" I ran after him.

He turned around with a surprised expression. I caught up to him next to the driver's door.

"Yeah?" he asked.

I shifted on my feet, uncertain what I'd intended to say. "Thanks. Thanks for doing this."

"I thought we already did that part."

"Oh. Yeah. I mean…Also, I'm sorry. I know I haven't been much of a friend lately."

"Okay." He folded his arms and leaned against the car. "I'm listening."

"I, uhm…I have a lot going on right now, things I need to figure out on my own. I hope you understand. But once this is over, I promise we'll have the conversation we need to have."

Mitch's features relaxed into a smile. He leaned forward, touched my arm, and grazed my cheek with a kiss. I caught the scent of men's cologne mingled with something unpleasant, like overripe fruit. It made me dizzy, and a little nauseous. *A serial killer…Maybe?* Did serial killers give off weird smells that could make a person nauseous?

"That'd be great, Mayela," he said. "Call me when you're ready."

With that, Mitch got into his car. As he drove away, I made note of the model and make as well as the license plate number. When he'd turned the corner, I walked back to Joni.

"What was that about?" she asked with narrowed eyes.

I shrugged. "Guess I felt bad for suggesting he might be a serial killer."

"You didn't tell him, did you?"

"Of course not."

"Well, do I get a kiss too?" she demanded. "I'm the one who scoped out the house and packed up your kitty gear."

I laughed and kissed her on the cheek. She smelled wonderful, like fresh coffee and sweet bread. "Thank you, dear friend."

"I want to follow you to your dad's."

"No, please. It's not necessary."

"I mean it."

"Go home, Joni. Get some rest. You've had a really long day, and I'm not going to add to it anymore. I'll be good from here on out."

"Are you sure?"

No, but I didn't want Joni getting any deeper into this than she already was. Serial killers were not the only thing I had to worry about right now. "I'm sure."

"Call me every ten minutes until you get there."

"Okay."
"I'm serious."
"I know."

Chapter 18

Aside from calls to Joni at ten-minute intervals, the drive to Dad's was thankfully uneventful. I drove a circuitous route and checked the rearview mirror often. Like I'd seen people do in the movies when they wanted to know if someone was tailing them. Mostly I was on the lookout for Mitch's car, but I didn't see him or anyone else that appeared to be interested in who I was or where I was going. I stopped by a pet supply store in Dad's neighborhood to pick up some litter. Twilight was gathering by the time I pulled into the well-lit space between his garage and the back entrance, which led to the kitchen. Dad greeted me at the door with a hug. His aroma of faint tobacco and old sweaters filled me with contentment and a deep-rooted sense of security.

"Good to see you, Sweetheart." Dad took the carry case from my hand and added, "You brought the cat?"

"Yeah. Mamá's coming, too."

"Tonight?" His eyes widened. "From California?"

"She'll be here around ten."

"Well, it's a little unexpected, but—" He shrugged. "—the more the merrier. It'll be nice to have everyone in the same house again."

The Lehman family reunion, convened to fend off soul hunters and axe murderers. "Thanks for being flexible, Dad. You said you had some beer?"

"Yup." He set the carry case on the floor and unzipped the door. It took him some effort to bend over nowadays. Midnight scuttled out, legs crouched and tail low. She shot a startled look at Dad and darted into the next room. "Always takes her a while to remember me. You want a beer now?"

"In a little while. I have a few more things to bring in."

"I'll help."

We retrieved the rest of my small inventory. As we set everything down in the kitchen, Joni called my cell.

"Where are you?" she demanded. "Why haven't you called?"

"Sorry. Time got away from me. I'm at Dad's."

"Whew! What a relief. I was worried, you know. It'd been twelve minutes already. Do you have a gun yet?"

I stepped away from my dad and lowered my voice. "We haven't talked about that, Joni. I just got here."

"Get your hands on a gun, okay? Like, now."

"I will." I stepped into the next room so Dad wouldn't hear us. "Everything's going to be fine. I'm where I need to be."

"I should go out there and stay with you."

Honestly. Enough was enough. I had my own panic to take care of. I couldn't spend the night managing hers. "Joni, you've done everything you can do for now, and you've been a great help. Mamá, Dad, and I can take it from here. We'll call the police if we need to. Get some rest now. I'll touch base with you in the morning."

In the silence that followed, I could hear her

fingernails tapping against some random surface.

"If you say so," she said at last. "I guess. Be safe. Please?"

"I will. Thank you."

When I returned to the kitchen, Dad was filling a pot with water. He'd laid his sauce ingredients out on the counter in a neat row, ready for processing.

"Can I chop something?" I asked.

"What?" He turned off the water, glanced at me then the vegetables. He'd gone a little hard of hearing now, too.

"The vegetables." I pointed to the counter. "Can I chop some vegetables?"

"Oh. No, sweetheart. I've got everything under control." He nodded toward the fridge. "Beer's cold. Why don't you serve up a couple, and we'll chat."

"I'm going to get Midnight settled first."

"Right. Well, the beer will still be cold when you're done. I'm guessing about thirty minutes to dinner."

"Sounds good."

After setting out Midnight's food and water on the floor in the kitchen, I picked up her bag of goodies and went to the living room. I put a blanket on her favorite chair and scattered a couple toys on the floor. I found her spare litter box in the utility closet and set it out in the downstairs bathroom. All this time, Midnight remained hidden, but I talked to her as I went, hoping she'd reappear. At the bottom of the bag, Joni had packed her kitty bed. I wasn't sure where to put that. Would Midnight and I sleep in the guest bedroom upstairs or on the foldout couch in the living room? I wanted Mamá to have the more comfortable guest room, but maybe she'd prefer the living room, to be as far away from Dad as possible.

Had they even slept in the same house since the divorce?

"This could be awkward," I confided in a whisper to invisible Midnight. "Hopefully fighting serial killers and fending off supernatural beings will distract them from their usual squabbles."

On the way to fetch fresh sheets, I stopped by Dad's study to check out his guns. He kept his stock clean and well-ordered in an antique wooden cabinet. The glass was polished to a high sheen. Dad's collection was small by Missouri standards and consisted mostly of hunting rifles, though he did keep a couple of handguns.

At his desk, I found the spare key where it had always been, in the top right drawer. The key was small enough to fit the hollow of my palm. I closed my hand around it, thinking I should open the cabinet and grab a handgun now. But it seemed rude to do so without Dad's knowledge, and I wasn't ready to tell him why I wanted a gun.

I wasn't ready, I realized, to even hold a gun.

Pocketing the extra key, I headed upstairs instead. My tiny jeans pockets were stuffed to capacity by now: one shungite crystal, one rosary, and one key to a gun cabinet. The complete beginner's toolkit for defense against mortal and immortal enemies.

To my surprise, sheets had already been changed in the guest bedroom. Dad had become a true paragon of domesticity in his old age. I selected more sheets from the linen closet and grabbed a couple pillows for the foldout bed. On the way back down to the living room,

I passed the kitchen. A strong whiff of fresh chopped garlic awakened my senses.

"The food's smelling good, Dad!" I called.

"Stop doing house chores and come have a beer," he replied. "It's time to relax!"

I laughed. It felt good to be home. Despite our differences, Dad always made me feel safe. In all the years of our sometimes-difficult relationship, I'd never doubted his love or his commitment to my wellbeing. He was a true father, my guide and companion, my stalwart protector since before I was born. Thank God Mamá found him when she did.

As I arrived at the living room, Midnight darted like a shadow from behind the couch.

"Oh," I said. "You've decided to make an appearance."

She fled to the dining room.

I shrugged and set to work on the foldout bed, knowing Midnight would be back soon to ask for her evening tuna. After taking the cushions off the couch, I gripped the foldout and pulled. As the bed frame emerged amidst metallic creaks and chirps, a sense of déjà vu blasted my awareness.

The feel of metal against my palms. The taste of copper in my mouth.

My hands went to my lips, as if to wipe the memory away.

The voice of a man. A shadow inside the light.

The woodlands behind the cottage. I stood there again, looking up at the sun shining through the forest canopy. A hot breeze cut through the humid summer air. Squirrels chased each other in agitated circles. Songbirds repeated nervous chirps. I moved along the path as if floating, not walking, propelled by some unseen force. Sweat dampened my skin. Raw thirst clawed at my throat. I wanted something to drink, a long rest in the cool shade. The cottage came into view. A flock of crows landed overhead, cawing ceaselessly. A man stood in my path, silhouetted by the afternoon light. Fear cast its icy breath over my heart.

"Mayela," he said. "I was hoping I'd find you here."

"Who are you?" I asked. Though his voice sounded familiar, his identity was obscured by the backlight. Branches shifted overhead, casting a ray of light upon his features, but his face was covered by a mask.

The memory melted away. I was back in Dad's living room on a cool September night.

"Mitch," I whispered, and I knew beyond a shadow of a doubt. It had always been Mitch. I'd never seen his face, but I knew the voice. I'd tried to run, but I couldn't escape. Everything happened so fast. He'd knocked me out and then…Then I was trapped. Hopelessly trapped. But I found a way, a door only I could see, opened by powers I didn't know I had. The moment I saw the breach, I'd acted on faith and instinct, leaping through the portal and landing in the Hunting Grounds.

I drew a sharp breath.

The Hunting Grounds wasn't a trap. It was my escape plan, my only path to safety. All this time, I'd thought the horror had started on the other side of the veil, when it was horror of this world that had driven me to Nathan in the first place. The true predator, the one Vicky Arevalo was searching for, was of this world. His name was Mitch McGraff.

And he knew where I was.

"Dad!" I shouted, running toward the kitchen. "Dad! We need to call the police right away. I know who—"

I stopped short at the kitchen door. Dad was sprawled across the floor, pale and still, dry pasta scattered around him.

"Dad?"

He didn't respond. My heart fell into my stomach. Tears sprang to my eyes.

"Dad!" I skidded to my knees and shook his shoulder. His body was limp, unresponsive. His pulse nonexistent. "No. Not this. Not now. Please, Dad!"

I reached into my back pocket, but my phone wasn't there. I sprang up and went to the kitchen table, rifled through my purse and duffle.

"Shit," I said as I searched. "Shit, shit, shit!"

Where had I put the damn phone? Throwing the purse on the table, I stepped over Dad's body to get to his landline and dial 911. There was no ringtone.

"You have got to be kidding me!"

I started toward the living room phone, then stopped. Understanding wrapped around my heart in a morbid grip. Dad's collapse was not a coincidence. I was witnessing a murder in progress.

Mitch was here. Right now, in this house.

Maybe I should have gone for the guns right then, but only one thing mattered to me in that moment. I knelt next to Dad, placed my hand on his thinning white hair, felt the last of his warmth fading. Tears stung my eyes. Grief tore a ragged hole through my chest.

Fuck you, Mitch!

How that bastard had killed him, I wasn't sure. I'd

heard nothing. There was no blood. And it had been quick. An injection? Asphyxiation?

Fuck you for killing this beautiful man. I hope there's a hell, and that you're never released from it.

Nathan's true name feathered through my breath. This was a moment to summon his powers. I could demand vengeance for the attack on me, for my father's meaningless death. Nathan would do anything I asked in exchange for the small price of my eternal soul.

Shit. The very thought made me furious. What kind of a choice was this? *Give me your soul or die at the hands of a serial killer?* Fuck that. No. Just no. All deals were off. Nathan had forfeited his rights by allowing things to come to this. If that meant I had to die a horrible death and start all over in the Hunting Grounds, so be it.

A shiver passed through me. *The Hunting Grounds.* I thought of my poor dad's soul right there, right now. Lost and confused. Alone and scared. The Hunting Grounds was nothing like what he'd been taught to expect. What if he got disoriented and never found his way out? What if he went mad and began to fade, like the old man who had scratched my arm?

Gripped by anxiety, I took his hand and held it to my heart.

"Dad," I murmured, closing my eyes. "Dad, can you hear me? Please hear me. Please, let me be with you."

In this way, for the second time, I returned to the Hunting Grounds. Not with my body as I'd done before, but through my spirit. Dark plains unfolded around me, vast and without form. Next to me stood my father, a pale image of his former self.

"Dad?" I said, hoping he would hear.

He started and looked down at me, bewildered. I realized that he did not see me as a full-grown woman, but as the girl that once walked with him through the woodlands of his parents' farm.

"Sweetheart," he said. "What are you doing? You don't belong here."

"I can't stay." I spoke more on instinct than real knowledge. "Dad, listen to me. You have to call on him. Call the one you believe in."

He studied me with a confused and sorrowful gaze. When he spoke, it was in slow tones, as if explaining a difficult truth to a child. "Prayer won't work anymore, sweetheart. He's not here. That's what Hell is—the absence of God."

"No." I shook my head, desperate for him to understand. "You have to listen to me, Dad. This isn't Hell."

"But it is." He extended his arm, indicating the dark formless plains. Ghostly figures began emerging from the mist. Drums sounded in the distance, heralding the hunt. "I knew in my heart this is what it would be, where I would end. I failed us all, sweetheart. I'm so sorry."

"That's not true!"

"The family fell apart." His shoulders were bent, his entire being folding in on itself. "I couldn't hold us together. It all fell apart."

"Oh, Dad!" I took his hands in mine, willed my adult form into his awareness. "Don't you see? We never stopped being a family! We always loved each other, all of us. Just in different ways at different times. And you, you saved Mamá and me! You took us into your home without questions or judgement. You gave us all your love, unconditionally. You were our protecting angel, Dad, and now you're going to the place of rest that you deserve. You only have to believe, Dad. Believe and everything will be okay."

The drums grew louder. Beasts howled in the distance.

"You shouldn't stay, sweetheart," he said. "This is a dangerous place. Not a place for my little girl."

"Dad," I pleaded. "Listen to me. If you would just…" What? What did he need to do? "Sing. Sing, Dad. Sing with all your heart and soul. Like you used to do in Sunday mass. Sing one of your favorite hymns."

He frowned. "Do you promise to go back home if I do?"

"Yes. But you have to hurry. Please."

He drew a phantom breath and began to sing.

"Joyful, joyful, we adore Thee, God of Glory, Lord of Love."

His voice sounded different, trembling and faint, but I recognized the melody and joined in:

Hearts unfold like flowers before Thee,

Praising Thee their sun above.

Fields and flowers, vale and mountain—

A glow broke on the horizon, soft like the rising moon. As we sang, the glow gathered strength and moved toward us, swooping low across the valley with increasing speed. Dad's hold on my hand tightened.

Blooming meadows, flashing sea.

Chanting birds and flowing fountains—

Light seared my vision. In an instant, Dad was gone. No longer bound to his soul, my spirit left the Hunting Grounds and flowed back into my body. I opened my eyes, the last verse fading on my lips, "Call us to rejoice in Thee."

Tears blurred my vision and streamed down my cheeks. Every part of me ached with inconsolable loss. Kissing Dad's hand, I laid it gently next to his lifeless body.

"Be well," I whispered. "Be at peace."

The familiar space of Dad's kitchen solidified around me.

An eddy disturbed the silence. Someone was shifting on their feet.

"How touching," he said without a hint of sarcasm.

My muscles tensed, ready for action, but I kept my eyes fixed on the corpse of my father.

"They'll say it was a stroke or a heart attack," he added, taking a step closer. "No need to do an autopsy."

All my fear and sorrow melted into white-hot rage. Springing to my feet, I grabbed the pot of water from the stove and spun around, intending to hit him. It might've worked if the water had been hot, but Dad hadn't turned on the burner before he died. The pot ricocheted off Mitch's shoulder, soaking him and the floor. I bolted past him down the hallway, toward Dad's office and gun cabinet. The hall seemed to lengthen in front of me. I pushed myself harder. If I could make it to the study and lock the door, I might have time to—

Mitch caught me first. I went down beneath his weight, just short of my goal. The floor hit my chest, knocking the wind out of me. Pain burst across the back of my head. Stars flashed through my vision. A blow like that might have subdued me the first time, but I wasn't going to surrender now. I kicked and flailed. Screamed and caught his gloved fingers with my teeth.

Then something bit me on the neck. I felt a burning sting, followed by cold liquid pumping into my flesh. Shocked by the unfamiliar sensation, I froze. The taste of metal flowed over my tongue. Spots blotted my vision.

Mitch bent close, one knee wedged into my back, breath hot against my ear.

"Don't worry, Mayela," he said as my body went numb. "I'm not finished. Yet."

Then the world vanished inside a mist of terror.

****

Moon River

The landscape that surrounded me seemed etched from a dream, whole but not quite solid. Confused, I leaned over a rail, straining to see. Below, dark waters rippled past a wooden hull. Above, steam billowed from tall stacks atop the vessel on which I stood. Toward the rear, a giant wheel churned the water, pushing the ship forward.

I was on a steamboat.

Why was I on a steamboat?

The last thing I remembered was my father's house, Mitch tackling me, the cold sting on my neck that left my body numb.

How did I get here?

Blue-lined clouds shrouded a full moon. Mist concealed a distant shore. Music rose off the river, bell-like tendrils of sound that wove together in a single, haunting melody. At first the song was indistinguishable from the slow ripple of water against the hull. Then the verse took shape in my mind and tumbled from my lips, the same song that played in Joni's shop the first time Nathan had appeared in my world. "Moon River."

From the front of the boat, a man called out, his voice strong and deep. "Mark one!"

Drawn toward the siren-like tones, I moved in the man's direction. As I approached the stern, a figure came into view. He was diminutive and dressed in a nineteenth-century white suit. His gray hair splayed like a wild bush. A moustache curled thick around his lips. He dropped a knotted chord in the water and let it sink before glancing up at me and tipping his hat.

"Evening, ma'am," he said cordially.

"Good evening." My response came more as a question than a statement.

Looking down, I noticed my dress was also nineteenth-century style—wrapped tight at the waist, with a charcoal skirt gathered into a bustle. Gloves covered my hands. Lace hid my face. I was a woman dressed for mourning.

"What is this place?" I asked.

"The boat," he replied.

"Oh." I pressed my lips together. I could see this was a boat. How to get past the obvious? "Who are you?"

"The line man." He pulled up the chord and cried out, "Mark quarter twain!"

I sucked in my breath. A boat with a line man. Was this it? Was I finally, truly dead?

But if I'd died, why had I landed here and not in the Hunting Grounds?

"You have a verse, miss?" he asked.

"A verse?"

"Every boat has its price. Our price is a verse."

"You mean, like poetry?"

"Yes, ma'am. A couple lines will do just fine."

"I don't read poetry."

"Then we can't have you on the boat, ma'am. If you don't know a verse, Captain'll say you've lived a wasted life. He'll have you thrown overboard. Damned shame, a pretty lady like you, but ain't nothing to be done for it. Captain's the Captain."

I glanced at the river below. A long, sinuous form broke the dark waters and disappeared again. There were monsters in the deep. Perhaps the water itself was a portal to the Hunting Grounds. "Would a song do?"

He frowned. "Captain's keen on poetry. Can't say he's ever accepted a song before. You don't know an ode or a limerick?"

I shook my head.

"Haiku? Anyone can write a Haiku."

"Truly, all I can think of right now is a song."

"Well, sing your song then." He leaned one arm against the rail and set his merry gaze on me. "We'll see if it pleases the Captain."

"Mr. Clemens," a woman interrupted us from behind.

"Miss Anne!" A broad grin broke on the line man's face. He bowed and tipped his hat. "Pleasant surprises all around tonight. How may I help you?"

I turned to see Nathan's Minion of Consequence, the dark-haired beauty Anne, also dressed in late Victorian fashion. Anne had coifed her hair beneath a tilted, feathered hat. She wore a lavender gown that accented her perfect figure. Her small, gloved hands rested on the carved head of a wooden cane.

She wears this style better than I.

I suspected Anne wore many styles better than I.

"This one owes no payment, Mr. Clemens." Anne nodded toward me as she spoke to the line man. "She's not here for the full voyage."

"Oh!" His eyes widened in surprise. He peered at me, as if taking a closer look. "Well, I'll be. I'm sorry, Miss! Usually, I recognize the dream walkers, but you sure look like you belong here. Like you'd come to stay. Please don't hold a grudge. I meant no insult."

"She understands, Mr. Clemens."

"Just doing my job, you know." He threw his line into the water. "You're welcome to wander, Miss. Lower deck is open to visitors, but don't go upstairs unless you have a guide."

"I'm here to serve as her guide," Anne said.

The line man tipped his hat. "I won't be asking any more questions, then. Be on your way."

"Mayela." Anne set her cool gaze on me, beckoning me to follow.

She led me along the side of the boat. Piano music sounded from the interior. Through open doors, I saw people laughing and drinking inside elegant rooms. Some danced, others gambled at tables. Anne and I turned a corner to arrive at a set of gated stairs. Opening a small purse on her belt, she drew out a silver key and unlocked the gate. Then she started up the stairs.

Behind us, I heard the distant call of the line man. "Mark four!"

"Wait," I said.

Anne turned, one brow cocked as if there were little I could say that would be of importance to her right now.

"What is this place?" I asked. "What's going on?"

"This"—she gestured to the boat around us—"is a

liminal space between worlds. One of many paths to the Hunting Grounds, and beyond."

"Why am I here?"

"To meet with Nathan."

"I don't want to meet with Nathan."

"Well." She shrugged. "It was your spirit that cried out for an audience, so here we are. He is anxious to hear what you have to say."

She paused, pursed her lips, then added, "You've made your choice, haven't you?"

"Yes."

"It will not be him."

I frowned. "How do you know?"

"That thread of steel in your voice." She continued up the stairs, compelling me to follow. The gate closed and locked behind us. "You are angry, and you think to punish him by refusing."

"I have good reason to be angry."

"Don't we all."

We turned the corner at the top of the stairs. I did not know where Nathan was or how long I had to interrogate Anne before he appeared. Reaching forward, I took hold of her wrist, finding it surprisingly solid. Anne stopped in her tracks and gave me a startled look.

"What did he do to you that inspired such loyalty?" I demanded.

"I told you." She extricated her wrist from my grasp. "He gave me vengeance against my husband."

"Yes, I remember. The one who had you killed."

"Beheaded. That blind fool."

"Yes, I know. But what was your vengeance?"

"Nathan showed me how to haunt my husband."

As Anne spoke, her voice gathered strength and fury. "Nathan taught me to whisper from the shadows, to place my reflection in panes of glass, to scream inside midnight storms. I dogged Henry for years. I drove him mad with my memory, with fear of his own sins and failures, with the promise of pending damnation. For the rest of his mortal life, he never trusted anyone, never found love, never had a night of peace. And when he died a foul-smelling, pathetic old man, I helped put my daughter on his throne. My daughter, you hear? A woman! The finest regent the mortal realms have ever seen."

The dots connected in my head.

"You're Anne Boleyn." I gasped.

She responded with a self-effacing smile. "Once, a long time ago, there was a foolish child named Anne Boleyn. Then she died and pledged her soul to a strange lord from another world. Now she's just Anne."

Anne began to walk again. I quickened my pace to keep up.

"Someone wants to kill me," I said.

"I know."

"If he succeeds, and even if he doesn't, it won't be enough to haunt him. It won't be nearly enough."

"Then ask Nathan for more."

"I don't trust Nathan."

"Trust takes time. You haven't much of that left."

"But he drove me to this choice! And it's an impossible choice."

"No choice is impossible, and this choice—let me be very clear—is not of his making."

"What do you mean?"

She stopped and met my gaze. "Nathan and his

kind are powerful, but not so powerful as to choose the time and means of our deaths. No, my liege did not create these circumstances, and as much as he wants to, he cannot undo them."

Part of me wanted to believe her, but how could I trust Anne? Any more than I trusted Nathan?

We rounded another corner and came to an open platform. Overhead, a handful of stars broke through wispy clouds. Below, the churning water continued its quiet melody. Nathan stood alone on the deck, facing away from us, looking out over the rail. His dark suit rested well on his broad frame, the old-fashioned jacket flaring at the knees. The sight of him sent my heart into palpitations. Had my spirit really demanded this? If so, I'd made a mistake. How could I say no to a being I so desired?

"Do you ever regret—?" I asked Anne, but she was gone.

The boat creaked beneath my feet, undulating with the flowing river.

No way to go but forward, through the field of swords.

I took a step toward Nathan. He turned around. We froze inside each other's gaze.

"Mayela," he said in a whisper filled with sorrow and longing. "How beautiful you are." Nathan closed the distance between us, reached forward to touch my cheek. "Too beautiful for the world into which you were born."

I took a step back. "I won't forgive you."

"I never intended any of this."

"What did you intend?"

He frowned and glanced away. "For you to live a

happy life; to fulfill your soul's potential in the company of your beloved husband. Yes, I dreamed of claiming you on the Hunting Grounds, of winning your trust and perhaps your heart, but not until after you died in peace, leaving behind a well-aged mortal body to become part of our world."

"Yet here we are." Anger welled inside. "My spirit in this liminal space, and my body at the mercy of that *thing*. You could have warned me. You should have warned me."

"I did."

"When?"

"Many times, in different ways. From the moment I recognized the rot in his soul, I sent whatever signals I could, through small creatures and harsh winds, frightened squirrels and chirping birds. Nausea in your gut. A chill across your heart. That last day on your grandparents' farm, it was I who urged the crows to caw ceaselessly as you walked the trails below. But these warnings were not heard. Our voices are too faint inside the noise of your world."

"You could have told me this week! Last night when we were together. I asked you, Nathan!" I paced, restless with the sting of betrayal. "I asked you if I was in danger. I asked you what propelled me into the Hunting Grounds, and you did not say."

"The covenant of free will—"

"Damn your rules and covenants!"

"I told you what I could before I left. I did. But, Mayela, you were in the strangest state. I begged you to listen to everything I said, but it was as if our lovemaking had drugged you." His hands worked against each other as he spoke. "I did not know what to do, how to help you remember. I am sorry. More than sorry. I know my suffering is inconsequential in all of this, but you must understand—to have such power and yet no power at all! All I want is to protect you, and yet I cannot. Not unless you call on me, Mayela. Grant me the power of intervention. Use my name."

I studied him, my supernatural lover, my guardian, and nemesis. What was I supposed to believe anymore? I felt completely adrift, lost inside the maze that separated our worlds.

"I can't linger here," I murmured, more to myself than to him. "My body needs me."

He caught my face in his hands, his touch reverent and careful, as if guarding a flame against the wind. I could not move, did not want to move, inside the intensity of his embrace. Gently, he lifted off my veil and surrendered it to the breeze. He took the pins from my hair, releasing my dark locks from their confinement. Then he set his lips upon mine. The kiss deepened when I didn't resist. Removing my gloves, I wrapped my arms around his neck and pulled him close, melting into our embrace. Somewhere between our souls, the promise of truth flickered, fragile yet bright, beating back the confusion of his world. Defying the violence that awaited in mine.

Fog flowed over the deck, shrouding the ship. The mist was cold and smelled of death. River, moon, and sky dissolved at its touch. Nathan sobbed as he was wrenched away.

"Live," he commanded, voice hoarse with sorrow. "Choose me, or do not choose me. But *live.*"

Panic took hold as he faded away.

"Wait!" I cried, but Nathan was gone, a wash of

gray inside the spinning night, his true name a distant echo scattering beyond my reach.

Chapter 19

I jolted back to consciousness. My limbs ached; my head felt thick as stone. Nothing covered my eyes and yet the darkness was absolute. Mitch had bound my limbs and taped my mouth shut. The grogginess faded. Sounds came into focus. An odd rumble enveloped me, undercut by an incessant slap below. Cautiously, I explored the space by shifting on my torso. I could not move more than a couple inches without hitting something. What was I in? A box? A coffin?

A trunk. The word formed in my head as I connected sounds and space to machine. Mitch had stuffed me in the trunk of a car while I was unconscious. Now he was driving somewhere, probably well outside of the city.

To finish me off.

My heart went into overdrive. Desperation took hold of me, and I worked my hands and feet against the bindings. Within moments, my wrists and ankles were raw. Frustrated and in pain, I stopped. *This isn't going to work*. He'd used something strong, like duct tape. I couldn't wriggle free of duct tape. Without some sort of cutting tool, I was trapped. And dead. Bloody visions filled my head—bodies abandoned in fields, rotting in the mud, scavenged by wild animals. Tears stung my eyes. My breath flared hot through my nose.

Oh, Nathan!

I wanted to call him. I did. I searched for his true name and felt it crisp upon my tongue. I would have used it, right then and there. Handed my soul over without looking back. But my mouth was taped shut. I couldn't say anything, and thinking the name wasn't enough.

Again, I writhed in the darkness. Blood pounded in my ears. The many ways I might die flashed through my mind.

Then I smelled it: a faint but familiar odor.

I stopped moving and sniffed again. Nail polish remover.

I furrowed my brow in disbelief. Ethyl acetate was inside this trunk. Not much of it, just a faint wisp that suggested…

Forcing my breath to steady, I closed my eyes and reached into the darkness with my senses. A smooth plastic surface bumped against my forehead. The object was squat and cylindrical, a little larger than my fist, with a metal cap.

A kill jar! What was a kill jar doing in Mitch's trunk? Mitch wouldn't have a kill jar in his trunk. Or ethyl acetate. Mitch wouldn't have these things because he didn't collect insects. I did. This was my trunk. He'd put me in my trunk and taken my car. Why?

I shoved the question away. I did not have time to decipher this man's game plan. I needed to figure out a plan of my own. The scent of ethyl acetate had given me a foothold, a spot of light inside the tunnel. Maybe there was something in here I could use.

Mitch had thrown out a lot, but given my cramped state, and the stray kill jar bumping against my head, it was clear he didn't throw out everything. Maybe he'd been in a rush. Maybe he didn't consider a clever entomologist could use her field gear as weaponry.

Squirming again, I searched my surroundings with my body. Every surface—arms, torso, legs—told me something. He'd ditched the bulky items first. The nets were gone, so no pole fighting for me. My large backpack had been removed, as well as the cooler and a box of replacement vials. I squirmed a little more, reaching farther forward and back. If I could just—

The car slowed, pulled over, and stopped.

My heart stalled.

Why was he braking? Had we reached a stoplight? An exit?

Was a cop pulling him over?

Had we arrived at the destination? My blood ran cold. Was this where he planned to kill me? Had he heard me bumping around?

An eternity passed while I remained frozen in silence, every shallow breath a roar inside my ears. I didn't have a chance like this. I did not have a chance. *Please, I need more time*, I prayed. *Please.* At last, the car moved again. We picked up speed, wheels slapping against pavement.

Relieved, I exhaled and continued exploring the trunk, mindful of the noise I might make. My elbow hit a soft lump of canvas.

Oh! I ran my arm along the object. *Oh, could it be? Is that what I think it is?* Yes. I couldn't believe my luck! Mitch had left my fanny pack. Dark, gray, and inconspicuous, it'd been shoved to the back of the trunk. I wanted to weep for joy, but there wasn't time. Carefully, I worked the pack toward my bound hands. I'd had this darling since grad school when they made field gear to last. She'd saved my skin on many occasions. Maybe today she would save my life.

The main pocket didn't contain much—my field notebook, pencils, flagging, a couple extra vials, my hand lenses. But in the small side pocket that I now unzipped, I had a pocketknife. Not a solid hunting knife like every proud Missourian should own, but a travel knife, about as big as my thumb. Somewhere along the way, I'd picked up this Swiss relic. I always carried it in the field. It had a toothpick, scissors, a nail file, and one very sharp blade.

Carefully, I extracted the pocketknife from my fanny pack, terrified of dropping the instrument and never finding it again. I ran my fingertips along the edges. I'd never opened this thing in the dark, much less behind my back. Which blade was the knife? I decided to try the edge with the biggest bulge. Jostled by the moving car, I pulled the edge out, worried the next bump might leave my fingers a bloody mess. It snapped into place. Success! With the blade exposed, I turned the handle in my bound wrists and started sawing at the tape. My cuts were small and awkward, but effective. The bonds loosened, then broke.

Praise the Lord! I could move my arms. Exhilarated, I ripped the tape off my mouth. *Fuck!* Wow, that hurt. Though not any worse than a standard wax. Quickly, I felt down my legs and cut the tape around my ankles. Then I closed the blade and secured it in my pocket. I had a lot in my pockets by now—the rosary, Dad's key, my knife. The shungite had disappeared, probably knocked out when Mitch tackled me in the hallway.

The car slowed again.

I tensed, fear clawing inside my chest. I was in a better position than I'd been ten minutes ago, but my muscles were cramped and sore, and my tiny knife not much to fight with. What was I going to do when we arrived and he opened the trunk?

We made a sharp turn. Wheels crunched over gravel. Rough jolts tossed items around the trunk, bruising my already sore body. I tried to brace myself, thanking my lucky stars I'd finished cutting my bonds and put the knife away before we hit this stretch.

A metal cylinder rolled against my knee. My hand shot out, catching the object before it escaped. Clutching the cannister to my chest, I felt it up and down, certain I'd found something important. An acrid smell emanated from the plastic cap, stinging my senses.

Tick repellent.

I had a half-used can of tick repellent. For the first time since I'd regained consciousness, I drew a proper breath. *I have a half-used can of tick repellent.* And with it, I had a plan. A crazy plan, but a decent plan. One that might save my life without having to sacrifice my soul.

The ride continued, interminable and bumpy. I cradled my tick repellent like a baby in my arms. At last, the car slowed then pulled to a stop. The engine sputtered and died. Deadly silence followed. My breath, though shallow, filled the space like low thunder.

The driver's side door opened and slammed shut.

My heart kicked into gear.

Footsteps sounded against gravel, rounding the side of the car, approaching the trunk.

This is it, Mayela, I told myself. *No fear. No*

hesitation. No mercy.

The latch clicked, and the trunk was flung open. I sat up and leaned into the blinding light, raising one hand in self-defense. “Mitch! Please. Don’t do this.”

“Shit!” he said.

That was all I needed. My eyes adjusted to the light, his silhouette coming into focus just as he reached toward me. Raising the tick repellent, I sprayed hard and long. Noxious aerosol hit him square in the face.

“What the—?” He lurched back, fists going to his nose, then to his eyes. He started to scream.

I scrambled out of the trunk. My legs, still stiff, slipped on the metal rim. I tumbled to the ground in an awkward heap. Gravel burnt my skin on impact. Dizzy and nauseous, I pushed myself to my feet. Mitch lunged at me. I sprayed him again.

“Bitch!” His eyes were shut tight as he stumbled in my direction. His arms flailed in front of him. I thought for sure I’d blinded him, but again, he lunged, hitting my hand with frightening accuracy. Pain shot through my wrist and elbow. The repellent, knocked from my grasp, flew out of reach into the shadows. Trusting my feet more than the knife in my pocket, I turned and ran.

Ahead of me loomed a ramshackle house with a sagging roof and boarded-up windows. Veering away from its ominous face, I plunged into the brush that lined the gravel drive. Shoulder-high grass slowed my advance, giving way to woody growth that tore at my clothes. Not far away, trees reached toward the starry night. I charged into their midst and dove, landing next to a tall tree and going still as a fawn beneath its arching limbs.

For several minutes, I heard nothing but my own

labored breath. A breeze rustled through leaves overhead. My palms burned with the sting of earth and gravel. My pulse slowed. I peered over the grass, taking stock of my surroundings. To my right, the car lights glinted, masked by the brush. On my left, the decaying house stared into the night like a gray-faced ghoul waiting patiently to be fed. A single bulb shed weak yellow light across the decrepit porch. Inside, everything was dark.

"Shit!" Mitch cursed to my right. "Fucking bitch!"

He came into view, meandering along the driveway toward the house, one hand covering his eyes, the other arm outstretched. Had I blinded him or not? I sure hoped so. If I had, he knew the terrain well enough to find his way to the steps and the front door. Fumbling in his pocket, he extracted a set of keys and let himself in. A light went on in the front room.

I picked myself up off the ground and crouched next to the tree. Aromas of night forest soothed my senses—loam and bark; moss and leaves; a soft, earthy mix that masked the smell of my fear.

What was he doing? Flushing poison out of his eyes? If that worked, he'd come after me again. Armed and ready, in no mood for pleasantries. Should I stay hidden or run? Run where?

Truth was, I felt safe in this spot. As a biologist, I knew all a fawn had to do to elude a predator was to sit still. I could sit still in a dark forest. All night if necessary. But once day broke? What then?

I glanced toward the car. My car. Fuck him for that. Fuck him for killing my dad, for knocking me out, and for kidnapping me in my own goddam car. Any chance he'd left my keys in the ignition? My phone on the front seat, maybe? He'd been careless about the fanny pack and the tick repellent. Out here, he'd be even more careless than he was at my dad's, less likely to take precautions on his own territory.

I took the knife out of my pocket and exposed the small blade. Steeling my nerves, I rose. I had to check the car. If I didn't, I might miss my best chance of escape.

I tried to avoid making noise as I pushed through the wild growth, but I was not light-footed like a deer or a lynx. From inside the house, I could hear his curses and shouts. I hoped that meant he wasn't paying attention. For now. Breaking free of the tall grass, I crouched and scurried across the gravel, keeping to the shadows as I approached the car.

The trunk was still open. Not good to drive off like that, but I decided against slamming the lid shut. Better to keep quiet. The door on the driver's side was unlocked, the window rolled down. I slipped inside. Knife in hand, I searched the interior. The keys were not in the ignition or behind the visor. The passenger seat and glove compartment were empty. Beneath the seats, nothing. My heart sank. If my keys weren't here, that meant they were on him or in the—

"Fucking bitch!" Mitch roared into my space and dragged me from the driver's seat.

He flung me against the car outside. Stars shot through my vision. Stunned and disoriented, I lifted an arm to shield myself. Mitch batted it away and pinned me, wrapping his fists around my throat. My esophagus revolted; my lungs lurched in panic. My fingers scrabbled against his thick digits, trying in vain to loosen his hold.

"I was going to take my time with you," he sneered. "Have some nice conversation and give you special treatment. But now, I just want you to die."

Mitch's face loomed large and distorted. His eyes were swollen shut, yet he seemed to stare straight at me, a pair of yellow orbs hovering over reddened, blistered lids. My air passage was giving way beneath the pressure, cartilage buckling in his vise-like grip. My lungs burned and screamed. Reaching forward with one arm, I found his throat and dug my fingernails into his Adam's apple.

Mitch chuckled, tongue flicking like a serpent between his lips. "Trying to choke me, Mayela? It's not going to work."

Spots blotted my vision, but I was not scared. I'd felt the shadow of death before. Hell, I'd died and come back to life.

"The one thing I want to know," he growled, "is how did you do it? How did you get away the first time? Not that I'm going to give you another chance."

My blood cried out for oxygen. I dug my nails deeper into his flesh, feeling for his pulse with the pads of my fingers.

"That all you got, little bitch? It's not enough."

Found it. Lifting my other hand, I drove the pocketknife straight into his carotid; a location I knew well, after all those semesters teaching anatomy and physiology. Mitch's face twisted in horror and surprise. Dragging the blade down his throat, I ripped open the artery. Blood sprayed hot in my face. Mitch faltered and let go. I hit the ground hard, sucking in gulps of precious air. Mitch fell to his knees clutching the gaping wound in his neck. He keeled over, shuddered in a fit of gurgling gasps, and then went still, sprawled across the gravel.

I dragged myself to my feet. Every breath burned in my throat. Hands trembling, I went to him, bent over, and finished hacking open his esophagus with my little knife. Then I opened the other artery.

"Just to be sure," I growled. I prayed he could hear me, that he knew he was about to die, and that he understood I had killed him. I hoped the last thing he felt when he left this world was fear.

Stepping back, I watched while the life faded from his body. Blood spread in a dark stain through his shirt and pooled wet on the ground beneath him. His fingers trembled, a shudder that traveled up his arms and overtook his whole body. Then Mitch went entirely limp, the violence of his final moments giving way to the peaceful, starry night.

I sagged against the car. My breath came in ragged gasps. My throat ached, my body burned with bruises, and my fists were sticky with blood. Though I had no more need for a blade, my hand gripped the knife and would not let go. Wild emotions surged inside my breast. I'd done it! I'd killed Mitch and saved myself. On my own, without Nathan's help, without the need to surrender my soul.

I pushed away from the car and tried to steady myself on my feet. *My soul is safe.*

But was it?

Mitch lay splayed across the gravel, bearing witness to a grim truth. I had killed a man. The aftertaste of his death took hold, spreading through me in bitter waves. I remembered the satisfaction I'd felt hacking open his throat. What would that cost me?

What had it cost me, already? How long would the stain of this act adhere to my spirit? How long would Mitch's shadow follow me after tonight?

"Oh, Nathan," I whispered.

But Nathan was not here. Instinct told me this marked the end of our negotiation. I'd made my choice; I refused to call his name or surrender my soul, even in the face of this horror.

A shiver ran through me, followed by sudden and terrible emptiness. Losing Nathan, I realized, would be like losing a part of myself. But this was how it had to be. This was what I wanted.

Wasn't it?

Live, he'd said. *Choose me or don't choose me, but live.* That's what I'd done.

"I'm sorry, Nathan," I whispered. "I hope you understand."

Kneeling near Mitch, I wiped my blade on his jeans. His soul would be on the Hunting Grounds by now. It gave me morbid pleasure to imagine him paralyzed by fear and pursued by monsters. I hoped something vile snatched him up. I hoped the Soul Masters would terrify and torture him for the rest of eternity.

"Good-bye, Mitch. And good riddance."

Straightening, I glanced around. Time to find a way out of here. I still didn't have the keys to the car. They might be in the house or on Mitch's person. I didn't want to search either. Reluctantly, I decided to start with Mitch. His corpse was stiff and heavy. It sickened me to touch him. I had to turn him over before finding keys in one of his back pockets. *Damn.* They weren't mine. The rest of his pockets were empty. So, I left Mitch where he lay and went to the house.

Boards creaked beneath my feet on the front porch. Rusted hinges squeaked when I opened the door. The furnishing in the front room was sparse—a metal desk against the wall, a worn couch, a small foldout table near the kitchenette. An overhead bulb illuminated the interior in faint, yellow light. The air smelled of wood rot, mold, and chlorine; of plastic and metal and blood-drenched deaths. In front of me stood a bolted door. Behind it lay a basement, maybe, or a reinforced room. Terror seeped out from around the door's edges and settled inside my stomach. *That's where he kept them.* That was where the others had spent their last days. Maybe that's where I had been, confined to a metal cage in the brief moments before I entered the Hunting Grounds.

The weight of every life he'd snuffed out came crashing down on my shoulders. Doubling over, I retched on the worn carpet. I wanted to collapse into sobs, but I couldn't. My heart was beating fast inside my ribcage, a ticking clock that warned me time was of the essence. I couldn't let myself mourn. Not here. Not now. I had to get out first, get as far away from this place as possible.

Placing one hand on the wall, I drew a sharp breath and steadied my balance.

My keys. Where would he have put my keys?

He would've entered here blind and in pain, anxious to rinse the poison out of his eyes. I couldn't imagine him carefully guarding the keys in a drawer or hanging them on a hook in such circumstances. No, he would've set them on a known surface or dropped them on the floor.

God help me if he dropped them outside. I'd be searching all night.

I went to the kitchen first; checked the sink, the floor, the table, and the countertops along the way. The sink was dry; my keys nowhere to be seen. He must've gone to the bathroom instead to try to clean up.

I glanced at the open door to the bathroom, a short yet interminable distance from where I stood. I hated this. The longer I stayed, the creepier it felt, as if the house could trap me of its own volition. I wasn't sure if Mitch had brought me this far the last time. I couldn't remember the exact moment or place of my escape, only that I'd been trapped in the dark and managed to get away. Even so, this run-down house was hauntingly familiar, as if it'd been part of my dreams and nightmares long before any of this began.

Taking a deep breath, I crossed the room, passing the metal desk along the way. He'd left photos scattered on the surface, all of them black and white. I recognized some of the women's faces. They were the same women Vicky Arevalo showed me in Joni's coffee shop. Only here, they did not smile. Mitch had caught them on film dead or dying, their faces contorted with fear and grief. The chilling solitude of their last moments washed over me, and a deep-seated rage surged inside my breast.

I could burn this place down. There was probably gasoline in the house and matches somewhere. I could send the whole thing up in smoke and watch it blaze to high heaven. But purging Mitch's den would also destroy evidence needed to put Agent Arevalo's case to rest. To give some closure to the families of these women, I had to leave this accursed house intact.

And I might need this, too, I realized. I'd just murdered a man, in a brutal and bloody fashion. There could be court days ahead of me, a plea of self-defense that would require proof I was here against my will, evidence I wasn't a spurned lover who had somehow "asked" for this. It was best to leave everything in place.

Turning away from the photos, I continued to the bathroom. At the entrance, I spotted my keys on the floor. I scooped them up and held them to my heart. Joy swept through me. Honest, pure joy of a sort I hadn't experienced in years. Strange to feel like dancing in this awful place, but I couldn't help it. I spun back to the front entrance, bloody knife in one hand and car keys in the other. I skipped off the sagging porch and started trotting toward the car. Laughter escaped my lips. Fresh air filled my lungs, crisp and calm.

Nothing could hurt me now. I was alive and on my way home.

Chapter 20

Mitch's body was where I'd left it, sprawled and still beside my car. Stepping gingerly around him, I opened the driver's door and tossed my knife on the passenger seat. Then I paused for one last look. A handful of late-season crickets gave music to the night. From somewhere inside the forest, a barred owl hooted. Overhead, the Milky Way stretched in a sparkling veil of stars against the beautiful black sky.

"Thank you," I whispered. "Thank you for giving me one more day. Please, let the others who were here before me find peace."

I got into the car and put the keys in the ignition. The gauges flickered on. The car started without protest. My old reliable sedan! I put the car into gear, only to be stopped by a loud pop and a long, harsh hiss.

Oh no. I braked, turned off the car, let my head sink onto the steering wheel. A flat tire? Now?

Leaving my keys in place, I got out of the car, slammed the door, and raised my fist to the heavens. "That's your response? Seriously? After everything I've been through, you blow out one of my tires?"

I mean, really. Enough was enough.

"Well, I've got news for you," I told the heavens. "I have a spare. I always had a spare. And I'm a helluva lot better at changing tires than at killing people."

The flat wasn't on the driver's side, so I went to the

passenger side to check the tires there. Oddly, they looked fine.

"Huh." I kicked them both to make sure. Another pop sounded, followed by a long sustained hiss. I realized the sounds weren't coming from my car. They emanated from the driver's side of the vehicle, in the vicinity of…

Mitch's body?

Wary, I crept back around to the driver's side. Mitch came into view, still splayed but no longer immobile. His corpse twitched and convulsed. Welts formed over his skin, growing into pustules that swelled and burst. Finger-like tendrils of flesh snaked out of the open blisters. I watched, frozen in horror, as tentacles emerged from every orifice—his ears and nostrils, his mouth, even the gashes I'd left on his throat.

"Oh, my God." I gasped.

Serpentine flesh spilled from Mitch's body and pooled into a shapeless mass, right next to my car.

"Shit!" I sprang into action, jumping over the fibrous mass and into the driver's seat. Closing and locking the door, I fumbled with the ignition while rolling up the window. Outside, the creature's body grew. I saw no discernable head or tail, no eyes, ears, or mouth. Just an expanding tangle of white flesh.

The car started, thank God. I gunned the engine. With an ear-piercing shriek, the monster shot a net of sticky tentacles across my windshield. The car lurched forward, then stopped. Wheels spun against gravel. Again, I slammed on the gas. The wheels strained and squealed. A smell of burning rubber filled the cabin. That thing had taken hold of my car!

"Shit!" I took my foot off the gas and hit the

steering wheel with my fist. "Shit, shit, shit!"

What was this thing? Where did it come from? What did it want?

The answer to all three questions landed like lead in my gut: This was the next contender, making his bid for my soul. My breath turned icy. Nathan had warned me. If I didn't choose him, another of his kind would have their chance. This tentacled demon was next in line, and it was not inclined to bother with a pretty face.

Again, I gunned the engine. Again, the wheels spun in place.

"No!" I couldn't fail. Not now. I glanced around the car. Tentacles extended over every window, but the doors were locked. All of them. That would help, right? Car doors were airtight. As long as they were shut and locked, tentacled demon thing couldn't get in. I'd hold out until dawn if I had to. Maybe the rising sun would burn it to a crisp.

A hiss sounded next to my shoulder. At the edge of the driver's door, just above the window, a thin strand of flesh appeared. Within moments, a mycelial network had spread around the doorframe. The hyphae pulsed and grew, extending over the door and into the air, reaching toward me. Desperate, I snatched the rosary out of my pocket. *Whatever works, right?* I plunged the metal cross into the squirming threads. They retracted, then sprang forward, wrapping around my hand and trapping my fingers inside a stinging web.

"Ow! Dammit!"

My dominant hand was immobilized. I twisted to grab my knife, still on the passenger seat, with my other hand. I began sawing through the tentacles, my cuts awkward and unsteady. Strands fell away, squirming, as

I hacked through them. More mycelia reached toward me.

"Come on!" I cut faster. At last, I broke free and scrambled into the back seat. There, I remained huddled in fear, cradling my seared hand against my chest. Tears stung my eyes. My skin burned icy hot, but I could still move my fingers. Hyphae were seeping through the edges around all the doors. Outside, tentacles flowed in a thick, gelatinous mass over the windows, cutting off my view.

Time slowed. The vehicle rocked as if drifting on an open sea. I heard my car groan beneath the faint hiss of demon flesh and the labored rhythm of my own breath. I considered this moment and everything that had come before it. Each step that had brought me here replayed in my mind—the whole, extraordinary journey of fear, confusion, mystery, and desire. All of that about to culminate with me being consumed by some mindless tentacled beast.

I pondered the one choice I could still make, and decided I had nothing left to lose.

Closing my eyes, I released Nathan's true name from my lips. Three times I called him. Statement of intention, reaffirmation, sealing of intent. In exchange for his help, I promised my soul, my body, my loyalty, my service. Whatever he asked for, I would give it. For all eternity if need be.

"Just do this," I murmured. "I don't care anymore. Do it."

I opened my eyes. The car continued to rock. Tentacles accumulated inside the cabin, hissing, thickening, stretching toward me. Frightened, I blinked back tears, feeling cold and small and terribly alone.

Where was he? Nothing had changed, despite my invocation. With a sinking spirit, I realized nothing would. I had waited too long and missed my chance. The negotiation period must have ended when I killed Mitch. That thing wouldn't be here if Nathan were still an option. Those were the rules. And Soul Masters always followed their rules.

Exhaustion and resignation set in. Hugging my knees against my chest, I began to cry. All my efforts to think this through, to fight back, to make the right choices. What good had any of that done? I'd given my best trying to find a way out of this horror, yet here I was, with blood on my hands and a giant tentacled beast about to swallow me whole.

The worst part was I loved Nathan. I did. Maybe from the moment he walked into Joni's shop. Maybe from the dreams I had had, long before all this began. But I could never see how it was supposed to work, me loving a creature who owned my soul. And I was right about that. It wouldn't have worked. Love only thrives between equals. If there was one thing I'd learned by middle age, it was this—*Love only thrives between equals*. So, it was better this way, him with his artists and revolutionaries and me with tentacled demon thing. Because how could I bear an eternity with a man I wanted to love but could not?

A violent jolt shook the car. I looked up through tear-blurred eyes. Otherworldly flesh still covered the windows. Dozens of pulsing tentacles inched toward me. Metal creaked and groaned under the strain. At any moment, this entire structure was going to collapse.

The car jolted again, lifting off the ground and hitting the earth.

"Idiot!" I shouted, angry. "You can't shake me out of here. You're just going to have to keep squeezing 'til it breaks."

The monster let go a blood-curdling screech. The car rose and hit the ground once more.

"Yeah, well," I muttered. "Fuck you, too."

A low roar rumbled through the floor. Everything went still. I held my breath, sensing inside the charged air that something important had just happened.

Did Nathan come after all?

Getting on my knees, I tried to see through the obstructed windows. Fire flashed across my vision. Thin blue flames slashed like claws through the mass of flesh outside, leaving scratch marks against the window. Dozens of tentacles inside the cabin went gray and withered. The tentacled monster screamed. Again, the blue flames struck, cutting through flesh and scoring the glass. More tentacles fell and shriveled. A narrow break in the white flesh covering my windows appeared. I scooched closer and peered outside.

The shadow of a leg wide as a trunk passed by my window, followed by a pair of feathered wings. Two broad limbs tipped by blue-flamed claws dug into the white mass of flesh and heaved. The demon howled as it was dragged off my vehicle. Tentacles that did not let go shredded and tore. I watched, riveted, as the creature was hurled toward the far side of the clearing. The ground shuddered when it landed in a formless heap.

Broken tentacles slid from my car. I could see the creature's rival now, though night obscured the details. Its predatory eyes glowed sapphire-cold. The head was hawk-like, somewhat compressed, with a long, sharp beak. Behind the feathered head, a long mane flowed down its neck in thick, twisted tresses. It had cat-like hindquarters, yet its forelimbs were feathered with talons. The creature also bore a pair of large, feathered wings. Talons, claws, and wings were tipped with violet-blue flames, the same sapphire color as the eyes. I recalled the name *griffon* from stories of my childhood, and thought this might be one, though I didn't recall that griffons were able to rear up on their hind legs.

Hope ignited in my heart. Nathan hadn't come, but there was a third contender. If this griffon thing won, maybe that wouldn't be so bad. Griffons had style. I'd take flame-tipped wings any day over worm-like tentacles.

"Mayela!" Someone shouted my name and pounded on the window behind me.

I jumped and spun around so fast, I put a crick in my neck. "Ow! Shit." With a gasp of surprise, I recognized the woman calling me.

"Anne?" I asked, rubbing my sore neck.

"What are you doing?" Her frantic voice was muffled by the closed window and locked door. "We need to get out of here!"

"Oh. Yeah." I clambered across the seat and let myself out on her side.

"I thought you'd never hear me." Anne took my elbow and dragged me away. "Come on!"

I stumbled, caught my balance, and then hastened to keep up with Nathan's number one minion. Anne was walking fast away from my car and toward the forest. She had dressed in fatigues, complete with a wide utility belt that accented her toned figure. A black beret was tilted just-so over her dark hair, combed back into a perfect bun at the nape of her neck. Apparently, Anne could make even battle gear look runway ready. The semi-automatic rifle strapped to her shoulder seemed as much a fashion accessory as any designer bag.

"This is a clever strategy." Annoyance crept into my tone as I ran to keep up. "Nathan sending you to get me on the sly, while winged beast and tentacled demon-thing are occupied with each other." When she didn't reply, I added, "You'd think he'd do the honors himself after all that fuss about the 'shimmering brilliance of my soul.' But whatever works, right?"

Anne stopped. I bumped into her. She gave me a withering stare. "That is not what is happening here."

In an instant, I understood. My heart leapt into my throat.

"Nathan," I whispered, looking back at the griffon.

"Yes, that's him," Anne snapped. "In a very bad mood, I might add." The ground lurched beneath us. Anne took my hand and pulled. "Let's go!"

I sprinted beside her. "What's that other thing?"

"His rival."

"I know that's his rival!" I grabbed Anne's arm, forcing her to stop. "But what is it?"

She hesitated, the uncertainty in her expression bordering on fear. Behind us, the tentacled mass was expanding in size, rising to the griffon's height. A bulbous head emerged over pillar-like tentacles that appeared to serve as legs. On the head, eyes began to pop out of white flesh, dozens at a time; pale yellow orbs that blinked as they focused on Nathan.

"See how it struggles to find shape?" Anne murmured. "That's one of the Unformed. They are considered outcasts among Nathan's kind. This one should have been destroyed long ago while it was still weak. Now it can only be contained."

The beast extended an array of tentacles, from which emerged spear-like points.

"Doesn't look like they're doing a good job of containing it," I observed.

"Who are you going to take that up with?" Anne shot back. "Management?"

I shrugged. "Just saying."

Thunder sounded overhead. Wind drove hard across the grass, roaring past us toward Nathan and the Unformed. Anne grabbed my hand, urging me to run again. The ground shifted beneath our feet, tilting upward and impeding our progress. Anne led me through the brush toward the woodland where I'd hidden earlier. When we reached the trees, she jumped, caught a low limb, and hauled herself up. Then she reached down to help me.

"But I don't understand." I clambered up to her side, breathless. "Why are they going to fight? There's no reason to fight! I made my choice, didn't I?"

"That's the dispute." Anne moved higher, settling in a crook between a broad branch and the trunk. "The Unformed One claims you had already refused Nathan when he appeared. Souls that have crossed the threshold are not allowed to recant a decision simply because we don't like the next option."

"The rules," I muttered. "The goddam rules."

"Nathan claims the bargaining period had not yet ended, and that his rival came after you too soon. Arbitration has not been forthcoming, so they will settle with a fight."

The wind gathered strength, swirling into a vortex that separated them from us. Where we were, the air was still and heavy. Inside the vortex, gusts buffeted plants, raising dust and debris. Nathan crouched on all fours, circling his rival. Tentacles spread like a fan around the bulbous head, ready to attack the griffon.

"This is wrong," I said. "I made my choice. My will should be respected."

"What do you suggest we do?" Anne replied, peering down at me from her perch. "If they didn't answer Nathan's call for arbitration, they certainly won't answer yours."

I nodded at the gun strapped to her shoulder. "Can't you shoot its eyes out, or something?"

"What, with this?" She shook her head. "A gun won't do any good. Not against them."

"Then why'd you bring it?"

"I needed something to complete the outfit."

Nathan and the demon hurtled toward each other. The impact exploded across the field, sending shock waves through the vortex and into the forest. I nearly lost my balance while the tree swayed and groaned.

"This is not going to end well," I said.

Anne did not respond. Her gaze was fixed on the contest.

Inside the vortex, shafts of lightning cut through clouds and dust, revealing a violent dance in broken sequence. Black wings were ensnared by tentacles. Fiery blue claws slashed through nets of flesh. Ivory cords sprang back, entangling limbs again. One creature, then the other, was thrown to the ground, each blow causing another tremor.

"How long will they keep this up?" I asked.

Again, Anne did not respond.

Troubled by her uncharacteristic silence, I climbed up to sit by her side. Her face was awash with fear. That scared me, almost more than anything else I'd experienced tonight. I hadn't, until this moment, imagined Anne as someone who could experience fear.

"What is it?" I whispered.

"Something's wrong. They don't…" Anne stopped, frowned, and shook her head.

"Don't what?"

"Hurt each other. Disputes are settled by what mortals might call first blood. They never fight like this, as if they intend to kill."

The dust cleared. Nathan and the demon had broken their grapple and now circled each other once more. Nathan favored one of his legs. A broken wing hung limp from his back. Tentacles littered the battlefield, but what had been cut off was regenerating from the bulbous head of that monster.

"They can kill each other?" I asked.

"Yes, but they don't. I mean, they haven't. Not in a long time."

"How is that possible?" I demanded, aghast. "What does it even mean, to kill an immortal? I thought the very definition of immortal is that you can't be killed!"

She bit her lip and looked away.

"What would happen to you and his other souls?" I insisted. "What will happen to me if Nathan doesn't survive?"

The demon let go an ear-piercing shriek and vomited a mass of tentacles from its mouth. Fleshy ropes whipped around Nathan's head and torso, trapping his wings and limbs.

"This is not happening." I started down the tree.

"No!" Anne caught me, halting my descent. "Don't you see? There's nothing we can do!"

"What do you mean, there's nothing we can do?"

"We're part of their realms now, don't you see? We belong to them. They settle their disputes between them, and we can only…" She stopped, her expression caught between terror and defeat. "We can only do as they say."

"Oh, Anne." I flung my arms around her in a tight embrace. "Trust me. I've got a plan."

With that, I dropped to the ground and ran toward the vortex. In truth, I had no idea what I was doing. Anne called after me. I ignored her distraught pleas. Driven by instinct and the shadow of a memory, I hurtled toward my would-be guardian and his rival. The ground grew steeper as I approached. The storm seemed to suck the earth toward its center.

I skidded to a stop in front of the wall of wind and crouched. The air was heavy and still around me, the pressure on my chest unbearable. Streams of dust and debris obscured my vision, separating me from Nathan and the Unformed.

Inside the vortex, Nathan was pinned to the ground. Tentacled limbs tightened around him like a hoard of boa constrictors. The demon loomed over him, yellow eyes blinking in triumph. A massive cord of flesh encircled Nathan's throat. He could not breathe, I realized. He needed to breathe, and he could not. Still, he resisted, snapping with his beak and slashing with claws, each strike coming weaker than the last.

I inched forward. The vortex whipped my face with pinprick stings. I had to get to him but crossing the wall of wind would be my death. The violent gusts would fling me away and tear me apart like a bag of dry leaves.

There's nothing we can do.

Was Anne right? Was I powerless to stop this? Yet I'd made it this far, to the edge of the storm, and this scene was palpably familiar, as if it were meant to be. As if I'd prepared for this moment long ago. *On the edge of a storm.*

At last, the memory blossomed full in my mind. I was a child on the playground, my mother at my side, a shadow behind. *This is the best time,* he'd said, and I had listened. I'd taken all that potentiality *on the edge of the storm* and woven a vision of prairie. Ever since I'd thought it'd been my imagination at work, but maybe it wasn't. Maybe that experience was more than child's play. Maybe I could weave something here as well. Something real.

Mayela! Nathan's anguished cry echoed through my heart.

I snapped back to the present. Nathan lay trapped beneath a writhing net of white flesh. His strength was spent, his fading sapphire gaze fixed on me. I felt his sorrow and heartbreak, the burning pain inside his lungs. Resignation filled his spirit. The glow in his eyes receded.

"No!" I cried and plunged my fists into the earth.

The dark soil responded, wrapping around my hands. Feather-light roots and tiny mycelia tickled my fingertips. Life retracted, then sprang forward, holding me tight and pulling my awareness into the earth.

We became one of being and of mind. Together with my allies, I tunneled through clay and loam, beneath the edge of the vortex, toward the tentacled monster. Though my body was anchored in place, my mind led the charge as we burst from the ground, an army of woody vines and toxic mycelia. Poisoned brambles engulfed the tentacled beast. Thorns poked at its eyes and sank into otherworldly flesh. Screaming, the tentacled monster thrashed and heaved, enraged by this new enemy. Then it stopped and caught sight of my earthly form crouched on the other side of the vortex.

Everything changed at once. Splintering the thorny branches, the tentacled beast barreled toward me. Terrified, my spirit plunged back into my body. I tried to pull my hands out of the ground and run, but the roots held me fast. I could not move. With a furious roar, the demon shot tentacles across the wall of wind, catching me in a sticky web. Ropes of flesh slid over my mouth and nose, then around my throat, cutting off my breath. Beneath the ground, the roots shuddered and fell away from my grip. My hands came free. I grasped at tentacles covering my face, only to have my arms immobilized by more.

Then Anne was next to me, cutting furiously through ribbons of flesh, becoming ensnared herself. Spots began to blight my vision. I was losing touch with this world, with all worlds, even theirs.

This thing doesn't want my soul, I realized. *It wants me destroyed!*

Blue flames seared my vision. The grip on my throat faltered. My lungs dragged in a sliver of air, and my vision cleared.

I saw Nathan's talons in front of me. Giant sapphire-tipped claws protruded from the demon's many-eyed head. With a violent sweep, the talons parted, rending the beast in two.

The tentacles that held me curled away and turned to dust. Behind the curtain of wind, the demon's mutilated head melted into the ground.

Ragged and spent, the griffon watched as the remains of his opponent disappeared. Then he staggered and fell, still as death against the windswept earth.

Chapter 21

I curled onto the grass in a fetal position, shaking uncontrollably. Anne gathered me in her arms, murmuring words that were garbled in my ears. She wrapped something around me. Gripping the crumply fabric, I realized it was a thermal blanket.

"You th-think of everything," I managed through chattering teeth.

"Not everything." She held me tight. "Next time, I'll bring something fit to slay a god, if I can find such a weapon. And if the gods let me have it."

"There won't b-be a n-next time."

Her brow furrowed as she watched the fading vortex. The wind was dissipating quickly, leaving little more than scattered leaves in its wake.

"This doesn't feel like the end," she said.

I caught sight of the griffon, sprawled on the ground a few yards away. He lay still. Too still. My heart contracted.

"Nathan." I tried to get up, but my limbs were weak and uncooperative.

Anne pulled me back into her embrace. "He needs time, as do you."

Her touch felt different from Nathan's. Warm and strong, but not so finely wrought. She had no scent, and when she spoke, I could not feel her breath.

"What was that?" she asked.

I shuddered and pulled the blanket tighter around my shoulders.

"What you did just now, with your hands in the ground," Anne insisted. "And the plants, the way they responded. What was that?"

Slipping my hands out from inside the blanket, I examined them front and back. My flesh was, thankfully, whole. No twigs or roots or random mycelia sticking out anywhere. I suspected it had not been the wisest move to invoke my untried and untrained powers, but desperate times required desperate measures. At least I'd survived. Hopefully, I hadn't given myself a fungal infection.

"Did Nathan see me?" I asked.

Anne glanced away. I could see how shaken she was, though I couldn't tell what had so unsettled her—my power or Nathan's near defeat.

"I don't know when he regained consciousness." Her voice was hoarse. "I was too busy trying to help you."

"Of course." I laid a hand on her arm. "Thank you."

She blinked and nodded. It occurred to me Anne couldn't cry in this form, and that she would be crying now, if she could.

"Nathan doesn't know about your power?" she asked.

"No. At least, I hope not. He can't know, Anne. None of them can know until…" Until when? Mamá had said until I understood their world, but when would I ever understand all of this? "Please don't tell him."

Anne pressed her lips together as she considered my request.

"You have a friend in me, Mayela," she decided. "But for that reason, I must also tell you: It is not wise to keep secrets from them. Their wrath can be fierce."

"Yeah." I nodded. "Think I saw a little of that tonight."

"He will not learn this secret from me, but you must tell him. Soon."

I pulled away from her embrace. My vision had cleared, and sensations of night were returning. Soft grass beneath me, a gentle breeze against my face, crickets chirping as if nothing had happened that might disturb their song. The vortex had vanished, leaving no trace of its existence on the land.

Nathan moaned.

Anne got to her feet and offered me a hand. "Come."

The griffon was gone, replaced by Nathan's semi-conscious human form. He clung to the earth, prone and naked, beautiful though lacerated from the battle. Anne knelt next to him and touched his shoulder, gently urging him to wake. I hung back, anxious for Nathan's wellbeing, yet subdued by the grim knowledge this creature now owned my soul. We had entered a new reality, where the romantic fantasies I'd once entertained would be left behind.

"Do you still need that?" Anne nodded to the blanket around my shoulders.

"No."

I took off the thermal blanket and gave it to her. As she wrapped it around Nathan, he sat up crossed-legged, rubbing his head with his hands. His eyes were shut. I could tell he was groggy and disoriented, much as I had been in the moments after I stopped invoking my powers.

Opening her backpack, Anne produced a small bundle of clothes. She laid these next to Nathan. Then she stood and beckoned me to follow her a short distance away.

I realized Anne meant to give him privacy as he dressed. This surprised me. Was it possible that in five hundred years, Anne had never seen Nathan in the buff? Pride sparked in my veins. After all, I'd managed to undress him in five days. Maybe that meant what he felt for me was, in its own way, real. That, and him nearly sacrificing his life to defend me from tentacled demon thing. Of course, none of this changed what needed to happen going forward. But it was nice to imagine he had a heart, and somewhere in that heart, he might have made a place for me.

While Nathan gathered his strength and got dressed, Anne and I stood at a discrete distance, facing the trees that had protected us. I could hear them now, oaks and elms whispering in the night, their language coalescing just beyond my reach. Mist was rising off the ground. A musky, pre-dawn scent saturated the air.

"I understand something now," Anne said. "Something I didn't understand before."

I glanced at her. "What's that?"

"Ever since I met Nathan, he has poured all his hope and power into us, his souls; into our often-ill-fated projects, into our stubborn desire to influence events in this world for the better. Five centuries gone by, and all this time he's never left anything for himself. Not until now, that is. For the first time, in recent days, I witnessed something I'd never seen before. I saw Nathan setting aside hope for himself."

Anne broke my heart with that. I blinked back the sting in my eyes and looked away. How to explain that whatever hope she thought I'd given him had ended here, tonight, with the decision I just made?

"Maybe you're right," I said, my throat thick with emotion. "I wouldn't pretend to know."

"Anne." Nathan called from behind, his voice a shaky command. We turned to see him approaching as he buttoned his shirt. His gait was strong, though he favored one leg. I wondered about his injured wings, now invisible. As he drew near, he set his eyes on me and said with tenderness, "Mayela."

I glanced away, uncertain.

"You are well?" he asked.

"As well as can be expected, all things considered." I met his gaze. "And your injuries? Your wing?"

"Fractured. It will require some care, but all will heal in time. We cannot linger. Anne, did you bring a phone?"

"Of course." She produced a cell from her utility belt. "I may have to walk a little to get reception. I'll make the call as soon as I can and be on my way."

"Thank you," he said.

Anne turned to me, her expression one of relief and gratitude.

"Welcome, Mayela." She placed a hand on my shoulder. "See you on the other side."

Then Anne started down the dark road, gait infused with confidence and joy as the shadows swallowed her form.

"Who is she going to call?" I asked.

"911." Nathan drew close and reached toward me.

"Mayela—"

I recoiled from his touch. I couldn't help it. Everything had changed now, even how I felt in his presence. "Let's just get on with this, shall we?"

"I'm sorry it came to this."

"Are you?" My words erupted in bitter tones. "You won, after all."

Nathan's shoulders deflated. He ran a hand through his hair, taking in the field of battle, my abandoned car, Mitch's sprawled corpse. "Is this a victory?"

I followed the direction of Nathan's gaze. Despite the tentacles that had boiled out of his body, Mitch's skin was whole, except for the bloody gashes I'd left across his throat.

"Anne explained to me what that thing was," I said. "But why did it come from *inside* of Mitch?"

"I'm not certain. Possession is not permitted anymore, though some among my kind have been known to violate the rule."

"You're saying that thing occupied him?" I asked, aghast. "Could it have controlled him? Is that why Mitch did what he did?"

"No. That's not the way possession works. My opponent could not have invaded your attacker's soul unless a perverse affinity existed between them in the first place. Mitch may have had an occupant, but he made his own choices."

Bile rose in my throat. I turned my back on Mitch and the whole bloody scene. I did not want to think about any of this anymore. "Can we go now?"

Nathan nodded and started toward the woods, beckoning me to accompany him. A path opened before us, grass and bushes parting at our feet as he led the way.

"I don't understand," he confessed as we entered the woodland. "The Unformed had me pinned, suffocating. Had my opponent finished me first it could have claimed all my souls. It was not wise to go after you before our battle had ended."

"Wisdom did not appear to be one of its graces," I replied.

"True. But how did you succeed in distracting it?"

"I…" What to say? "I threw a shoe."

Nathan stopped and faced me with a quizzical expression. "You what?"

"I threw a shoe. You know, like Clara and the Nutcracker Prince."

He gave me a blank look.

"You're five hundred years old, and you haven't seen The Nutcracker Suite? Or read the fairy tale by Hoffmann?"

Nathan shrugged. "No."

"Well, the story's only been around two hundred years, so I guess you aren't that far behind on your reading. When the seven-headed Mouse King is about to defeat the Nutcracker Prince, Clara throws her shoe at the Mouse King. The distraction is just enough to allow the Nutcracker to drive his sword through the Mouse King's heart."

"So, I'm the Nutcracker Prince?"

"And tentacled demon thing was the Mouse King."

"But you still have your shoes."

I sighed. "It's a metaphor. What I'm trying to say is, I found a way to make him believe I was a threat. It worked long enough to get you back on your feet. That was all."

Nathan hesitated, as if about to ask something else, and then continued walking.

"It was a grave risk," he said quietly. "I am most grateful."

"I had to do something. I wasn't going to let it win."

We came to a small clearing. Nathan paused in his gait. Broad trees surrounded us in a wide circle. Their baritone murmurs reverberated through the earth. Overhead, the dense canopy rustled in a soft breeze.

"This will do," he said.

"For what?"

"To cross over." Nathan let go a long exhale and turned to face me. "Mayela, I know what you've decided for your soul, and I can sense what you've decided for your heart."

It hurt to hear him voice the truth. I set my jaw against the pain. "Nathan, you have to understand—"

"I do. I am not happy, but I understand. You believe this an impossible situation in which to cultivate love. Perhaps you are right; I do not know. But I want to assure you I will ask nothing of you when we are on the other side. With the decision you made tonight, you designated me as your guardian, nothing more. All I desire is for you to be at peace. On this you have my word."

That was a fine declaration for someone who'd already secured my soul. And my heart. And my body. Honestly, what was he thinking? He had to know I would never be at peace having him so near and yet so far out of reach.

"Thank you," I said, tight-lipped.

Nathan watched me a moment as if expecting

something more. The hope in his eyes gave way to resignation. He turned away from me to a pair of nearby trees that formed an arch with their branches. With one hand he traced the curving limbs, starting from the roots and reaching toward the canopy, marking a continuous circle. Light streamed from his fingers; night fell away at his touch. When the portal was complete, I saw stars on the other side, shot through with bright streams of color, breathtaking in their brilliance.

"Here begins your future," Nathan said, extending a hand toward me.

A lump settled in my throat. My feet rooted into the ground.

"I haven't…" I let go a short sob. "I didn't say good-bye to Mamá."

Nathan's face fell. "Oh, Mayela. I'm so sorry! I was not thinking. Of course, you must see your mother. We will arrange something. With your gift of moving between worlds, body and soul, you will be able to speak with her. This is not your last day in the mortal realm. Indeed, if you wish it, you will have much work to do here."

With a stiff nod, I took a step toward that beautiful, starry gate. There was much to be desired on the other side. A realm of artists and revolutionaries, a universe of new discoveries, a demigod who loved me even if I did not see a way to love him. A few more steps, and I could leave this messy, dangerous, worry-ridden world behind. I would be protected and at peace. That was all he wanted, after all. For me to be at peace.

Yet something held me back. As I wavered on the edge of eternity, the true nature of my dread took shape in my mind. Every instinct told me if I walked through that doorway now, I would leave behind half of who I was. The part of me inherited from my father—that mysterious, wild, untamed being who had yet to fully emerge and claim her power—would be lost forever.

My hands clenched. I took a step back.

"Nathan," I announced, facing him. "There's something I need to tell you."

His hand dropped to his side. A frown crossed his brow. "Whatever it is, we can talk after we cross the threshold. Anne will have informed the authorities by now. The police are on their way. To linger is risky."

"No. I'm sorry. We have to do this, right here. Right now. The thing is, I…" I moved away from him and started pacing. My heart pounded inside my chest. "I'm not fully human. My father was immortal. A soul hunter. Like you."

I wasn't sure what I expected from this announcement, but Nathan's stunned silence took me by surprise. He stared at me, jaw agape, as if I'd picked up a rock and hurled it into his face.

"I, uhm, think I know how you feel," I offered. "I was pretty surprised myself when Mamá told me. I only found out a few days ago, when all this started. I mean, I didn't even believe in this stuff, in creatures like you, so you can imagine—"

"That's not possible," he said.

"I know! That's what I thought. But then the pieces started falling together, and it all made sense. Things I saw as a child that no one else could see; the way I crashed into your world, body and soul, and came back on my own; and now—" I stepped toward him, my voice gathering momentum. "—Tonight, when we fought the tentacled demon thing, I didn't throw a shoe. I plunged my hands into the earth and commanded the plants and fungi to attack! They responded, Nathan! They grew at my fingertips, vines and brambles and corrosive mycelia. I made a living net that invaded the vortex, attacked that monster, and drew it away from you."

"No!" He held up his hands. "You aren't listening to me, Mayela. What you're saying is impossible."

"What do you mean, impossible?" His denial had stoked my fury. "I'm telling the truth!"

"There has to be some other explanation."

"Why?" I demanded. "Because there's only room for one demigod in the state of Missouri?"

Nathan closed the distance between us. "If what you say were true, whoever sired you would've claimed you years ago. You'd be well into your training, perhaps even preparing for your metamorphosis."

"Mamá hid me. What happened between her and my father was not consensual. So, she ran as far away as she could, before I was born, and vowed never to let him find me."

"But without training, you would've…" He stopped short, as if holding some unnamed terror upon his lips.

"I would've what?" I prompted, a chill running down my spine.

Nathan cast an uncertain glance toward the place beyond the woods, where he'd battled the tentacled demon. Anne's words returned to me full force. *One of the Unformed*, she'd said. A creature that was incomplete, unable to find its shape. An outcast among Nathan's kind, a horror among my own.

"I would've become something like that?" I whispered. "One of the Unformed?"

"Hybrids must be inducted within the first three decades of their mortal life," he replied as if reciting a lesson from his school days. "They must be inducted or destroyed."

"Or destroyed? Isn't that a little extreme?"

"Any hybrid constrained to a mortal vessel will go mad if their powers manifest without proper guidance. At least, this is what we are told." He shook his head and turned his gaze inward. "What I've always been told."

"Well, I can see how this might drive a person crazy. I mean, I've barely kept my head above water the entire time."

"Yet here you are." He caught my gaze and held it.

"Yes, but…" Quiet realization warmed my heart. "I wasn't without proper guidance. I had you."

A tremor invaded his voice. "I didn't know…I never imagined…"

Emotions swallowed Nathan's words. He blinked and stared at the ground, hands clenched at his sides.

Stepping past him, I approached the portal and gazed through the arched branches at the star-drenched sky beyond. There, I saw a reflection of everything we'd invoked these past few days—dinner on the Plaza, candles in my bedroom, roses in my kitchen, a fire on the back porch. All our ordinary and extraordinary conversations. Making love to him on the cusp between two worlds. I recognized the beauty of what we'd given to each other; a gift powerful enough to overcome confusion, fear, and unimaginable violence; strong enough to bridge our separate worlds. Strong enough to defy death itself. My heart unfolded in a burst of light, beckoning me forward into new possibilities.

"I'm ready." I realized. Going back to Nathan, I took his hand in mine. "I'm ready to cross over now, with you. I'm not sure what I am, or what I'm meant to be, but I want to learn. You can show me, Nathan. Please, show me how."

Dark gaze steady on mine, he pressed my hand to his lips and breathed in the scent of my skin. Then he let me go and took a step back. "No."

I blinked. "What?"

"I cannot do what you ask of me."

"Why?"

"Induction is the sole responsibility of the immortal parent. I cannot intervene."

"Wait." I lifted my hands to stop him. "You're saying I have to be trained by my father or I'm not in the club?"

He drew his lips in a thin line and nodded.

"That's ridiculous!"

"I'm not saying I agree, but I cannot—"

"He. Is. A. Rapist. What part of that do you not understand?"

"Mayela—"

"You know what I think about your rules, Nathan? Your rules suck!"

"Please, listen to me."

"All that talk about inciting revolution among *my* kind? Maybe it's time to start a revolution among your own!"

"Enough!" he thundered. "I cannot train you! And I must relinquish my claim over you. It is the only way."

The words hit so hard they knocked the wind out of

me. Breathless, I stared at him in disbelief. "You're going to let me go altogether? Just like that? But I…I chose you, Nathan. I want to be with you."

"Did you? Do you?" His tone carried an undercurrent of melancholy. "The choice must be made freely, Mayela, and you were backed against a wall. I was so desperate to have you I was willing to ignore that, to turn a blind eye to the fundamental injustice of your circumstances. In truth, our entire negotiation should be declared null and void. Any among my kind would recognize that were you to take this to arbitration."

Sirens sounded in the distance. Anne's phone call had been received and heeded. The police were on their way.

"Then I choose you now," I said, anxious with the realization that time was running out.

"Mayela," he sighed, his face awash with pain.

"I choose you!" Desperation invaded my voice. "I mean it. I mean it now, and I meant it before, with all my heart and soul. I meant it when I sought you out on the Hunting Grounds, and again when I summoned you here tonight. I choose you, Nathan. It's always been you. Just you. Only you."

"I cannot take you with me," he insisted in gentle tones, "knowing what I know now. If I bring you into my realm, pretending to be your guardian while training you in secret, it puts everything—everyone—at risk. You, me, all my souls, all the work we are doing; my entire realm could be destroyed the moment the truth comes to light."

"But you can't just—" Tears broke through my words. "You can't leave me alone like this, with powers

I hardly understand and monsters in the shadows waiting to come after me. You can't, Nathan. You can't do that."

"You will be well-protected," he said, though his voice was hoarse with doubt. "Follow your mother's guidance. She knows her craft well. Above all, trust yourself and your instincts."

"Nathan!"

He silenced me with a desperate kiss, lips pressed hard against mine, arms wrapped around me in a tight embrace. "I love you, Mayela."

"Then don't do this."

"I love you, and I release you. I absolve you of all obligations to me. The bonds forged between us are severed, in accordance with the laws of my kin. Nothing is owed. All debts are forgiven. You are free to choose again."

"Nathan, please!"

"I release you." He stepped away. "Go, Mayela, and be at peace."

Then he vanished, slipping fast through the portal. The threshold of light vanished behind him.

Silence descended on the glade. I stared, bewildered, at the place where my guardian and supernatural lover had just stood. Arching trees marked nothing more than empty space, as full of shadows as my own heart. I was paralyzed, afraid to move because the moment I did, the pain of his absence would forever be seared into my being. A future without Nathan would drag me forward, condemning me to the unbearable knowledge that I would never again return to this place in time, when everything, all his love, had been within my grasp.

Lights flashed across the high trunks, red and blue flickers that ignited fear and disorientation. What strange creature had descended upon the woodland now? I was too weary to care or fight anymore.

But these lights were not a new host of demons. They were from my world, projected from a patrol car that approached Mitch's dilapidated cabin a short walk away. I heard car doors open, followed by commanding voices of police officers. My future had arrived, but I was not ready. I fell to my knees and gripped the grass with my hands. Sobs shuddered through me, trauma and grief bleeding out of my soul, extracted as a river of tears that watered the earth.

Chapter 22

The sun shone bright that mid-October day when Mamá and I spread Dad's ashes on his parents' farm. Cremation had not been part of my dad's faith practice, but Mamá insisted this was his will. She'd dreamt of him, she said. He'd come from the other side to tell her he wanted the remains of his mortal body scattered in the woods. Six months ago, I might've insisted on a Catholic burial for him, but after all I'd experienced, who was I to argue with Mamá?

October was my favorite month in Kansas City. Summer had finally loosened its muggy grip, allowing autumn to burnish the trees in copper, scarlet, and gold. The breeze was cool and crisp. The bright sun illuminated a cerulean sky. As Mamá and I walked the woodland paths behind the cottage, she sprinkled Dad's ashes along the trail and hummed softly. I did not recognize the melody, but it was perfectly tuned to the music of the forest—the scramble of squirrels up trunks, the chirps of late-season birds and lingering migrants, and the rush of wind through high branches.

At the stream crossing, we paused and sat on a rustic bench Dad had built decades before, when I was little and our threesome a cohesive unit. When Sunday picnics were still a thing and Mamá and Dad's relationship, forged on shaky grounds, was held together by the strength of a child's laughter. There on the edge of all our memories, Mamá hung her head and wept. I put my arm around her shoulders and held her close. My eyes stung, but I couldn't cry anymore. I'd shed too many tears in recent weeks. I would cry again for Dad many times, I knew. But not now. Not today.

Reaching into my pocket, I pulled out a tissue and gave it to Mamá. She accepted, grateful, wiped her eyes, and blew her nose. For a long while she stared at the forest, her trembling breath marked by sniffles. When at last she managed to speak, her words were choked.

"I wanted to love him," she confessed. "I did. I wanted to be the wife he always hoped for. I just couldn't."

"Oh, Mamá," I murmured, and she was crying again, leaning into my embrace. "You did the best you could. You made the decisions you had to make. That's all any of us can ever do. Don't blame yourself for not falling in love with him. That was never up to you."

"Mi corazón." She thumped a hand over her chest, trying to smile but coughing instead. "My heart is rebellious and haughty."

"No, Mamá." I kissed her on the cheek. "Your heart knows what's best for you. Whether or not it's convenient, and whether or not you agree."

That earned a weary smile. Mamá straightened and dried her tears. We rose and completed the path in silence, holding hands as we circled back toward the cottage. I had not returned to my grandparents' farm since my disappearance in September. I'd expected the setting to trigger unpleasant emotions. But whatever imprint Mitch's one-time appearance had left was not strong enough to undo my family's sacred space. The sense of welcome and peace I'd always found here had somehow endured.

Back at the cottage, I made some hot tea. Mamá and I sat on the porch, cradling our mugs and taking in scenic fields and woodlands. Birds fluttered through the underbrush as the sun dipped toward the western horizon, casting an auburn glow across the landscape. As much as I loved this place, I wasn't sure if I could keep it. I hated to sell off Dad's legacy, but where would I find the time or the money to maintain so much land?

And what would I do, out here all alone?

Mamá set her glass aside. "We should move here, you and me."

"What?" I looked at her, not entirely surprised she had read my thoughts.

"We should fix up this cottage and live here, on your father's farm."

"But…" I paused, wondering which objection to start with. "What about Carolyn? Do you think she'd move all the way out here?"

Mamá shook her head. "I will speak with her, but I don't know if she will want to give up her mountains and beaches and sailboats."

"We have sailboats," I offered. "And beaches, too. On the lakes."

Mamá gave me a withering look. "Carolyn and I will work something out. Long distance if we have to. I love her dearly, but it's time for me to come home."

Whoa. I was overjoyed by the thought but, "Mamá, you need to think about this. You've been so happy with Carolyn, and with everything in California. You know how different things are, here in the Midwest. I can't let you give up the love of your life just to—"

"You are the love of my life." Determination flared inside her eyes.

I knew from long experience what that posture meant. There would be no arguing against this, especially not from her daughter.

"I'm coming back to Kansas City," she said, "and we will live here on the farm, together."

I glanced around the veranda, taking note of the sagging and moldy parts. There were many. "This place needs a lot of work. And it's a long commute to campus."

"You really think you're going back to the college?"

I sipped at my tea, unsure of my answer. After the attack, I'd requested accumulated family and medical leave. At first, my dean was not happy to see me jump ship mid-semester. Then the story broke that I'd gouged the throat of a serial killer. Some ambiguity persisted with respect to the legal repercussions of having killed Mitch, so I was told to take as much time as needed, at least until the media attention died down.

On campus, marches and candlelight vigils had been organized in my support. Students, current and past, had sent countless cards expressing their sympathy for the horror I'd faced. Many added what an amazing teacher I was and how awful it would have been to lose me. To think, if I hadn't nearly died at the hands of a serial killer, I might have never known how much they valued my presence in the classroom.

"It's meaningful work," I told Mamá, aware I wouldn't have admitted that even three months ago. "Besides, how else will I pay the bills?"

"The ground beneath the city is poisoned," she said. One month ago, I wouldn't have had a clue what she meant by that. "I'm not saying I can't protect you in the city, but here, it would be easier. We can weave stronger, more resistant wards on the farm. We'll be safer, and you'll have space to learn what you need to learn."

"Space to improvise, you mean." What could I learn without a teacher? "I just hope I don't blow anything up."

"From what we've seen, your gifts do not involve flame throwing." She offered an encouraging smile and patted my hand. "*No te preocupes, hija.* We will find a way."

Mamá seemed to be having an easier time embracing my new identity. Then again, she'd always known. I had yet to fully process my true nature, much less what it meant for my future. I'd give anything to go back to my former life and resume a simpler existence, but I knew that wasn't possible.

"We'd have to put on a new roof," I said, "and fix a heck of a lot of other stuff. We could probably cover repairs with the money from selling Dad's house. If not, I'll apply for an equity loan." I paused. Financially, it could work, but this would take a lot of time. Why didn't my superpowers include house repair? "We can over-winter at my place in the city while the contractors get started. Then if everything goes well, maybe we can move out here next year sometime?"

Mamá nodded, and so it was decided.

We gathered our things, locked up the cottage, and headed back into town.

As days bled into nights and back again, I tried not

to think about Nathan. But I saw his face everywhere—on strangers in the produce section in the supermarket; among people walking their dogs in the park; seated with families at tables in restaurants. I understood my mind was playing tricks on me, that Nathan wasn't here and wasn't coming back, but that didn't make things easier.

At night I dreamt about him. I saw Nathan nestled high in an immense tree, its long dark branches hung with brilliant stars and colorful worlds. Surrounded by this stunning beauty, Nathan covered his face and wept. At his side, a three-headed snake kept vigil. I felt his sorrow, yet I had no sympathy. He'd abandoned me, after all. Left me numb and alone in the woods, suspended between sadness, anger, heartbreak, and relief. Relief because I never wanted to belong to him or even be like him. Anger because I loathed his decision anyway. Heartbreak and sadness because if he'd loved me, truly loved me like he claimed, he would have found a way for us to be together. He could have at least tried. I was worth that much. I was worth an honest effort.

One afternoon in late October, the doorbell rang. I was surprised to find Agent Vicky Arevalo standing on my porch.

"Dr. Lehman." She gave a curt nod. "I hope this isn't a bad time. I was wondering if I might speak with you a moment?"

"Sure." I opened the door to let her in. There'd been several interviews already, most by appointment with my lawyer present. This unannounced visit troubled me. "Should I call my lawyer?"

"I'd like this to be off-the-record if that's okay."

She removed her shoes and set them neatly by the door. "I just have a couple simple questions. I'm trying to tie up some loose ends."

"Okay." I knew my lawyer would not agree, but something about Vicky Arevalo inspired my trust. And awe. Secretly, I wanted some one-on-one time with her, too. "Would you like some tea or coffee?"

"Tea would be great."

I led her to the kitchen and gestured for her to take a seat at the table. "I've got everything. Herbal? Black? Green?"

"Earl Grey?"

"Coming right up."

She glanced around the kitchen as she sat down. "Is your mother here?"

"Mamá's out shopping for crystals. You need to talk to her, too?"

"No. I'd rather this be between the two of us."

Uh oh. That sounded kind of ominous. "Well, she'll be out for a while."

I finished preparing the tea in silence and brought the mugs to the table. Vicky took a whiff of the aromatic steam as I settled next to her.

"Shopping for crystals, huh?" she asked.

I shrugged. "It's a thing Mamá picked up in California."

"Interesting." She set her mug on the table, wrapped her hands around it, and leaned toward me. "I'm here to tell you we're almost done. This case is as tight as can be. I don't anticipate you'll have to put up with any charges or court time. All the forensic evidence matches your testimony. What happened at your father's house, inside your car, and everything in

McGraff's little cabin of horrors. We even found the used can of tick repellent in the grass near your car. I must say, that was a brilliant move on your part."

My gut tensed at the memory. "It's a miracle any of it worked."

"I'm glad you killed him."

Startled by the conviction in her tone, I met Vicky's gaze.

"I want you to know that," she continued. "I'm glad he's dead. McGraff was very sloppy this time. His desperation was evident every step of the way. If he'd succeeded, he might've been able to go back and clean up a few things, but…" She paused and shook her head. "I think we would've gotten him this time, Dr. Lehman. No matter what. McGraff left an easy trail. It's almost as if you were destined to end this. For everyone."

I took a sip from my tea. My body had gone cold, and my hands were trembling.

"Some destiny," I said with a shaky voice. I had not overcome the trauma yet. *This will take time*, I reminded myself. And time, as I'd recently learned, was superabundant in our universe.

Vicky took in my reaction. "I'm sorry. I don't mean to upset you. On the contrary."

"It's not your fault. I'm still processing, that's all."

"Still." Her tone softened. "That was careless of me. And disrespectful. I'm sorry."

"It's okay. Really."

She nodded, chewing on her lower lip as if debating her next words.

"You said you had some more questions?" I prompted.

"Yes." She let go a soft exhale. "Something's

bothering me. I know this is difficult for you, Dr. Lehman, but I want to be sure Mitch McGraff was the only assailant you encountered that night."

My pulse slowed. "What do you mean?"

"Did you see anyone else at the scene of the crime?"

"No." I stared into my tea, worried she might detect I was lying. What had they found? Footprints? Paw prints? Tentacle tracks? As far as I could tell that night, no trace of a supernatural struggle had been left behind, but I was not a forensic scientist. "Why do you ask?"

"It's a feeling really." Her hands worked against her mug. "Nothing more. Every time I return to the scene, I can't shake the sense that we've missed something. Something important. I don't know how to explain it. I get this tingling at the nape of my neck, and a voice inside keeps insisting someone else was there."

"Mitch was the only person who attacked me."

"But maybe he had an accomplice who cut and ran? Someone who escaped when he realized the game was up?"

"I don't think so," I said.

"According to your testimony, you didn't spend much time in the house."

"No. No way. I was in and out of there as fast as possible."

"So, someone could have been hiding in there, or anywhere on the property, deciding whether to finish you off or simply run."

"I guess." Wow, this woman had an instinct. No wonder she was an investigator. Could she tell I was hedging on the truth? "It seems there would've been another car there, don't you think? If you're right."

Vicky Arevalo sat back in her chair. "I've thought about that. I've thought about a lot of things. To be honest, all the evidence is against my hunch, but when I get this feeling, I'm rarely wrong. I don't want to walk away believing the case is closed if it's not. More people might die if I make that mistake."

"I understand." I did. Truly. "All I can say, from what I experienced, is that Mitch seemed to be running a one-person show."

Vicky nodded and took a long draw from her tea. "My partner and I have also spoken with Ms. Marovic, and some of the customers in her coffee shop. A curious detail turned up in those conversations, something you never mentioned to me. You went out with a man the night before Mitch McGraff kidnapped you?"

"What, you mean Nathan?" His name popped out before I could stop. I could have kicked myself. My heart went into palpitations. "You think he's involved in this?"

"Do you?"

"No." I shook my head, perhaps too vigorously. "No, I don't."

"Joni told me you met him right before all this happened, and that she'd been very happy for you. Then everything was blown apart by your father's murder and the attack."

That about summed it up. "Yes, what she said is true."

"You haven't heard from this man since?"

"No. I mean, he's a nice guy and everything, but he was just passing through KC on business. We went out on a date, had dinner on the Plaza. It was fun, but not the beginning of a great love, or anything like that. He's not my type, really." After a moment, I added, "For starters, I prefer someone who lives here."

"Do you know where he is now?"

"No." Not really.

"You said Nathan was his name?"

"Yes."

"Do you have a surname?"

"No." What else could I say? If I told her *de la Rosa*, she'd track down every Nathan de la Rosa in the country, and for what purpose? Nathan's earthly persona wasn't real.

"Any contact information?"

I hesitated. With a sinking feeling, I saw I'd been cornered. Any further evasion would only arouse Agent Arevalo's suspicion. I had to give her something. "I think his number is still on my phone, if that would help."

"Yes, it would. Thank you."

I left the table to retrieve my cell, telling myself this was not my problem. Nathan had to fend for himself now. It wasn't my responsibility to hide his existence or protect him.

"Normally, I would've deleted his number by now," I said, returning to my seat. "But with everything else that's been going on, I think he's still on my list. Here it is."

She wrote down the numbers as I read them. Whether this would work for her was beyond me. Could she call Nathan on the other side? Would he answer? If so, what would he tell her?

Then, the much harder question—Would Nathan

answer me if I called?

I didn't want to know. Nor did I want to be tempted. As soon as Vicky finished writing the number on her notepad, I deleted him from my contacts.

"Well." She tucked away her notes and stood. "I think I've taken up enough of your time."

"You haven't finished your tea."

"No rest for the weary." She started toward the front door. I followed. "I can't tell you how grateful I am to you for putting an end to this, Dr. Lehman. We'll never know how many lives you saved, and you have brought important closure for the families already affected."

"It wasn't enough."

"It never is."

We reached the foyer. Agent Arevalo put on her shoes, then met me with a grim and honest gaze. When all this was over, maybe next year, I'd invite Vicky Arevalo out to the farm. I'd make tapas and serve some wine. Maybe we'd have a conversation that didn't involve serial killers. Maybe we'd even laugh. Then I'd know whether this connection I felt with her was simply hero worship or the start of a real friendship.

"I could never do what you do," I blurted.

She cocked her brow in surprise. "After how things went down between you and McGraff? I'm not so sure."

"That was survival. What you do, to be able to deal with this stuff every day, I couldn't even touch that."

"It's exhausting," she acknowledged, opening the front door. "This job has tested my limits, and my faith in everything, but I have no regrets. There's nothing like stopping a killer. Those moments when we achieve justice, they burn so bright, I'm afraid I'll go blind if I look too long. So, I close my eyes and move on to the next case. There's always another case."

"If only we could snap our fingers and make the bad guys disappear."

"I'd give anything for that." Vicky Arevalo stepped through my front door and into the afternoon sun. "I'd give my very soul."

Chapter 23

On the second Tuesday in November, I went to the polls to vote. Between confronting a serial killer, battling soul hunters, and losing my supernatural lover, I hadn't paid much attention to the presidential campaign. Not that I needed to. I'd made my decision long ago. I didn't agree with all my candidate's policies, but I trusted her experience. Certainly, she was better than the alternative, a man who invoked divisive rhetoric to please unruly crowds. In my mind, the choice couldn't be clearer. I was excited to elect our first woman president. I also felt grateful I'd secured a little more time in this world to see it happen.

Joni, who'd dyed her hair blue in recent days, came over on election night for a small watch party. I prepared nachos and bean dip, along with a vegetable plate. Mamá took charge of the margaritas. With the food laid out and our glasses served, we settled in to celebrate the making of history.

We didn't get the history we expected. Evening wore into night. State after state fell for the candidate none of us supported. Our fiesta turned into a session of grim solidarity. By eleven o'clock, I'd fallen into resentful silence. Joni, morose, hung her head in her hands. Mamá was cursing in Spanish at the TV.

"Maybe it's time to end this party," I said.

Everyone agreed.

No official call had been made, but midnight had arrived, and the writing was on the wall. As Joni picked up the dishes, Mamá tried to stand and lost her balance. I caught her elbow and guided her to her room. I'd never seen her this drunk, or this angry.

"*Mierda*!" she cursed. "*¿Cómo es posible*? ¡*Metieron ese hijueputa en la Casa Blanca*! ¡*Mierda*!"

"Don't worry, Mamá." I helped her into her pajamas. "It's going to be okay."

"This is not okay!"

I turned down the sheets and settled her into bed. "It's just four years, Mamá. That's why we have term limits. Four years, then we'll be done."

"You know how much damage that *bestia* can do in four years?" she shouted, her fist raised to the air.

"We'll vote him out in 2020. You'll see."

"Ha! You think you know how these people operate? You think he won't try to dismantle everything to keep himself in power?"

"Honestly, Mamá? I don't think he's that smart."

"Because you haven't been paying attention."

I sighed. "You may be right."

"You think you know about dictators? I can tell you about dictators! I grew up under a dictatorship."

"I know, Mamá." I kissed her on the forehead. This was not the moment to argue for the strength of our constitutional democracy. "Go to sleep. We'll talk in the morning."

"At least your father, *qué descanse en paz*, won't live with the shame of having voted for that *hijueputa*."

"*Buenas Noches*, Mamá." I retreated to the door of the bedroom. "Please rest. And don't worry. Everything will look better in the morning."

"*Mierda*," she hissed as I turned out the light.

Back in the kitchen, Joni was rinsing dishes and putting things in the dishwasher.

"Your mom okay?" she asked.

"She'll be fine." I leaned against the counter. Exhaustion was setting in. "She had too much to drink. And then, she was gut-punched by an entire country tonight."

"Can you believe it?" Joni dried her hands and tossed the towel aside. "We put a racist misogynist into the White House. I mean, it's not the first time we've done that, but this guy actually brags about being racist and misogynistic, and we *still* elected him!"

"Final returns aren't in yet," I offered, weakly.

She huffed. "We all know where it's going."

I straightened and stretched. "I'll finish cleaning up here. You should head home. It's late."

"Aw, honey." She came over and hugged me. "What a year, huh? I'm so sorry. I was hoping tonight would be a bright spot after all the awful things you've been through, but wow. Just wow."

I took her arm in mine, and we started toward the front door.

"My mind feels numb," I said. "I don't know what to think; how to even begin wrapping my head around this."

We arrived at the foyer.

"How did we not see this coming?" Joni muttered, putting on her shoes. "We should've seen it coming. We should've done more to prevent this from happening."

"Maybe," I conceded, but Nathan's lament was echoing through my mind. *To have so much power and yet be powerless*. "Or maybe we did the best we could, and this still happened."

"What do you mean?"

"This guy was elected because tens of millions of people, all across the country, made their own independent decisions. How could we have stemmed a tide like that?"

"I don't know!" She threw up her hands in anger. "More canvassing, more donations, more...*something.* We should've done more of something."

I shook my head. Defeat weighed heavy on my shoulders, the accumulated load of four decades of frustrated effort. My most important decisions, it seemed, had yielded little more than disillusion, pain, and heartbreak. My career, my marriage, my strange supernatural heritage—What was it all for if I couldn't make a difference?

"The truth is, I'm worn out," I confessed. "Twenty years ago, when I started grad school, I thought we would change the world. No, I thought the world was changing, and that we would be a part of the change. But the things I care about, the values I hold dear? Most people don't give a damn. They don't want to listen, Joni. They don't want to see what we're doing to each other or to the planet. And they don't want to change."

She held my gaze a moment. "Well, that's depressing."

"Sorry." I forced a laugh. "I'm in a mood. Life has not been pretty of late."

"Oh, sweetheart." Joni's eyes misted over. "I'm so sorry! I keep forgetting. You have enough on your mind without thinking about politics."

She wrapped her arms tight around me. I held my

friend close, overcome with bittersweet emotion and gratitude for having her here.

Joni pulled away, wiping tears from her eyes. “We should get some sleep. Call you in the morning?”

“Yes, please. Maybe I’ll be in a better place by then.”

“I hope so. We’ve got a lot of work to do if we’re going to take this guy down in four years.”

Sweet Joni, always preparing for the next fight. I wished I felt the same spark, but there was little left inside beyond my empty heart and wilted ambitions. Hopefully, this pit of despair was a passing result of my recent trauma. “Text me when you get home tonight, okay?”

“Will do.” She left, shutting the door behind her.

Silence wrapped around me like a well-worn and comforting cloak. Midnight slipped out of the shadows. She followed me as I returned to the living room to gather the remaining dishes. The TV was still on, though muted. A final call hadn’t been made. The frenzied looks on reporters’ faces indicated a historic upset; the victory no one saw coming. I turned off the broadcast.

With my arms full of dishes and Midnight at my heels, I continued to the kitchen, dimming the houselights with my elbow as I went. By the time I started loading the dishwasher, only the lamp over the sink remained lit.

As I worked, the election results plagued my thoughts. What did this mean for my country? More to the point, what did it mean for me? Three months ago, I lived in a world of physical realities that could be measured, analyzed, and understood. Now, I straddled two worlds—this one, and the enigmatic realm of the Soul Masters. I understood I could no longer act on this side of the veil without considering consequences for the realm beyond, anymore than Nathan acted in his world without considering consequences for my kind. But what power did either of us have to incite true transformation, here or there?

I shook my head to escape the expanding maze of my own deliberations. It was too late, and I was too tired to obsess over this. Hoping to clear my mind, I took out my phone and turned on some music, choosing a playlist of my students' favorite songs. The mix was eclectic, full of joy and potential, a reflection of my students' unfailing belief in their power to change the world. As much as I complained about my teaching career, I could always say this—the future belonged to my students, and that gave me hope.

I turned up the volume. Before long, I was dancing, hips swaying to the rhythm, feet tracing circles across the floor, hands spiraling through the air. Midnight joined in, skittering across the kitchen and pouncing on unseen shadows. She made me laugh. My sadness diluted by her antics, I paused, breathless and dizzy.

"What do you think, Midnight?" I asked, playing with the lyrics from the song. "Are we broken, or are we just bent?"

Midnight, in true cat fashion, was not listening. She rolled on the floor next to the back door, stretching her paws toward the garden in pure cat delight.

I knelt to pet her. "Do you think we'll learn to love again?"

Midnight sprang up and pawed furiously at the door, overcome with her famous coo-purr.

I laughed again. “Silly kitty! You know I’m not going to let you outside! Especially this time of night. What are you going on about?”

My breath caught on the answer. Hardly daring to believe, I rose and peered out the window. *Could it be?*

Inside Mamá’s circle of stones, flames leapt from the firepit. A man stood watching, hands in his pockets, back turned to me, his familiar figure silhouetted by flickering amber light.

“Nathan,” I whispered and opened the door to greet him.

****

Threshold

Kansas City, Missouri. November 2016

Nekhen felt the sweet touch of Mayela’s soul like the rush of a cool breeze before a spring shower. No sooner had he turned around than she was upon him, arms flung around his neck, face burrowed against his chest. He stiffened in surprise. Given the circumstances of their parting, he had expected anger, resentment, and no small amount of distrust. He did not deserve such warmth and affection.

“I missed you,” she murmured.

The words melted his heart, exposing the suppressed agony he’d endured all these days after letting her go. Enclosing Mayela in his arms, he whispered, “I missed you, too.”

Mayela tightened her hold. Nekhen pressed his lips into her soft hair and breathed her aroma of roses, sage, and loam. With time, he could bury this *missing* beneath other concerns, but the hole created by what might have been would always remain. And always, for Nekhen, was a very long time.

Mayela extricated herself from their embrace. Joy filled her aura, and her face shone with gratitude. "It was good of you to come. I've thought about you every day, all the things I should've said but didn't. Our good-bye was so rushed, so broken, so full of upset, and I—"

"Mayela, please. Say no more. I only ask that you forgive me for—"

"Don't apologize." She held up her hands. "Not for anything. We did the best we could, didn't we? Besides, I'm the one who's sorry. I didn't know when to tell you about my origins. I still don't know what to do with who I am, but I trusted you, and I trust the decisions we made. All of them. It's okay. Everything is okay."

Except everything wasn't okay. That's why he had returned. Nekhen's heart contracted at the magnitude of the challenge before them. He drew an unsteady breath and gestured to the chairs. "Can we talk?"

"Yes, of course."

As they settled in, Nekhen took off his jacket and placed it around her shoulders. His mortal—half mortal—love had rushed out of the house without a sweater, and the November night was cold. Shivers coursed through her shoulders. Mayela thanked him and snuggled into his jacket, leaning toward the crackling fire.

"My condolences for your country," he said.

She cast him a sideways glance. "It's going to be that bad, huh?"

"There will be strife and violence. Many will suffer and die."

"Wow. That sounds apocalyptic. You have a crystal ball that tells you this?"

"Five hundred years of history have taught me what always happens when someone who cannot see past themselves attains great power." In her world, and in his. "Tomorrow, you and your mother should go shopping."

She lifted her brow in amusement. "That's very Reagan-Bush of you. Unfortunately, shopping does not solve America's problems, as much as we'd like to believe otherwise."

"You will need knitting needles."

"I don't knit."

"You will learn. Buy some knitting needles and pink yarn, for you and your mother."

"Nathan." She sat back in her chair, confused. "What on earth are you talking about?"

He shrugged. "You said you trusted me."

"O-kay," she replied, doubt evident in her voice. "Any other divine guidance, while we're at it? A recommended shade of pink, perhaps? Baby pink? Carnation pink? Fuchsia?"

"Whatever shade you prefer."

"Got it." Mayela shrugged in concession. "Now that you've delivered the strangest oracle in history, is there anything else you came to say? Anything important?"

Yes. But before they got to that, "I received a call from Vicky Arevalo."

"Oh." Her face fell. "That phone number still works?"

"Yes, and there's an answering service. When I'm not in this world, I make sure to check regularly."

"I hope I didn't cause you any trouble."

"You did the right thing. To keep my information

from her would have aroused suspicion. In any case, I am prepared for such eventualities. Agent Arevalo has what she needs. There's a record of my dropping off the rental car at the airport, and my name is on the passenger manifest for a flight out of Kansas City. She will also find proof that I checked into a hotel in Atlanta on the day you were attacked."

"Clever." Mayela nodded. "So, the devil went down to Georgia?"

He rolled his eyes. "I have allies there. There's good work to be done in Georgia. Momentum to change the world."

"If you say so."

Clearly, she did not trust him as much as she said. "I told Agent Arevalo I hadn't been in touch with you since leaving Kansas City, but that having learned of your ordeal, I would call on you again."

Mayela caught her breath, then exhaled softly. "And here you are."

Such sweet hope in her voice, like dawn breaking after a long night. Dare he imagine she could love him again? Quelling the urge to touch her cheek, he folded his hands tight against each other and turned toward the fire. "But not because of a promise made to an FBI agent."

"Then why?"

"Mayela." He hesitated, wary of igniting her wrath again. "The night I left you behind and crossed the portal on my own, I lied to you."

She frowned. "About what?"

He shifted, uncomfortable in his seat. It was not in his nature to intentionally deceive, and he regretted having done so with her. "I thought you might've figured this out on your own by now. When I said, 'I release you,' I did not in fact release you in full."

Mayela sucked in her breath and jumped to her feet. She began pacing around the fire, her face a mix of astonishment, trepidation, and—Could it be?—Joy.

"Oh, my God!" she exclaimed. "Why didn't I think of it before? The intention had to be repeated three times, didn't it? Just like when I called your name. Statement of intent, reaffirmation, sealing of intent. You said *I release you* only twice!"

He nodded.

She returned to his side and took a seat. "What does it mean?"

"I'm not sure it means anything. We are on uncharted territory. From the beginning, my claim was suspect, given your origins and the circumstances under which you were asked to make your choice. Now that I know the truth, our laws obligate me to stay away so your father can exercise his rights. But that night, though I understood the rules and the consequences of violating them, I was unwilling to sever the last thread between us. So, I left the act undone. I wanted more time to gather information and consider possibilities."

"And now? What are you thinking now?"

What was he thinking, indeed? Wadje would not be happy if she knew her son were here.

"I have been listening to murmurings on the other side of the veil. No one speaks of you, Mayela. Given everything that's transpired, I find this remarkable. If any among my kind know of your origins, they are holding their silence." He furrowed his brow, returning his gaze to the flames. "I have also thought much about the Unformed One that came for you that night. I have wondered why the creature contested for you at all. The Unformed have no rights among us, no path for claiming and keeping souls."

"I'm not sure it wanted to keep me. I had the clear impression, toward the end, that thing intended to destroy me."

"I agree."

In the silence that followed, realization washed through her features. "You think it knew what I am."

"It knew, or whoever sent it knew."

"But who would…?" Mayela sat back, placing a hand over her mouth. When she spoke again, her voice was reduced to a horrified whisper. "My father. My father found me and wanted me destroyed. He sent that thing to do it. That thing, and Mitch. Mitch was meant to tear apart my body, and tentacled demon thing was going to finish my soul."

"There's no way to be certain, Mayela. The creature is gone and your father, whoever he is, remains silent. But given everything you've told me, it seems a likely scenario."

"That means he could come back and—"

"There's no way to be certain," Nekhen reiterated.

"But what if it's true? What if that asshole knows where I am and decides to—"

Nekhen took Mayela's hand in his. "We will cross that bridge when—and if—we come to it."

The terror drained from her face. She looked at Nekhen in surprise, as if seeing him for the first time. "We?"

"I have also given much thought to what you said about the need for revolution in my world. I believe you are right. What happens beyond the veil is inextricably linked to what happens here. That means there can be no justice among your kind until there is also justice among my own."

A smile graced her features. Colors of lilac and gold spread through her aura. "What do you propose?"

"I am going to do what you asked of me, Mayela Lehman. I am going to teach you."

"Yes!" She jumped to her feet in joy.

"We will conduct this business with discretion," he added quickly. "I will reside in my realm. You will reside here. We will meet between worlds, as necessary."

"College professor by day, demigoddess by night!" Mayela clapped her hands. "I can do this. I know I can."

"This is not a game, Mayela. The risk to both of us is great."

"I understand." Though as far as he could see, she did not. "When's my first lesson?"

"I believe we are well past your first lessons."

"Right. When's my next lesson, and what will I learn?"

Nekhen drew a breath. Already, he wondered if he had made a mistake. He had never inducted a half-mortal. He had only his mother's example, which wasn't the finest, and his own instincts to go on. "I thought we might start with dream whispering."

"Oh." She frowned. "What's that?"

"It's a technique we use to insinuate ourselves into the nighttime journeys of mortals. We contact people poised to make a difference and encourage them to follow their convictions. One of my souls, Humboldt, has been leading a team of dream whisperers in Europe.

Perhaps you'd like to observe them in action?"

"I'm going to Europe?"

"You would visit the liminal space of our targets, who happen to be in Europe."

"So, I'm going to Europe, but only in my dreams?"

"From a certain perspective, yes."

"I see. But why the liminal space of Europeans? Why not the liminal space of Americans?"

"I thought Humboldt's initiative would interest you. He wants to spark a movement of seismic proportions on climate change. The best prospects right now are in Europe. There's a young woman who shows particular promise. I'm optimistic about Humboldt's efforts. I suspect we will see a breakthrough in the next year or two."

"Nice." She nodded. "I mean, to be honest, I was hoping we'd go straight to the chapter on how to turn into something with wings and claws, but dream whispering sounds—"

"Mayela." He rose to rebuke her. She stiffened at his tone, but there was nothing for it. Levity in this endeavor was unacceptable. "Perhaps I haven't been clear enough. Before you agree to this path, you must understand. We may not survive. If my kind discover what I am doing before your powers are fully manifest, they could destroy us both, as well as the souls we protect."

Mayela furrowed her brow in response. Turning away from him, she stared into the fire, arms crossed over her chest, as if seeking answers from the flames. Nekhen noticed icy trepidation twisting through her aura, undercut by a steely thread of determination.

At last, she lifted her gaze to his.

"They might try," she offered. "But we can take them down, can't we? You and me together, with a little help from Anne?"

Then she broke into a mischievous grin and winked.

Nekhen surrendered with a laugh, drawing his love into a warm embrace. She tilted her head to meet him, wrapping her arms around his neck. Sparks reflected in her eyes. Her breath ignited a fire on his lips.

"Yes," he said, opening his heart in full to receive the enduring brilliance of her soul. "I believe we can."

A word about the author…

K.R. Gastreich is a recipient of the OZMA Award for fantasy fiction and the Andrews Forest Writer's Residency, as well as a winner of the Women on Writing Flash Fiction Contest. Her fantasy novels feature high-stakes romance, gripping battles, and darkly lyrical prose. In addition to The Silver Web trilogy, she has published short stories in Zahir, Adventures for the Average Woman, 69 Flavors of Paranoia, and World Jumping. A proud native of the American Midwest, K.R. Gastreich lived for many years in Texas and then in Latin America before returning to the Kansas City Metro where she grew up. When not writing, she enjoys hiking, camping, studying dance, and spending time with her family. To learn about new releases and other events, visit K.R. Gastreich's website at krgastreich.com, or follow her on Instagram @EolynChronicles.

krgastreich.com

Thank you for purchasing
this publication of The Wild Rose Press, Inc.

For questions or more information
contact us at
info@thewildrosepress.com.

The Wild Rose Press, Inc.
www.thewildrosepress.com